ABDUCTED
INNOCENCE

OTHER TITLES BY SANDRA BOLTON

A Cipher in the Sand

The Emily Etcitty Mysteries

Key Witness

ABDUCTED INNOCENCE

THE EMILY ETCITTY SERIES

SANDRA BOLTON

THOMAS & MERCER

Text copyright © 2017 by Sandra Bolton
All rights reserved.

Published by Thomas & Mercer, Seattle

www.apub.com

Amazon, the Amazon logo, and Thomas & Mercer are trademarks of Amazon.com, Inc., or its affiliates.

ISBN-13: 9781477848685
ISBN-10: 1477848681

Cover design by Ray Lundgren

Printed in the United States of America

To my children,
Tim, Terry, and Todd

1

N avajo police officer. Emily Etcitty picked up the incident report dropped on her desk by Officer Joe Hosteen. She raised her eyebrows and flashed him an annoyed look, which he responded to with a sardonic smile and shrug. She had finished her shift and was filing the final reports—and looking forward to spending time with Abe, her musician boyfriend, at his place near Bloomfield.

"Sounds like female stuff to me," Hosteen said, giving it little significance and, therefore, delegating it to Emily. "Captain Todechine said a woman might handle it better."

Emily skimmed the dispatcher's report. "A missing girl out at Teec Nos Pos."

"Yeah, missing for only four hours when the family called it in. Probably nothing but another pissed-off teenager acting out."

"This was called in over three hours ago, Joe. Why didn't you give it to me right away?"

Officer Hosteen's eyes were black and sharp as pinpoints, his nose and bone structure chiseled angles, his mouth a thin line. He reminded Emily of a Picasso painting. There was nothing soft or sympathetic about Hosteen. He and Emily had clashed on several occasions in the past over police procedures and didn't particularly like each other. Now that both were in contention for promotion to sergeant, the friction had increased. Only one would be selected.

"I was tied up on another case. This missing-girl report didn't strike me as being particularly urgent—probably a runaway who took off to Grandma's house when she didn't get what she wanted."

Emily studied the report slowly and methodically for a second time, pausing at the end. It was not uncommon for a thirteen-year-old girl to go missing for a few hours; it was, however, unheard of for one to disappear during her *Kinaaldá*, the Navajo puberty ceremony practiced by traditional families celebrating a girl's transition into womanhood.

"You didn't even read this, did you?" She pursed her lips and stared at him. "I'll head on over there and talk to the family," she said.

You sexist pig, she thought to herself.

The trip to the village of Teec Nos Pos on the Arizona side of the reservation took an hour and a half. On her way, Emily drove past the looming monolithic rock formation the Anglos called Shiprock. Someone had given it that name because it resembled a clipper ship sailing the gray-green desert. Emily knew it by its correct name—*Tsé Bit' a'i*, Winged Rock, after the great bird who brought the Navajo from the north to their present land.

After she had left the familiar landmark and the town of Shiprock behind, the land opened up once again to scattered mesas, washes, canyons, and the occasional trailer or hogan. Traffic thinned out on

Highway 64 to sporadic pickup trucks, giving Emily plenty of time to let her mind drift back to her own *Kinaaldá*. She remembered how proud and excited she had been to wake up and discover signs of her first menstrual cycle, knowing the spots of blood on the sheet meant there would soon be a four-day celebration ending with a feast. A young girl brought up in the Navajo tradition would not run away at a time like that.

The sun had dropped behind a sandstone cliff and was casting fiery-orange flames across the western sky when Emily reached the nearly deserted village. She made a quick stop at the Teec Nos Pos Trading Post to ask directions to Jim Benally's residence.

"Two miles out of town, you'll see a dirt road—make a right turn," said the shopkeeper. "About three more miles, you'll be there. Half the town is looking for Darcy. I'd be there myself if I didn't have to keep the store open."

Damn, Emily thought. *Dozens of other footprints have probably obliterated the girl's tracks, and it's going to be dark soon.*

She hurried back to her Chevy Blazer, sped toward the Benally home, and arrived fifteen minutes later. Before leaving the SUV, she called in her location to headquarters.

The scene that greeted her looked disconsolate. A long wooden table placed under a spreading cottonwood tree was covered with casserole dishes and desserts that remained untouched. Flies buzzed around plates of roast lamb, mutton stew, green chili, and beans that sat congealing in the chilly evening air. A traditional round corn cake that smelled slightly burned had been abandoned. A medicine man chanted prayers, but no one appeared to be listening. Several women huddled together trying to comfort one another while one of their group—probably the mother—cried despairingly. Children clustered together in front of a hogan, their faces somber, their eyes round. She saw no men or teenage boys. Emily assumed they were all looking for the girl. She approached one of the women, introduced herself, and, speaking in Navajo, asked for the mother of the missing child.

"I am Nina Benally, Darcy's mom," a plump woman dressed in fancy clothes snuffled through tears. "Why have they sent only one person? Why have you taken so long?"

"*Yá' át' ééh alní íní,*" Emily said, saying the traditional evening greeting. She shook the woman's hand softly while diverting her eyes and giving Darcy's mother time to calm herself. "I came as soon as I received word your daughter was missing. Tell me what happened today."

Nina Benally sat up straight and drew in a long breath before speaking. She uttered her words slowly, deliberately, as if trying to preserve dignity in front of an officer of the law. "It is the final day of my daughter's *Kinaaldá*. I dressed her this morning in her woven-rug dress, turquoise and shell jewelry, and washed her hair with yucca suds and combed it with the grass comb." There was pride in her voice, but tears streamed down her face as she continued. "I tied her hair with buckskin in the traditional way." The mother's lips quivered as she fought to control her emotions.

Purple shadows loomed over the mesa. It would soon be too dark to see prints. Emily knew time was crucial if she was to find any trace of the girl today, but also understood she must not hurry the mother. "Please go on, Mrs. Benally. What time was it when you last saw your daughter?"

"Today was to be the final day of her races before we began the feast and celebration—one this morning and then the evening run. She left after sunrise, about seven thirty, excited, so proud, and wearing a big smile. The children followed her, as is the custom, but my Darcy ran so fast she left them all behind. They came back without her and told us she had been teasing them and laughing when they last saw her. She never returned from her morning race. It is only a little over a mile. What could have happened to my daughter?"

Emily waited, listening to the woman's sobs until they subsided. "Mrs. Benally, it will help if you can answer some questions. Do you know the time when the children returned?"

"Nine o'clock, maybe. The kids had already been looking for Darcy. We waited for her until noon. When she still hadn't come back, I worried something had happened, so my husband went into town to call the police. He is out on the trail now, looking for our girl." Nina Benally could no longer keep up the facade of dignified composure. She made a keening sound while praying, beseeching the gods to deliver her daughter home safely from whatever evil had taken her away.

Emily placed her hand on the woman's shoulder and patted lightly. "Thank you, Mrs. Benally. I will do everything in my power to find Darcy. If you have a recent picture of her, it would be a great help."

The family had called headquarters at noon to report the girl missing, but Hosteen had sat on the report until after three thirty.

Why had the asshole waited so long?

Emily left the woman and walked to a group of children. "*Yá'átéé sha'alchimi.* Greetings, children. I want to help find Darcy. Will someone show me where she began her race this morning and which direction she went?"

All but one of the children cast their eyes down, looking too frightened to leave the protection of the pit fire and the adult women.

"She started here, at the hogan, and ran to the east," a round-faced boy of about ten said. "They are afraid of the skinwalkers," he added, indicating the other youngsters. "But I will show you the way."

Of course. She ran toward the east in a circular path, symbolizing the movement of the sun, the cycle of life. She would face the sun to return. How could I have forgotten so much?

"With your mother's permission only, and you have to promise not to run ahead," Emily said.

After radioing in her status, Emily retrieved a flashlight and camera from the Blazer. A breeze had picked up, bringing a sudden chill. April

5

in the northeast highlands of Arizona can be sunny and warm one day and snowy the next. She donned her jacket and met the boy in front of the hogan.

"My mother said I can show you the path as long as I am not out of her sight," the boy said. "She rubbed corn pollen on me for protection."

"All right, let's go, but only a little ways. When we reach the path, you have to turn around. It's getting dark."

"I'm not afraid of skinwalkers," said the boy.

"I know. You are brave, but this is police work. I just need to know where to start."

"Here," said the boy when they were about fifty yards from the hogan. He pointed to a narrow path scuffed with numerous tracks. "Do you want some corn pollen?" He had stopped sounding so brave and looked anxiously back toward the safety of the hogan and fire.

"No, but thanks—I can manage now. Run back to your family. I'll wait until you are there." As she watched the boy scamper away, she thought about the stories she had listened to as a child about skinwalkers. Those malevolent witches, according to legend, were capable of transforming themselves into coyotes, wolves, bears, or any animals they wished. Shape-shifters, they were called. It was rumored they used mind control to make people do anything they wanted, especially harm themselves in some way. Emily shook off a chill, telling herself she didn't believe any of it. She beamed her flashlight on the trail, searching for moccasin tracks amid the disparate tread marks of sneakers.

They were easy enough to find—small, flat indentations usually off to the left. When Emily came upon an entire footprint, she took a picture, thinking it looked like a size six or six and a half woman's. The weight on the forefoot was embedded deeper than the heel, and the soles were smooth, indicating the probable print of a Native American—a people accustomed to running by putting the forefoot down first. Emily surmised the girl was probably of medium weight. She made a mental note to ask the mother about her height and weight when she retrieved the photograph.

A coyote howled from a mesa top, startling Emily and sending a shudder down her spine. She reacted automatically by reaching for her gun, stopping with her hand on the butt of the Glock 19 in her hip holster.

Shake it off, she told herself as she continued forward.

She was looking for the spot where the other children had turned back, leaving only the girl's tracks. Relieved, she noted that the men in the search party had ridden their horses along the side of the trail as not to disturb the tracks.

About a mile down the path, Emily came upon a dirt road. She crossed it, saw that the trail remained unmarked by footprints on the other side, and discerned that the dusty lane showed signs of fresh tire treads. The vehicle had made a sudden stop, judging by the skid marks. It appeared to have backed up, made a U-turn, and headed in the direction from which it had come. The horses had also stopped there. The riders had dismounted, followed the moccasin tracks, and then returned to their steeds. The horse tracks continued along the road in the direction of the vehicle. Emily snapped a few close-up shots, being careful not to step on anything, then returned to the spot where she had last seen Darcy's prints. They appeared jumbled. The dirt was disturbed as if there had been a scuffle, and there were other shoe prints—not children's sneakers, but large cowboy boots, maybe two different pairs.

As she bounced the light around, something else caught her eye. Partially hidden behind a rabbit bush was a single deerskin moccasin. She decided it was time to call for assistance. If a skinwalker had taken Darcy Benally, he wore size eleven or twelve boots and drove a four-wheeled vehicle. It looked like dinner with Abe would be a little late.

2

Friday, April 6, 1990

Mattie Simmons's Churro Sheep Ranch

Bloomfield, New Mexico

Abe Freeman watched from the gate of the corral while his dog, Patch, chased the last of the Churro sheep into their enclosure. His little three-legged mutt was a natural, but of course he had received excellent training. He had learned the ropes of herding from the two dogs at Emily's grandfather's sheep camp. Abe locked the gate and marveled at how much his life had changed in the past two years.

He had fulfilled his promise to Sharon, his first love. Her death was still a painful memory. He had carried a small vial of her ashes to the Pacific Ocean, where he'd scattered them in the bay off the coast of San Francisco.

I told you someday we would see the Pacific, baby. Well, here we are, not quite like we planned, but it's the best I can do.

The next day, Abe had found a job as a dockworker. He lived frugally, saved his earnings, and thought more and more about New Mexico and Emily Etcitty, the Navajo cop who had once arrested him as a murder suspect—and later became his lover. On a late October morning, he loaded his dog and gear into his camper, found a pay phone, and called Emily at her mother's house near Huerfano. "I want to come back if you can put up with me," he told her.

Abe had been in New Mexico for a week, staying at the trailer with Emily's grandfather and her brother, Will, when Emily showed up with news about a wealthy Texas businesswoman who kept a breeding herd of Churro sheep at her ranch outside of Bloomfield. The woman needed a caretaker, someone who could tend the sheep, deliver the lambs to Navajo buyers, look after the property, and keep up the sprawling New Mexico Territorial ranch house. In turn, the woman would provide a reasonable salary plus living quarters in the guesthouse—a small two-room adobe that fit Abe to a tee.

Abe counted the ewes and their suckling lambs and herded them into the barn. April was the middle of the lambing season, and he was in charge of two hundred breeding ewes and twenty rams, plus the four llamas that served to guard the flock from coyotes and marauding dogs. Also, there were still thirty yearlings to deliver to Navajo herders that month. He thought he might have miscounted but wasn't sure. He had only come up with twenty-nine young sheep.

The jangle of a telephone interrupted his woolgathering, and he left the barn to answer the call. He didn't have a phone in his place, and no one but the owner and Emily knew the number in the main house. Abe quickly unlocked the door and picked up the receiver.

"Hello?"

"Hi, Abe. I'm sorry. I'm going to be late," Emily said in a breathless voice. "I'm out at Teec Nos Pos, involved in a case—a missing girl. Had to hike a couple of miles, and don't know what time I'll be finishing up here tonight."

He tried to hide his disappointment. The steaks and bottle of wine he had splurged on would have to wait. "Don't worry. Do what you gotta do. We can have a late dinner." Even though he knew it came with the job, Abe felt his heart rate increase when Emily worked late. His brow furrowed and his grip on the phone tightened. "Are you all right out there? Anyone else with you?"

"Not yet. I radioed for assistance, and they're on their way. As soon as the crime-scene investigators arrive, I'll turn things over to them. I need to return to headquarters, write my report. When I'm done, I'll head on to your place."

"I'll be waiting. And be careful. Anything special I can do in the meantime?"

"Have a hot bath ready, and a warm bed with you in it. There's a definite chill in the air."

"You got it. I'm going to build a fire in the *kiva*, make it nice and cozy."

"Sounds great. I've got to go now, question the mother and father of the girl some more. See you in a couple of hours."

After he had hung up, Abe frowned, relocked the door, and followed the flagstone path back to the guesthouse. He popped the top on a beer and sat down in the rocking chair, his mood having changed from eager anticipation to broodiness.

It's probably nothing—a girl has an argument with her parents and takes off—maybe to a friend's house or a boyfriend's. Kids are like that, he reasoned. *But what if it is something more? Emily is like a little bulldog with a pork chop when she gets on a case. She sometimes thinks she's a one-woman police force. No telling when she'll get back.*

Abe swallowed a swig of beer and tried to push a nagging thought out of his mind: *What if something terrible did happen to that girl and Emily is alone out there, in the dark?*

He knew the Navajo people avoided going out at night—that they believed evil things carried by the wind happened in the darkness. No young girl would choose to be out there alone. Neither would Emily—even though she was a seasoned police officer, a fact he often had trouble coming to grips with no matter how many times he told himself, "It's her job."

Abe emptied his beer and tried to shift his thoughts to other, more pleasant things, like Emily in his bed later that night lying naked in his arms, and the warm-all-over feeling he would have when he woke up in the morning and she was still there.

They'll find the girl and everything will be all right, he told himself.

Three hours later Abe finished the dinner preparations while Emily lay soaking in the big, old-fashioned, claw-foot bathtub. The clean scent of rain-drenched sage he always associated with her intermingled with the smells of fried potatoes and onions in the kitchen. Abe poured two glasses of wine and carried them into the bathroom, sat on the side of the tub, and handed a glass to Emily.

She looked up at him, her skin sleek and glistening, her small, firm breasts peeking over the edge of the water, her smile not quite erasing the worried look in her eyes.

"Other people are working on that case, you know. They'll find her, Em."

"All I saw were tire tracks, some shoe prints, and her moccasin. Someone took her against her will, Abe. Why would anyone do that?"

Abe sighed because there was nothing he could say. Emily had explained to him that Darcy had disappeared while running a race as part of her *Kinaaldá* ceremony, a joyous and proud time for adolescent girls.

Why indeed would anyone abduct her during such a celebration?

Later that night, concerns of the day were momentarily forgotten as their desire for each other grew. Their bodies pressed together in the age-old dance of lovemaking, becoming increasingly more urgent. Seconds before she thought Abe would explode, Emily let out a moan, and they came together as one.

Afterward, lying side by side, Abe took Emily's hand in his. *"La petite mort,"* he said.

"What?"

"The little death—and worth dying for, sweetheart."

3

Saturday, April 7, 1990

Mattie Simmons's Sheep Ranch

Bloomfield, New Mexico

Abe awoke the next morning to a pink-streaked sky and the sound of the wind rustling through young cottonwood leaves. He looked at Emily, still sleeping, her black hair fanned on the pillow. They had talked long into the night, speculating on the case of the missing girl. Abe knew, no matter how hard he tried to distract her, that Emily's preoccupation would continue.

He gently brushed a strand of hair from her eyes and got out of bed. The sun poked its fiery head above the eastern horizon, spreading shimmering light on patches of new grass. Along the river, pale-green willows alternated with silver-gray Russian olive trees. It was a beautiful day, and Abe looked forward to the ride after breakfast to Teec Nos Pos with Emily—and the rest of the weekend together.

While he was outside recounting the yearlings, Emily joined him. She looked like a schoolgirl, dressed in blue jeans and plaid flannel shirt, her hair pulled back in a ponytail.

"Good morning. I made coffee." She handed him a steaming mug. "What's up? You look worried."

"Hey, sweetheart. I didn't want to wake you—you looked so peaceful." He ran a hand through his shoulder-length curly hair. "It looks like one of the yearlings is missing. I should have checked into it yesterday but forgot. Want to take a walk this morning? Maybe we can find some trace of it in the pasture."

Abe noticed Emily's distraction, how quiet she had become while they traipsed along the fence line. "What's on your mind, Em?"

"Sorry, Abe. It's the missing girl. I can't stop thinking about her or wondering what happened. I know what it's like to lose a child. Hosteen is supposed to follow up on the case while I'm off. I hope he puts the time in. He seemed so casual and unconcerned yesterday."

"Look," Abe said, cupping her chin with his hand and forcing her to look into his eyes, "they'll find her. She can't be far. And you may not like Hosteen, but he's a pro."

Emily shook her head and tried to smile. "You're right. Let's find that yearling." The 250 acres of grazing land were fenced off into five separate fields, allowing the sheep to be rotated and the grass to grow back when eaten down. Abe and Emily walked the roadside fence line of the fifty acres designated to the yearlings but found no sign of an animal kill.

"What do you think?" Abe said.

Emily pointed to a cut wire on the fence. "I think you've got a sheep rustler."

"Shit. These lambs are all designated to go to deserving Navajo families, namely, those involved in rug weaving. On the market, each one is worth about two hundred twenty-five dollars. But I guess you know that better than I do." Sometimes he forgot Emily was not just his girlfriend, not just a Navajo Nation police officer, but also a member of a clan of longtime sheepherders.

Closer inspection of the area around the cut fence revealed a pair of boot prints, which led to a dirt road bordering the pasture. Any incriminating tread marks had been erased by those of several other vehicles that had driven along the road.

"Yep," Abe said. "A rustler."

4

Herman Tallbrother's Sheep Camp

Teec Nos Pos, Arizona

I 'll call it in." Emily didn't tell Abe how frequently sheep rustling occurred, or how hard it was to catch the guilty party once the thieves removed the ear tags. "This is San Juan County Sheriff's Department's jurisdiction." She also neglected to tell him the county didn't give a damn about Navajo sheep.

"This fence needs fixing now. I can deal with the rest later, Em. I can't stick around and wait for 'Deputy Dave' to show up. Got to get those lambs loaded and delivered. Those folks are waiting for their check."

While Abe repaired the fence with new sections of wire and clipped away the loose ends so the sheep wouldn't get snagged, Emily returned to the house and made toast and scrambled eggs. Most of the time she thought this domesticity was all right, but occasionally worries nagged at her. Like now.

What if Abe leaves again? He always seems so unsettled. Maybe he'll never be able to love me as much as he loved Sharon. Can I live with that? Do I want to? Am I ready to give up my independence?

For Emily, when it came to men, trust remained an issue. Past experience had left scars that were slow to heal. She quickly brushed her concerns aside when she heard Abe at the door.

"Just in time," Emily said, putting two plates on the table.

Abe sat down at the table across from Emily. "I like it when you're here with me." He smiled at her over the brim of his coffee cup. "Patch helped me cut six yearlings from the herd and corral them. I've got the truck backed up to the gate and the loading chute ready. We can take off right after breakfast." Since Abe's truck was used more for utility than traveling now, he had removed the camper shell and equipped the bed with a stock rack and back gate. It would hold six young sheep without a problem.

"Good. Looks like a beautiful day for a road trip." Though everyone in the northwest plateau wished for spring rain, it didn't look like it would happen that day. A brisk breeze chased wispy white clouds across the robin's-egg-blue sky. Emily grinned back at Abe. "I know someone I can talk to about the lost lamb."

Abe raised his eyebrows and gave her an inquisitive look.

"If anyone knows about missing sheep, it's Charley Nez."

"Why Charley?" Abe asked.

"He's a wheeler-dealer, his fingers in a lot of different pots, and he has contacts all over the rez. If a Navajo stole sheep, he'd know something about it. It might take some coaxing to get information out of him, but Charley has his price."

"I know Charley. I give piano lessons to his daughter. I'll call him when we get back. As I said, I'm sorry to put you to work on your day off, but it sure makes things easier for me."

Emily pitched in with the dishes, and Patch helped Abe load the lambs, nipping at their heels until they climbed the chute. He closed the tailgate, making sure it was secure, and surveyed the surrounding countryside. The bottomland along the San Juan River was lush green compared to the barren high desert outside Farmington and in Arizona, but even it would wither and die if there weren't enough spring rains. Last year's winter snow had been sparse, leaving little to soak into the water table. Water, or the lack thereof, was an ongoing concern for the Navajo sheepherders and other ranchers in Northwest New Mexico.

It was barely nine o'clock when they took off for the sheep camp ten miles north of Teec Nos Pos. By the time they neared their destination, distinctive pink-and-orange rock formations, red mesas, and steep canyons had begun transforming the desert into a surreal wonderland.

Wedged on the seat between Patch and Abe, Emily barely noticed the striking scenery. She was still thinking about the missing girl and wondering if Hosteen had followed up on the note she had left on his desk the night before. Emily needed to explore all possible angles, and wanted to know if there had been other young girls reported missing in the previous five years, or if any of the investigators had interviewed the search party on horseback at the Benally place. *I should have done it myself,* she thought, then admonished herself for not being able to leave work behind on her day off. Work had been her life and her redemption for mistakes of her past. If she had not made such bad choices, her little boy might be alive. The man she had chosen to live with and who had fathered her child had taken her baby from her during a drunken rage. He'd stumbled, with the boy in his arms, and they had both fallen into a rain-swollen ravine. Little Christopher's body was not found until three days later. Emily closed her eyes at the memory and tried to focus on the present.

Abe tapped his fingers on the steering wheel as he drove, playing an invisible piano, a habit he had developed because of the music that always coursed through his head. He stopped to look at her. "You're so quiet. What's on your mind, sweetheart?"

Emily's eyes lingered on Abe's for a moment before she gazed out the window. "Darcy Benally. She's out there somewhere—alone, scared. I can't stop thinking about her. I want to find her, Abe. I should have run a search on the computer myself, but I was in too much of a hurry to get to your place."

"The others are working on it, Em. Maybe they've even found her by now."

"Maybe," she said, but her voice sounded doubtful. "Do you mind stopping at the Benally place after we deliver the sheep? I'd like to talk to the mom and dad again."

"No problem, if it will put you more at ease," Abe said.

"Thanks. I promise I'm all yours the rest of the weekend." She rewarded him with a peck on the cheek.

Abe hummed snatches of a haunting nocturne while Patch stared out the window at passing cacti and sagebrush, and Emily silently brooded over the missing Navajo girl—until she realized that Abe was asking her a question.

"Earth to Emily. Are you there?"

"I'm sorry. What did you say?"

"We're coming into Teec Nos Pos, but I need to find the location of the Bitter Water Clan sheep camp. Any ideas where to start?"

"Pull in at the trading post up ahead. The shopkeeper will know. I'll go inside and ask." Because of her familiarity with the landscape and her ability to speak Navajo, she would be better able to get directions.

The parking lot in front of the picturesque sandstone-colored adobe building contained several cars and SUVs with out-of-state plates.

"Tourists passing through from the Four Corners Monument or on their way to Monument Valley," Emily said as she opened the door and stepped down from the cab. She ducked under a sign proclaiming the trading post had been established in 1905 and entered the building. The proprietor, a tall Anglo wearing a straw hat, was busy discussing the price of an intricately woven rug with a tourist outfitted in pseudo–Santa Fe style, so Emily looked around until she spotted a young Navajo woman near the register.

"*Yá'át'ééh.*" The two women exchanged pleasantries in Navajo before Emily got to the point of her business. "We're delivering some yearling lambs to the spring sheep camp of the Bitter Water Clan. Can you tell me how to get there?"

"*Aoo*, sure. It's not hard to find," the woman responded, gesticulating with her hands while giving directions. "Herman Tallbrother took his sheep up there last week. The halfway camp is located near the creek, before you climb out of the canyon."

Emily bought two orange sodas, thanked the woman, and wished her a good day.

Abe wrinkled his nose at the orange drink and declined the offer. "Thanks, but I'll pass. So? Where do we go from here?"

"Follow Highway 160 until you cross a dry creek bed, and turn left onto the first dirt road. Their camp is about eight miles in. Name's Tallbrother, if you didn't know." Emily took a long pull on her orange soda. "Coldest drinks around, and the only place on the Navajo Nation that buys Churro yarn from Diné sheepherders," she said. "World-renowned rugs are woven around Teec Nos Pos."

Just as the salesgirl at the trading post had indicated, the camp was not hard to find. Three older-model Ford and Chevy pickup trucks were parked in a clearing near a small hut constructed of wooden poles and canvas tarps. Two of the trucks had trailers attached, and the third contained a two-hundred-gallon water tank in the pickup bed. An elderly woman worked a spindle under the roof of an open outdoor kitchen area, and two other women were busy hand-cleaning freshly sheared piles of wool. A young girl played with three mixed-breed dogs. Near a wooden corral containing about twenty sheep and a llama, two men were busy with hand shearers, cutting wool from a couple of hog-tied sheep lying on their sides on a tarp. When they finished, they released the animals' binds, and the pair of freshly shorn, naked-appearing ewes scampered off to join the flock. A teenage boy gathered the wool, then singled out another sheep for shearing. Everyone stopped what they were doing and looked up when Abe's truck pulled into the camp.

"Wait until they come to greet us," Emily said to Abe.

"They're expecting me." Abe opened the glove compartment and retrieved a brown manila envelope. "I need someone to sign the sales agreement."

"Do they pay you?" Emily asked.

Abe shook his head. "No exchange of money involved. I guess they've worked out something with Mattie Simmons. They're supposed to give her a rug for each sheep delivered. She'll pick up the rugs later and sell them in Dallas, to collectors."

"An authentic Teec Nos Pos rug is worth a lot of money—a lot more than one yearling lamb. What else is the Bitter Water Clan getting out of the deal?" She couldn't help thinking this seemed like another case of the "white man" ripping off the "dumb Indian."

"A percentage of the selling price. I don't know for sure how much because I haven't read the agreement. The contract goes back in another self-addressed envelope and is mailed directly to Ms. Simmons. Once she sells the rug, she sends the weavers their share."

"Hmm. I've heard most of the weavers are not very happy with the money they're getting." Emily was still pondering this when a stocky man with a deeply creased brown face approached the truck. He was followed closely by a second man, younger and taller, but the resemblance left no doubt the two were brothers.

Abe and Emily stepped down from the truck when the first man approached. Patch didn't waste any time hopping out to sniff around and meet the dogs, who seemed friendly enough. The man extended his hand to Abe.

"Herman Tallbrother," he said. "My brother, Tom."

"Glad to meet you," Abe said, shaking hands with both men. "Name's Abe Freeman, and you probably know Emily Etcitty. I've got six yearlings from Mattie Simmons's ranch in the back of the truck for you."

The teenage boy wandered over and peered through the slats at the sheep. "They're Churros, all right, Dad," he said. "Want me to unload them?"

"Wait," his father said. He climbed into the bed of the truck and examined each sheep until satisfied they were all in good health. "Okay, Junior, put them in the corral. Careful you don't spook them."

Abe pulled the loading chute out of the back and let the tailgate down. The yearlings bleated loudly, looking confused and terrified until they spotted the other sheep.

The boy, aided by the dogs, made quick work out of corralling them with the rest of the herd.

Emily and Abe accepted an offer of coffee and sat at a table in the tarp-covered kitchen. The delicious aroma of fry bread filled the air as the women began preparing a fresh batch for their visitors. While Herman Tallbrother studied the sales agreement, Emily let her eyes drift to the camp. She spotted a loom with a large, partially completed rug and recognized the pattern as a traditional Hero Twins, woven with shades of brown, gray, and black yarns. The pattern was tight and expertly done. *Worth at least $9,000 or $10,000,* she thought as she accepted a hot piece of fry bread from the woman. She smiled and thanked her, but did not miss the disapproving looks she received from all the women. They might as well have said their thoughts out loud: *Stick with your own kind. Isn't a Navajo man good enough for you?*

The papers were signed, one copy given to Herman Tallbrother and the other sealed in the envelope. The men shook hands. Abe whistled for Patch, but before they got back in the truck, Emily decided to question the clan about Darcy Benally. She was sure they had heard of the kidnapping in this tight little community.

"Did you find out anything new?" Abe said when they were back on the highway.

"A couple of things." Emily pushed back a stray strand of hair. "One I already knew—the Diné don't approve of Navajo women cozying up with white men."

Abe put his hands in his pockets, looked down at the dirt, and kicked a rock near his foot. "Did they come right out and say it to you?"

"No, they didn't have to. It's easy to pick up on silent Navajo rebukes." Emily patted Abe on the knee. "Don't worry. I'm used to disapproval. The main thing I wanted to know was if they had seen or heard anything new about the missing girl."

"And . . . ?"

"Well, the Tallbrother men and Junior participated in the search party, so they know someone in a vehicle kidnapped the girl. Junior supplied a piece of interesting information. I wanted to know if they had noticed any unusual vehicles hanging around. I didn't expect much, but one thing he said got my attention."

"Yeah? What?"

"Last week, they were buying supplies at the trading post for the sheep camp. Junior didn't want to go inside, so he hung out on the porch. He said a white van with tinted windows pulled up. He couldn't see who was inside. After about ten minutes, it left. He thought it strange they kept the motor running the whole time."

"No one got out? Kind of weird."

"Yeah, and it just so happened the Benally family was inside the store at the same time."

"Did he notice the make or model of the van?"

"A Chevy utility van, white, newer model. He didn't get a license plate number, though, because he didn't think it was important at the time. The van left when the Benallys came out of the trading post. Junior talked to Darcy and her mom and dad for a few minutes before helping his father and uncle load the truck. Said he forgot about it until I started asking questions."

"Kind of a slim lead, Emily. Lots of white Chevy vans out there."

Emily sighed. "I know, but it's all I've got for now. I'm curious about whether they know anyone with a Chevy van or have seen it around." Emily let her eyes wander over the landscape. Steep canyons and jutting sentinels of red sandstone contrasted with new growth of grasses and wildflowers. Even the scant spring moisture that had arrived was enough to transform the desert into a veritable oasis. "The turnoff is up ahead on the left."

Abe rolled down the window and watched Emily as she walked toward a cluster of people in front of a hogan. There was a large gathering at the Benally place—extended family, clan members, neighbors—still looking for Darcy, waiting for any word from the police.

"I'll wait in the truck while you talk to them," Abe said. "Take your time."

Ten minutes later she returned. "No one remembers seeing a Chevy van, and they don't know anyone who owns one."

Abe turned the key in the ignition and glanced at Emily. "A dead end, you think?"

"Maybe. There's one more person I'd like to talk to while we're out this way. Okay, Abe?"

"Does that mean I get to be your sidekick again?" Abe said with a rueful grin. "Backup to the bodacious lady cop?"

A year ago he had become a reluctant partner in their pursuit of Easy Jackson's killer. But Abe had a strong motive—he had been accused of the murder at the time. By helping Emily, he had cleared his name but had also put his life in danger more than once.

"You don't have to—there's no obligation."

"I wouldn't pass up the opportunity to help you, babe. It's the least I can do. So, where are we headed now?"

"Darcy's grandmother mentioned another person who might have noticed the Chevy at the trading post—old Tom Crow—a half-breed who lives alone in Shiprock near the cutoff to Route 666. She said he was walking around with a spray bottle and a rag when they left, doing what he usually does. Watching people and trying to earn a little pocket money by washing tourists' windows. When he gets money, he usually spends it on booze. Tom only has one good eye, but he never misses much. If there had been anything out of the ordinary, he would have noticed."

"Route 666. The number of the beast," Abe said.

Due to the many unexplained phenomena occurring on Route 666, the desolate span of highway was referred to by many as "The Devil's Highway" or "The Highway to Hell." Emily had told Abe she discounted the stories about demons, devils, and fiery semis rumored to haunt that particular stretch of road, but no one could downplay the number of unexplained accidents occurring there each year. Most law enforcement officers attributed the unusual sightings and high accident rates to excessive alcohol consumption. Since it was against the law to sell alcohol on the reservation, calculating businesspeople had established liquor stores and bars at both ends of that particular length of roadway. In Emily's mind, drunkenness explained a lot.

"It's not far out of our way, I promise," Emily said, "and there's nothing satanic about the name. It was the logical choice for the sixth spur of old Route 66."

Abe grinned at her and narrowed his eyes. "You sure? 'Let him who has understanding calculate the number of the beast, for it is the number of a man. His number is 666,'" he quoted.

"Revelations," Emily said. "Drilled into me by the mission schools."

Tom Crow lived in a tumbledown shack on a junk-laden piece of land a mile beyond the intersection of 64 and 666. Emily found him sitting in an old lawn chair in front of his house, a bottle of Ripple clutched in his hand, one bleary-but-good eye trained on the new arrivals. With skin the color and texture of wrinkled parchment, hair a wispy cloud of gray smoke, and clothes smelling like they hadn't been washed in a month, the shrunken man scowled at Emily as she emerged from the truck. A yellow dog, all skin and bones, barked halfheartedly and got Patch's attention.

"Who're you?" Tom Crow mumbled.

"Tom, it's me. Emily Etcitty. Remember when I bailed you out and bought you dinner?"

"Who?" He took a long swig of wine. "Oh, yeah. You're the lady cop. Whatta ya doin' out here?"

"I need your help now, Tom. I want to know if you saw a white Chevy utility van at the Teec Nos Pos Trading Post at any time last week."

Tom Crow closed his eyes. In the prolonged silence, Emily thought he had fallen asleep. She was about to shake his shoulder when he opened his eyes and spoke.

"Sons a bitches never give a guy a break when he's down on his luck. Seen that van lotsa times. Don't even roll their fuck'n window down when I tap on it askin' if they want a wash job. But I seen 'im. Seen 'im when he cracked his window and told me to get lost. Seen 'im drive down this road, too, goin' north, comin' south. Drivin' this same ol' Highway to Hell. He'll get there soon enough, stingy bastard."

Emily's pulse quickened. "This is important, Tom. Can you describe the person in the van?"

"Hell, no. Saw his eyes for a second, top of his head is all." He yawned and took another drink from his bottle of cheap wine. "Told ya. Window was cracked." He spit a stream of tobacco into the sand. "I'm getting tired of talking. It's past my nap time."

"Just a couple more questions, Tom. Is there anything at all you can remember about the van or the guy inside—like the color of hair or eyes? Did you notice the license plate?"

"Colorado plates, I know for a fact." The yellow dog who had been lying near the chair began scratching halfheartedly at his ear. Tom Crow looked at the truck and at Abe sitting in the driver's seat. "Dark, curly hair—looked kind of like that fellow there," he said, nodding at Abe.

5

Saturday, April 7, 1990

Highway 666

Near Shiprock, New Mexico

L ooks like me?" Abe said. "Great. Am I the go-to guy for every crime committed out here?" They were back on the highway, headed toward Shiprock and a diner in Kirtland Emily wanted to stop at for lunch.

"Old Tom is ornery. He never got a good look at whoever was inside, just the top of his head. But he did say the van had Colorado plates. I'm calling this in as soon as we get back. I also want to find out if Hosteen turned up any other cases involving missing girls. After we grab a bite to eat, let's head home."

"You can't let this go, can you, Emily? Not even for a day." Abe felt a wash of disappointment. He had wanted them to have some time together without the distractions of work.

"Sorry, Abe. Because of the missing girl, it's personal with me. This is who I am. It's what I do."

Abe sighed. "I know your job is important to you, but we have so little time together. It feels like you are somewhere else."

She put a hand on his leg. "I'm here with you now, and I'm hungry. Pull in up there on the right—Doc's Diner."

The parking lot overflowed with pickups, fracking trucks, and eighteen-wheelers loaded with pipe and rigging. Abe found a small space that would accommodate the Toyota and squeezed in.

"Looks like they've got a crowd," he said. "I don't want to keep Patch waiting long."

"They're always busy, but they have fast service, and the food is great. Come on. We can get it to go if you want."

They stepped into the crowded diner, and Abe scanned the room for an empty booth or table. The customers had segregated themselves—one side of the room was crammed full of Navajo workers and families, the other with Anglo men in various-colored coveralls branded with the names of oil or natural-gas companies. Emily's brother, Will, had told him how the low-paying entry-level jobs—roustabouts and roughnecks—were delegated to the Native Americans while the higher-paying positions were given to the white men. Abe cursed under his breath when he noticed the cold, reproachful stares coming his way from *both* sides of the room. He quickly ushered Emily toward a booth where a pair of burly men in red coveralls were picking up their tab and preparing to leave.

As the men walked by, they leered at Emily. Abe heard them snicker. "I bet he orders red meat," one said. "Seems to be his preference." They both laughed, and Abe, feeling his stomach knot up and his pulse quicken, turned around, balling his hands into fists. The barriers he had so carefully built up during his lifetime broke down when he heard the man's remarks about Emily, and a blind rage took over. He'd had enough of the offhand comments, the silent rebukes, and the racial slurs.

29

Abe planted himself in front of the larger of the two, a potbellied brute at least six inches taller, with a shaved head and a scruffy beard. "You say something to me, or does shit just naturally fall out of your mouth whenever you open it?"

He saw the rigger's face turn red as his eyes narrowed in anger.

Emily stepped forward, placing a hand on Abe's arm. The other went automatically to the place where she usually carried her holstered Glock.

"Don't do anything stupid," she said to the rigger.

"You Injun-lovin' son of a bitch," the man said, ignoring Emily as he drew his fist back and prepared to throw a blow. Abe was smaller, but brawny and fast. He caught the big rigger with a belly punch and heard the wind whoosh out of him like an inflated tire. The other man jumped in, grabbing Abe by the shirtfront.

"Navajo Nation police officer," Emily said, moving in front of the man and brandishing her badge in his face. "Step back and drop your hands to your side. Unless you and your friend want to spend the night in a jail cell full of red men, you had better turn around and walk away."

The man hesitated, looked around the diner at all the eyes fixated on him. "Screw it," he said. "Let's get out of here." He released Abe, threw a twenty on the table, and helped his buddy, who was bent over, gasping for breath. They no doubt knew better than to get in trouble with Navajo law enforcement on reservation land.

"What an idiotic thing to do," Emily said, glaring at Abe.

She didn't have to tell him. He knew it was dumb. He had even spent most of his life avoiding that kind of violent behavior.

"I know. But why do we have to put up with this shit, Emily?" he said, gesticulating with a swing of his arm at the patrons in the diner. "Why can't they accept us?" Most of the crowd had turned their eyes away or resorted to stealing sidelong glances at the pair.

"Get used to it," Emily said. "If you're going to live here, accept the way it is. My people have lived with this kind of discrimination all our lives."

I should be used to it, Abe thought. Sharon had been a beautiful dark-skinned woman, so the two of them had often been on the receiving end of racially biased remarks, especially from his own mother.

"Let's go," he said. "I'm sorry I made a scene, but not sorry I busted the fat asshole. He deserved it, and I'll tell you what—it felt good."

What happened to the old Abe? The guy who used to smolder inside but turn away from confrontation? I'm not looking for trouble. I don't want to hurt anyone or anything—but I'm not walking away anymore.

He grinned, feeling pleased with himself. "I'll fix you lunch at the house. It'll be better than anything you could get here."

They walked out of the diner and got in the truck.

"It had better be good," Emily said. "Because I'm famished and pissed. You know, if I hadn't pulled out my badge, they'd probably still be scraping you off the floor. Promise me you won't pull any more stunts like that."

Abe patted Patch on the head. "We'll be home soon, boy," he said. But instead of promising her anything, Abe winked and began humming Vivaldi's "Spring" from *The Four Seasons*, his free left hand drumming on the steering wheel in time to the music.

"You're forgiven," Emily said, licking her fingers after devouring the last bite of her Reuben sandwich. "For the moment."

Abe grinned, took a swig of beer, and carried their plates to the sink. "I'm going to hose out the back of the truck and check on the sheep. Want to keep me company?"

"Go ahead. I'll join you in a couple of minutes. First, I need to call headquarters to let them know about the van with Colorado plates, and see if Hosteen came up with any other missing girls."

When she stood, Abe wrapped his arms around her. "This is our time, Em. Will is going to be here all day tomorrow, and you are leaving tomorrow afternoon. We have the rest of today alone. Let's make the most of it." He took her face in his hands and kissed her, felt the heat rising in his body. The desire to make love right that minute nearly derailed his plans to go outside and work, but she gently pushed him away.

"After this call, I'm all yours. No more distractions." Emily gave him a lingering kiss, her moist lips parting, her tongue teasing his. "We can spend the rest of the afternoon in bed. How does that sound?"

Abe grinned. It seemed like a good idea—and proved to be even better than he thought. Their lovemaking began with a fierce intensity, both bodies demanding more until they collapsed in exhaustion. Their mutual desire quenched, all other thoughts put to rest for the time being, they slept in each other's arms.

Will arrived the next morning while Abe was busy preparing potato latkes. He might have abandoned his Jewish religion and his family when he left New Jersey, but not the food he had grown up eating. Latkes were one of his favorites, and he wanted to share the special treat with Emily and Will.

He watched as Will Etcitty climbed down from his old Chief motorcycle, his scruffy black cowboy hat pulled down to partially hide his scars. Will stood outside, beeping the horn on his Chief—the Navajo way of announcing someone's arrival. Abe was always glad to see Emily's brother. He had learned a lot about sheep from him, but he didn't look forward to the task that lay ahead. Will had come to help Abe castrate the young male lambs and to dock their tails.

Emily interrupted her preparations of green chili, tortillas, and eggs. It was going to be a Jewish-New Mexican breakfast in the best tradition. Both she and Abe were hungry after their arduous night of lovemaking.

"Come in, Will, and stop making so much noise. The coffee is ready, and breakfast is coming right up."

Will Etcitty had quit drinking—and gradually gotten down to an optimal weight. After being laid off from his geologist position with a mining company, he had focused his life on the teachings of his aging grandfather. He had mastered the traditional songs and prayers of a Navajo healer, and had learned the proper uses of medicinal herbs and how to read sand paintings. Now he was recognized by his people as a *hataalii*, a powerful medicine man, and was much in demand for ceremonies.

Will maneuvered his strapping body into a kitchen chair and, grasping his mug with both hands, took a sip of hot coffee. *"Yá'át'ééh abíní,"* he said. "Are you ready for some Rocky Mountain oysters, Abe?" he chuckled softly.

Abe carried a plate of crisp latkes to the table. He saw the grin on Emily's face as she brought over three plates of fried eggs and a pot of green chili.

"Okay, I give up. What the hell are you talking about?" Abe said.

"Sheep nuts," said Will. "'Course, they're kind of puny coming from little lambs. But deep fried with a little hot sauce, they're damn tasty." He laughed when he saw the expression on Abe's face.

"I'll try just about anything, but I'm not even going to think about lamb nuts." Abe dug into a crispy latke smothered in green chili. "Gotta say, though, New Mexico green chili tastes pretty darn good on Jewish latkes." He took another bite, chewed slowly, and looked at Will. "What are you up to next week, buddy?"

"I'm performing a *Kinaaldá* ceremony near Mexican Water for the Nez girl. Charley got in touch with me yesterday; I'm going to be there Tuesday and Wednesday." He stopped chewing when he noticed Emily's expression. "What's the matter, sis?"

6

Monday, April 9, 1990

Huerfano Substation

Navajo Nation Tribal Police

E mily sat at her computer and scrolled through the database on missing persons in New Mexico, going back the past ten years, pausing when she came to cases involving Navajo girls. Most had been runaways, as Hosteen had suggested. Nearly all had turned up eventually—either dead or alive. She had come to work an hour early to discover whether there had been similar kidnapping incidents in the past and, so far, had come up empty. It was chilling to realize how many girls had been reported missing. Then, a picture of a young Navajo girl caught her eye. Emily's pulse quickened, and she stopped scrolling.

02/05/1982—Mary Jo Claw
Date Missing 02/05/1982 from Kirtland, New
Mexico
Age: 13

> Mary Jo Claw was last seen at the Claw residence outside of Toadlena, New Mexico. She was wearing a traditional dress and running on the final day of her *Kinaaldá* ceremony. If anyone has any information concerning her whereabouts, contact the Navajo Nation Police.

The entry continued with a physical description of the girl and her clothing. No trace of her had ever been found, and there were no suspects.

She would be twenty-one years old now, Emily thought. *If she's still alive.*

Emily scribbled information on a yellow pad and continued her search. Before Hosteen arrived, she had found reference to three more missing girls. All had been celebrating their *Kinaaldá*—and none had ever been found. And she had only researched New Mexico. The vast Navajo reservation extended into Arizona, Utah, and a small section of Colorado as well.

She became so engrossed in her work that she didn't notice Hosteen when he sat down at his desk across from hers. He hadn't been available when she had tried to reach him Saturday afternoon—out of range, the dispatcher said. He had Sunday off. It infuriated her to think he might have been intentionally ignoring her.

"Mornin', Etcitty," Hosteen said. "What're you doing here so early?"

Emily glared at him and quickly returned to her computer screen. "Have you bothered to take a look at these files on missing girls, Joe?"

"As a matter of fact, I did. Why are you so pissed this morning?" He put a bakery bag from Safeway on his desk.

"Why couldn't I reach you all weekend?"

Hosteen set his cup of coffee down and stood looking at her with intense slate-gray eyes, his arms folded across his chest. "I was on the road. I went out to the Benally place to talk to the father and other men involved in the search. They didn't find anything. Then, I had someone I needed to talk to way out in the Checkerboard area—took me all day—and I was off on Sunday, like you. Or, don't you ever take a day off?" he asked, his voice edged with annoyance.

Emily blew air out of her mouth in a long, exasperated sigh. "So the men on horseback never saw anything suspicious? Well, something is adding up here, and we should have jumped on top of it right away. There's a pattern of young girls disappearing during their *Kinaaldá*. Why didn't anybody pick up on this?"

"How should I know? I've only been working this area for the past two years, remember. And if you're interested, I already made a computer printout of the missing girls who fit the description. And I was out in no-man's-land talking to some of the parents." Hosteen put his hands on his hips, his voice rising in anger, drawing the attention of Captain Todechine, who had just entered the building.

"What the hell's going on? Don't you two have anything better to do than snipe at each other?" Todechine's massive frame towered over Emily's desk as he stood glaring at his two candidates for sergeant.

"It's about the missing girl, sir," Emily said. "I think we need to act quickly on this."

"Hosteen's on it," he snapped back.

The ass kisser, Emily thought.

Emily said, "Well, sir, the Chevy van I called in on Saturday? I think we should put an APB on it."

Hosteen continued standing, not saying anything.

"An APB based on what, Emily? That someone saw a white Chevy van in the parking lot a few days before the Benally girl disappeared, and they didn't see anybody get out, so they assumed it was suspicious? Do you know how many white vans go into that parking lot on a daily basis?" Todechine learned forward and pounded a fist on Emily's desk before answering his own question. "About a thousand tourists on their way to Monument Valley or the Grand Canyon or out to buy a few Indian trinkets before they leave the Wild West. Jesus Christ." Captain Todechine straightened his back, ran a hand through his buzz-cut white hair, shook his head, and scowled. "I'm getting a lot of flak from the community. I want the two of you working together on this. Stop bickering and get me something solid," he said. He swung around and walked into his office, slamming the door behind him.

Emily and Hosteen stared at each other. Neither smiled—neither wanted to partner with the other.

"Well, shit," Emily said. "Are you going to share with me who you talked to and what you found out?"

"Saturday morning I did exactly what you're doing right now—followed up on it by tracking down the families. Give me some credit, Emily. I was wrong not to act on the Benally case right away, and I felt sorry about it, but I'm a good cop. So lighten up."

Embarrassed for assuming Hosteen was avoiding her, Emily apologized, though she still did not like the idea of working with him. "Look, I'm sorry, Joe. I was out of line."

Yes, she had to admit to herself, *he is a good cop, and if I don't prove myself better than he is, he'll get the promotion—not me.* "Did you get any new information?"

"All right. Apology accepted. Help yourself to a doughnut, but hands off the chocolate one." He looked at her list and pointed to three names. "I only had time to meet with these three families. They're scattered all over the Navajo Nation and Checkerboard area. They came up with the same story each time. The girls just disappeared—no trace of them ever found. No suspects, only a few tire tracks. They all vanished in isolated areas accessible by dirt roads only, and crisscrossed by a grid of pipeline roads leading in all directions."

"Since you accepted my apology, I'll accept your offer of a doughnut," Emily said. She made a selection, avoiding the chocolate, and took a bite. "There's one more name on the list." She paused to lick powdered sugar from her fingers. "Mary Jo Claw. Let's take a ride out to the Claw camp and see what we can find out."

Their destination was three and a half miles outside of Toadlena, New Mexico, a drive of eighty-one miles on an unpaved Indian Service Route. Emily reproached herself for her outburst as they got into Hosteen's police-issue Ford Explorer. She simply preferred to work alone, enjoyed the solitude while driving through the reservation's remote boondocks. She hoped Hosteen wouldn't talk too much.

"It's a goddamn desolate wasteland out here," Hosteen said when they were off the main highway. "I don't know how you people can stand to live in such a place."

The remark did nothing to endear her to her new partner, and she shot him a contentious look. "What do you mean by 'you people'? Don't you consider yourself a member of the tribe, Joe? Or are you ashamed to be Diné? If you can't see the beauty in this land, I find it hard to believe you are Navajo."

"Get off your high horse, Emily. I'm as much Navajo as you, but I was born in Albuquerque. My mother left when she was a teenager, ran away like I figure some of these girls did because she saw there was no future for her here. She put herself through college, got a decent job, and provided me with a better life."

"Have you ever tried to find family members here? I bet you don't even know your clan name," Emily said, giving him a skeptical look.

"I know this," Hosteen said, matching her tone. "Fifty-five percent of the adults in the Navajo Nation are unemployed, and the poverty rate is forty-six percent. The alcohol and drug use are twice the national average, and so is the suicide rate. Do you seriously think I want to stay here and raise a family?"

Emily winced. She knew the statistics behind what he said were true, but also knew there was more to life on the reservation than numbers. Her decision to remain on Dinétah and do whatever possible to improve conditions for her people had been made long ago; her ties remained longstanding and profound, with little tolerance for attitudes like Hosteen's.

Coward, she thought. *Sellout.*

"Why do you stay here, Emily? You could live better in Albuquerque or Santa Fe."

Emily thought about her childhood, the hours spent sitting at her grandmother's knee listening to stories—the Navajo Creation legend, trickster coyote, the magic of Spider Woman, and many more. She envisioned the powwows, the Sash Belt dance, the Basket dance, herself as a young dancer in a fringed blanket dress, and the communal sharing of food and celebration. But mostly it was the land—it held on to her as tightly and tenaciously as the root of a bindweed plant.

"If I have to explain, you don't get it and never will, Joe." She chewed her lip, irritated with him for pointing out what every white person who came to the reservation remarked on.

Except Abe.

Wanting to change the subject and focus on the job ahead, she said, "We're almost there, and dammit, try not to let your prejudices get in the way while we do this interview."

The Claw homestead consisted of a weather-beaten trailer with a rusted old Dodge truck parked alongside. The ruined remnants of a sheep corral stood broken and abandoned about a hundred yards beyond the trailer. The land appeared desolate and unforgiving—with no indication of the presence of children or animals. Two heavyset women, their eyes narrowed in overt hostility, lips clamped in identical frowns, sat on metal chairs in front of the trailer. They watched as the Explorer pulled up.

"Honk your horn and roll the window down," Emily said. "See if they'll let us get out. I understand you don't speak Navajo."

"Not too much," said Hosteen.

Emily rolled her eyes. "Well, that's helpful. What if the people we interview don't speak English, like plenty of old-timers?" To his shrug she answered, "Let me do the talking."

Hosteen gave the horn three blasts and waited while the women looked impassively at the occupants of the Explorer. Finally, one of the women stood up and walked stiffly toward the police vehicle, stopping at Emily's open window. Emily knew that because of lack of proper nutrition, nearly one in three Navajo were diabetic or pre-diabetic. Watching the heavy woman struggle to walk on swollen legs was a clear indication that this woman was one of the sufferers.

It wasn't always like this, Emily thought, *before all that white flour and lard.*

She was brought back to the present by the woman's raspy voice.

"We didn't do nothing wrong. What do you cops want?"

"Yá'át'ééh," said Emily. "You're not in trouble. We're looking for some information about the girl that disappeared five years ago. Can you help us?"

A shadow crossed the woman's face, clouding her flat Indian eyes. "The cops never found her—why are you here now? Did you find my daughter's body?" she asked in a tremulous voice. "Did you find Mary Jo?"

"No. Are you her mother?"

The woman heaved a heavy sigh. "Yes. Get on down." Looking back over her shoulder at the other woman, she said, "Nonni, grab two more chairs outta the kitchen, and heat up the coffee."

The only people remaining in the Claw household were the two middle-aged sisters, Blanche and Nonni. Blanche, the mother of the missing girl, said her husband had run off a couple of years after she lost her daughter, and her parents had both died.

"So that's when I told Nonni to move in with me. She didn't have no husband or kids of her own, and I didn't have no one left."

The coffee was thick as tar and mixed with some kind of bitter-tasting herb. Emily took a sip, trying not to make a face. She glanced at Joe, registering his grimace as he set his mug down. "Tell me about your daughter's *Kinaaldá*," Emily said.

Blanche Claw lowered her substantial body into the sagging lawn chair with an audible moan. "It was her grandma who arranged it. Mary Jo being her only grandchild, she wanted her to have a traditional *Kinaaldá* when she came of age." The woman wrung her hands. "We had a big party ready for when she returned from her run—singers, a feast. She didn't come back. I never learned what happened to her. Afterward, her father drank more and took it out on me. One day he ran off. Then my mama died—later Dad. I didn't care about the sheep or nothing else after that." Blanche's eyes became watery, and her sister patted her trembling hand.

Hosteen, who had remained quiet up to this point, broke into the conversation. "Mrs. Claw, if you speak English, I'd like to ask you a question. I noticed you had some trouble walking? Arthritis?"

"Yes, and diabetes," she answered in English. "Runs in the family."

"That's a shame," said Hosteen. "My mother has diabetes, too. How long have you been afflicted?"

"All my life, just about," said the woman. "Nonni here has diabetes, too, and so does—did—my girl."

"So I guess there are people from Indian Services who come out here and check your blood sugar to see how you're doing?"

Emily studied Hosteen, wondering where this was going.

"Sure do," said Blanche, nodding her head.

Her sister, Nonni, nodded along with her. "There's that home health-care person comes out every two weeks, and a social worker. Used to have a tutor come out here for Mary Jo before she went missing."

"You had the same people coming all the time?" asked Hosteen.

"Sometimes—pretty much, I guess," said Blanche. "Course the tutor don't come no more."

Emily's pulse quickened as she realized where Hosteen's line of questioning was headed.

"Could you give us the names of all the people who made home visits at the time your daughter disappeared, Miss Claw?"

"Well, if I can remember all their names. They come and go." She closed her eyes in concentration. "You don't think one of them . . . ?"

Once they were back in the car, Emily had to admit it, reluctant though she was. "Smart questioning, Joe. I should have thought of that."

"You would have," he said. "In time." He smiled, looking smugly pleased with himself—or so Emily thought.

"Let's stop in Shiprock at the Department of Family Services and see what we can find out about these names Blanche Claw gave us," said Emily. "I'm curious to know if any of them still work on the rez."

"That's where I'm headed," said Hosteen. "It makes sense. Someone familiar with the land had inside information about when these different girls were having a *Kinaaldá* ceremony. But first, we need to talk to the other parents—the ones I saw yesterday—to see if they were receiving home services from the same people as well."

"Right," Emily said. "I'm getting ahead of myself. I know we should, but we don't have much time. It'll be quicker to check the records at Family Services." She paused and stared out the window as the image of Shiprock, a hazy peak on the horizon, appeared. "There's going to be a *Kinaaldá* for the Nez girl out at Mexican Water on Wednesday. I plan on being there."

"To keep an eye on things?" said Hosteen. "Good idea."

"To participate," Emily answered in a near whisper.

Hosteen gave her a sidelong glance. "I'm coming along."

"Lina and I run at sunrise," Emily said.

7

Monday, April 9, 1990

Mattie Simmons's Churro Sheep Ranch

Bloomfield, New Mexico

Monday morning, as the rising sun set fire to billowing cumulus clouds, Abe crawled out of bed, stretched, and yawned. He wished he could sleep longer; his body ached after a day of wrestling and castrating lambs, but today there were piano lessons to give, and before that, animals to feed and water and pens to clean.

He was out by the sheep pens filling a watering trough when a pickup pulled up and honked.

A woman with close-cropped red hair sat behind the wheel. A tow-headed teenager was seated on the passenger side. "We brought your sheep back," the woman said. "We would have brought it sooner if I'd seen it, but Danny hid it in the shed." She switched off the ignition, and the engine shuddered to a stop.

Abe walked to the older-model Ford and peered into the bed. Sure enough, there was his yearling, tethered to a tire to prevent it from jumping out. The lamb baaed loudly when he approached and appeared to have a bandage wrapped around its right hind leg.

"Why do you have my sheep?" Abe asked the young man as he opened the tailgate and gently set the animal on the ground. "What happened to its leg?"

"I . . . I . . . was only trying to help. It was caught on the fence, and you weren't home. I didn't steal it." He nervously rubbed his hands on his pant legs. "I'm sorry I had to cut the fence."

Abe looked at the kid. He appeared to be about eighteen or nineteen. Gangly limbs, freckles scattered across a pale face, green-speckled hazel eyes like his mother's darting from side to side, not meeting Abe's gaze.

"Okay, I fixed the fence. At least you brought him back."

"Danny," the mother said, "why don't you take Mister . . . ?"

"Freeman. Abe Freeman. Just call me Abe. I don't go by mister."

"Abe." She smiled. Her eyes were the same color as her son's, only more alive. "Why don't you take Abe's sheep to the corral with the others?"

"Okay," said Danny. "Can I stay and watch him awhile? Make sure he's gonna be all right?"

"Yes, for a few minutes." When Danny scooted out of the truck, the woman held out her hand. "Ellen Jorgenson. I guess you noticed my boy is a little slow, but he's good-hearted, and he didn't mean no harm to your sheep."

Abe shook the woman's proffered hand. "No harm was done. If he hadn't cut the yearling loose, a coyote or something would have got him for sure."

The woman smiled again, brightening her features. "We live up the road about half a mile, Danny and I. Sometimes I let him walk down these dirt roads just for the chance to get some exercise and fresh air, though he never goes far. That's when he saw your sheep. He loves animals. Loves them more than people."

"I can appreciate that," Abe said.

Danny jogged back to the truck, with Patch following right on his heels. He reached down and playfully ruffled the little mutt's coat. "I like your dog. What's his name?"

"Patch," Abe said. "See those black markings covering his right eye? That's why I called him Patch."

Danny nodded, a questioning look lingering on his face. "But why does he only have three legs?"

"Patch was in an accident, hit by a car. My girlfriend and I rescued him. He's practically good as new now."

The young man's face became serious. "I was in a car accident, too."

Ellen Jorgenson looked at her son, who sat on the ground playing with Patch. "Danny and his dad were driving home from Sonic one night. I just had to have me a chili dog with some onion rings. On the way home, a drunk driver crossed the center line from the opposite direction, hit their car head-on. My husband died instantly, and Danny ended up with massive injuries and a steel plate in his skull. He was twelve years old when it happened—he still is."

"I'm sorry. It must be tough for you."

Ellen sighed and turned her head away, watching her son. "Yes, it's hard, but it's been eight years now. I still have my boy. He's what keeps me going." She leaned her head out the open window. "Danny, come on now, son. We gotta get goin'." Before she started the truck, she scribbled something on a scrap of paper and handed it to Abe. "Here's my phone number. If you ever need help with the animals, give me a call. He may not be real smart, but Danny's a hard worker, he's honest, and he'll do as he's told." The stress lines on her face appeared to ease. "I thank you for not calling the cops."

The young man waved, and Abe raised his hand in farewell as the truck rumbled away. He folded the paper and slipped it into his pocket, doubting he would ever need it. He examined the cut on the yearling's leg. He would have to hurry to make it on time for his ten o'clock lesson.

The wound was not deep and showed no sign of infection. Danny had wrapped it with clean strips of muslin. Abe finished feeding the animals and, with Patch's help, herded them into separate fields, making sure the section they were in was not overgrazed.

Managing a sheep ranch had turned out to be more complicated than Abe had imagined—rotating pastures, checking fence lines, and making sure the animals remained healthy. But then, so had his life in general. He still tried to spend a couple of hours each day practicing the piano on Mattie Simmons's Steinman grand, and he earned a little extra cash by giving lessons two days a week at a local middle school. In fact, it was Lina, Charley Nez's daughter, he would be teaching that day. Abe smiled and shook his head. Lina was a chubby girl with a sweet, dimpled face. Timid at first, she now attacked the piano with gusto. What Lina lacked in aptitude, she made up for in enthusiasm.

The night before, Abe had spoken to Charley Nez on the phone and asked if he had heard of anybody trying to sell a yearling. Charley said he hadn't, but he would keep his eyes open. Then he had told Abe about the girl's upcoming ceremony.

"We're having a celebration for Lina—it's her Kinaaldá. You're invited. Come early," he said. "So you can be there when she finishes her race and cuts the corn cake."

As a matter of fact, Abe was looking forward to the event. It would be his first opportunity to watch Will at work as a ceremonial singer, and he enjoyed the dances and music. But it was a two-hour drive from Bloomfield to Mexican Water, and he would have to get an early start. Charley Nez said they were conducting the ceremony there instead of at their home in Kirtland because of the hogan, plus the fact that it was a sheep camp with plenty of room and an outdoor cooking area. Abe would be pushing it if he was going to make it in time for the sunrise run.

I might need Ellen Jorgenson's son, after all.

He decided to call her number when he returned from his piano lesson and ask if Danny would be interested in taking care of the sheep for a day.

He can come tomorrow and walk through the chores with me, and then I'll decide if he can handle it or not.

8

Monday, April 9, 1990

Department of Family Services, Navajo Nation

Shiprock, New Mexico

Emily and Hosteen worked on separate computers in the Office of Personnel Management for the Shiprock Agency of the Navajo Nation. It was a slow, tedious procedure, partly because of the massive turnover in Bureau of Indian Affairs and tribal employees. To make the task more difficult, they learned that some had transferred to a different agency so their records weren't accessible.

"Looks like we're going to have to visit all the personnel offices in the Navajo Nation to get a match," Hosteen said. "This is going to take a long time."

Emily, stiff from bending over a computer monitor for the past two hours, rubbed the back of her neck. "Or, we could make a few calls to Window Rock and sweet-talk some people into doing the personnel search for us—have them fax us the names of social and health-care workers who were employed during the time frame when the girls went missing."

"Good thinking. We have a couple of names to start with—Amy Stark, a social worker, and Phillip Harris, home health-care provider. He's still employed, but there's no recent info on Stark. I'll check Harris's schedule in the Admin office on the way out. If he's anywhere close, we can drop by for a visit." Hosteen pocketed his notepad and pulled his tall, solid frame to a standing position. "I'm ready for lunch. How about you?"

Emily realized they had been together all morning without sniping at each other, and it felt good. *Maybe he's not such a prick,* she thought.

"I could go for some Chinese, and the Wonderful House in Farmington is on our way to the Checkerboard. But first, I've got one more name to add to our list: Wayne Mackey. A social worker. He was recently transferred here from the Northern Agency. Toadlena falls in that region. Maybe he worked there when Mary Jo Claw disappeared." Emily shut down the computer and stood. "Let's eat. After lunch, we'll call Admin in Window Rock and take a drive out to talk to the families you saw yesterday. It's going to be a long day, Joe."

One of the difficulties of working for law enforcement on the Navajo Nation stemmed from the fact that its territory encompassed twenty-seven thousand square miles. No matter where you were, it took a long time to get to where you were going. The Checkerboard area, home to two of the families on their list, wasn't even on the reservation. It comprised a vast section of BIA land east of Farmington, under the joint jurisdictions of the federal government, county, and Diné.

It was after seven by the time they completed their interviews and returned to headquarters. A cold wind blew down from the north, stirring up the dust and sending tumbleweeds skittering across the road, and an icy chill through Emily's bones. She felt achy from the long day of riding in Hosteen's vehicle and couldn't wait to get home. But first she wanted to read the fax sent from Window Rock, the seat of government, and the capital of the Navajo Nation.

"Listen to this," she said to Hosteen. "Amy Stark quit her job and moved on in 1986, but both Mackey and Harris are still employed by the Navajo Nation. Harris transferred from the Northern Agency two years ago. Now, both he and Mackey work the Eastern and Checkerboard. What was the name that family out by Crownpoint mentioned as their social worker?"

"The only name they knew him by was Mac. We'll run a check on both these guys first thing tomorrow."

"We need to catch them at home and question them in person." Emily yawned. "I want a hot shower, some of my mom's green-chili stew, and a good night's sleep. Feel like I've been eating dust all day." Emily walked toward the door, stopped, then turned around to face Hosteen. "We almost got along today—amazing." She grinned. "I hope it lasts." Before she left, she added, "About that Chevy van . . ."

Hosteen laughed, displaying perfectly aligned white teeth. "Forget the van, Emily. We'd be looking for a needle in a haystack, and we don't have time."

Emily had a nagging hunch the van was significant, and it frustrated her that no one else did. "Well, like I said. Almost."

Emily still lived with her mother. She liked the convenience and her mother's companionship. She'd had a rebellious streak as a teenager that ended with the tragic death of her young son. The feeling of remorse would forever haunt her. Her mom was her rock.

Emily came out of the bathroom in her robe, a towel wrapped around her wet hair. "Mom, where's my blanket dress? The one I wore for my *Kinaaldá* ceremony?"

"It's in the cedar chest. Why do you want your dress now?"

"I'm going to wear it Wednesday, to run with Lisa Nez. And my moccasins. Do you think you could fix my hair before leaving for work—the way you did it back then?"

Bertha Etcitty was a no-nonsense woman. She put her hands on her hips and peered over her reading glasses at her only daughter. "Why? Are you starting puberty again—having a second childhood?"

"Mom, this is important. It's part of the investigation I told you about. I want to make sure nothing happens to the girl."

"Well, why don't you just run in your jogging pants and tennies instead of a dress and moccasins?"

"Because I want to look like a young girl celebrating her *Kinaaldá*. I need to draw this guy in if we're going to catch him. Don't worry—I'll have my Glock and a radio with me at all times, and there'll be plenty of people around. I won't let anything happen, but I don't want to scare the perp away either. Joe Hosteen will be close by as backup."

Bertha wrinkled her nose at the mention of Hosteen's name. She had heard enough stories from Emily to have formed the opinion he was an arrogant asshole who rejected his Navajo blood. "Have you discussed this plan to lure the perp in with anyone else, or are you thinking in your stubborn mind that you can do this all by yourself?"

"I discussed it with Abe. He and Will are going to be there, too, Mom. Don't look at me like that."

Bertha's face brightened a little when she heard her son's and Abe's names mentioned. "Tsk, tsk, tsk. It sounds like you're going off on your own again, Emily. I'll bet the captain doesn't know anything about this." She shook her head. "Okay, I'll help you get ready. Now eat your stew before it gets cold."

After eating, Emily placed a call to Charley Nez's home. Charley's wife, Millie, answered the phone.

"Millie, this is Emily Etcitty with the Tribal Police. How are you?"

"I'm good, Emily. Excited and busy—fixing the food and getting ready for my daughter's ceremony. Charley butchered a sheep. Is there a problem?"

"No problem, but you heard about the missing Benally girl, right? Just to stay on the safe side, I'd like to be there at your daughter's ceremony."

"Of course you're invited, Emily. Your brother is going to sing, and perform the blessing."

"I know. Millie, I don't want to just be there, though. I want to wear my *Kinaaldá* dress and run alongside Lina."

There was silence on the other end of the phone. After a moment Millie spoke up, concern in her voice. "You don't think . . . ?"

"No, no," said Emily. "It's simply a precaution."

9

Tuesday, April 10, 1990

Mattie Simmons's Churro Sheep Ranch

Bloomfield, New Mexico

At eight a.m. Emily and Hosteen met with Captain Todechine to discuss their progress on the case.

"We came up with names of two people who might have come in contact with the victims and had been in the vicinity at the time of their disappearances. We're going to try to question them today," Emily said.

"Who're we talking about?" asked Todechine.

Hosteen handed a copy of the report they had generated the night before to the captain. "Two males—Phillip Harris and Wayne Mackey—a home health-care worker and a social worker. They'd both be in a position to know when and where a *Kinaaldá* was about to be celebrated."

"And since their work involves home visits, they'd be familiar with the territory," Emily said.

Todechine arched his eyebrows. "Check them out and let me know. One more thing." He picked up a note from his desk. "This came in from the evidence technicians. The tracks where the Benally girl disappeared—they came from Toyo Tires, seventeen-inch P235/75R15s."

"Meaning what?" said Hosteen.

"Meaning they could have belonged to a 1990 Chevy G20 van. Get on it," said Todechine.

"I knew that van was the key!" Emily said, unable to contain a self-satisfied smirk.

Hosteen winced.

Emily stopped to talk to the desk sergeant, Arviso, and asked him if he could spare anyone to run a trace on a 1990 Chevy van with Colorado plates.

Arviso looked up and frowned. "Probably thousands of them out there. It's going to take some time, and I've got all officers out on the road."

"We're under pressure from the captain, Sarge," Emily said. "We need to know if the registration matches either a Phillip Harris or a Wayne Mackey. It concerns the investigation of the missing girl."

Arviso gave her a long-suffering look. "I'll see what I can do."

"Thanks, I owe you one. If you find out anything, give me a call. Hosteen and I'll be in my vehicle checking the addresses on those two." She caught up with Hosteen and said, "Joe, I'm driving today."

The truth was, Emily disliked being the passenger. Passenger meant "passive" in her mind, and she wanted to be in control of the situation that day—they were closing in on something big. She could sense it.

Hosteen didn't say anything, but he slid into his seat looking sulky, like a man unaccustomed to riding shotgun with a woman.

The addresses they had for the two men turned out to be duds— vacant, dilapidated buildings. They tracked down the owners and learned they had never even heard of either man, and said that no one had lived in either house for years. Their mail was delivered to a post office box in Farmington.

Next, they stopped at the personnel office and asked where the two were scheduled to work that day. They discovered both had put in for an emergency leave of absence, Mackey claiming his mother was ill.

"Damn," said Emily. "Both have address duds and put in for leave at the same time? That's too coincidental, don't you think?"

Hosteen raised an eyebrow. "Hmm. We'll talk to their coworkers, maybe get some insights about these two. Like where they hang out, who their friends are—anything that might help."

"Right. *Dzil ná oodili* is the nearest health center. Someone there should be able to fill in a few blanks."

Interviews with coworkers there and at Human Resources failed to turn up anything other than a vague description of two Anglo men— both in their early or late forties with no distinguishing marks. Mackey was described as having a ruddy complexion, being a little overweight, and having light-brown hair. Harris was wiry, shorter, and darker-skinned. Coworkers remarked he spoke with a Texas accent, but both men kept mostly to themselves. They all said the same thing—the pair often carpooled to work and shared a government vehicle when making home visits, but rarely interacted with other staff members.

The day was nearly shot, and, so far, they had failed to produce any useful leads.

"We might as well call it quits," said Hosteen. "We're not getting anywhere, and I'm damn tired. Are you still planning to run in that race tomorrow?"

"Yes, of course. I told Charley Nez I'd be there, but it's going to be an all-day affair." She slumped in her seat, tired and cranky, not wanting to talk. The crackle of the radio broke the strained silence.

"Ten-four, dispatcher. What've you got?"

"Got one match on your suspects. A 1988 Chevy Vanagon, regis-tered in Montezuma County, Colorado, to Wayne Mackey. License-plate number: Uniform—Papa—Yankee—Five—Four—Niner. Home address listed at 1159 Chapman Road, Cortez, Colorado. I've got his mug right here in front of me. Do you read?"

"Ten-four. Put out an APB right away, and notify the Cortez Police Department of a possible hostage situation at that address."

"Ten-four, Etcitty."

After the call, Emily turned to Hosteen, her skin prickling. "Did you get that down, Joe? He has to be one of our kidnappers. Now we need to make sure the girl is all right and nail his sorry ass."

10

Wednesday, April 11, 1990

Mattie Simmons's Churro Sheep Ranch

Bloomfield, New Mexico

Mexican Water lay a half hour's drive from Teec Nos Pos, on the Arizona side of the Navajo Reservation. Abe had set the alarm for four thirty a.m. to make it to the *Kinaaldá* in time for Emily's sunrise run with Lina Nez. It was pitch-dark when the shrill buzz pulled him from a restless sleep. He sat up abruptly, sweat beading his forehead, the remnant of a disturbing dream tainting his thoughts. In the dream Emily was calling for help, her arms stretching out to him as she began to sink into sand, but Abe could not move. His limbs felt as heavy as a load of bricks, and he could not lift them to reach her, no matter how hard he tried.

Abe shook his head. He went into the bathroom, splashed cold water on his face, and hurriedly dressed. He went out the door, reluctantly leaving Patch behind, and left a house key under the mat for the Jorgensons. The day before he had shown Danny where he kept tools and animal feed, and had told him how much grain to give the sheep in the morning. Patch would help the young man separate the animals into their proper grazing areas, and as an added assurance, he had written everything down on a notepad for Ellen.

As the truck rumbled down the dark and deserted highway toward Mexican Water, Abe replayed the previous night's conversation with Emily. They had identified two possible suspects in the kidnapping of the young girls but so far had not been able to locate either.

Sounding breathless and exhausted, Emily had said, "Cortez Police went to the address given by Phillip Harris when he applied for his Colorado driver's license. It's the home of his widowed mother, Sophia Harris, but she swore she hadn't seen her son for over three years—not since he left the Mormon Church and became involved in some cult. Cortez cops and the Montezuma County sheriff's department are keeping a twenty-four-hour watch on the house just the same. At least we have a face."

"What about the other suspect?" Abe had asked.

"No trace of him yet, but we know he hangs out with Harris, and the two of them made home visits to the victims and were familiar with all the back roads on the rez. Arviso is going to look into any possible cult activity in the vicinity."

Abe had worried about Emily, at age thirty-two, dressing like a young girl and running in a race, using herself as bait to draw out a couple of psychopaths. "Don't do it, Em. Keep an eye on things and be ready, but don't put yourself in danger. Play it by the book this time."

Emily had laughed. She kept insisting there was nothing to worry about.

"I want to be near the girl, Abe, and I'll be armed. I talked to Charley. The morning trail is two miles in and two miles out. There's only one road that intersects that trail, and a couple of clan members are going to station themselves there and near the midway point. At dusk, we will run for the final time. It is a different path but heads toward the east, clockwise, in pursuit of the setting sun. It's a shorter route, and there are no roads that cross or run alongside the trail. Then Lina can cut the *alcaan*, the big corn cake she made to honor the sun, and we can celebrate her coming-of-age. It's all about the cycle of life, balance, and harmony, Abe."

Abe hadn't realized there would be a morning *and* an evening run. That meant he would have to be there the entire day. In fact, the traditional ceremony lasted for four days, but because of employment obligations of family members, Charley and Millie Nez had to cut their festivities down to one big day of celebration.

"Be careful, Emily," he had said before hanging up.

When Abe reached the hogan at Mexican Water, he saw Lina Nez lying facedown on a blanket, her arms stretched out perpendicular to her body. She wore a brightly woven dress tied with a sash belt and adorned with turquoise-and-shell jewelry. Leggings and buckskin moccasins completed her ensemble. Will, kneeling at her side, appeared to be giving the girl a massage. He chanted in Navajo as he stretched and pulled on her limbs. His medicine bag, or *jish*, was draped around his neck. Abe watched in silence, unaware until she spoke that Emily had appeared by his side.

"Will got here yesterday and spent the night singing. He's molding her body now," Emily said. "Making sure she grows straight and vigorous in the image of Changing Woman, the mother of creation, and daughter of night and dawn."

Abe turned to gaze at Emily, awed by her appearance. "You look like a young girl yourself, a beautiful young Indian princess." Emily had dressed in a manner similar to Lina, but her blanket dress was woven in a red-and-black pattern, as opposed to Lina's blue, black, and white. Ornate turquoise-and-silver jewelry draped around her neck and wrists.

Her hair, like Lina's, was pulled back and combed into a traditional Navajo bun, and tied with long strands of white yarn.

"What is Will singing about?"

"*Hózhóójí.* The Blessing Way," she said. "It's sung at a girl's *Kinaaldá* to ensure a life of good health, emotional strength, prosperity, and a positive outlook." She wrinkled her nose, and her eyes turned misty. "I guess it didn't work so well for me, considering I was such a fuckup when I was young."

Abe touched her face and tilted it so he could look in her eyes. "You're the bravest, most caring person I know. It just took you a while to find yourself. This *Kinaaldá* business is bringing back memories." He brushed an escaping tear from her cheek.

Emily shook her head and laughed, regaining her composure. "Stop being a worrywart. It'll be over soon, and we will have the bad guys." She looked toward the eastern horizon. The first rays of sunlight kissed the red buttes and rock spires, casting a rosy glow on the juniper-flecked desert. She saw Lina stand up and beckon to her. "It looks like we are about to begin," Emily said to Abe. "Remember, no eating the corn cake until after the races. Cutting and serving it is Lina's job."

Emily joined the girl standing in front of the hogan. Holding hands and smiling, they faced the flaming aurora of a beautiful sunrise.

11

The morning run was completed without a hitch, though Emily had to slow down frequently to encourage the chubby Nez girl. Lina was out of shape and apparently not used to physical exercise. The long festivities of the night before and restricted diet of nothing but cornmeal mush had left her body weak and exhausted. Emily knew the girl wanted to run farther and faster to show her endurance and prove that she would be a strong woman, but her body could not oblige what her mind desired.

"Just a little farther," Emily had said to the wheezing girl, bent forward and holding her sides. "You can rest in the hogan until the evening race." She had been vigilant about checking the brush along the path for signs of anything unusual and had seen nothing. They were on their way back, less than a mile from the hogan. The small band of children who tagged behind them at the beginning of the race had quickly fallen by the wayside and returned to their parents. "I'll tell you what, Lina. Walk a little ways until you catch your breath. When we are close, you can run again. It will be our secret." She winked at the girl and received a dimpled grin of gratitude in return.

Judging by the sun's position in the morning sky, Abe determined it was nearly ten o'clock. He stood off by himself, surveying the small gathering. Friends and family members would not begin to arrive until dusk. After Lina cut the corn cake, the older women would start serving the rest of the food and drinks. Will continued to sing, nodding his head in time to the rhythm, his voice soft and mystical. The women tended to the tortilla-making and stew pots while the men stood in small groups, smoking and telling stories. Abe felt like the misfit he was and wished he could be somewhere else. But he would stay until Emily finished the final race and was headed home, safe and sound. He heard cheers, looked up to see the two runners coming down the path, and breathed a sigh of relief.

He grinned when he saw Emily's flushed face, and she smiled back. Will had finished his session of prayer songs. He stood up to take a break and greet the runners as well.

Abe ambled over and put his arm around Emily. "Well?"

"So far, so good," she said. "Poor Lina is worn out, though. She is going to take a nap before her hair is recombed and we run the second race." Emily filled a cup from the water tank and downed it.

One of the women held out a plate piled high with slices of roasted lamb, green chilies, and tortillas, and beckoned to them.

"Fasting is not a requirement for this job," Emily said. "Come on."

"You go ahead," Abe said, hanging back, feeling intrusive. Charley Nez would have none of it.

He brought Abe a Styrofoam cup filled with coffee, and a paper plate full of steaming meat and chili wrapped in warm tortillas. "Eat, my friend, and thank you for coming to my daughter's *Kinaaldá*. It made her happy to see you here."

Abe thanked his host, grateful for the hot meal after his early morning wake-up. He joined Emily and Will.

"Nice singing, Will."

Will, his mouth full, nodded in response. Between bites, he said, "Stick around. More to come. It gets better."

"Where's your sidekick?" Abe asked Emily.

"Hosteen? He should be showing up anytime. He can't stay all day, though—has to go to Cortez to question the mother of a potential suspect first."

The sound of an approaching vehicle caught Abe's attention, and he watched as a white Ford Explorer with the insignia of the Navajo Nation Police pulled into the parking area. The tall, lanky man who emerged from the vehicle reminded Abe of an origami creation unfolding.

So this is the infamous Joe Hosteen.

Emily saw him, too, and excused herself. She stood beside Hosteen, their heads bowed together in a private discussion. Despite himself, Abe felt a pang of jealousy. After their conversation, Hosteen got back in his SUV and drove away.

A short time later, Emily disappeared inside the hogan. It was close to noon, and a brisk wind began kicking up the desert sand, making the juniper trees whistle and last year's dead tumbleweeds roll into irregular hillocks. Abe huddled with a group of men, drinking coffee, making small talk about sheep, and listening to Navajo jokes he often did not get. The day moved slowly. He missed Patch and wondered if Danny was doing all right, knowing there was no way he could call and find out. The guests chatted and watched the sky, waiting for dusk so the celebrating could begin.

By the time Emily and Lina emerged from the hogan in the late afternoon, a crowd of about fifty guests had arrived—the women dressed in their fanciest velvet blouses and turquoise jewelry, the men in blue jeans, cowboy boots, and ribbon shirts. The mood became celebratory. Will sang to the accompaniment of two additional drummers, and some of the women initiated a circle dance. The two runners smiled, looking freshly primped and rested. Lina's face beamed with excitement as she caught Abe's eye. Abe watched as she approached a group of young children and, one by one, lifted them by their arms.

After the song, Will sidled up beside Abe to explain. "It's part of the ceremony. She's stretching their bodies so they'll grow straight and tall."

Abe nodded while he scanned faces in the crowd. Most were Navajo, but he spotted a few Anglos bunched together, off to the side. *Teachers, possibly?* One man wearing a ball cap stood alone, leaning against a white pickup truck. He appeared to be speaking on a walkie-talkie. *Suspicious, or just another guest making contact with a friend?* Every stranger looked suspicious to Abe. He chewed his lip and wondered when Hosteen would return.

Will had been singing prayer songs on and off all afternoon. His voice sounded scratchy, and his eyes burned red with fatigue. He patted Abe's shoulder and said, "I have eight prayers to sing while the girls run. After that, I can rest and let the others do the singing and dancing." As the sun dropped in the western sky, Will returned to his drum and began chanting to a soft, rhythmic beat.

Emily and Lina stood side by side once again, this time facing the setting sun. The wind whipped at their skirts as they began the final race. Hosteen had still not returned. For a reason he couldn't understand, Abe felt the skin prickle on the back of his neck.

The once-puffy white clouds now rumbled, gray and angry. Emily jogged beside Lina, who had slowed considerably from her beginning pace. Something moved in the brush. *It's just the wind,* Emily told herself. Nevertheless, she felt more secure once she put a hand on the butt of the weapon she had holstered over her buckskin leggings.

Something lay in the middle of the path ahead of them. When Emily realized what it was, her blood chilled. The coyote pelt had been freshly skinned, and the head had been left attached—the eyes, sorrowful and accusing, burned into hers. Emily froze in her tracks, grasped her Glock in both hands, and pivoted in a circle, responding to each sound made by the wind whistling through the *piñon* and sagebrush. Lina let out a cry and began backing away. Stumbling over her own feet, she whimpered, fell to the ground, and cowered, her arms shielding her head and face.

"Coyote has turned into a skinwalker and is coming for us."

Emily hurried to Lina's side and knelt down to help her. "Stand up and stay close to me. Coyote didn't do this." Keeping the Glock steady in one hand, she grabbed the radio with the other. But before she could turn it on, she felt a stinging sensation on the back of her neck. She brushed at it, thinking a scorpion had bitten her. Then she saw the dart—a syringe and hypodermic needle with a distinctive tuft of fibrous material at the end—fall to the ground. A cold sweat broke out on her forehead. Based on her experience with sedating rogue animals, Emily knew it would only be a matter of seconds before she lost all muscle control.

Already, the hand holding her Glock felt numb. She tried to aim it in the direction she thought the dart had come from. She began to feel the full effects of the drug and discovered she couldn't move her arm. Her fingers lost their grasp on the Glock, and the two-way radio fell at her feet. She tried shouting, but nothing came out. Her legs crumpled under her. With her eyes wide in horror, Emily watched helplessly as a hooded figure grabbed Lina and covered her face with a handkerchief. The girl went limp, and the man picked her up as if she were a sack of flour. Emily's police mind remained sharp even though her body was immobilized. She knew what the outcome would be. She had been hit with a tranquilizer dart containing a fast-acting paralyzing agent. She was completely immobilized and might die soon—and she had failed to protect Lina.

12

Abe shoved his hands into his pockets and shuffled his feet. It was getting cold and dark. *Emily should be back by now. And where the hell is Hosteen?* He decided he would go out on his own to find out what was keeping the runners. He grabbed a jacket from his truck. While in the parking area, Emily's partner pulled up and jumped out of his vehicle.

"Are they back yet?" Hosteen yelled, a note of urgency in his voice.

"No. Where have you been? You were supposed to be here hours ago."

"I got held up—a wreck on 666. Who the hell are you?"

"I'm Emily's friend—Emily's boyfriend. They should have been back by now. This was supposed to be a short run. I'm going to look for her." Abe turned to walk away, but Hosteen stopped him.

"We'll go together. It's quicker this way."

Abe heard the urgency in Hosteen's voice and felt a chill. "What's wrong? I thought there were no roads along this trail. I'm going to follow the path."

"There's a pipeline that runs near here. Check the camp one more time to see if they made it. If Emily and the girl have returned safe and sound, great. No problem. If not, tell Emily's brother and Charley Nez to get a search party together. Hurry up—there's a storm coming." Hosteen had already jumped behind the wheel of the Explorer and had the engine idling.

Abe didn't argue—he took off running. When he returned and hopped in Hosteen's waiting vehicle, he said, "There's no sign of them. Will already took off down the path on his motorcycle. A search party on foot is right behind him. Do you know something you're not telling me?"

"Just a gut feeling something's not right." A streak of lightning momentarily illuminated the Explorer's interior, casting an eerie glow on the Navajo's chiseled face. Hosteen spun out of the parking lot and tried his radio. "Out of range, and dammit, here comes the rain." A few big drops splattered the dusty windshield.

"Shit," Abe said when it began to rain harder. "I never liked the idea of her doing this." He drummed his fingers on the dashboard. "Can't you speed up? We have to find them. What's your plan?"

"I'm going as fast as I can. And, to start with, we locate the pipeline, look for any sign of recent disturbance—broken branches, bent or broken grass, tire tracks—whatever doesn't seem right." He gave Abe a sideways glance. "You got a name, buddy?"

It sure as hell isn't "buddy," Abe thought. Why hasn't Emily even mentioned me to her colleague—now partner?

"Name's Abe Freeman."

"Hosteen," the cop said, his mouth an unsmiling seam. He turned on the side-mounted spotlight and drove slowly down the rain-drenched right-of-way.

"How are you going to find a pipeline in the dark? It all looks the same out there." Abe's trepidation increased. He needed to do something besides ride around in the dark next to this asshole, who was supposed to have helped protect Emily and the girl.

But so was I.

"I should have followed them on the last race."

Hosteen ignored Abe's remarks. "One of the boys at the station got some maps from the National Pipeline Mapping System. They show all the main gas lines, state by state and county by county. There's a pipeline near here—connects with a major line near Farmington and ends in Kayenta. The gas company had to clear the brush to make way for the line, and they use it when they check for problems. It's not really a road, and it's off-limits to everyone but the pipeline workers. It runs along here somewhere. I want you to keep an eye out for a yellow marker sign designating an underground line."

Abe let out a frustrated sigh, but after a few minutes said, "I think I see a marker up ahead."

Hosteen froze the spotlight on a yellow pipe and a small clearing on the right. "This is it. It's where we start. Are you coming or staying here?"

"Hell, yes, I'm coming."

Hosteen grabbed a flashlight, and the two men scrambled up a slippery slickrock embankment only to quickly descend into a rocky ravine. Once out of the ravine, the land leveled out into a treeless, meadowlike strip. Hosteen swung the flashlight across a narrow ribbon of land bordered on one side by the canyon and on the other by oak brush and juniper. "This is the pipeline. The girl's running path should be no more than thirty or forty yards to the right of those juniper trees. If anyone came after them in a vehicle, it had to be somewhere along here. Start looking for any signs something or someone came through here."

Abe rummaged through his jacket pocket for the small flashlight he carried on his key chain. It wasn't long before the narrow beam picked up the distinct markings of snapped juniper branches and tire ruts heading through the brushy area. "Over here!" he shouted.

Even in the rain, they could tell a vehicle had backed about ten yards into the brush.

"They came in here, then left. See where a car drove out?" Hosteen tried his radio again but still could not get a signal. "Goddammit. I need to get a roadblock set up and call for assistance. I don't like the looks of this. Freeman, I want you to get back to the trail and find the search party. See if they came up with anything. I've got to drive somewhere I can get a signal and radio this in."

Abe felt the blood drain from his face and a cold chill course through his body as the realization hit him. He breathed in short gasps, didn't seem to be able to get enough oxygen. "You think someone came in here and took Emily and the girl? I'm going with you." Rain dripped off his ball cap and light windbreaker, and he shuddered. "You might run into them along the way."

"No, you're not. You're going to do as I say. Now get going before the search party arrives and walks all over the possible evidence. That's the best way to help right now."

Abe considered arguing but changed his mind. *Will rode his motorcycle down here,* he thought. *I'll take it and follow those tire tracks myself. Will can watch things at the camp.*

"All right, Hosteen. Quit wasting time talking—and you better have the cops looking for a Chevy van."

He turned and crashed through the brush until he saw Will, illuminated in the rain by the light of his motorcycle, kneeling over something in the path and chanting in a tormented voice.

Emily! he thought.

He ran toward Will. When he neared the motionless shape in the road, he realized Will was looking at an animal of some kind—a coyote. It was only the hide and head. Will, startled by the noise, swung around and clenched his fists, his face contorted in anguish. He dropped his hands to his sides when he realized who it was. His eyes brimmed with tears as he stared helplessly at Abe.

"They're gone," he said. "See the dart on the ground? It's from a tranquilizer gun. They must have immobilized Emily before she could do anything. I'm going after them."

Abe's stomach churned when he saw the dart, the empty syringe still attached. "No, Will, wait. Let me take the bike. We found tracks from their van I can follow, and you should stay here to talk to the family—they need you. And somebody has to keep people away from the crime scene."

Will rubbed his forehead and inhaled deeply. "You don't understand. I let my people down. I let Emily down. How could this have happened?"

"It's not your fault. Please, Will, stay and keep watch. And don't let anyone touch the coyote or dart, or anything else. Keep them off the crime scene. There might be tracks—if the rain doesn't wash them away." Abe could feel his heart pounding, the taste of fear in his mouth, the tightness in his muscles. He knew he had only a little time before the tire tracks near the pipeline disappeared as well. "We're wasting time, Will. Hosteen will be back as soon as he can call in for assistance." He reached into his pocket. "Here're the keys to the truck. You can take it to my place and stay there tonight."

"I'll stick around here for a while. I'm gonna do a powerful ceremony—*Nayeejii A'cha Soodiziz*, the Dangerous Way Protection Prayer—for Emily and Lina. And for you. I'm gonna sing it till all of you get back. Go on. But be careful, brother."

Abe put a hand on Will's shoulder and looked him in the eye. "We'll find them," he said, trying to convince himself as well as Will. He knew Emily might be dying from the tranquilizer dart, and he hated not knowing how or where to reach her. He quickly mounted the bike, rolled it off the kickstand, fumbled with the switches, and jumped on the starter a couple of times. When the Chief rumbled to life, he turned the bike around and headed back through the brush in the direction he had come.

The rain turned to a drizzle, leaving the pipeline slick and tread marks hard to see. It didn't matter, though. Abe knew the direction they were headed, and with the canyon on one side and dense brush on the other, there was no place to turn off. This section was relatively smooth and flat—nothing but the slippery surface to keep him from driving fast.

He had covered about three miles when he noticed a well-lit area and what appeared to be a flame in the sky ahead. As he got closer, he realized the fire was coming out of a flare stack at a natural-gas pumping station. A portable generator attached to a truck supplied power for a floodlight. A dirt road, heading north-south, intersected the site. Unfortunately, the trucks and equipment vehicles parked nearby made it impossible to distinguish one set of tracks from another. A group of men stood close to a cluster of tanks, pipes, pumps, and drilling rigs. Abe scanned the vehicles, looking for any sign of a white Chevy van. When he didn't spot it, he approached the workers, hoping someone had seen it and could tell him which direction the van had taken.

Too late, he realized his mistake.

A half dozen men, dressed in red coveralls, stared at him as he dismounted the bike and began walking his way. One, a heavyset man with a potbelly, clutched a plumber's wrench in his hand. Abe stopped in his tracks, locking eyes with the racist lout he had decked at Doc's Diner. While the others looked on with smirks on their faces, the oil-rig worker slowly walked toward Abe, swinging the wrench back and forth.

"Well, whaddya know? Look at the piece of shit that just blew in. I bet you're the punk who's been messing with these valves, too. Trying to make more trouble for us, aren't you, squaw-lover?"

Abe put his hands in the air. "I didn't come here to make trouble, and I haven't touched anything." Abe's mouth went dry, and he licked his lips. "Look, if you're itching for a fight, just name the place and time. We can settle things later. All I want from any of you is information, and I'll be on my way. It's urgent. I'm looking for some missing girls. Someone took them. Did anyone see a white Chevy van go by?"

"What if we did, asshole?" said the guy with the wrench.

"Just tell me which way it went."

The brute stopped less than a foot away. They stood eyeball-to-eyeball when the rigger grinned, swung the wrench, and smashed it into the side of Abe's right knee.

Abe gasped in pain and doubled over, grasping his knee with one hand. He held up the other in surrender. "Just tell me which way, you son of a bitch," he croaked before an uppercut caught him in the solar plexus, and he tumbled to the ground.

The gas-line worker, like an animal smelling a kill, began kicking him in the side and head. "That'll teach you to mess with me, you worthless piece of shit." He raised the wrench above Abe, ready to deal another blow, but the other men jumped in and pulled him away.

Abe lay in the mud, gasping for breath, struggling to remain conscious. He heard shouting: "McCaffey, you crazy fool. You're going to kill him. Let's clean up the job and get the hell out of here before someone else shows up." The floodlight went out, car doors slammed, engines roared—then there was nothing but the steady drip of rain.

"Goddammit. I told you to stay at the crime scene. What the hell did you think you were going to do?"

Abe's eyes fluttered open wide enough to recognize the angry face of Joe Hosteen. The Navajo police officer helped him to a sitting position, and Abe groaned in pain. He shivered from the cold, blood oozed from his split lip, his head throbbed like a beaten stepchild, and his knee felt twice its normal size. When he tried to stand, the knee buckled and he stumbled to the ground with a grunt.

"You need a doctor," Hosteen said.

Abe waved him off. "I'll be okay. Gotta move around is all." He clambered to his feet and cautiously tested his leg. "Did you find anything?" He cringed and bent over, holding his knee as a new spasm of pain shot through his body.

"No. As soon as I got within range, I called the dispatcher. They put out an APB, but nothing yet—backup crew and crime-scene investigators are on the way, and Emily's brother is standing guard." Hosteen shook his head in disgust. "Jesus Christ. What did you think you could accomplish by taking off on your own?"

"Thought there was a chance I could catch up with them, or at least see which way they went." Abe held his jaw and wiggled it back and forth. Nothing appeared broken. And though one eye was nearly swollen shut, his tongue told him all his teeth were intact. "Saw a work crew here, so I stopped to ask if they had seen a white Chevy van. This guy jumped me—McCaffey, they called him."

Hosteen raised an eyebrow.

"We had a run-in a few days ago. He made some crude remarks about Emily."

"Get used to it."

"That's what Emily told me," he said, rubbing his knee.

"Can you make it back to my vehicle? I'm dropping you off at the hospital. Then you can file a complaint."

Abe shook his head. "Where's Will's bike?" he asked, looking around.

"Back there." Hosteen pointed with his head. "Someone must have kicked it over."

"Help me stand it up. I'll ride it back and talk to Will, try to find out if they learned anything. I'm not quitting—I'll try to find their tracks." He moved toward the motorcycle, stopped, and faced Hosteen. "There was an Anglo guy at the ceremony. I saw him standing beside a white truck—Ford, I think. He was alone and talking on a portable radio. When I went to my truck to get a jacket, he was gone."

"I'll check it out. Listen, Freeman, you're in no condition to do any riding. You need to take care of your knee. I know Emily's your girlfriend and you want to find her—I don't blame you—but don't try being the Lone Ranger. Go home, stay out of the way, and let the Indians do their job." Before he left, he gave his number to Abe. "Call me if you hear anything."

13

Unknown Location

Emily's eyes shot open. She tried moving and discovered that her arms and legs were pinned down, strapped onto something flat—a cot or gurney. She was inside a moving vehicle. Men's voices, sounding hollow and distant, echoed in her head.

"Oh, fuck."

"What the hell's wrong?"

"I remember the girl's case. She's diabetic."

"Shit. What do we do now?"

"I don't know. We can't let the boss know we screwed up. I'll figure out something."

She lifted her head and immediately felt a rush of nausea. "Lina?" she whispered, twisting her head from left to right as she searched for the girl. A wash of dizziness swept over her, and she closed her eyes. Emily wasn't sure if she was actually hearing voices or just dreaming.

She drifted off to sleep again, then awoke, thinking she was drowning. Her body was drenched in sweat. Struggling against her bonds, Emily opened her eyes to see a man's face peering down at her.

"Ah, you're awake. Good. I was afraid the dose of ketamine in the dart might have been too powerful, but your vital signs look good. I did practice on the coyote first, though, and estimated his weight before I increased the dosage for you," the man said.

She blinked, blinded by the glare of an intense beam of light on her face. Her head pounded and her stomach clenched in panic. "What were you talking about? Where's Lina?" she said, her voice sounding far away and disconnected from her body.

"Nobody was talking. Don't worry about the girl. She's sleeping peacefully." The man's accent was Midwestern, a flat monotone. He shined the light on the inert figure of Lina, strapped to another gurney. "I just took her pulse rate and blood pressure—a little low, but there's nothing to worry about. She should be waking soon. Chloroform doesn't stay in the body long, so I gave her a little more to prevent her from waking up too early and becoming overanxious."

They were moving along a bumpy road. Emily choked back the bile in her throat. "Where are you taking us?"

"You're going to like it there. We didn't plan on bringing you along, but you were in the way—a problem. So, lucky you, you are one of the chosen ones now, too. There is no greater honor than to be selected by our Divine Prophet and leader."

When Abe returned to the crime scene, the police had already arrived and taped off the area. Will, rain dripping from his battered hat, stood off to the side by a clump of bushes listening to a group of Navajo men. Charley Nez, his face contorted with rage and grief, was shouting at him in Navajo.

Will looked up when he heard the motorcycle, and Abe saw his friend's stricken features in the glare of the headlight. The others turned their backs, and Will walked wearily toward Abe.

"They don't want me around. Some of my people are saying I brought an evil curse—that I am practicing *clizyati*, the Witchery Way. That I have performed a perverted ceremony, invoking evil." He stopped when he saw Abe's bruised, blood-streaked face. "Get behind me on the bike, and I'll take you to the truck. We'll load it up, and I'll drive. I can't do any good here—I've already told the cops what I know."

Abe nodded and slid back, giving Will room to climb onto the motorcycle. He was soaked to the skin, shivering, and feeling each ache and pain brought on by the beating. "We've got to go after them, Will."

When Will stopped beside Abe's truck, he pulled the loading ramp down and rolled his bike into the Toyota's bed, jumped in the driver's seat, and turned the key in the ignition. Abe limped in beside him on the passenger side. They rode in gloomy silence until reaching the highway.

Will pulled a cigarette from the pack of Marlboros in his shirt pocket and shook one out for Abe. "I've got to take you home, Abe. You're in no shape to go after anyone. You didn't find Emily, but do you want to tell me what you *did* find?" Though he seemed to be trying to sound calm, Abe could hear the tremor in Will's voice and see the shaking hand that held the package.

Abe put the cigarette between his bruised lips and accepted the proffered light. If there was ever a time to start smoking again, it was now. "Trouble, and not the kind I was looking for."

Smoke began to fill the vehicle's interior, so Will cracked a window, his eyebrows forming question marks under the brim of his black hat.

"I was following the tracks of whoever took Emily and the girl. I ran into a work crew at a pumping station, so I stopped to ask if they saw anyone." Abe inhaled deeply, filling his lungs with noxious smoke, knowing he wasn't doing himself any good but savoring it just the same.

"Turned out to be the same asshole I had a run-in with last week. He slammed my knee with a wrench, sucker-punched me, kicked me a few times for good measure. He might have killed me if the others hadn't pulled him off. Guess I lost consciousness for a while. Pricks only had to tell me which way the vehicle went." His right elbow on the window frame, his pounding head resting in his palm, Abe groaned. "We have to look for them, Will—now—before it's too late. What do you think they want with these girls? With Emily? They might . . ." He didn't want to give voice to the thought that had been tormenting him. "They might kill them. Maybe they're that crazy."

Will's voice trembled when he spoke. "Abe, don't think like that. I want to go after them as much as you, but where are we going to start in the dark—in the rain—in the condition you're in? Tomorrow, we start early. Now you're going home to soak in a hot bath, take a couple of aspirin, or smoke a joint. You're no use to anyone in the condition you're in, and neither am I. The cops are on it. I've got to go home, break the news to Mom, and line up some more family to help in the search."

Abe had forgotten about Bertha. The news that Emily was missing would be hard on her, but he wasn't ready to quit. "I know, Will, but I'm betting it was a Chevy that took them, and it turned north, into Colorado. We could go after it now."

"Go where, Abe? There won't be any tracks to follow on the highway." This time, it was the Navajo with the voice of reason—unlike before, when Will had persuaded him to go along on a wild-goose chase to Arizona in search of a killer. "Better we wait, talk to the cops, and see if they got any leads."

Abe ran a hand through his hair, took a long draw on the cigarette, and stared out the window into the black night. "I don't know what to do, Will." He blew out a long stream of smoke. "What did the cops find at the scene so far?"

"The tranquilizer dart. They're sending it to the lab for analysis. Sis's radio was on the ground, and there were two sets of prints leading off into the brush. The ones going out appeared deeper than those coming in, meaning they were carrying something heavy."

The weight of the day felt like it had fallen on Abe's eyelids. He leaned his head back and fell into a fitful sleep.

He was awakened a short time later by the sound of a siren. A white Ford Explorer, emergency lights flashing, raced past them from the opposite direction. Abe rubbed his forehead, felt pain ripple through his body. "Hosteen going back to the scene," Abe said, his voice thick. "I wonder what he found. I'm going to call the station when I get home. What's your take on him, Will?"

"Don't know much about him. He left the rez as a little kid. Seems a bit standoffish. Keeps to himself. Emily doesn't have too many good things to say about him." Will shrugged. "His mother was an activist, and a few people didn't like it. She butted heads with the higher-ups one too many times, and they made a pariah out of her. The family wouldn't take her in, old man was gone, so she disappeared one day. I guess Hosteen was born in Albuquerque."

"How good a cop is he?"

"I hear he's blunt but smart. Doesn't care about making friends. Ambitious, nontraditional, like his mother."

For the duration of the trip, Abe could think of nothing more to say.

Will, his face dark, appeared lost in a controlled rage. When the Toyota turned into the driveway of the sheep ranch, Patch ran out of the barn, barking at their arrival.

Abe rubbed his knee, feeling a sharp pain. "Thanks for driving, Will," he said after gingerly stepping down from the truck and bending to scratch Patch behind the ears.

"Who's the kid?" Will asked when the tall, gangly young man stepped out of the barn door and waved at them.

"Danny Jorgenson—lives a half mile up the road. I paid him to take care of the animals today. He still has the mind of a kid, but his mother helps him, and he's a good worker. Wonder why he's still here."

"Abe!" Danny called. "You didn't come home, so I told Mom I want to sleep in the barn and take care of Patch and the sheep. Can I stay, please? Mom said I could if it was okay with you. Please?"

Another weary sigh slipped past Abe's lips. "You can stay tonight, Danny. Are you sure it's warm enough in the barn?"

"Yeah. I've got my sleeping bag and a thermos of hot chocolate. All the sheep are in," he said with a note of pride in his voice. "I took real good care of them." Danny frowned as he got a closer look at Abe and Will. "What happened to you guys?"

"Nothing you need to worry about, Danny," Abe said. "I need to talk to your mom, though. Might want your help a little longer."

"Yes! Yes! Yes!" said Danny, raising his palm for a high five. His eyes gravitated to Will's burn-scarred face. "Were you in an accident, like me?"

Will nodded his head. "Yep."

Danny reached out and ran a finger down Will's cheek. "Does it still hurt?"

"Sometimes, but it is getting better," Will said to the freckle-faced young man with tousled strawberry-blond hair.

Danny smiled. "I'm getting better, too. I've got to get back to the barn now. Abe, can Patch sleep with me tonight? I already fed him, and I made him a nice soft bed in the hay."

"Okay, Danny. Go on, now." Before he limped toward the main house, Abe turned to face Will. "Let yourself inside the guesthouse. I don't have a phone in there, so I'm going into the main house to call the station and Danny's mother." After a moment he added, his voice filled with dread, "I know you're going to have to break the news to Bertha, and it's going to be tough."

When he returned to his place, after learning the police had no new leads and making arrangements for Danny to stay on a little longer, Abe saw that Will had lit kindling in the fireplace and was adding logs to a crackling fire. Though Abe had no appetite, something in a Crock-Pot smelled good, and the house looked cleaner than it had ever been.

"Danny's mother, Ellen," Abe said, taking the lid off the pot and inhaling the aroma of Texas-style chili. A pan of corn bread sat on the counter.

"You look like shit. Take a hot bath, and put some of this in the water. After I call Mom, we can eat something. Gotta keep our strength up," Will said, handing Abe a handful of dried plant material.

"What's this?"

"Yucca and other herbs. Soothing to the body. You'll need it if we're gonna find Emily and Lina. I'm making a medicinal tea—it'll help you sleep." Will finished feeding logs into the stove and filled the kettle. He reached into his medicine bag, pulled out a small packet, and dropped a pinch of something into the water.

At one time, Abe would have scoffed at his friend's cures—but no longer. He had borne witness to the power of Navajo medicine many times in the past. He only wished Will had something powerful enough to show him where Emily was being held.

Once in the bathroom, he pulled off his sodden clothes, groaned, turned the water on as hot as he could stand it, and dropped the yucca powder under the spigot. Abe would have preferred a shower, but the foaming suds and soothing aroma provided instant relief to his knee. He submerged himself in the steaming water and felt a stinging sensation around his eye and cut lip. When Abe emerged, the water had turned a rusty brown from his mud- and blood-encrusted head. No wonder he had given Danny Jorgenson such a fright.

14

Wednesday, April 11, 1990

Women's Compound

Unknown Location

The vehicle came to a stop, but Emily could see nothing from her confinement in the pitch-black interior. Curtains had been pulled across the windows, blocking any light from entering. They had stopped once earlier, but only briefly. She heard the faint murmur of men's voices, the creak of a metal gate, and then they were moving again.

Someone thrust the glare of a flashlight in her face, and she heard a different male voice, a West Texas twang. She felt a blindfold being tied tightly over her eyes.

"Who the hell are you? Where are you taking us?" she yelled before a strip of tape prevented her from saying more.

"That's no language for a lady," the unknown voice drawled.

"She's a spunky one. Older than the girl here—carried a gun, too," the flat monotone remarked.

"She'll learn," the second voice said. "Get ready. The girl's waking up."

"Just in time."

Emily tossed her head from side to side and strained at the straps binding her wrists and ankles. She heard whimpering and a scream before Lina was also gagged. Someone released one of Emily's arms from its constraints, and she swung it wildly in self-defense before it was quickly shackled and handcuffed to the other. The remaining straps were loosened, and Emily kicked at unseen hands before being pulled to her feet and led down a ramp. She stumbled, heard the girl's muffled whimpers, and unconsciously twisted around to look for Lina before realizing blindfolds still covered her eyes. Her heart pounded like a war dancer's feet on red clay, and she lost all sense of time and place. Sweat broke out on her forehead at the same time as a shudder ran up her spine.

Where in the hell are we, and what are they going to do with us?

She felt and heard the crunch of gravel under her feet, then something solid, like concrete. Another gate opened and clanged shut with the sound of a lock clicking in place. Emily and Lina, prodded by the two unknown men, shuffled along a cement pathway until one of the voices told them to stop.

"Stairs up ahead. Watch your step."

Emily silently counted the steps. *One—two—three—four.* There were six in all before they paused on a flat surface and she heard knocking on a wooden door, a sound like a sliding bolt, the turning of a knob. The door opened with a whispered whoosh, a rush of warm air, and the strong smell of soap and bleach.

"Two? I thought there was just one," a disembodied female voice said.

"We had to take this older one. The boss might have some use for her."

"Well, bring them inside," said the woman. "Let me see what you've got."

The men shoved her through the doorway, but Emily remained blindfolded, gagged, and unable to move her hands. She sensed more than saw the change from darkness to bright light as her moccasins scraped against a rough wooden floor.

"Are they virgins?" asked the woman.

"The girl was having her ceremony for womanhood. She's as pure as heaven's snowy flake. I don't know about the other, but she can stay on as a breeder or worker."

Upon hearing these words, Emily cringed, and the taste of bile began to rise in her throat. She forced herself to swallow the bitterness so she wouldn't gag.

"Hmm," the woman murmured.

"Have them washed and dressed appropriately by eight o'clock in the morning," the banal male voice said. "The Prophet will be here for inspection and approval."

"Glory is to the Prophet," the woman said just before Emily heard retreating footsteps and the closing of a door.

Emily wanted to run, but the shackles made that impossible. And she couldn't leave Lina. Furthermore, where would she go, blindfolded and cuffed? She was also groggy and weak from the drug used in the dart gun.

Best to wait for the right opportunity, find out what kind of lunatics I'm dealing with, figure out a way to get out of here or call for help, she thought.

The woman was talking again. "Listen carefully. Do exactly as I say, and neither of you will be punished. I'm going to take off your blindfolds. If you cooperate, I'll remove the tape from your mouths."

Emily blinked against the brightness. She was in a long hallway with doors on either side. The woman standing in front of her appeared middle-aged, tall and sturdy, with gray-streaked hair pinned up in an old-fashioned bun. Her plain blue dress had a rounded collar, long sleeves, and a hem reaching to the floor. Her washed-blue eyes revealed as much life as the corpse of a drunk Emily had once found in a roadside ditch. Quickly looking around for Lina, she saw the girl standing a few feet from her. Lina's eyes had the terrified glint of a deer caught in the spotlight of a hunter. Her skin was a ghastly pale, and beads of sweat dotted her forehead. As their glances met, she saw the girl's eyes tear up. Seconds later Lina crumpled to the floor.

Emily instinctively made a move to help her, but at the same time, the fish-eyed woman blew a whistle attached to a chain around her neck. A half dozen women, dressed and coiffed in the same puritanical manner, emerged from their rooms and surrounded the two Navajos.

"Take the girl to the shower room, and remove her heathen clothing and devil's adornments. Make sure she is scrubbed clean and dressed in a fresh muslin gown, and confine her to her room."

Two of the women reached down and picked up Lina, grasped her by the legs and armpits, and carried her down the hallway. The woman who appeared to be in charge turned and fixed her eyes on Emily. "There is soap, a towel, and a shower in your room. Your bedclothes and tomorrow's dress will be laid out. We will pray Satan releases his hold, and you will be prepared to serve our Lord and Prophet. You are blessed you have been chosen as one of the few." She reached her rawboned hands toward Emily's face. "I am removing the tape from your mouth now, and I want you to be still and quiet."

Emily flinched as the sticky adhesive was ripped from her lips, but instead of heeding the warning, she began protesting. "Listen, I am a Navajo police officer. There are a lot of people looking for us right now. If you don't want to spend the rest of your sorry life in a prison cell, let the girl and me go free or—"

A solid slap across the face stopped her in midsentence and rocked her backward.

You crazy witch, she thought to herself. *What kind of madhouse have they taken us to, and why? I've got to be quiet and patient until I can figure out a way to get out of here.*

"Take this one to the holding room at the end of the hall. Get her a nightgown and new clothing. Make sure the door is padlocked before you leave," the woman said to the remaining four, who stood impassively by her side. The speaker turned to Emily. "I will check on you in half an hour. If you are not bathed and dressed appropriately, someone will assist you—by force, if necessary."

Late that night when Abe emerged from the bathroom dressed in clean clothing and feeling stronger, he looked around for Emily's brother. "Will?" he called from the open door. Puzzled, he checked the truck and noticed the motorcycle was missing. He had not heard the rumble of the engine starting up.

Will must have left while I was running the bathwater, he thought. *Maybe he wanted to talk to his mother in person.*

Abe knew Bertha Etcitty would take the news of her daughter hard. He decided to go inside, try to eat something, and drink the cup of tea Will had brewed while he waited. Afterward, feeling exhausted, he collapsed on the couch, put his feet up, and felt his eyelids drop.

His eyes flew open with a start; sweat dripped down his face and back. He had fallen asleep and dreamed a recurring nightmare. Fiery demons were chasing him, and his legs were so heavy and leaden he could barely move. Emily had been calling him, her arms outstretched but beyond his reach. The fire in the *kiva* had died down to embers, but the house felt overly warm. Abe rubbed his eyes and looked at the clock on the mantel. One thirty.

Where's Will? Has he gone to his mother's house and decided to stay there, or is he out looking for Emily on his own? Abe paced around the small room. *I won't be able to sleep now. I'll call Bertha Etcitty and find out what's going on.*

He made his way back to the main house and dialed the familiar number, hoping he wasn't waking anyone.

As soon as it rang, someone picked up the receiver and answered in an anxious voice.

"Hello? Will, is that you?"

"Bertha, it's Abe. I thought Will might be there with you."

Bertha Etcitty typically presented herself as a formidable pillar of strength, but at this moment she sounded to Abe like any desperate, heartbroken mother when one of her children faced danger. For her, it was both her daughter and son. Abe could tell by the crack in her voice that Will had told her about Emily's disappearance and had taken off on his own.

"No, he left right after telling me about Emily and Lina. Abe, Will didn't know this before, but Lina is diabetic. She needs her insulin. When I told him, his face turned to stone." She sniffled. "I thought he might have gone back to your place. I just hope he didn't go drinking again. He was so upset. He said the Nez family refused to speak to him after . . . after their girl was taken. They never told him about her diabetes. He thinks they blame him for what happened, and now he blames himself."

Abe exhaled a long breath. News of Lina's diabetes added increased urgency to the case. "It's not his fault, Bertha. He was there doing his job. I feel like I should have . . ." He let the words hang without saying what he truly believed. He should have watched her more carefully.

Abe heard Bertha catch her breath and let out a sob.

"I don't know what to do—my daughter *and* that little girl. I need Will here to help me find Emily. I can't handle this alone."

"You're not alone, Bertha. I'll locate him and bring him home, then we'll work on getting Emily. I promise you. Do you have any idea where he might have gone?"

"Thanks, Abe." Bertha sniffled. "There's a couple of places he used to hang out. Wait for me. We'll go together. I'll be there in fifteen minutes."

"There's no need for you to come here. Just tell me where to look," he said, but his words were lost in the click and dial tone at the other end.

He had learned long ago there was no point in arguing with Emily's mother.

Grabbing his wallet and keys, Abe went out to wait in his truck. The rain had ceased, and the clouds parted, opening the curtain on a star-studded sky. In any other circumstance, he would have marveled at the beauty, but tonight he was barely aware of it. He could only think about finding Emily—and now her brother.

You sure picked the wrong time to screw up, Will.

The Etcitty house wasn't far, and in less than ten minutes he saw the headlights of Bertha's Honda Civic coming down the road. She pulled in beside Abe's truck and climbed out. Her mouth was creased in a grim line of determination. "We'll take your truck," she said, and slid onto the seat behind him. When she saw Abe's cut lip and swollen, bruised eye, her eyes widened, and she gasped. "What happened to you? Did Will . . . ?"

"No, of course not. It's a long story and isn't important right now. Where are we headed?"

Bertha shook her head. "Smokey's, on the corner of Third and Broadway, right here in Bloomfield."

They didn't speak again until they reached the vicinity of Smokey's Saloon, a dimly lit dive preparing to shut down for the night.

"Drive around to the back, and keep looking for Will's motorcycle," Bertha said.

After circling the block, Abe turned into the alley. "Doesn't appear as he's here. Where else do you think he might have gone?"

"Bernie's," she said without hesitation. It occurred to Abe that Bertha must have conducted this search herself many times in the past. "It's a little ways out of town, on Highway 550. Lots of Navajos go there."

A fifteen-minute drive brought them to a rundown building on a dirt lot. The lights were out, and there were no cars in the parking lot, but it wasn't hard to spot Will's motorcycle parked at an angle in front of the Quonset-hut-turned-beer-joint. A rumpled, stooped man sat leaning against a side wall, a shabby black hat pulled down to hide his face.

"That's him," said Bertha. "*Bil naak'ai'*. He's passed out. Help me get him into the truck."

The smell of stale whiskey and vomit permeated the interior of the cab as soon as they situated Will's unresponsive body on the seat. Abe rolled the passenger window down and told Bertha to drive the truck back to his house—that he would take the motorcycle. Riding Will's old bike for the second time that night, he felt even more troubled than before. Abe needed Will; Bertha needed Will. The Navajo people needed him as well—his songs and prayers would help sustain them until they found Emily and the missing girls. After Abe reached his house and parked the motorcycle beside Bertha's car, he continued to sit, brooding, not knowing what to say to comfort Emily's mother.

"Let's bring him inside," he said after a few minutes. "He can sleep it off on my couch."

Bertha shook her head. "No. Put him in my car. I'll take him home, get him cleaned up, and we'll be back early in the morning."

Abe raised his eyebrows, forming two furrows in his brow, and gave Bertha a questioning look. She was a determined, thickset woman without an ounce of fat on her, but Will stood a head taller than his mother. "I don't think you can manage him alone. I'll follow you."

"No," said Bertha, shaking her head again. "I've done this before. You go on, get some rest. I'll see you in the morning, at seven. I'm coming with you to find Emily. I'll call the school and take emergency leave."

"I don't know if that's a good idea, Bertha. Maybe you should stay close to home. What if Emily tries to call you?"

But the woman was adamant. "We will search for my daughter together. The more people, the better chance we have of finding her. I'll have my niece stay at the house."

15

B efore they escorted her to a small room at the end of the hallway, the women stripped Emily of her silver-and-turquoise bracelets, her handcrafted silver conch belt, and the conch bells and beads attached to her dress. They took her mother's turquoise necklace, her beaded moccasins, and her silver hairpins. Her long, black hair fell from its carefully combed Navajo bun into loose strands, draping her face and shoulders like a veil. She felt violated and enraged, robbed of her identity. As she shuffled her bare feet along the wooden surface of the floorboards, she told herself to stay calm.

Wait for your chance. She repeated this mantra over and over. *Don't fight them until the time is right—until they remove these chains and you can figure this out.*

She remained passive while they led her into a cold room with one small, barred window situated too high to allow her to peek out at her surroundings. The room was furnished with a straight-backed wooden chair, a small table, and a cot-size bed. On top of the tightly made-up bed lay a long, plain, white-cotton nightgown and scratchy-looking underwear reminiscent of earlier times. The walls were painted white and were bare—except for a single poster listing a set of rules.

One of the women, a faded midfifties brunette with muddy brown eyes, clad in a ridiculous pink dress made from the identical pattern as the others', took a set of keys from her pocket and unlocked Emily's handcuffs and shackles. After removing the chains, she indicated a door in the back of the room. "Go now, shower and cleanse your body. Take your bedclothes, and place your heathen dress outside on the floor. We will wait fifteen minutes. If you're not out by then, we will come in and assist you. Remember, we are the only ones who can lock and unlock doors."

Emily quickly looked around the small bathroom. She saw the essentials—toilet, sink, shower, a bar of soap, towel, toothbrush, and toothpaste. A second small window was installed above the toilet.

Yiiyah, Emily thought. *It's a crazy religious cult kidnapping girls. What am I going to do? I've got to keep my cool for now.*

She bit her lip, showered, put on the ridiculous underwear, and pulled the Puritan nightgown over her head. When she emerged from the bathroom, the woman who seemed to be in charge was waiting.

"From now on you will be dressed correctly and adequately covered at all times," the woman said, indicating the chair where a long pink dress—made in the identical style as the others—and a pair of thick leggings lay. High-topped boots sat on the floor by the bed. "Modesty is a virtue, and the body is a sacred vessel that must be kept pure and ready for the Prophet. When you hear the bell in the morning you will get up, wash, comb your hair, and get dressed so our spiritual leader will not be offended by your unholy immodesty. Someone will come for you to make sure you have combed your hair correctly. Do not be late." She left the room, slamming the door behind her.

Emily heard the lock click. She stared with loathing at the outfit laid out for her. She tossed the clothes off the bed and pushed the chair under the window, trying to look out. Acres of cultivated land, a part of a water tower, sheds, the tops of buildings, and a tall white spire came into view but did not give her any clue as to her whereabouts. Even though the area was well lit, a tall wall completely encircled her prison. Emily climbed down and replaced the chair, then kicked it in a fit of frustration and anger. She scoured the room for anything she might be able to use as a tool or weapon, but there was nothing except the list of rules staring back at her.

SINGLE FEMALE RULES FOR DAILY LIVING

1. Wake-Up Call is 5:00 a.m.
2. Only Plain Soap and Water Are Allowed for Bathing and Cleaning
3. You Will Wear No Adornments in Your Hair or on Your Body
4. Keep Your Room Immaculate
5. Remain Silent Unless Spoken To
6. Worship Service Led by the Matrons Is from 6:00 a.m.–7:00 a.m. Daily
7. Breakfast in the Dining Hall is 7–7:30
8. Chores Will Be Assigned by the Matrons after Breakfast
9. Lunch Is at Noon, Dinner at 6:00 p.m., and Evening Worship at 7:00 p.m.
10. Bedtime Is 9:00 p.m.
11. REMEMBER: CLEANLINESS, MODESTY, AND PUNCTUALITY ARE VIRTUES THAT PLEASE OUR LORD AND PROPHET.

I hate these crazy people, she thought as she paced the room. *What was that movie?* Stepford Wives. *Cloned women who can't think on their own. Or the book I read a while back*—The Handmaid's Tale *by Margaret Atwood. This place is madness. But so far they haven't hurt me—or Lina either, I hope.* Her thoughts went back to the first missing girl, Darcy Benally. *Maybe Darcy is here as well, and I'll be able to see both girls in the morning. Poor Lina must be traumatized. If anyone lays a hand on her, I swear I will kill them.*

After Bertha Etcitty had driven away, Abe stood outside and gazed listlessly at the stars. He had no idea what they were going to do tomorrow, or where to begin their search. Abe missed his dog and wished Patch was with him to offer some small comfort. He sighed and rubbed his head. Ever since the concussion he'd gotten two years ago when he'd run blindly through the desert seeking help for Will, he'd been plagued by recurrent headaches. The kick McCaffey had landed on the side of his head didn't help either.

McCaffey—yeah, that was the name I heard the men say when they pulled him away.

Abe hurried into the main house and began searching for a phone book, not caring if he disturbed more than one sleeper at that hour with his calls.

There were three McCaffeys listed in the Farmington area. An irate older woman answered the first number he dialed. She said there was no man in the house and slammed the receiver down before he could get another word in. With the second call, he hit pay dirt. The phone was picked up on the fourth ring by a male voice he knew he had heard before.

"McCaffey?" Abe said.

"Yeah. Do you know what time it is? Who the hell are you?"

"It's three o'clock in the morning, and I'm the guy you tried to kick the shit out of last night."

"What the fuck—"

"I know your name, I know where you work, and I know where you live. I've got friends on the Navajo Police Force. All I have to do is press charges, and you are probably out of a job, in jail, and possibly facing a charge of attempted murder." Abe waited through the silence on the other end of the line.

"What do you want from me?" McCaffey hissed. "Why'd you call?"

"I want the same thing I did when I stopped to ask you a question, asshole. I want to know if you saw a white van on the pipeline road—and if you did, what direction it headed." Abe waited for the reply.

A long pause followed. "And if I tell you what I saw, you won't press charges? Is that what you're saying?"

"I'm thinking about it."

"Yeah, well, shit. A white Chevy utility van came down the pipeline road. Made me mad. They're not supposed to be out there, and someone's been vandalizing the gas line."

Abe's heart thumped. "Which way did it turn? North or south?"

"North—toward 666. Okay, I gave you what you wanted. Now are you going to back off?"

"Maybe," Abe said, and hung up. In the morning, he would call Hosteen to see if the cop had any new information.

He returned to his house, collapsed on the couch, and had almost drifted off when he heard whining outside the door. As soon as the door cracked open, Patch let out a sharp bark and wagged his tail.

"Boy, am I glad to see you," Abe said, scooping up the dog in his arms. "Have you been taking good care of Danny and the sheep?" Abe scratched his dog and ruffled his fur. Back on the couch, he fell asleep almost immediately, his arm draped across Patch, who was curled up on his chest, sleeping as well.

16

Once again Abe's eyes popped open to a sound at the door. This time, it was a little after seven in the morning, and the persistent knock was accompanied by an agitated male voice.

"Abe. Abe. Wake up. I can't find Patch. Is he in there?"

Danny Ferguson must have panicked when he awoke and discovered the dog missing.

Patch jumped off the couch and began barking. Only half-awake and still groggy, Abe stumbled to his feet, felt the pain in his knee, and limped to the door. "It's okay, Danny. He's right here with me."

"I was scared he ran away or got stole," Danny said.

Abe smelled chili and realized he had left the Crock-Pot on warm all night. "Patch wouldn't run away. You hungry?"

Danny, his hair sticking up, brushed at the straw stuck to his shirt and pants, and sniffed at the same smell. "Nah. I've got to get the chores done, and Mom said she would bring me some hot chocolate and cinnamon rolls this morning."

"Sounds good. Go ahead. Take Patch with you. You can feed him when you're done. I'm going to have to take off early again this morning, or I'd help you. I'd like to talk to your mom when she gets here, too."

"Okay, Abe." Danny whistled, and Patch bounded off with him toward the barn.

Abe yawned, filled the coffeepot with water, put two large scoops of Folgers into the basket, and limped over to the main house to call Hosteen while he waited for Bertha and Will.

"Joe Hosteen," said the voice on the other end.

"Hosteen, it's Abe Freeman. You told me to check back with you. Have you got anything new?"

"Freeman, I'm surprised you're up and about. Just got my coffee and getting ready for a briefing with the boss before we hit the road." There was a brief pause while Abe assumed Hosteen was taking a drink. "Here's what we've got so far. Names and mug shots of two former Bureau of Indian Affairs employees we're pretty sure are involved. So there's an APB out on those two and the white Chevy utility van. Had a search team working on it all night. The girl is diabetic—she needs her daily dose of insulin. She could go into shock, possibly die, if she doesn't get it."

The thought of Lina dying for lack of her medication felt like a knife twisting in Abe's gut. He swallowed hard. "How much time does she have?"

"No one knows for sure. It could be within a day, or she could hold out longer, depending on whether her body is manufacturing any insulin at all."

"We've got to find them as soon as possible. What about that van you traced to Cortez? Did you find the owner?"

"It was a white utility van registered in Montezuma County, Colorado, to a Wayne Mackey—a social worker employed by the tribe. We think he's got a partner, Phillip Harris, who's a medical technician. They did some fieldwork on the rez and the Checkerboard, and both disappeared before the girls came up missing. We're not a hundred percent certain, but they're our main suspects."

"Harris and Mackey. White guys. Any idea where they might be headed?" Abe asked.

"Nothing definite, but we questioned Mackey's mother. She said he left a couple years ago to join a religious cult, and she hasn't seen him since."

"Do either of them have an arrest record?"

"Some misdemeanors, nothing too serious or heavy. It doesn't look like personnel did much of a background check when they were hired by the rez, though."

"Where does the mother live? Is somebody keeping tabs on her?"

"Yeah, Freeman. She lives in Cortez, and we've got it covered. I know you're worried, but lots of good cops are out there looking for Emily and the girls. Just remember what I said, and stay out of the way."

"Okay," Abe said.

Right, he thought.

"Keep me posted, Hosteen."

"I'll try. By the way, it's Joe. Hey, you want to press charges against McCaffey?"

"Not right now," Abe said. "I'd rather you put all your energy into finding Emily and the girls. I called McCaffey early this morning. Told the asshole either he said which way the van headed or I'd press charges. Took about thirty seconds before he fessed up. The van turned north, toward Colorado. That's where I'm headed now." He hung up before he could hear Hosteen's protest. When he got off the phone, he saw Bertha's Honda, followed by Will on his Chief, pulling into his driveway. Ellen Ferguson's truck was parked beside the barn.

Will looked like hell. The burn scars on his face were more promi-
nent than ever. Right now he was the palest Indian Abe had ever seen,
but he met Abe's eyes and gave him a thumbs-up, indicating, Abe
hoped, he was back on track again. Ellen came out of the barn with a
plate containing fresh cinnamon rolls and joined the group. She glanced
at Abe's black eye and scrapes but didn't comment.

After introductions, Abe invited everyone inside. Maybe the others
could use some coffee and one of Ellen's cinnamon rolls. He was too wound
up to eat, even though he hadn't had anything in more than twelve hours.
Last night, lacking any appetite, he had gone to bed, leaving the chili still
warming in the Crock-Pot. While Ellen and Bertha picked at their rolls,
Abe shared what he had learned from Hosteen about Mackey and Harris.

Will listened quietly, sipping his coffee but turning down the offer
of food. Apparently, everyone was too anxious to eat. When Abe mentioned the direction the van had headed, Will spoke up. "We'll go down
every side road going north on 666 until we find something. If we run
into any local ranchers, we ask if they've seen a white van pull into any
of the ranch roads or any unusual activity. We can each take a section
and meet at a designated spot at noon."

"We're going to run into some locked gates and 'No Trespassing'
signs," said Bertha.

"After we cross the border into Colorado, we're on the Mountain
Ute Reservation and will be until about twelve miles south of Cortez,"
Will said. "They won't be on the reservation anywhere. Neither Navajo
nor Utes would let them stay."

"Maybe we can get a map of that stretch of highway," Abe said.
"Who would have one—county assessor? Might save us some time, and
we can find out who owns the land."

"Good idea," said Bertha. "Abe, you see if you can get hold of a
map. It's Montezuma County. Will and I are going to start looking
around and asking questions. We'll meet in Cortez at noon. There's
a Mexican Restaurant called La Casita on Main Street." She turned

toward Will with a stern, matronly look. "Will, you're going to be needing something in your stomach."

"I'm okay, Ma. Look," he said, addressing everyone at the table. "I stumbled last night, a moment of weakness. I'm not proud of it. But I got back up. It's not going to happen again."

"Well, I know son, but you still need to eat."

To appease his mother, Will grabbed a cinnamon roll.

Abe looked at Ellen. "Do you think Danny can handle the work if I have to stay away a few days? I'm not coming back until we find Emily and the two girls, and I'd like it if you both stayed at my place while I'm gone."

"Of course, Abe. It'll make it easier all the way around, and I can keep an eye on things for you. Just do what you gotta do. Find those lower-than-a-rattlesnake's-belly bastards who took the girls. And don't worry none about your little dog. He's in good hands." Ellen turned toward Bertha and took her hand in both of her own. "I'm so sorry this happened. But I just know you're going to get your daughter back."

"We better get started," Abe said. He pulled a couple of twenty-dollar bills out of his wallet and gave them to Ellen. "In case you need anything."

"Did those men beat you up?" Ellen asked, making eye contact with Abe and lightly touching his bruised face.

"No—that's a different story," Abe said, brushing her off. "If you're all right with everything, we're leaving now."

There was one thing he had to do first. He had never left Patch for any length of time, except for his stint in the hospital and the night he spent in jail when Emily arrested him as a possible murder suspect.

When the little dog bounded up to Abe at the sound of his whistle, Abe picked him up and scratched his floppy ears. "You be a good boy and help Danny out," he said, petting Patch's head. "You can't go this time. I've got some work to do, but I'll be back soon. Promise."

Emily thrashed around on the narrow bed and punched the pillow. She hadn't felt this helpless since she was forced, at the age of five, to leave her family and attend the government-run boarding school. When the official van had pulled up, she had hidden behind her grandmother's long skirt, clinging to her leg. They had to drag her away kicking and screaming.

She finally fell into a brief and restless sleep, marked by a dream that coyote had changed into a skinwalker and took the form of a hideous woman wearing a long pink dress.

A clanging bell from outside her door brought her to a sudden, disoriented wakefulness.

"Get up, wash up, and get dressed. You have fifteen minutes," the shrill female voice blared. Emily rolled out of bed and onto her feet. Her clothing lay strewn across the floor where she had thrown it the night before. The chair leaned on its side against the wall. The predawn, casting barred shadows into the room, did nothing to lift her spirits.

What next? Emily said to herself. *I wonder what these freaks have in store for me and the girls today.*

After replacing the chair, she went into the bathroom to wash. Fifteen minutes later she was clothed in knee-length, white-cotton pantaloons and a shift, long wool stockings, and a pale pink dress that came to the tops of her boots. A quartet of middle-aged women who frowned in disapproval fussed over her long, black hair.

"Sit down," the tallest of the four said. "Your hair will never do." One woman pulled a hairbrush from a deep pocket and roughly pulled it through Emily's hair, forming two tight braids that she pinned to the top of Emily's head. Emily couldn't see what they had done but assumed it had to be a style similar to theirs.

Despite the rule about no talking, Emily could not remain silent. She wanted some answers. Maybe someone would be humane enough to tell her something. "Where are the other girls? Why are we being held prisoner here?"

"Shh," hissed a woman with salt-and-pepper hair. "Someone will punish you if you speak out of turn."

"Those Navajo girls—they've done nothing wrong. Their parents are brokenhearted. Are you a mother? Think about how it feels to lose your child. Let them go, and I'll stay and do whatever you say," Emily said. "I lost my son. I know how it feels."

A woman with a thin face and sad eyes whispered, "Quiet, or we will have to report you to the matron. We are performing the will of God as written in the Scriptures and proclaimed by our Prophet. Your gift will please our Lord. Now do not speak again."

Emily held her tongue, but she thought she had detected a glimmer of pity or pain in the woman's downcast eyes when she had mentioned losing a child.

Abe followed Will's motorcycle, with Bertha's Honda bringing up the rear. The little caravan made its way to Shiprock, where Highway 64 intersected with Route 666. They continued traveling north until reaching Tom Crow's shanty near the Colorado border. Abe saw Will pull over, so he followed suit. Bertha was right behind him.

"Why are we stopping here?" Bertha asked. "I don't want to waste any more time talking. We need to find Emily."

"Let's see what Tom has to say," Will said. "Maybe he noticed something, or he can tell us who owns land out this way."

"It won't hurt," Abe said.

Tom must have heard the commotion of the three vehicles and wondered what was going on. He stumbled out of his shack, bleary-eyed and stubble-chinned. Clenched in his right hand was a half-empty bottle of MD 20/20.

"I don't remember sayin' anything about there bein' a party at my place," he said, squinting at the faces of his guests. "I'll be damned. If it ain't Wilbur Etcitty," he said, his eyes stopping on Will's features. "Heard you got burned pretty bad. Want a drink, Will?"

Will grimaced. "No, Tom. We're looking for my sister and two young Navajo girls. We think those men in the white Chevy van with Colorado plates took them."

"Holy shit," said Tom, shaking his head. "Your sister is a lady cop, right? She was just here the other day asking me about a van." Tom took a draw on the bottle of rotgut red wine. "Son of a bitch." He wiped his mouth with the back of his hand. "I knew those white men were no good." Crow blinked and seemed to notice the two other people. "Who's this with you?"

"This is my mother, Bertha, and my friend Abe Freeman. We need your help, Tom."

The mangy old dog Abe had noticed the first time he visited sauntered out of the open door of the shack and let out two halfhearted barks before curling in a circle near Tom's feet. Seeing him made Abe think about Patch, and the loyalty dogs had for their owners, no matter the conditions.

"Do you spend much time in Cortez?" Will said.

"I go there now and then," Tom said. "Got a couple drinkin' buddies."

"When you go, ask your friends if they've heard anything about a religious cult out on 666," said Will. "And, just keep watching the highway, Tom. You got a telephone?"

"Nah, never had a need for one. But write down a number, and if I see or hear somethin', I'll get word to you."

"Thank you, Tom Crow," said Bertha. She reached into the pocket of her blue jeans and pulled out a ten-dollar bill, but Tom waved her off when she tried to hand it to him.

"I'm not takin' your money, Bertha Etcitty. I worked with your husband, Sam, for fifteen years in the uranium mines. I seen what it done—ruined a whole bunch of us workers, and them mine owners didn't give a hoot. You gotta get your girl back—them other girls, too. Dirty scum sumbitches—takin' little Navajo girls. Shit."

Abe wrote Hosteen's telephone number on a scrap of paper and handed it to Tom. "If something suspicious turns up, call this number."

When the threesome left, Tom Crow was still standing on his stoop, shaking his head, and cursing "the filthy pigs that took them girls." Abe drove to Cortez and the tax assessor's office while Will and Bertha began their individual investigations of the side roads bordering the Ute Mountain Reservation.

After Emily made her bed and cleaned the room to the women's strict specifications, they escorted her down a long corridor. Emily remained quiet, as they had admonished her she would have to be put back in "restrainers" and locked in her room if she did not. But she remained stealthily observant of her surroundings, memorizing each door, noting every window, looking for any possible means of escape. Her prison, as she thought of it, was at the end of the long hallway. As they walked, she counted six doors on her right and six on the left, which she assumed must be living quarters for the women. They were numbered, as in a hotel or dormitory. Other doors had signs painted on the wood above their frames—LAUNDRY, KITCHEN, and DINING ROOM on the right; SEWING ROOM, CHAPEL, and WAITING ROOM on the left. On each door, a portrait of a narrow-faced man with gray hair and piercing eyes stared back at her. Looking at him sent a chill through Emily. She wondered where the girls were, and if they were all right. The women stopped at the door to the chapel and hustled her inside. Emily heard the lock click behind her.

The room, painted entirely in white, lacked any adornment on the walls. Narrow windows, again too high to look out or in, lined the back. The only pieces of furniture in the room appeared to be a small altar and pulpit near the back. A banner hanging above the pulpit read:

FOR BEHOLD, I REVEAL UNTO YOU A NEW AND EVERLASTING COVENANT:
AND IF YE ABIDE NOT THAT COVENANT, YE ARE DAMNED, FOR NO ONE CAN
REJECT THIS COVENANT AND BE PERMITTED TO ENTER INTO MY GLORY.

The woman she assumed was the leader of the group stood behind the pulpit. Emily scanned the chamber for the girls but saw nothing except what appeared to be lines of puffy clouds on the floor—some in hues of pale pastel pink and blue, but the majority white. After a moment, it became apparent she was looking at prostrate young women, their heads bowed on the floor. She wondered which, if any, could be Lina or Darcy, but was suddenly ordered to assume the same posture. Emily raised her head as a soft sound, like muffled sobs, broke the eerie quietness of the room, but the strident voice of the matron in charge soon obliterated all else.

17

Thursday, April 12, 1990

Cortez, Colorado

Concentrating on his destination, Abe sped through the Ute Mountain Reservation, past Sleeping Ute Range and the village of Towaoc, Colorado, ten miles south of Cortez. Abe was so engrossed in his desire to find Emily, not only was he oblivious to the sweeping, rugged terrain of Southwest Colorado, but also to the Colorado State Patrol officer parked just beyond the reservation border—until he heard the wail of a siren and saw the flashing blue-and-red light.

Abe pulled over, cursing to himself for the delay.

"Officer, I can explain," he said to the lawman, who was clad in blue pants and shirt, his head topped with a navy-blue hard hat bearing the emblem of a winged wheel and the letters "CSP."

"Go ahead and tell me all about why you were doing seventy-five in a sixty-miles-per-hour zone, mister," the officer said as he pulled out his citation book. "I need to see your license and registration, sir."

Abe reached for his papers and handed them to the cop. "It's an emergency, officer. I'm trying to find two missing Navajo girls and my girlfriend, Emily Etcitty, a Navajo police officer. You must have heard about the kidnapping. One of the girls needs her daily shot of insulin. It's urgent." He retrieved his insurance and registration from the glove compartment and gave them to the cop.

The Colorado State Patrol officer, iron-jawed and unsmiling, scrutinized Abe's New Jersey driver's license and his documents. He handed them back, an unreadable look on his face. "Where are you headed in such a hurry right now, Mr. Freeman?"

When Abe finished with a rapid explanation, the officer scratched his head, frowned, and said, "Okay. I may be crazy, but I'm buying your story. Follow me." Led by the flashing lights of the patrol car, Abe was escorted to the front door of the Montezuma County Court House, more than making up for lost time.

After thanking the officer, Abe bounded up the steps and into the foyer of the unremarkable, three-story rectangular building. A directory on the wall told him the assessor's office was on the third floor. He took the steps two at a time, intent on his mission—until the sound of his name thundering through the hall stopped him in his tracks.

"Freeman!"

Turning around, Abe found himself eyeball-to-eyeball with Joe Hosteen.

"What the hell are you doing here?" Hosteen asked.

"No law against me being here, is there, Hosteen?"

"Seems kind of coincidental is all. Headed for the assessor's office?"

"Yeah, just so happens I am. You?"

"Never mind me. Thought I told you to let the law handle this."

Abe sighed. Maybe he could reason with the guy. "Joe, listen. We both want the same thing—to find Emily and the girls, and the sooner, the better. Emily's mom and brother are out there now, scouting the back roads in southern Montezuma County. We think the girls are being held somewhere in that area. I came in here to check property records. For Christ's sake, I have to do *something*."

Hosteen studied Abe with unflinching black eyes. He rubbed his chin and finally spoke. "I'll save you some trouble. I already looked at the records. Let's get out of here, and I'll tell you about it."

When Emily and all the girls left the chapel, they were not sent to the dining hall for breakfast, as the schedule indicated. Instead, they were marched into the corridor, where they were told to line up and wait for the appearance of the Prophet. They stood in two lines, facing one another from opposite sides of the hallway, the girls in white on the left, the women in pink and blue on the right. Emily, in her pink dress, tried to make eye contact with Lina, who was standing nearly across from her, but Lina's swollen, tear-stained eyes were downcast, her face devoid of color.

The women trustees, as Emily mentally referred to them, walked up and down, admonishing the young girls to stand up straight, smile— and some of them did, their young, innocent faces beaming.

The east-facing front door flew open, and the long shadow of a tall, thin man filled the hallway. She heard the intake of air from the women, and for a few moments, a looming shadow was all Emily could see. It filled her with a sense of dread. Two men followed the tall one. The door closed, and before one of the women hissed in her ear to keep her eyes straight ahead, Emily was able to discern the features of the one called the Prophet. The man appeared to be in his late forties or early fifties. His face was cadaverous, and his hair was thin and turning gray. A nervous tic caused the left side of his mouth to twitch, but his eyes burned with fearsome intensity. They were daggers, black as her own, sunken under thick brows. He locked his eyes on her, and his stare was so piercing she felt as if he were plunging knives into her soul. The Prophet wore a tailored, Western-cut black suit; his longish hair was slicked straight back. He stopped and studied each girl, sometimes caressing their hair and face, before moving on to the next. Emily seethed when he tilted Lina's chin up. The child shuddered and shrank away as if a rattlesnake had made a strike. The man continued looking at her, the left side of his mouth twitching spasmodically, and then he whispered in the ear of one of the other men before moving on.

The way some of the other young girls' faces glowed when the Prophet approached them made Emily cringe and wonder how such an evil person could have so much power. He stood in front of her now, appraising her body, sneering, joking with the two men.

"Looks like the Lord sent us another Injun to tame. He must not think we do enough good work to please him. Got our hands full with this one, I'll bet."

"She's tainted," the man with a Texas twang said. "But, I wouldn't mind puttin' up with her. She'd be praisin' Jesus in no time."

The men snickered while the Prophet continued to appraise her face and body.

"Turn around," he said.

The African slaves must have felt this same sense of degradation when they were being examined by rich, white buyers, Emily thought.

She felt as if he were mentally undressing her and swore under her breath, regretting she could not curse in the language of the Diné. She looked at the other two men and recognized them as the ones who had kidnapped Lina and her. They were explaining the reason she had been taken along with the girl, speaking in front of her as if she were not a fully functioning human being with a mind and life of her own. She turned around and faced him once again, biting her tongue to keep from lashing out at all three.

"She'll make a good worker—looks healthy enough. Maybe a good breeder, too, if it pleases our Lord. Don't let her out of your sight," the Prophet said to the matron, who nodded her acquiescence.

He moved along the line of older women at a much quicker pace, his mouth sometimes split into a crooked smile. But it appeared his interest was mainly in the young girls dressed in white. Emily spotted

Darcy standing several spaces away from Lina, and her heart lurched. She could see anger burning in the young Navajo's eyes. With her chin jutted in defiance and brow furrowed, Darcy glowered at the men.

Good, Emily thought. *She has a fighting spirit.*

She gave the girl a quick nod of approval and mouthed in Navajo, "Be brave. I will get us out of here." She wished Lina would show some spirit as well. Quiet defiance had been Emily's key to survival through the tumultuous years of boarding school, and she believed it was still a necessary skill for the young. She tried to make eye contact with Lina Nez, but the girl kept her head down, silent tears rolling down her face and falling on the cumbersome boots.

No one had mentioned a name for the one they called the Prophet, but Emily had plenty for him: creep, sick bastard, child rapist. She watched as he stopped in front of a fresh-faced blond of about fifteen. He put his hands on her shoulders.

"This one will be my new wife." His voice boomed, carrying the weight of complete authority. The girl smiled, blushed, and stepped out of the line, ecstasy lighting her pale-blue eyes. "Phillip and Wayne. As a reward for your courage and dedication in rescuing these two young women from a life of sin, I will choose another wife for you."

The faces of the two men who had kidnapped Emily and Lina—and most likely Darcy—stretched into smug grins, though they quickly faded when the Prophet turned his attention to the line of ladies in pink. He evidently had the last word on who would marry whom.

The filthy pigs want a virgin, Emily thought. *That's what the girls in white are, and the head creep is saving them for himself.*

The women in pink were middle-aged, not nearly as attractive a prize as the young girls, but the men didn't protest when the Prophet passed by Emily and laid his hands on the shoulders of two women, who stepped out of the line, obviously having nothing to say about the matches. When he had completed the selection of wives, the Prophet approached the matron.

"You are doing the Lord's work and will receive your reward in heaven. Continue." He turned and led his procession out the door, leaving behind a smell akin to decay in a basement full of dead mice.

Emily contained a sigh of relief—she and her girls had been spared. But she wondered how long it would last. Lina looked sickly and weak. *What was it I overheard the men in the van saying?*

She couldn't remember. The drugs had muddled her mind, but she knew, somehow, they didn't have much time.

After the entourage of men and their new wives left, the remaining women marched into the dining room for a generous serving of oatmeal and a glass of water. Coffee was evidently not an option in this prison camp. A long prayer session followed, extolling the virtues and wisdom of the Prophet, after which they were assigned to their chores for the day. Emily was sent, with a group of six other women, to work in the garden. It would be her first opportunity to see anything other than the inside of her prison enclosure, and she welcomed the chance.

When she stepped out the front door, blinded by bright sunshine, Emily had to blink before she could focus on her surroundings. After a moment, she was able to make out an eight-foot wall, topped with spirals of razor wire, surrounding the women's building. A tall iron gate remained closed—and apparently locked. She could see no familiar landmarks, mountains, or anything identifiable beyond the high walls except the gleaming white steeple. But the soil under her feet was pale and rocky, not so different from the land of the Diné, and she felt comforted by the thought that she might not be far from home.

Large plots of land inside of the enclosure were cultivated and prepared for seeding, and some already sprouted young plants. The women led Emily to a shed filled with an assortment of garden tools, bagged manure, fertilizer, compost, and chicken feed. One of them handed her a shovel and hoe and sent her to work planting potato eyes on a newly plowed plot. While Emily pretended to be engrossed in her work, she surveyed the lay of the land, the dimensions of the wall and its distance from the building, rock projections, guard posts—anything that caught her eye. The only other buildings inside the closed compound were the tool shed, what appeared to be a pump house, and a chicken coop with a fenced pen. She knew there had to be more structures on the other side, but she had no way of determining what or how many.

Emily worked alongside a woman of about forty, whose dull brown hair was streaked with strands of gray, her weary eyes cast down. It was the same woman she had noticed in her room, the one she had asked whether she was a mother. After the woman had dug a six-inch hole in the soil, Emily dropped in a potato eye from the hefty sack fastened around her shoulder and covered it with dirt. They worked without speaking for two hours, but there was something about the way the woman looked when Emily had asked about a child that made her think she could break through the barrier of silence.

"My name is Emily. What's yours?"

The woman shot her a quick glance but said nothing.

"I need to talk to someone. I'm frightened. I miss my family. I don't know where we are. Won't you please talk to me while we work?"

"We're not allowed to talk here at the Harmony Home Ranch," the woman said, a tone of bitterness tingeing her words. But after a few minutes, she added in a whisper, "Betty. My name is Betty."

So this place has a name, but I still don't know where I am, Emily thought.

"Thank you, Betty. You are the only one here who has shown me any kindness. This ranch, where is it located?"

"Utah, near Cortez." The woman ducked her head and began viciously attacking the soil with her hoe, then stopped, looking around to see if anyone was watching. "They banished my boy and my husband," she blurted out before returning to her task. "My son was sixteen when they ran him off."

Cortez! I'm not that far from home. If I can win Betty's trust, maybe I can get away.

Emily stared at Betty and saw the trail of a tear cut a path through the woman's dirt-smudged face. "Why did they do that—run your son off?"

"Keep working. Don't look at me." When Emily returned to planting, the woman began talking again in a hushed voice. "The Prophet said there were too many men—not enough women. He saw my husband and son as a threat to his power."

"Why didn't you go with them?"

"I couldn't. I didn't even know what happened or where they went," she said in hushed tones. "It's been two years, and I haven't had a word from them, where they are, or if they're dead or alive. I'm kept here, a prisoner like you—a breeder and a source of welfare money." The blade of the hoe pummeled the ground with ferocity. "They don't know I can't bear any more children."

"I don't understand. Why did you come here in the first place?"

"We believed in the Prophet, in his goodness, and his message—it was God's voice coming through him—telling us how we should live. All of us believed."

"And now?" Emily said as she moved up the dirt row behind the woman.

Betty hacked relentlessly at the brown earth, but before she could answer, the loud clang of a cowbell summoned them to lunch.

18

Thursday, April 12, 1990

Cortez, Colorado

I don't have time to sit around and drink coffee right now," said Abe in response to the Navajo lawman's suggestion they go to the corner café. "What I need is information. I want to find Emily and those girls, and people are waiting for me."

Hosteen cocked an eyebrow. "Guess I beat you to the punch. I can save you some time and trouble. Look, Freeman, I'm as determined to find them as you are. Emily's my partner, and Lina needs immediate care. I should have been there, so I'm following every lead to find out where they are."

Abe stared at Hosteen, debating with himself whether he should listen to what the man had to say or go ahead and check on his own. "What did you learn at the assessor's office?"

"Let's get coffee, and I'll tell you about it. You look like you could use something a little stronger, but this is not the time." Abe felt his stomach grumble. His last meal had been nearly twenty-four hours ago. He had been in a hurry to get on the road that morning and had been too nervous to eat or drink anything. He could go for a cup of coffee. "Okay, but let's make it quick."

They walked the half block to Angie's, a small diner advertising freshly baked bread and the best doughnuts in town.

After settling in a booth, Abe ordered coffee and repeated his question. "What did you learn at the courthouse?"

Hosteen studied the menu and smiled up at the young waitress. "I'll try one of your Danish pastries and a cup of coffee. You sure you don't want something to eat, Freeman?"

Impatience and annoyance gnawed at Abe. "Just coffee," he growled—his agitation showing by the constant drumming of his fingers on the Formica tabletop. As soon as the waitress left two cups on the table, he looked at Hosteen. "You said you could save me some trouble. Seems like you're wasting my time. I need to get going." He stood, ready to leave, but the officer waved him down.

"Harmony Home Ranch," Hosteen said. "In 1980, they bought ten thousand acres south of Cortez and began some extensive construction. Looks like they used their own people for nearly all the work—plumbers, electricians, carpenters. Even made their own cement."

Abe slid back into the booth and studied Hosteen. "What's the connection?"

"I logged on to the land data system and property records for the last ten years in Montezuma County. After a cursory examination of the abstracts for land bought or sold in the last decade, that one that stood out as peculiar. Somebody had a hell of a lot of money and applied for a mess of building permits—septic, water, electricity. But they didn't want to pay taxes—claimed they should have an exemption because they are a nonprofit religious organization and describe themselves as providing 'a safe and loving home for unwed mothers.'"

Abe jumped to his feet, nearly spilling the coffee. "That's the place. Why the hell are we sitting here while you order some goddamned pastry?"

"Hold on," said Hosteen. "I just got this information. You and I are the only ones who know about it. Why'd I share it with you? Don't know. Maybe because I can see how much you care about Emily, or because you are close to her mother and brother, and they're out there looking for her, too. The thing is, no one can just burst onto private property based on suspicions—not even the cops. We need enough evidence and probable cause to get a search warrant. Sorry, man, it's the way the system works."

Abe ran a hand through his hair and sat back down. He knew Hosteen was right. "Okay. So how do we go about getting the evidence we need?"

"What do you mean 'we'?"

"I want to be a part of this, damn it. I can help."

The waitress delivered Hosteen a fat Danish oozing cream cheese. "Looks great," he said. She smiled shyly and walked away. He took a bite, closed his eyes, and chewed. "Mmm."

Abe looked at him and waited while the man nonchalantly devoured the sweet pastry. After he had finished, Hosteen took a swig of coffee and regarded Abe.

"I told you before. Let the law handle this."

"Hosteen, I'm going to do this either with you or on my own. You can't stop me from trying to find Emily."

Hosteen stared at a spot over Abe's shoulder for a long minute before speaking. "When are you meeting up with Emily's folks?"

"Today at noon, here in Cortez at a restaurant called La Casita."

"It's a couple of blocks up the street. Good food. Don't think I'll be too hungry, but I'd like to be at the meeting." Hosteen swiped at his mouth with a napkin. "In the meantime, we've got two hours. I'm going to take a drive out to the Harmony Home Ranch. Do you want to ride along?"

"Yeah, of course. We'll take my truck. Draw less attention. What's the location of this so-called ranch we're looking for?"

Hosteen unfolded his long body from the confines of the booth and handed Abe the tab. "Almost all the way back to New Mexico. It borders the Ute Reservation. Sure you want to drive?"

Abe nodded. "If you have no objection to riding in a beat-up old Toyota, my truck is in front of the courthouse. Let's go."

A contemplative silence marked the first few miles of the trip. Abe couldn't help wondering what sort of opinion Hosteen had of him. "We should be running into Bertha and Will somewhere out here," he said, breaking the ice.

"Bertha? She's Emily's mother, I guess? How long have you known the family?"

The story of how he met Emily and the Etcitty family was not something Abe wanted to share with the Navajo lawman. So he kept his answer short and cryptic. "A couple years."

"How'd you and Emily meet?" Hosteen persisted.

"It's a long story." Abe exhaled an exasperated breath.

What right does this guy have to question me about my relationship with Emily? No way am I going to tell him anything. Nosy asshole.

Abe said, "Right now, I'm just interested in finding Emily. Judging from what we've learned, I think Emily and the girls might be at this ranch you were talking about. Do you know something you're not telling me, Hosteen?"

Hosteen took a pack of Juicy Fruit out of his shirt pocket and offered Abe a stick. When Abe shook his head, the lawman unpeeled one and popped it in his mouth. "A habit I picked up when I quit smoking," he said, chewing slowly. He rolled the wrapper into a ball and dropped it back into his pocket. "We have reason to believe the men who snatched the girls belong to a religious cult—maybe a breakaway sect from the Mormons. The word is that they still practice polygamy. I got a hunch when I read about this Harmony Home Ranch. I haven't had enough time to check into it further, but I called headquarters, and they're going to assign someone to investigate cult activity in this area."

"Makes sense—kidnapping young girls for wives. Fucking creeps."

"There's nothing substantial yet," Hosteen said. "Once we get inside, we should know more."

"So why don't you have a search warrant?"

"It's still only a little after ten in the morning, the day after our ladies were snatched. Cortez is a small town with limited resources. Judge Mobley is out of town, and he's the only one who can issue a warrant. One of our men is tracking him down, but he's on a fishing jaunt somewhere around Navajo Dam, and they haven't been able to reach him yet. He's scheduled to return late tomorrow night."

A jackrabbit, his long ears pressed flat, tail between his haunches, leaped a zigzag pattern across the road. Abe slowed, allowing the animal to pass. Bright sunlight, promising a warm day, glinted off the flat, dun-colored plateaus. Creosote bush, yucca, sagebrush, and greasewood hugged the high plains of the Four Corners area while buzzards, flying in concentric circles, surveyed the barren landscape.

They were five miles from the Ute village of Towaoc when Abe spotted Bertha's Honda parked at the side of the road. Emily's mother, shading her eyes with one hand, peered at a sign on a locked steel gate. She turned at the sound of Abe's truck pulling onto the gravel and looked at the two men as they approached.

"Bertha, I was hoping to run into you," Abe said. "Have you met Joe Hosteen, Emily's partner?"

Before speaking, Bertha took a minute to solemnly regard Hosteen. When she spoke, she did so in Navajo, introducing herself and her maternal and paternal clans by name, and telling him where she was from. She waited for his response.

"I'm sorry," said Hosteen, coloring, not meeting her gaze. "I don't speak Navajo."

A frown creased Bertha's face. "It's a shame, Joe Hosteen, that you have lost your language. Never mind. I am Emily's mother, Bertha Etcitty. I suppose we should shake hands like the *bilagáana*." She extended her right hand and asked, "What have you learned about my daughter's disappearance?"

"We ran into each other at the courthouse," Abe said before Hosteen could speak. "Joe got there before me and had already done some background checking in the assessor's office."

"I don't know anything for sure about Emily and the missing girls, Mrs. Etcitty. But I'd like to know what's really going on behind that gate." Hosteen glanced up at the sign. HARMONY HOME RANCH was written on an ornate iron scroll. "The description in the assessor's office got my attention, and I asked Abe if he'd be interested in riding out here. He said he planned on meeting up with you and Emily's brother at noon, so I figured we had plenty of time. How'd you end up here, Mrs. Etcitty?"

"I studied the layout of all the ranches on this side of the highway. Most of them are easy to access, but this one is a fortress. Something about it . . . tell me why this particular ranch caught your eye," Bertha said, showing interest in Hosteen.

"I noticed the amount of acreage they bought and was curious about where these people came from and what they're doing here," said Hosteen. "They're outsiders, possibly a cult."

"It would be nice if Will were here," Abe said. "Have you seen him?"

Bertha tilted her head toward the highway. "He's working the other side. Should be along pretty soon unless he ran into something or someone. I told him to meet me back here when he finished up. It's the first place I checked out and, after seeing the rest, is the only one that doesn't look like a regular cattle ranch."

Hosteen nodded and walked to the gate for a closer look. Thick vertical steel bars stood at least eight feet high. The electronically controlled gate required a code for access. A trench about twenty feet wide and ten feet deep ran along the fence line, and large boulders had been placed near the gateposts. Eight strands of barbed wire, stretching in both directions, presented further discouragement to anyone considering breaking in.

"Sure looks like they don't want company," Hosteen said.

"I feel something evil here. This is where they're holding my daughter," said Bertha. "Emily and two little Navajo girls are in there somewhere—and maybe more girls we don't even know about. I want to break that damn gate down."

Before anyone could respond, Will arrived on the scene. He parked the Chief, nodded to Hosteen and Abe, and solemnly studied the gate—the sign welded to the top, the secure fence. He went over to his mother, wrapping his arms around her. "If she's in there, I'll find her and bring her home. I won't let you down this time, *Shimá*."

A shudder shook Bertha's body. When she regained her composure, she faced Abe and Hosteen. "Will and I are going after Emily. I don't know what your plans are, but I'm getting my girl out of here."

As much as Abe wanted Emily back, he knew they couldn't rush headfirst into a highly barricaded site without running into resistance. "We need to figure out the best way to do this, Bertha. Some way we can succeed within the limits of the law. And making sure no one gets hurt." He turned to face Will. "You know I'm right. We can't screw this up."

"We're going to arouse suspicion if anyone from the ranch comes down the road and sees all of us out here. Especially since I'm in uniform," Hosteen added. "More than likely, they carry portable radios so they can alert the people inside if someone is snooping around. If the girls are hidden, we'll have no proof they're being held captive, and we won't be able to do anything. Judging from the building permits I saw at the assessor's office, there are a lot of people living on this ranch." He ran a hand through his thick black hair. "We don't know if they have weapons either. I'm getting a search warrant as soon as I can."

Will's battered face looked even gaunter after his drinking binge of the night before. Bloodshot eyes peered out from under the rumpled brim of his hat. He looked first at Hosteen, then at Abe. "The rest of you can go. Do whatever you want—wait for a search warrant. I'm gonna try to follow this fence line. They couldn't have made a trench all the way around, and even if they did, there has to be a way to get across." Before anyone could stop him, Will fired up his Chief. "I'll meet you in Cortez at the café," he yelled as he began working his way through the rough terrain along the south edge of the fence.

"He's a damn hardheaded fool," said Hosteen. "Freeman, I told you to let the law handle this. Instead, you bring in the family. Why don't you all just go on home and let me take care of this?"

"If he's hardheaded and stubborn, he got it from me," said Bertha, glaring at Hosteen with her arms crossed over her chest. "Do you think I'd sit at home, not knowing what's going on, and wait for the cops to make some kind of move? We're talking about my only daughter."

Abe stood beside Bertha, trying to hide how much his knee was paining him. He knew he was in no condition to scale fences and hike into the ranch. Still, he had no intention of leaving. He felt they were close to finding Emily, and he wanted to be there. "I'm staying with Bertha. There must be something we can do."

"You can stay out of the way and let me do my job," Hosteen said, his voice edged with frustration. "I don't want to babysit you."

Two pairs of unflinching eyes stared back at him.

In a gesture of surrender—hands up, palms out—Hosteen faced the stonewalling pair. "All right, all right. I'm calling this in and asking for backup; I need to go to the Montezuma County Sheriff's Office, see if he can expedite a warrant. If you want to be useful, go back to Cortez and see what you can learn about this Harmony Home Ranch bunch. Ask around town, but try not to be too obvious. I'll meet you back at La Casita around noon. Now let's clear away from this gate before we're spotted."

After dropping Hosteen off at the Montezuma County Courthouse, Abe parked on a side street and waited for Bertha, who was not far behind. He caught a glimpse of his face in the rearview mirror—purple bruise under his left eye, swollen split lip. He looked like a street brawler with a gimpy leg. He wondered if anyone would bother to talk to a mug like his. *I've got to try,* he thought. He also pondered where to start: local businesses, government agencies, library, newspaper? Someone had to have information about that ranch and the people out there, and he was determined to find out who.

19

Thursday, April 12, 1990

Women's Compound

Harmony Home Ranch

The lunch break was short—washing up followed by a lengthy prayer and a bowl of chicken soup that only had a hint of chicken. After the meal, Emily was due to return to the potato patch. As the women and girls sat at the long dining-room table, their heads bowed while the matron prayed and extolled the merits of the Prophet, Emily surreptitiously scanned each face, searching for Lina and Darcy. They were not at the table, and that worried her.

Where could they be? Maybe Betty can provide some information.

Back in the field with the gunnysack of potato eyes, she waited until it was safe before questioning Betty.

"Where are the girls?" she whispered.

Betty quickly glanced from side to side. "God's plan for young women. All the new girls are kept isolated for the first two weeks and instructed in their proper role as wives."

"Brainwashing, you mean. Why wasn't I included?"

"You're not a virgin. The Prophet likes to initiate all the new virgins. He may give you away as a wife to one of the other men."

"Over my dead body," Emily hissed. "I need to get out of here so I can let people know what's going on. Will you help me, Betty?"

When one of the matron's assistants walked by, the two women bent back into their work, heads down, mouths shut. She appraised the rows they had planted, then frowned. "Step it up, ladies. Stop lollygagging or you'll be working instead of eating supper tonight."

Slaves, Emily thought with disgust. *These poor women are nothing but sex slaves and worker bees.*

When the woman was out of earshot, she whispered, "Tonight, Betty. Will you help me? Can you unlock my door and the front door?"

"No. I don't have keys to the locks. There's nothing I can do."

Ever since she had been taken captive, Emily's focus had been on how to escape from the compound and notify authorities. Without someone to unlock the doors, she would have to climb out of her window and scale the eight-foot wall surrounding the women's compound—unnoticed—a difficult, if not impossible, feat. Ascending walls like these had been part of her police training, but not in a ridiculous dress, and not with coiled razor wire strung along the top. There was also the unknown on the other side of the wall, but she would face that obstacle when she came to it. First she had to convince Betty to help her.

"Is this any way to live, Betty? Don't you want to get away from here—see your son and husband again?"

The other woman kept her head down, blinking away tears she tried to hide. "I don't know what I can do."

"I need different clothes—jeans and a long-sleeve shirt, gloves, and wire cutters. Can you get your hands on anything like that?"

Emily waited for a response while Betty chopped at the earth with a hoe. With her brow wrinkled and mouth set in a frown, she appeared to be in deep concentration. At the end of the row, her head still down, she spoke in a halting voice. "I still have some of my son's clothes. If I help you, will you get me out of here?"

"Yes, of course."

"I have laundry duty tonight. While everyone is in the chapel, another woman and I will pick up the dirty laundry from each room and bring in clean linens. I'll hide the clothes between the sheets and towels and leave them in your room, under the bed."

"All right, good. The wire cutters?"

"I'll look for some when I return my tools to the shed. If I can pick any up without anyone noticing, I'll put them in with the clothes." She shuddered. "Lordy, if I get caught . . ."

"Whatever happens—if they stop me—I will never implicate you. I promise." After a period of silence, Emily said, "Can I count on you, Betty?"

"Yes." She nodded emphatically. "I want my family back. I want my life."

Abe and Bertha parked their vehicles on a side street near the courthouse and met under the shade of a giant blue spruce. "We know this much about Harmony Home," Abe said. "They're a weird religious cult, an offshoot of a mainstream church. And, according to all those building permits they applied for, they've been doing a lot of construction. Why don't you check with the local hardware stores, building-supply companies—anyplace you think these people might have frequented? This is a small town. They must have gotten some folks' attention."

"I know what to do, Abe, and I know where the businesses are." Bertha pursed her mouth in a frown. "Tired and worried and mad as I am, I'd just as soon scream and slap the hell out of somebody. But I'll try to keep my cool. We'll meet back at the café like we planned and share what we learned, if anything. I sure hope Will shows up. I'm afraid of what my son might get into his head to do." She exhaled a long sigh. "Where are you headed?"

"I got an idea, Bertha. Do they have a newspaper in this town?"

"The *Cortez Journal*. Their office is down there, close to the Safeway—East Roger Smith Avenue, I think. Why do you want the newspaper?"

"Maybe someone else was curious about the goings-on at Harmony Home Ranch and did a story. I don't know—it's worth a shot. If I'm lucky, they might have even gotten inside for an interview and taken pictures. I'll go through their archives."

Bertha nodded. "There's plenty of Mormons in this part of the country. I've been thinking they got kicked out of the Church of Latter-Day Saints and formed their own crazy religion—practicing polygamy and all."

"Makes sense. And it's why they want these young girls," Abe said. "Sick bastards."

"Well, let's get a move on. If Joe Hosteen doesn't get a warrant, I'll still find a way to get in there without one. Montezuma Street is at the next intersection. Take a right and you'll run into East Roger Smith. Turn left. It'll get you to the newspaper office." She turned and walked briskly away.

The flat, rectangular building housing the *Cortez Journal* was exactly where Bertha described. The flags of Colorado and the United States hung from a pole in front of the main entrance. Abe pulled a tattered notebook out of his glove compartment, groped around for something to write with, and entered the foyer. A woman was hunched over a computer at a large wooden desk situated catawampus, near the center of the room. Numerous framed pictures of children or grandchildren shared space with stacks of papers, Post-it notes, and a telephone, keyboard, and monitor.

He approached the woman, notebook in hand, having decided in advance to say he was writing an article on self-sustaining communities in the Four Corners area and had heard rumors about the Harmony Home Ranch. He introduced himself as a freelance writer, Lance Jeffrey, and asked if the managing editor was in.

"Which magazine?" The gray-haired receptionist peered up at him through horn-rimmed glasses, raised her eyebrows, and pursed her lips when she saw his battle wounds. A nameplate on her desk read, "Tina Brewster: Secretary/Receptionist. The Superglue That Holds This Place Together."

"*High Country News.*" Abe smiled to cover the lie. It was the only title he could come up with. He hoped it would work. He had seen a stack of magazines in Mattie Simmons's house with *High Country News* on top, and thought it seemed appropriate for this area. "I guess you can't help but notice my face—just took a tumble when I was out hiking."

"Uh huh. Well, hold on. I'll see if the mister is free." She picked up an old-style phone and pressed a button. "Phil, there's a writer out here says he's with *High Country News* and wants to ask you a few questions . . . He's looking for information on those strange people out at Harmony Home . . . Yeah, okay."

"He can give you ten minutes before he has to cover a city council meeting. Mr. Brewster's office is through the door on the left. Go on in, he's expecting you."

"Thanks. You two related?"

"You could say so."

Phil Brewster stood up to meet Abe with an outstretched hand. "Brewster," he said, shaking Abe's hand, "but call me Brew. Looks like your last interview didn't go so well if that black eye is any indication." He nodded toward a worn, overstuffed love seat, adding, "Sit down and make yourself comfortable." After sliding into a frayed leather chair behind his cluttered desk, he swiveled to face Abe. "Now, how can I help you?"

Brew and his wife, Tina, like many couples who have been married a long time, shared characteristic mannerisms. The managing editor, pink-faced and portly, glanced up from the papers spread across his desk. He, like his wife, came straight to the point. "You're not actually writing an article for *High Country News*, are you? What's your story?"

After a moment's hesitation, Abe decided to be straight with the man. He had felt foolish the minute he told the lie about working for a magazine. *Why wouldn't a newspaper be interested in getting an inside scoop on a local kidnapping?*

He silently chastised himself and then said, "You're right. I don't work for any magazine. I'm trying to find my girlfriend and two Navajo girls. They were kidnapped from the reservation, and I have reason to believe they're being held at the Harmony Home compound. I'm looking for any information that will help in securing a search warrant so we can investigate the ranch. I'd appreciate whatever information you can give me. Please, I'm concerned about their safety—the Navajo families are worried sick."

"What makes you think they're at Harmony Home?"

"We suspect the two men who abducted them are members of a cult that practices polygamy, and the ranch is their headquarters."

Brew looked at his watch. "I know about the kidnapping. It's a big story. You got ten minutes. My top reporter is out of town, and I need to cover a council meeting. A bunch of old windbags and egotistical hotheads, but I'll want to talk to you more later—get the full story." Phil Brewster cleared his throat and pushed his bifocals up his nose. "Tina called it right. Those people out there are peculiar. Once a month, some of the women come to town to cash their welfare checks. They always look the same—long pastel-colored dresses, hair pinned up in an old-fashioned style, no makeup or jewelry. Plain is what they are."

"What about the men?"

"Hardworking, good carpenters, not too friendly. Some of the men work here in town doing construction and such, but they are a tight-lipped bunch and keep to themselves. I wanted to go to the ranch and do a feature story, look around, take some pictures, and talk to the person in charge, but he wouldn't have any of it. So all I got was a telephone interview."

"You have his name, though, right?"

"Said his name was Rupert Langley. Not sure if it's his real name. Gave me a story about building a self-sustaining community and sanctuary for unwed mothers and their children—as well as providing them with a good God-fearing Christian education. That's why so many of the women are on food stamps and the government assistance plan for women, infants, and children—WIC. His answers to other questions were curt. I had Tina do a background search on the name he gave me, but nothing came up. I wrote the story, even though it didn't amount to much."

Brew stood up and Abe followed suit.

"Thanks for your time. If it's possible, I'd like to see the article."

"Sure. Tell Tina I said you can go through the archives. Sorry to rush off. Hope you find your girls. Since the cops put out an APB, I'll post their pictures if you have them, run a story. I can't mention Harmony Home yet, though. By the way, there's a rancher by the name of Hank Lovato—has a small plane. I overheard him talking at the Dew Drop Inn the other day. Said he was flying his Cessna over Harmony Home Ranch, and when he looked down, he thought he saw a goddamned village with a big castle smack-dab in the middle. You might want to get in touch with him."

Abe's heart beat a little faster. "Thanks. I'll have a Navajo police officer contact you concerning information about the missing girls." He stopped Phil Brewster before he made it out the front door. "What did you say the rancher's name was? Do you think he might have taken pictures?"

"Don't know. You'll have to ask him. He's in the phone book. Hank Lovato, out at the Twisted T Ranch."

Abe scribbled the rancher's name in his notebook, adding the notation "pilot" and, before he forgot, jotted down "Rupert Langley—Harmony House leader—kidnapper." When he returned to the front office, he looked for the editor's wife.

"Mrs. Brewster?"

"Call me Tina."

"Tina. I need a couple of favors, and I will level with you. I lied. I'm not a reporter. I'm looking for a kidnapped lady police officer and two young Navajo girls. They might be at the Harmony Home Ranch."

"Well, that sounds more believable. I wasn't buying the story about *High Country News* anyway. What's your real name, mister?"

"Abe Freeman. I need to go through your archives, and I'd like to get in touch with Hank Lovato. Can you get me the number?"

"Sure thing, sugar. The morgue is down those stairs. Old newspapers are filed on racks according to the year and date. The article Brew wrote on the Harmony Home Ranch was five or six years ago, sometime in the summer, if memory serves me right. There're a few more short articles listing building permits and such that happened before Brew tried to get the interview. So much construction going on—it's what got him interested in the first place. Watch out when you go down. Lights are on the left, but the stairs are narrow."

Abe thanked Tina and headed in the direction she indicated. The basement where they stored past issues reeked of ink, old paper, and mildew. He browsed the long rows until he found the racks for 1985 and 1986, and quickly skimmed through the summer editions for anything relating to the Harmony Home. It was slow, tedious work. Most newspapers stored their past editions on microfiche now, he knew, but he finally found pay dirt.

While he read the article, Abe jotted down a few notes. Brew had been right. The information was sketchy, and Langley attempted to portray a rosy image of Harmony Home. It was nearly noon when he finished, but he wanted to talk to Lovato before he met with Bertha and Will.

After Tina handed him the rancher's number, he decided to ask for one more favor. "Tina, I'm pressed for time. Would you mind . . . ?"

"Calling him for you? Why didn't you say so in the first place?" After dialing, she handed the phone to Abe.

Bertha and Hosteen were already sitting at a corner table when Abe arrived at La Casita a little after twelve. Bertha, fidgeting with her napkin, looked more anxious than ever. The little café was filling up with a lunch crowd, but there was no sign of Will. Abe took a chair beside her. "How're you holding up? You look tired."

"As good as can be expected, and I'm no more tired than you. At least I don't have a bum knee or bruises and cuts all over my face. You look like you've been in a barroom brawl. I'm thinking too much— about Emily with those awful people, and about Will."

"They'll be all right. Let's give Will a little time. Joe?" he said, acknowledging the Navajo police officer. "Any luck with the search warrant?"

Hosteen rubbed his chin. "First thing in the morning. Judge is coming back late tonight. It's the best we can do."

They waited while the waitress wiped the table, dispersed place mats, silverware, water, and menus.

Abe sipped his water. "I have some news. I've got a name for the person in charge at Harmony Home Ranch. It may not be his real name, but maybe you'll come up with something when you run a check on it, Joe."

"Give it to me. I'll call it in."

"Rupert Langley is the name he gave the editor at the *Journal*. Editor's name is Phil Brewster. He didn't give much credence to the name, especially after he couldn't find anything when he tried a background check. Maybe the cops will have better luck. Anyway, the paper wants to run a headline story on the kidnapping—put the girls' pictures out there. I said you'd get in touch."

Hosteen scribbled the names on a notepad and slipped it into his shirt pocket. "Will do. Radio and TV are running stories as well. Anything else?"

"The paper hooked me up with a rancher who has flown over the compound in his Cessna, and I gave him a call. As far as I know, he's about the only one who can provide a description of the layout inside the fence."

Before Abe could add more, Will—dusty but unharmed—ambled through the doorway, his eyes searching the crowd for familiar faces.

Bertha spotted him and waved to get his attention. When he joined them at the table, she studied his haggard face. "Are you okay, son?"

After downing the contents of his water glass, he faced his mother with a tired smile. "I'm doin' all right, but the ranch out there is about as hard to enter as a bank vault. Rocky canyons and *arroyos* on both sides, a steep mesa in the back. The only way to get in is on foot or through the gate. How are you holding up, Ma?"

Bertha looked to be on the verge of a breakdown. Nodding her head, she blinked back tears.

"*Shimá*, I want you to go home," said Will. "There's nothing more you can do here. We can handle it, and you need to take care of yourself—be at the house in case Emily calls."

Hosteen, who had been quietly listening, broke into the conversation. "He's right, Mrs. Etcitty. Go back home. You can be our liaison with the families of the girls. It would be a huge help."

"Bertha," said Abe, "as soon as we learn anything, we'll let you know."

Emily's mother stood, excused herself, and went to the restroom. The men frowned, Abe dawdled with his napkin, and Hosteen scratched his head.

"She'll go," said Will. "And it's better this way."

When Bertha returned to the table, she said, "You promise you will keep me informed about what happens? And I mean *right away?*" Before she turned to leave, she added, "I didn't learn much today. Talked to a man at the hardware store who said those people just about bought him out. They spend a lot of money in town, but they are probably set up now to live off the grid, he said. I got too depressed after I heard that and couldn't deal with talking to any more people. You're right. I'm no use here."

Will stood up and put an arm around his mother. "Are you okay to drive?"

"Yes, *shiyáázh,*" she said. "You bring our Emily back home, and stay safe."

"I'll be singing for the holy ones to protect her and the two girls, and to give Lina the strength to hold on. Go on now, *Shimá.*"

Hosteen sipped his water, waiting a few minutes in the silence left by Bertha's departure before continuing. "About the rancher with an airplane? I wonder if he took pictures."

Abe shared his recent conversation with the rancher, Hank Lovato. "No photos. Said he didn't have his camera with him, but if he ever went back, he would be sure to bring it."

"What kind of plane has he got?" Will asked. "Any chance he'd take us up?"

The waitress returned, pencil and pad ready to take orders, but no one had looked at the menu, so Hosteen told her they weren't ready. Even though they hadn't eaten all day, the men were more interested in what Abe had to say than in food. They ordered coffee all around, and the waitress bustled off.

"He has an older-model Cessna 172 Skyhawk. Seats four. We'd have to give him something for gas and his time, but yeah, I think he might," said Abe.

"Give him a call as soon as we leave. See if you can set something up," Hosteen said. "Think I'll go visit the sheriff. Maybe I can talk him into forming a *posse comitatus* after we get a search warrant."

Will set his cup down and looked inquiringly at Hosteen. "What's this *posse comitatus* business all about"?

"To quote the law-enforcement manual, 'It's the common law authority of a county sheriff to conscript and arm any able-bodied man to assist him in keeping the peace or in pursuing or arresting a felon.' Sometimes a sheriff will deputize civilians when he's shorthanded."

Abe drummed his fingers on the table and exchanged a look with Will. "Do you think he'd deputize us? Two guys off the street? Seems kinda crazy."

"He's got the authority to deputize anyone he wants, so yeah, if he felt there was a need," said Hosteen. "He can even deputize me. I'd just as soon you two went home and waited it out. But I'm kind of shorthanded myself, and we need to get as much information on the cult as we can to make sure the judge won't hesitate to sign a warrant."

Abe and Will nodded in agreement.

"Okay," said Hosteen. "Let's order something—it's going to be a long day."

Hank Lovato agreed to meet them at the Cortez Municipal Airport at two o'clock sharp. They took Hosteen's police SUV, Will riding in front and Abe in the back, a steel cage separating him from the two Navajo men. Abe was reminded once again of when he had first met Emily. He had been on his way to Chaco Canyon, running from his past and the haunting memory of his girlfriend's death. A drifter he had met the previous night had been found murdered, and Abe's knife was discovered near the body. Emily had taken him into custody. After being released from a night in jail, he had been ordered to remain in the area as a material witness until his name was cleared. He ended up staying with Will and his grandfather at their isolated sheep camp.

That's how it all began. Now Emily, Bertha, Will, and Grandfather Etcitty are my family, he thought. Abe shook his head, clearing his mind of the reverie—they were nearing their destination.

"Lovato said the airport's easy to find—right off Highway 666, on our left coming from Cortez. We're supposed to look for a '62 Skyhawk, white with a blue stripe on the side, red on the tail. He said he'll be waiting."

Lovato's directions took them three miles south of Cortez and down County Road G to an assortment of low-slung, industrial-looking buildings and hangars, and a small terminal with a single runway. On the tarmac in front of the terminal, a man wearing a cowboy hat and boots was disconnecting the tail tie-down of a small single-prop plane.

"Must be him," Abe said, approaching the man. "Hank Lovato?"

A weathered brown face turned in their direction, and burnt-umber eyes assessed the three men. Lovato, stocky but muscular, straightened and extended a calloused hand. "You Abe Freeman?" he said, shaking Abe's hand. "Introduce me to your friends."

Abe had been brief in explaining to Lovato why the three wanted to see the cult compound, saying only that he had reason to believe criminal activity was being conducted inside those walls. Lovato didn't pursue the topic further.

Lovato asked, "Ever been up in a single-engine prop? Well, never mind. It's a kick—you're gonna love it. Go on; get in. Find a seat and buckle up. I'm about done here."

Abe slid into the seat next to the cockpit while Will and Hosteen settled in the back two. When Lovato finished inspecting the outside of the plane, he strapped himself into the cockpit and began a preflight check of the control panel instruments. Apparently satisfied with the readings, he turned on the master switch and opened the throttle.

"I got a chance to listen to the radio during my lunch break, and I heard the story about the missing Navajo girls and police officer. Just put two and two together, so this flight is on me. If those bastards out there had anything to do with it, I'll help any way I can to nail their asses." Lovato checked to make sure there was no one behind the plane and turned on the ignition switch, holding it until the engine caught.

The Skyhawk bounced down the runway and slowly began its ascent. A cloudless blue sky promised good visibility, but contrary winds buffeted and rocked the small plane. Abe glanced back at Will, noting the pained expression on the man's face and his tight grip on the armrests.

He's terrified of flying, Abe thought. *But he's doing this for Emily.*

"Hang on," said Lovato as a violent gust pitched them up and down. "Coming up on the right."

Abe peered out the window at a barren landscape scarred with *arroyos*, washes, hogbacks, and outcroppings. Mesas sprung up out of the buff-colored desert, now showing pale patches of spring green. Random buildings denoting isolated ranches were scattered over the harsh terrain. Miniature cattle dotted the land. Looking north, the rugged La Plata and the San Juan Mountains loomed menacingly. A thin ribbon of blue snaked through the brown earth, parallel to the black strip of highway.

"Navajo Wash," said Hosteen, who had been quietly studying the land. "It's running fully now, but come summer it'll be bone-dry, except during the monsoon rains."

How well Abe remembered those summer rains and the flash flood that had trapped Emily in a raging torrent of mud and water.

Has it already been two years? I managed to save her then. Can I do it now?

Ten minutes later the sight of what he thought must be an apparition caught Abe's eye—the sun glanced off a gleaming white cathedral spire surrounded by a carpet of green grass, houses, outbuildings, shops, and cultivated plots of land.

"Jesus Christ," said Abe. "It is a goddamned city."

The aerial view of the cult's property presented an astonishing and formidable fortress. The enclosed buildings were backed up to a steep mesa and surrounded by a high wall with guard posts at each corner. A shimmering white temple capped with spires and encircled by manicured lawns and flower beds loomed, tall and imposing, at the center of the ranch. The area where the women were working lay behind yet another wall. A cement sidewalk led directly from the front of a dormitory-like structure inside the wall to the entrance of the temple. Abe counted at least twenty large houses, several hangar-size storage sheds, barns, and silos, plus a fleet of heavy equipment. It appeared the ranch had its own water tower and sewage-treatment plant, plus an array of solar panels. In fact, they had everything they needed to live off the grid and be self-sufficient—cattle, goats, chickens, orchards, cultivated fields.

"Can you get closer?" asked Hosteen, who was readying the camera he had brought along.

The Cessna dropped and swooped low, revealing more details. They were close enough to make out the shapes of people—women in long pastel dresses bent over the earth, wielding shovels and hoes. Their faces turned up at the sound of the plane but quickly reverted back to their task when a tall woman in blue walked by. Abe could not distinguish their features, dressed as they were, and with hats covering their hair.

"Emily could be one of those women," said Will.

Abe's heartbeat increased with each click of the camera shutter. As the plane zoomed closer, his eyes settled on a structure—a dormitory-like building enclosed behind a high wall. "You're right—Emily and the girls. We've got to figure out a way to get in there," said Abe. "And get them out."

Later that afternoon, after gathering all the information they could find regarding the Harmony Home Ranch and its occupants, Abe, Will, Hosteen, and Sheriff Turnbull met with Phil Brewster at the *Cortez Journal* office. Together, the five men worked on the proper preparation of the affidavit that needed to accompany the search-warrant request.

"The facts need to be spelled out explicitly and provide sufficient probable cause to issue a proper warrant," Hosteen told them. "We have to write this in a way that will give us permission to search the entire premises and to question everyone who lives within the confines of the ranch without being in violation of privacy rights."

After three hours' work, Hosteen and Sheriff Turnbull seemed satisfied with the document. Tina Brewster typed it up, providing the sheriff with two copies and Hosteen with one. It had been a long day that was running into night, but they finally had something to show for it.

20

Thursday, April 12, 1990

Women's Compound

Harmony Home Ranch

When the women completed their day of yard work, they trudged, dusty and back-weary, to the dormitory. The matron, waiting at the open door, instructed them to remove their shoes before entering, shower, change into clean clothing, and report to the chapel in half an hour. After completing a day's labor, they were required to study Scripture and thank God for the incredible privilege of serving him and the Prophet.

"Your clean clothing is laid out on your beds. As most of you know, you are not allowed to keep personal possessions of any kind in your room, but I have assigned each of you the correct size. Leave the soiled items and towel by the door for Betty to gather."

Every word coming from the woman's mouth was an affront to Emily's ears, another slap in the face, but she pretended to meekly comply while her mind focused on a means of escape. Earlier in the day, she had observed a small plane flying directly overhead and wondered about it. There was no way she could signal the pilot, and it left quickly. She'd wanted to scream with frustration.

While the others gathered in the chapel, Betty and another woman had the task of going from room to room with a laundry cart. Betty had promised to hide the tools and her son's clothes in the cart and slide them under Emily's bed when the other woman wasn't looking. Emily had wanted a crowbar, but Betty said she would not be able to take an item so large from the toolshed without arousing suspicion.

"You'll have to make do with a screwdriver," she had said in a breathless whisper. "I have the wire cutters and rope. They're under my dress."

Emily knew that Betty was taking an enormous risk in agreeing to help her, but she also believed that the woman's desire to leave this place and find her husband was stronger than her fear. Now, as the matron's voice droned on and on, Emily's heart pounded while she played out her plan in her head.

Stay calm, she reminded herself. *One step at a time.*

Abe would have stayed in a motel in Cortez overnight, but he needed some gear and a change of clothes. In his haste to start looking for Emily, he had forgotten everything. When he tried to call Ellen to let her know he was coming home, no one answered.

She's not at home because she's at my place with Danny.

He tried a few more times, then drove the eighty-four miles from Cortez to Bloomfield. Anxiety, anger, and fatigue gnawed at his mind and body. The judge would not see them until tomorrow morning at eight o'clock, and the sheriff wouldn't make a move to deputize anyone until Hosteen had a search warrant in hand. He and Will had argued with the Navajo cop, lobbying to break into the compound on their own. Hosteen said he'd have them arrested if they tried—that they'd screw up the investigation. In the end, they grudgingly relented.

Of course, Hosteen was right, but when Abe approached the ornate gate to Harmony Home Ranch, he pulled off to the side of the road. Staring at the gate, clenching and unclenching his fists, he felt as if his blood would boil and his head would explode. He got out of the truck and walked to the gate. Grabbing hold of the bars, he shook them as hard as he could and yelled at the top of his lungs. "Emily! Damn you people to hell, you filthy sons of bitches. If you lay a hand on her or those young girls, I'll hunt you down and kill you!" Sitting back down in the driver's seat, spent and exhausted, his body trembled so much he could barely drive.

When he turned off the ignition in his dark driveway at ten thirty, he knew sleep would not come easily. He saw the Jorgensons' truck parked near the front of his house, the lights off, Danny and Ellen evidently tucked in for the night. Abe walked to the barn and heard Patch scratching to get out. When he pushed the door open, moonlight fell across the sleeping form of Danny Jorgenson, illuminating his guileless boy-man face, completely relaxed in untroubled slumber.

Patch danced at his feet, tail wagging, whimpering softly. Abe reached down and stroked the dog's coat. "Okay, boy. I missed you, too. Quiet now. We'll take a walk."

There was no need for a flashlight under the radiance of the full moon. Abe found the path leading to the river and followed it until he reached the large cottonwood gracing its bank. A fallen log lay at the edge of the river. He sat, closed his eyes, and breathed deeply, soothed for a time by the smell and sound of water coursing over rocks. Abe was not cut out for confrontation and violence—he had once been a quiet, introspective man, a peace-loving musician. His life had changed dramatically since coming to New Mexico. Tomorrow morning he would be carrying a gun, and be expected to use it if necessary—a thought he still could not quite come to terms with. "Why is there so damn much evil in this world, Patch? How could anyone take children—or a girl who needs medication—from a happy family celebration and lock them away for his own filthy pleasure?"

Patch looked up at him while he continued addressing the dog as if he expected an answer.

"I want Emily back. I don't want her hurt, and I don't want her involved with scum like this anymore. I'm tired of this shit."

Patch barked and Abe shook his head, sniggering mirthlessly at his foolishness. "Okay, okay. We'll walk." They wound their way along the riverbank and circled back to the house. When he returned, he saw a glow in the window, and Ellen Jorgenson, her bare feet tucked under her, sitting in the rocking chair. She looked up expectantly when he opened the door, but he shook his head, anticipating her question.

"I'll get my things and leave now," she said. Walking to the couch, she began gathering the blanket and pillow where she had evidently been dozing.

"Thanks for staying, Ellen. Sorry I'm so late. I'm leaving for Cortez again first thing in the morning. Do you mind if Danny stays another day?"

"Of course I don't mind. Danny will be thrilled, and I'll stay with him tomorrow and as long as need be. I wish I could do more."

Abe tried to suppress a yawn. "You've done more than you can imagine, Ellen."

"You look beat. I'll go now. You need your rest."

Abe nodded. "Thanks. You don't know how much I appreciate your help. I'll square it with you and Danny when this is over, promise."

She smiled and walked to the door. "No need. Good night, Abe."

Emily walked back and forth across the small room, too wired to sit still and wait for the opportune time to escape. Betty, as promised, had left a towel-wrapped parcel under the bed containing men's pants, a shirt, and a cap. There was more—a pair of wire cutters, a screwdriver, a long rope, and a file. After the lights-out hour, Emily stood on a chair in the bathroom and worked methodically and quietly to remove the window and frame. Once she took the frame out, the thin metal bars were easy to dislodge.

The women went to bed early, but she had no way of telling the exact time, so she watched the moon. When it reached its highest point, she would leave. She had already changed into the young man's clothes, several sizes too big, and felt grateful that Betty had thought to include a belt. As she paced the room in her clumsy boots, she pondered her escape.

Should I follow the road and take a chance I won't run into anyone, or should I bushwhack it and follow my instincts?

Having no idea about the lay of the land, she decided to try following the road. The full moon would provide enough light, but would also make her more visible to others. In the dark men's clothing, her hair tucked under the ball cap, she hoped no one would notice her.

Emily noted the moon's position. It was time to move. With the rope and tools stuffed into the pockets and waistband of her pants, she climbed onto the chair once again, grasped the edges of the window opening, pulled herself up, and wriggled through. Looking down, she saw that a drop of about twelve feet awaited her. Luckily, thick grass covered the ground.

Tuck and roll, she reminded herself as she pushed her body out and away from the window.

She hit the ground, knees bent, with a thud. She went into a roll. Crouching low, her legs throbbing from the jolt, she hurried to the shelter of a shrub and waited for any sign someone might have heard her. From her hidden vantage point, she scanned the wall, looking for the darkest, most advantageous location to attempt her climb. The bright moon, both her friend and nemesis at this point, provided a clear view. When after several minutes no lights appeared in the windows, and no one emerged from the dormitory, she made a run toward the nearest shed and pasted her body against its wall. Advancing in short spurts, she arrived at a section of wall near some trees, and partially hidden in shadows. Emily assumed this would be the most dangerous part of her escape. She would be in open view of anyone looking her way, and she did not know what lay on the other side. She uncoiled the rope, checked her pocket for the wire cutters, and took a deep breath.

No turning back now.

After sprinting to the wall, she crouched again.

A large coil of razor wire, attached to steel poles at ten-foot intervals, topped the wall. The poles supporting the wire bent outward. Emily made a loop in the rope, lassoed a pole, and pulled herself to the top.

She looked around, breathing heavily, relieved no one had seen her, knowing more challenges were ahead. The sharp-edged razor wire, coiled and treacherous as a poisonous viper, curled directly above her head. Emily held tightly onto the rope while she cut strands of wire with her free hand. The thick line resisted, but she kept at it until a coil sprang loose, snapping back and slicing her cheek, nearly causing her to lose her grip.

"Son of a bitch," she hissed, wiping her bloody face with a shirt-sleeve. This was another time when Emily wished there were swear words in Navajo. They would be so much more meaningful than the English that didn't do justice to the way she felt.

She dropped the wire cutters in a back pocket and, grasping the top edge of the wall, pulled herself up, surveying the surroundings while she caught her breath.

Get the rope, she reminded herself as she scooted toward the pole where it dangled. She wouldn't need it to get down from the wall, but she figured it might come in handy later. She hung the rope over her shoulder and studied the grounds. Her high vantage point provided a view of the spreading ranch outside the prison compound's walls.

Numerous structures, some of them appearing to be private dwellings, were laid out in gridlike fashion around a towering temple that shimmered, white as a moonlit ghost, in the surrounding spotlights. The other buildings were dark, shut down for the night. Street lamps and spotlights lit the road, and she saw a small structure she thought must be a guard post.

While she studied the road leading away from the compound, a vehicle approached, driving slowly, its spotlight probing the sides as if looking for anyone trying to enter or escape—as if looking for *her*. She ducked and flattened her body against the wall, realizing she would not be able to follow the road without being detected by whoever was in the guard post or on patrol. She had previously considered slipping into the back of a van and hiding until someone drove it out of the gate, but Betty had informed her it would be impossible. All the vehicles were locked and the keys returned to the Prophet's right-hand man at the end of each day. Whenever someone needed a car or truck, the keys had to be signed out by the driver.

Now, as she observed the road, she rethought her plan.

Stay away from buildings and roads.

She decided to remain in the shadows, move away from the compound, and take her chances in the open country. She swung her legs up and over the side of the wall, holding tightly to the edge, then twisted her body around and lowered herself to the ground.

The spotlight of the patrol vehicle swept the fence, and Emily crouched, waiting for it to pass. Once it turned, she headed away from the houses and dashed, almost crawling, toward a clump of trees. She ran through the orchard, using the trees as shields to check if anyone was following her. When she reached the other side, she was far enough away from the lights of the compound to let the full moon guide her. A deep ravine with flowing water ran along the back side of the orchard, and an irrigation system channeled water into the orchard. *Acequias,* the Spanish called them, though Emily doubted this place shared water with any of its neighbors.

Beyond the channel of water, Emily could make out the dark outline of a mountain range dominated by a singular sharp peak, and all at once she knew where she was. *"Dibe Nitsaa,"* she whispered in wonder. One of the six sacred mountains of the Diné, named Mount Hesperus by the Spanish, *Dibe Nitsaa* was located in the Plata Mountains north of Mancos, Colorado. She was on land that had once been part of Dinétah, the traditional homeland of the Navajo people.

This ravine in front of me must be Navajo Wash, she told herself. *If I follow its southerly course, I'll meet up with the highway and be heading home.*

Tears of relief streamed down her cheeks as she silently thanked her ancestors for leading her to this point.

The journey was easy at first. She washed her blood-streaked face with cold water from the canal and made good progress through flat pastureland, always keeping the channel of water in sight. Emily checked the moon's position again. She figured she had been walking for close to three hours when the terrain gradually began to change. Outcroppings of rocks, cacti, and sage dotted the land. As the moon dropped lower, so did the terrain. The wash tumbled into the ravine, sometimes disappearing from view. When the moon descended to a point just above a range of mountains, she reached the edge of a deep canyon and a five-foot-high, tightly strung barbed-wire fence. She might be able to cut the fence, but she knew she would still have to climb down into the ravine, cross it, and make her way to the top to get off the compound and look for a road.

Go for it, she told herself as she extracted the heavy-duty wire cutters from her pocket, thanking Betty once again.

Clutching whatever handhold she could reach—roots, rocks, juniper branches—Emily sidestepped, slowly descending the slick slope of the ravine. She could hear water below, churning over rocks at the bottom. Dark shadows obscured her vision.

As she reached for what she thought was a root, it moved, and she heard an unmistakable rattle. She jerked her hand back before the snake could strike and tried to back away, but lost her footing in the process and began a rapid slide down the rocky slope. Emily fought to maintain her balance on the uneven surface, but snagged her foot on a root and fell, tumbling over brush and sharp rocks. She didn't stop until she landed on a boulder at the bottom, near the water's edge. Her arms and face were scratched, bruised, and bleeding, her leg bent at a grotesque angle. Emily tried to move, and searing pain, worse than anything she had endured since giving birth to her son, shot through her knee and up her spine. "*Shiká anilyeedá!* Someone please help me!" she cried until numbness, along with a certain detachment, crept into her body.

21

Abe leaned against his truck in the gray predawn, checking for Will's headlight every few minutes, his dog watching every move. He hadn't slept well, and his knee still ached, but not as much. He had called Will earlier. They would ride in Abe's truck to meet up with Hosteen at the sheriff's office in Cortez. "Bring the guns," Abe had said, referring to the shotgun and antique pistol that belonged to Grandfather Etcitty. "They may not deputize us if we don't have our own weapons." Tense, edgy, his stomach churning and mouth dry, he had turned down Ellen's offer of breakfast, opting for only a cup of coffee, but now he wished he had eaten something. He had poured the remains of the pot into a thermos to drink later, as his stomach was too unsettled for a second cup.

"It's Friday the thirteenth, Patch," he said, stooping to ruffle the dog's fur. "A hell of a day for a showdown." A single beam appeared on the road, and Abe opened the truck's door in anticipation of Will's arrival. When Patch tried to jump in, he stopped him. "Not today, buddy. No place for a dog." *God, how I wish things were peaceful and normal, the way they were before Emily disappeared.*

Will parked the Chief in front of Abe's house and opened the passenger door of the pickup, placing the shotgun and an old revolver on the floor behind the seat, and sighing heavily. "Life was a hell of a lot easier to deal with when I stayed drunk." He slumped in the seat beside Abe. "Let's get those sons o' bitches and bring our girls home."

Abe pumped the gas pedal until the engine caught. "You look like shit," he said, glancing at Will's stony face, bloodshot eyes, and grim-set mouth.

"Humph," Will snorted, slumped in his seat. "You're not too cute yourself, asshole. Don't count on wowing any women today."

"Yeah. Well, there's only one woman I want to impress, and I don't think she's going to care what we look like when we find her."

Will remained silent during the remainder of the trip, and the small talk ceased, each man seemingly lost in private thoughts while the scenery, straight out of a Western movie, flew by. The sun peeked over a mesa top, casting a brilliant palette of orange and pink across the eastern sky. Bruised, purple cumulonimbus clouds were beginning to form along the northern horizon, carrying with them the threat of afternoon thunderstorms. The morning air felt cool but bore a slight odor of rotten eggs, attributed to the chemical methyl mercaptan that was added to odorless natural gas as a way of detecting leaks. An ugly yellow-gray cloud hovered low in the west—emissions from the massive Navajo Generating Station. They turned north, away from the twisting San Juan River that flowed through Farmington, and onto Highway 666. The land stretched into a high desert prairie sprinkled with the spring colors of new grass, yellow blanket flowers, pink prairie primrose, and gray-green sage. Abe glanced at Will, thinking he might have fallen asleep, but he saw the Navajo's eyes were open and staring straight ahead.

"Yesterday's plane ride . . . Will, I know you don't like to fly. You did good, buddy."

"Humph," Will mumbled as they drove past Sleeping Ute Mountain and onto the last stretch before Cortez and their meeting with Hosteen. Will was obviously in no mood for conversation.

Pickup trucks—some newer models, others weathered and worn—were lined up in front of the building shared jointly by the judicial department and the sheriff's office. Hosteen had recruited six additional Navajo men to join the posse—two off-duty officers from tribal police, and four civilian volunteers. They hunkered in separate groups near the entrance of the Montezuma County Sheriff's Office, the Navajo turning their heads as one to watch when Abe parked, and he and Will emerged from the truck. It was early, not yet eight o'clock, and Hosteen stood off to the side with the two Navajo lawmen and the sheriff, waiting for the arrival of Judge Mobley and his signature on the search warrant. Hosteen looked up and nodded when Abe and Will approached.

Charley Nez, Lina's father, stood among the volunteers. He shot a steely-eyed look at Will before spinning around, showing his disdain for the new arrivals.

"*Yá'át'ééh abini,*" Will said, greeting the group with the traditional Navajo "Good morning." All the men returned the greeting and acknowledged Abe and Will's presence in a polite manner—except for Charley Nez. Will walked up to him so they were face-to-face.

Nez clinched his fist as if ready to fight. "You brought this trouble on my child, *yee naaldlooshii*. You are a skinwalker, posing as a *hataalii*."

Will raised his hand, and Lina's father took a step backward but remained in his hostile stance. "Charley, I am not your enemy. We are together in this bad business—brothers, one people—searching for your daughter, Lina; Henry Benally's daughter, Darcy; and my sister, Emily, who also has a mother in grief. You all know my *shimá*, Bertha

Etcitty. She taught some of your children, brought you supplies when you needed them. You know my grandfather, a respected elder, a singer who came whenever anyone sought his help. You trusted them. Now, trust me. Any bad feelings you have against me, we will resolve at a later date. We need to remain united in this effort to find our loved ones, no matter how much anger you feel toward me."

Charley Nez did not respond, but dropped his clenched fists and hung his head, staring at the ground.

Abe had watched in silence, relieved that Charley Nez had not acted on his anger. Now was neither the time nor place for a confrontation. A few minutes later a dark sedan pulled into a reserved parking place in front of the sheriff's office, and a portly white-haired man stepped out. He smiled at the group standing near the entrance and signaled to the sheriff and Hosteen to follow him inside. Forty-five minutes later, the two men emerged. The sheriff, standing on the top step of the building, held a sheaf of papers in one hand and addressed the crowd.

"Gather 'round men, and listen up. My name is Tom Turnbull, and I'm the sheriff of Montezuma County. I want to thank you all for coming here and volunteering." Despite his small stature and slow East Texas accent, Sheriff Turnbull came across as someone you wouldn't want to cross. There was not an inch of flab on his trim, muscular body; his eyes were sharp, and his voice was booming. "Judge Mobley has signed a warrant enabling us to search the entire premises of the Harmony Home Ranch and to confiscate any and all evidence listed in this affidavit. It is within my power as the sheriff of Montezuma County to deputize you so you can assist me in fulfilling this investigation. After you repeat the oath of office, I will swear you in as onetime deputies and read you the terms of this affidavit. If there is anyone who thinks he can't follow these terms, you best turn around and head on back to the reservation now. Understood?"

The volunteers nodded in agreement, and Sheriff Turnbull read the oath.

"Repeat after me, filling in your name. I . . . do solemnly swear . . . that I will support the Constitution of the United States . . . the Constitution of the State of Colorado . . . the Home Rule Charter for Montezuma County, Colorado . . . the Ordinances of Montezuma County, Colorado . . . and that I will faithfully perform the duties of the Office of County Sheriff . . . of the County of Montezuma, of the State of Colorado, in which I enter."

After the men had repeated the oath, the sheriff swore them in and read the scope and limitations of the warrant aloud. "Since we do not want to alert anyone we're coming, we will be utilizing a no-knock warrant," Sheriff Turnbull said.

"What does that mean?" Abe asked Hosteen.

"Means we can break down the gate if necessary and enter unannounced."

"One more thing," the sheriff said. "It is crucial we find the Nez girl and provide medical attention as quickly as possible. There will be a medevac helicopter, and EMTs with her required insulin dose, at the site. Now, men, if you brought a weapon, you are authorized to carry it, but it is only to be used in a life-threatening situation or if I give the order. Understood?"

All appeared to be in agreement, so the sheriff had one of his deputies pass out rubber gloves and plastic evidence bags to all the men. "Use these if you see anything questionable, and don't leave prints on anything."

They formed a caravan and drove to the gate of Harmony Home Ranch, the sheriff in the lead, followed by one of his deputies in a heavy-duty truck. Hosteen and the two Navajo cops followed behind him, with Will and Abe and four more vehicles tailing. There were eleven stone-faced, determined men in all.

When they stopped, parked in a line along the side of the highway, Abe swallowed hard, trying to ease the dryness in his mouth. They'd soon learn what lay behind that barricade.

Will we find Emily?

His stomach clenched in a knot as the deputy took a battering ram out of his truck and slammed the steel-barred gate until the lock busted.

Emily's eyes fluttered open to bright sunlight, and once again her body was racked with paralyzing pain. Looking at her leg, she knew it was broken and could not support her weight. The sky, though mostly clear, was ringed with dark, puffy clouds. Rain would follow, and the water in the wash would rise rapidly. She tried to move away from the edge of the wash, each inch causing her to cry out in anguish. Cold sweat drenched her forehead, but she had to move. By using her arms to support her weight and sliding on her backside, Emily slowly dragged her body to higher ground. The broken leg dangled uselessly, impeding her progress and sending sharp jolts of pain all the way to her spine. To distract herself, she hummed a song she had learned as a child from her grandmother. "The Happy Song," Grandmother had called it, and said it was to take your mind off your problems.

"Hi yo hi yo ip si na ya. Hi yo hi yo ip si no ya. Hi yo hi yo," she chanted through clenched teeth.

The snap of a branch made her stop. Something—or someone— was in the brush and moving toward her. Bear, mountain lion, a search party? Not knowing if it was friend or enemy, Emily reached for the screwdriver in her pocket and pulled her body behind a thick juniper bush. She froze, adrenaline rushing, her senses alert, waiting and watching.

The dim outline of a tall, bulky figure emerged from a path through the thicket.

Bear, Emily thought. *A skinwalker did this—brought me here to die, and now he has taken the form of a bear.*

But as the figure drew closer, Emily saw it was a human form wearing a floppy hat and leading a donkey. The person stood tall and straight, a thick, solid body clad in a long buckskin skirt and shirt, braids protruding from under the hat. The woman pulled a forked wooden tool from a knapsack on the donkey and began to probe the earth, carefully extracting a plant, complete with roots, and put it in a bag.

Emily watched, holding her breath as the woman neared. The donkey brayed, and the woman stood still, looking around with apprehension. When she spotted Emily, she shouted and backed away.

Ute. She must be Ute, Emily thought.

The Ute Indian Tribe and the Navajo had been long-standing, traditional enemies. Historically, the Ute raided the camps of the Navajo, stealing horses and sheep; the Navajo would retaliate by riding into the Ute camps and kidnapping their women. They were neighbors now, and all the grudges and bad feelings of the past had been forgotten, or at least forgiven, Emily hoped.

"Help me!" Emily cried out in a cracked voice.

The Ute woman jumped back, grunting loudly, and pulled a hunting knife from a leather sheath at her side. She brandished the knife, waving it in a threatening manner and shouting indecipherable words in what Emily thought must be the Southern Paiute language.

"I think my leg is broken," Emily said, indicating her injured leg. She tried to lift her head, felt dizzy. Her skin was clammy, drenched with sweat, and she recognized the symptoms of shock. She fell back, breathing through her mouth. "I need help. Please, I don't understand what you're saying. English. Do you speak English?"

The Ute woman, still wielding the knife, cautiously approached Emily and probed her body with the toe of her moccasin. When she touched the broken leg, Emily gasped and recoiled, feeling as if she had been jabbed with a red-hot poker. The woman bent down, the knife in her hand, and Emily swung her arms in an unsuccessful attempt to fend her off.

"I'm a Navajo police officer. Etcitty, Emily Etcitty," she muttered through clenched teeth. The knife plunged down, and Emily began to scream, pounding the air with her fists in self-defense. But the blade made a clean rip in her pant leg, exposing the protruding broken bone. The Ute woman stood and stared at the twisted leg, mumbling under her breath, then retrieved a blanket from the donkey and placed it behind Emily's head. Returning to the donkey, she got a gourd canteen and gave Emily a sip of water, all the while speaking words Emily could not understand. After giving Emily a final look, she covered her with a shawl, mounted the donkey, and rode away.

"No!" Emily cried out. "Don't leave me here." She tried to move her body in the direction the woman had gone but found it impossible. The sky darkened, and flashes of light sent jagged cracks through the thunderheads. Emily began to shake, her breathing slow and shallow, her heartbeat irregular and faint. She closed her eyes, allowing darkness to envelop her once again.

No alarms sounded, and no armed guards came rushing when the gate swung open. The posse returned to their vehicles and followed the sheriff's lead down a well-maintained gravel road broad enough to accommodate large trucks and heavy equipment. The sparse high-desert landscape gradually transformed into lush green fields. Tight barbed-wire fences divided the land into sections, some planted in barley, oats, and hay. Other pastures held grazing cows with their newborn calves, ewes with their lambs, and goats.

Abe was amazed to see the contrast between this land and the sur-rounding ranches. "Where's all the water coming from for irrigation when the rest of the area is nothing but red dirt and sage?" he asked Will.

With squinted eyes and his mouth pulled into a frown, Will sur-veyed the landscape, taking his time before he answered. "The only source of water around here I know about is Navajo Wash—unless they drilled some wells, which they might have done."

Since living in New Mexico, Abe had learned a lot about water rights and the importance of water in arid country. *Acequias,* communal irrigation canals, were supposed to be shared equally with all the members of a community. The villages elected a *majordomo* whose job entailed ensuring that water distribution remained equal. It looked like Harmony Home Ranch used more than its fair share, if irrigation water came from the Navajo Wash. He quickly dismissed the train of thought—he had more important things on his mind, like finding Emily and the girls.

They had driven close to five miles without seeing any other vehicles or structures, except for a distant tall, white spire, when the landscape began to change. On the left, an array of solar panels stretched out, blanketing a half acre of land. A sewage-treatment facility appeared on the right, followed by a water tower. Other indicators of an organized community began to emerge. Another steel gate and a high wall brought the caravan to a sudden standstill. Coiled razor wire topped the wall, giving it the appearance of a prison stronghold rather than a home for unwed mothers. A man in his early twenties—pudgy, pink-faced, shirt buttons bulging, hand on the butt of a pistol, stepped out of a guardhouse near the gate and walked to the sheriff's vehicle. Turnbull emerged from his SUV and confronted the guard. Abe could not hear the exchange of words, but he watched as the lawman presented his identification and the search warrant.

The guard scowled as he read the document, handed it back to the sheriff, and took a handheld walkie-talkie from a side holster. An angry exchange of words ensued, and the sheriff's deputy jumped from the vehicle with his gun pulled. The young guard dropped the walkie-talkie.

Abe drummed his fingers on the dash, feeling the tension building with each passing moment. "I wish I knew what was going on."

"Let's find out," Will said, stepping down from the truck. Abe joined him, and by the time they reached the sheriff, Hosteen and the other Navajo cops were already there. The guard, though still refusing to open the gate, glanced nervously at them.

His pink face turned bright red as he continued to argue with the sheriff. "I can't let you in without authorization from the Prophet. I've got my orders." His eyes darted toward the Navajo men as they formed a tight semicircle around him.

Sheriff Turnbull shook the warrant in front of the man's face. "This is all the authorization you need, son. Now open this gate or we bust the damn thing down. Whichever way, we're coming in."

The guard, sweat soaking the armpits of his denim shirt, shook his head and went inside the guardhouse as he mumbled under his breath. The sheriff and deputy followed right on his heels. While the sheriff looked on, he punched in a series of numbers, and the gate swung open.

"I'm going to be in a world of trouble," he whined.

"You're already in a shitload of trouble, son," said Sheriff Turnbull. "Stay here with him, Frank, and watch the gate. Cuff him if needed. We don't want this boy skedaddling or making any warning calls."

"You can't do this. I haven't done anything wrong. This is private property. I'm just doing my job."

Ignoring the young guard's outburst, the sheriff addressed his deputy once again. "Frank, I want you to make a note of whoever comes through here. Make sure no one leaves. Keep an eye out for Phillip Harris and Wayne Mackey, the two suspects Hosteen briefed you on. I gave you all a copy of their mugs and the license number on the vehicle, but I'll bet my next paycheck they changed it." He turned and gave the gate guard a hard look. "You know those two, don't you? You see them leave anytime today?"

The guard shrugged. "I don't recognize those names."

"You better not be lying. It'll go hard on you, guaranteed." The sheriff turned his attention back to his deputy. "Get on the radio if you have any problems, Frank. Keep me posted on what's comin' in and tryin' to go out."

Frank nodded and positioned himself inside the guardhouse.

"Okay, men. Get back in your trucks, and let's get moving."

Once inside the gate, it was hard to believe they were still in the Southwest semidesert. Buildings began to pop up—identical two-story homes grouped together in a sort of cul-de-sac around a central plaza that gave the appearance of tract homes in a suburban community from the sixties. Massive hangarlike buildings, warehouses, and various smaller structures clustered around a central square. At one such structure, a clutch of women clad in long, pastel dresses stood beside a group of children. They stared at the intruders, their eyes round with surprise or fear—as if a band of aliens had just landed on their planet. The women quickly hustled the children inside one of the buildings and closed the door. In the center of the plaza stood an imposing white temple.

"Holy shit," said Will. "Where does all the dough come from to build and maintain this place?"

"I'm thinking the women's welfare checks and the men's payroll from jobs in town go into the big boss's general operating fund. It must add up to a hell of a lot of money," Abe said. "Look. A private jet and runway."

"Rich bastard is scamming his own members, raping young girls, and living like a king."

"Rules this place like a dictator. He must have the people here brainwashed. Remember Jim Jones and the Kool-Aid? They'd probably drink it here if he said it was good for them." Abe glanced at several men lined in front of a machine shop of some kind, their unsmiling faces etched in harsh lines.

He saw the walled area behind the temple and felt a new surge of anger. "Will, see the building back there with a wall around it? Yesterday we saw women working in there. I'll bet you anything that's where they're hiding Emily and the girls. Damn, I wish we could break in there right now. This search-warrant business is going to take all day."

Will narrowed his eyes and stared at the women's compound, but remained tight-lipped.

"All right. I know it would be a mistake," Abe said. "We have to do this by the book so the pervert can be arrested and sent to jail where he belongs. Did you see all those little kids? Think about how many of them he might have fathered while he was getting his jollies with young girls."

The sheriff's vehicle stopped directly in front of the sidewalk leading to the temple steps, and the rest of the posse pulled in, forming a line behind him. At the sound of the vehicles, men dressed in coveralls and work boots emerged from workshops and houses to stand abreast. They appeared unarmed but formed a human barricade in front of the temple. Sheriff Turnbull stepped down from his patrol car and faced them.

"I'm Montezuma County Sheriff Tom Turnbull, and I'm here to serve a search warrant and conduct a legal search of these premises and all structures on these premises. Anyone who attempts to interfere with this procedure will be held under temporary arrest for obstruction of justice by one of my ten deputies. I have papers and an affidavit signed by Judge Mobley that outlines the terms of this warrant. Now, somebody tell me where I can find Rupert Langley."

The men stared at the sheriff, stone-faced and mute.

"Boys, come on out here." Turnbull beckoned to the posse. When they were all lined up, flanking each side of the sheriff, he turned to the ranchmen again. "I'll give you one more chance. This here warrant doesn't have to be presented directly to Langley. I have the authority to show it to any of you, but I'm giving you the courtesy of speaking to your boss and explaining things first. Now, I'll ask you—"

He was interrupted in midsentence by the roar of a jet engine firing up. By the time he turned toward the sound, a Beechcraft turboprop was rolling down a runway. Abe felt a slow burn building within his body.

"I'll bet a year's pay that's Langley. The son of a bitch done cut and run," the sheriff said to no one in particular. "Where's he going in such a hurry?"

Abe clenched his fist. "Dammit. How'd he know we were coming?"

The ranchmen crossed their arms, still saying nothing, but a smirk cut across the face of a short, balding man.

Sheriff Turnbull pulled a handheld radio out of its case. "Dispatch, run a check on a flight plan for a commuter jet that just took off from the Harmony Home Ranch. I believe it's a Beechcraft Baron. See if you can find out who it is licensed to and where it's headed, and get right back to me. Over." After returning the radio to its case, he turned his glare on the ranchers. "Okay, you with the silly grin," he said to a slope-shouldered man in overalls. "Step on over here." He pushed a copy of the warrant into the now-flustered man's hands. "I am conducting a criminal investigation into the kidnapping of two young Navajo girls and a female Navajo police officer. You are duly served this warrant granting me and my deputies the right to search any and all vehicles, buildings, houses, or persons on the property known as Harmony Home Ranch. It also gives us the authority to confiscate anything we might consider evidence in a criminal case. We'll start right now, with this here church."

The massive door to the temple swung open, and a thin man with a narrow, pinched face stood in the entrance. He wore a black suit and black dress shirt buttoned tightly around a long turkey neck. Snow-white hair hung to his shoulders, and the skin on his face was parchment thin, broken by blotches of bright-red capillaries on his cheekbones and his nose. His voice, when he addressed the sheriff, reminded Abe of a rusty gate.

"Our Prophet has unexpectedly been called away. I am his private secretary, Fred Henrikson, and I am authorized to act on his behalf. How may I help you?"

The smirking man in overalls rushed up the broad steps and handed the warrant to the secretary, who pulled a pair of bifocals from his jacket pocket and began to scan the papers, his mouth turned down at the corners in distaste.

"Like I just told these men, I'm Tom Turnbull, the sheriff of Montezuma County, and I'm looking for some missing girls. So, your boss just got called away *unexpectedly*? Executive business meeting or something? You just step aside, Mr. Henrikson, and we'll begin our search right here and now. If any doors need unlocking, I'd be mighty obliged if you'd cooperate. That way we won't have to cuff you and break the place up."

22

Unknown Location

Colorado Backcountry

When she regained consciousness, Emily felt sure the cult members had found her. Her body was pinned down on a flat mat, and she was unable to move her legs or arms, just as she had been when the kidnappers first took her and Lina hostage in the van. A sharp pain shot through her right leg when she tried to sit, causing her to cry out. Her eyes fluttered open. She was not in a van taking her to some secret hideaway, nor in a locked room or a prison for young girls.

Two amber-colored, almond-shaped eyes stared back at her. The animal bleated, kicked up its heels, and scampered away.

A goat, Emily thought groggily. *Where am I?* She remembered falling, breaking her leg, and the appearance of the strange woman. *The Ute woman must have brought me here. I have to tell her to call for help—Abe, Will, someone at headquarters—let them know about the cult and the girls.*

"Hello? Where are you? Please. I need to talk to you." She closed her eyes again, exhausted from the effort. A memory came floating back. *The Ute woman did not understand English. I don't understand Ute. I'm so tired. Can't keep my eyes open. Have to rest.*

She blinked until she could focus, unaware of how much time had elapsed, and peered at her surroundings through eyes as narrow as slits. Her head was pounding, and her broken leg was bound between two wooden slats with strips of rawhide. She tried to pull herself into a sitting position but became dizzy and immediately fell back again.

Onto what?

A *travois* was propped at an angle so her head remained slightly elevated, resting on a pillow of rabbit fur.

She turned her head to the left and noticed a makeshift shelter of brush and grass backed up against a rock wall. It looked like the temporary dwellings the Ute used to make and left behind when they traveled on hunting or food-gathering trips.

What was it called? Wickiup?

In front of the *wickiup*, a fire pit smoldered with hot coals smelling of *piñon* smoke, something pungent. Baskets woven from willow or grasses hung on the outside of the primitive structure; others perched on rock shelves were filled with various roots and leaves.

Emily felt as if she had fallen into the past, an earlier time when the Ute and Navajo raided each other's camps for horses and slaves. Would she be a Ute slave now? Emily yelled again. "Hey! You've got to help me, please!"

The Ute woman stepped out of the *wickiup*, glowering at her.

"Me Emily Etcitty. Navajo. Police officer. You," she said, pointing at the woman, "find a telephone. Call 911—the police or sheriff." Emily pantomimed dialing and holding a phone to her ear while the Ute woman stared, her leathery face revealing nothing. "Shit," Emily said, closing her eyes in frustration and raising her voice. "I have to get out of here."

"You don't have to yell," the Ute woman replied in a calm voice. "I'm not hard of hearing."

Ignoring the pain in her leg, Emily pulled herself upright at the sound of the woman's voice. "You speak English? Why didn't you say so before? You need to call the tribal police, sheriff, someone."

"Humph. Of course I speak English. Went to those damn government schools same as you where we couldn't speak anything else. Can't call anyone, though. No phone anywhere near here. Besides, I don't go where there are people."

"Listen. Don't you understand? I need a doctor. My leg's broken."

"I saw your leg. I fixed it. When it heals, I'll be gone and you can leave, walk out, and call the cops."

"Please. I can't stay here and wait until my leg heals. The ranch I ran away from, they kidnap young girls during their puberty rite—Navajo girls, and maybe Ute girls as well. They brainwash them, and the bastard cult leader takes them as wives. Rapes them is what he does, fourteen- and fifteen-year-olds, tells them they please God by having his children. There are two young Navajo girls there now." Emily's voice broke as she strained to move. "Damn it, I have to tell someone."

The woman silently stared at Emily, her face devoid of emotion except for a tightening around her mouth and a narrowing of her eyes. "I can't go to the white man's town to call for help, and I can't go back to my people."

"Why can't you?"

The Ute woman turned and walked away without providing an answer while two curious goats traipsed to Emily's side and began nibbling on her shirt. "Scram!" she yelled, waving her arm, frustrated by the woman's reluctance to send for assistance and her inability to do anything about it.

Abe let his eyes roam over the interior of the massive temple. No expense had been spared in constructing the building. The cavernous interior was lined with gold-plated and marble statues. But not of Jesus, or any of the saints, or even of Mary, but of a curiously modern-looking man. He held a book while young girls knelt at his feet. The expensive-looking stained glass allowed light to cast a rainbow of color on a snow-white marble altar. Above the altar, etched in marble with gold-plated letters was a sentence: THE TIME IS GETTING SHORT, AND THE WICKED PEOPLE ARE ABOUT TO BE SWEPT OFF THE LAND, AND GOD'S PEOPLE WILL BE LIFTED UP TO REDEEM ZION.

"Huh," the sheriff scoffed after reading the cryptic message. A quick look at the main chapel revealed nothing but pews, benches, and more accolades to a Prophet. "Where do these doors lead?"

The secretary gave the sheriff a condescending look. "The Prophet's private residence and my office and quarters," he said in a simpering voice. "And some quiet rooms for meditation and counseling. Nothing of interest to you, I'm sure."

"Open them up, and I'll decide for myself what's interesting."

Abe and Will exchanged looks of disgust.

"Meditation and counseling, my ass," Will said under his breath.

The eerily white interior of the temple was supposed to give the impression of purity, Abe figured. But to him, it conveyed defilement, lecherousness, exploitation—the residence of evil. In Abe's mind, the long table in the center of the room covered with satin cushions took the form of a bed where the Prophet seduced young girls. A white satin couch surrounded by a circle of chairs provided furniture for a side room. There were numerous doors—more side rooms. Abe felt his stomach turn while searching the sanctimonious chambers and dwelling of a monster who had the gall to call himself a prophet. Still, no matter how thoroughly the men searched, nothing came up that might implicate anyone in a criminal act. In fact, the room, furnishings, doorknobs, all appeared sterile—as if recently wiped clean. The sanitized room and the fact there was no telephone, computer, or files was enough of an anomaly to arouse suspicion.

The sheriff stood in the center of the opulent office space, frowning. "Where's all the paperwork pertaining to the business of running this place, Henrikson?"

The man shrugged. "I have no idea what you're talking about. You are in a house of worship, not a business office."

Sheriff Turnbull narrowed his eyes and exhaled a whoosh of air. "I don't believe you. I'm holding you in temporary custody for obstruction of justice. But right now, you are going to give me the keys to unlock each and every building, gate, and vehicle in this damn place. And don't try telling me you don't have the keys. I see a big ring hanging on your belt loop." Finished with the cult member, he faced the posse. "Men, I want four of you to stay here and go through this church with a fine-toothed comb. Wear gloves, and if you see anything even remotely suspicious, bag it. Be especially thorough in the living quarters and office. Okay—Jim, take three men and turn this place upside down," he said to his deputy. Turning to another one of his men, the sheriff said, "Radio Cortez and see if they came up with a flight plan on that plane. Let me know if you discover anything that might give us a clue as to where he's headed. The rest of you, including this here prisoner," he said, slapping a pair of handcuffs on the secretary, "come with me."

Abe and Will joined four other men and followed the sheriff down a hedge-lined sidewalk. "What's behind this locked gate and wall?" the sheriff asked, tilting his head toward the women's compound.

"It's the women's private quarters," the secretary said. "We must respect their modesty and not disturb them."

"Bullshit. Open the gate."

Abe's heart pounded, his stomach muscles tightened, and his breath quickened as he watched the metal gate swing open. The enclosed area was the place they had observed from the plane. It was where he felt confident they would find Emily and the two girls.

166

He closed the distance between himself and the sheriff—Will and Hosteen beside him, the look in their eyes saying they knew it, too. They passed women tending garden patches, working the same as yesterday, long dresses dragging in the tilled earth, bonnets or hats shading their faces. Startled, the women raised their heads to stare, wide-eyed, at the men before quickly turning away. The men in the posse also stopped to gaze at the women, the Navajo men possibly wondering if their loved ones might be among them, hidden under one of the strange outfits. Abe stared, too, hoping one of the shapeless, pastel-clad figures might be her. "Emily!" he shouted, but the women kept their heads bowed—all but one with a tired face and sad, gray eyes.

She looked directly at Abe when he called Emily's name and made a barely perceptible shake of her head before turning away.

"What is the meaning of this?" A large woman in a blue dress, her face florid with anger, stomped in heavy boots toward the posse. "Men are not allowed in here without permission." She turned her glare to the secretary, ready to demand an explanation, but the sight of the Prophet's private secretary shackled in handcuffs left her openmouthed and speechless.

"No reason to be alarmed, ma'am. I've got a warrant to search these premises," the sheriff said, showing her his badge case and papers. "You can come along and cooperate, or you can get cuffed like your friend here for impeding a legal investigation of a crime. What'll it be?"

The woman, her face blotched and even redder, stammered, "God will punish your wickedness." She turned to walk toward a two-story building, the sheriff and posse members following right behind. "Whatever could you want here?"

"Joe," Abe said to the Navajo cop, "I want to talk to one of those women before I go inside."

"I doubt anyone will talk to you. They all look scared to death, and no doubt they believe it's sinful to talk to strange men. I didn't see any Navajo faces in the bunch. You have anyone particular in mind?"

"Yeah, as a matter of fact I do," said Abe, picturing the woman with gray eyes. "Tell the sheriff I'll be in when I finish. I've got a hunch she knows something."

Will had been studying the women working the plowed patch of ground as well. "I'm hanging here with Abe. We won't take long."

Hosteen looked at both Abe and Will and shrugged his shoulders. He must have recognized the doggedness in their faces. "I'll let the sheriff know what you're up to. Just don't jeopardize any potential witness, Freeman."

Abe nodded. "I understand—it's just a feeling I have. The gray-eyed woman was the only one who actually looked at us, and I saw her shake her head."

"I saw it when you called Emily's name. She's hiding something. Let's see if we can find out what it is."

"All these women look like they're scared shitless."

"Yep, partner. I can feel the evil in this place. If this woman knows something, maybe she'd like to get it off her chest."

Abe surveyed the plot of cultivated land again, looking for the gray-eyed woman. It was hard to discern one from another because they all wore identical dresses and kept their eyes averted. He tried to remember some characteristic that made her stand out, other than her eyes. She was wearing a blue dress and a straw hat. "I think she's the one," he said to Will, indicating a figure lagging behind the others at the end of a row of new seedlings.

When Abe and Will approached the woman, she trembled—her wide-open eyes darting quickly from the house to the two men before she hid her face and began hacking wildly at the weeds growing alongside sprouts of corn.

"She's scared all right," Will said as they walked across the garden plot toward her.

"Excuse me, miss," Abe said. "We're not going to hurt you. We just want to ask a few questions."

She shook her head and began attacking the weeds with a frenzy.

"Miss . . . ," Will said, his voice soft and pleading, "the Navajo woman someone kidnapped and brought here is my sister, my only sibling. Our mother can't sleep. All night she cries and prays for Emily's safe return. We mean you no harm. Please tell us if you know anything about Emily Etcitty and the two young Navajo girls."

The woman glanced around to see if anyone was watching. "I can't talk to you," she said without lifting her head, her voice barely above a whisper. But after a moment, she blurted, "She's gone. I don't know where she went. She left in the middle of the night. Please don't tell the matron I said anything, or something bad will happen to me. I hope Emily's all right. She said she would help set me free."

Abe's mouth dropped open, dumbfounded by the news, not sure he heard her right the first time. "Are you saying Emily was here, you talked to her, and she escaped?"

Will's widened eyes showed his shock, and he looked at the woman with such intensity she began to tremble. "When did she leave?"

"Around midnight, when we were all asleep. I brought her clothes and some tools earlier in the evening. The matron discovered her missing this morning and sent word to the Prophet. There are two young Indian girls here as well, but I don't know where they're kept." The other women had stopped hoeing and had turned to stare at her. She paled and cast her eyes down. "What's going to happen to me now? Please, you've got to get me out of here. I think they'll have me stoned to death when they find out I helped Emily."

Abe's heart pounded like a metronome set at a fast tempo.

"Emily's out there, somewhere," Will said. "Why hasn't she contacted us?"

Abe shook his head. "We need to tell Joe Hosteen and the sheriff about this and get a search party going. She may be hurt."

23

"Come with us," Abe said, taking the woman's elbow. "No one's going to harm you. You need to tell the sheriff what you know. We'll get you out of here—take you with us when we leave. What's your name?"

"Betty, Betty Prescott," she said with more courage in her voice. "My husband and son were run off from here, and I was left behind—kept in this building and made to work all day. Just like most of the other women and girls. We all believed in the words of the Prophet at one time, but . . . he lied to us. All lies."

Will ran up the steps leading into the house and shouted for the Navajo cop. "Hosteen! Joe Hosteen! Where the hell are you? Sheriff Turnbull, we've got someone out here with information about Emily and the girls."

Upon hearing Will's words, men began appearing from the open doors of the dormitory rooms. When Abe entered the house with Betty in tow, four Navajo and the sheriff met them in the foyer of the women's compound.

"What's this about?" said the sheriff.

Abe spoke first. "Sheriff, this is Betty Prescott. She can vouch for the fact Emily and the two girls were here." Abe looked at the expectant faces of the girls' fathers. "Mr. Benally, Mr. Nez, we may be getting close. This woman helped Emily escape from this house last night. You better talk to her, Sheriff. I'm going to start looking for Emily."

"Yes, the Indian lady was locked right in there," Betty said, pointing to a door at the end of the hall that had not yet been opened. "I snuck her a screwdriver and wire cutters, some of my son's clothes."

Looking at Abe, the sheriff said, "You just hold on, young man. You're durn right I'm going to talk to her, but don't you try going off half-cocked when you don't have any idea where to look or what to do. You're still my sworn deputy, and we haven't finished our work here."

Turning his attention to Betty, he added, "I want you to start from the beginning, and tell me exactly what you know about Miz Etcitty and the two Navajo girls, Miz Prescott. We'll go in one of these rooms so we can talk in private. Hosteen, you come in here with the lady and me. The rest of you men keep searching this place from top to bottom. I'm interested in the room where they kept Emily Etcitty. Look it over real good. Just make sure you don't leave prints. And you can cuff the lying son-of-a-bitch secretary and his so-called matron in charge to a pole or something, just as long as they can't go anywhere. They've got a lot of explaining to do."

Hosteen punched numbers on his handheld radio. After he had signed off, he spoke to the sheriff. "I informed my boss that Emily and the girls' presence at Harmony Home Ranch has been confirmed by an eyewitness. He's sending more men to assist in the search. The state troopers have a helicopter available. I suggest you call them, Sheriff, and for any other assistance you can get since we're in your jurisdiction."

"I'll make the call, Hosteen. Just as soon as I finish this interview."

"That's my sister out there," Will said to the sheriff. "I want to find her."

"I know you do," the sheriff said. "I don't blame you, and these men want to find their little girls. Come in here with Hosteen and me while we talk to this lady. I don't want you and your friend taking off on your own, hear?" he said, looking directly at Abe. "These are the keys to all the rooms," he said, tossing the ring to Abe. "Open them up, and you men get to work."

Will, though he appeared agitated and ready to bolt out the door, followed Hosteen into the room where the sheriff waited with Betty Prescott. Abe caught the ring of keys. They all looked the same. He spent some time going from room to room, opening doors, trying all the keys until he found the ones that sprung the locks. He saved Emily's room for himself and chewed a thumbnail while staring at the key ring and the lock on the door. After a few unsuccessful attempts, a key slid in smooth as silk, and the lock popped open. As soon as he stepped inside, Abe sensed Emily's presence. He slipped the disposable gloves on and picked up the odd pink dress thrown across the made bed. He held it up to his face, taking in the faint aroma of rain-washed sagebrush she always carried. He saw clean sheets and towels where Betty had left them. The small table had no drawers—nowhere to stash personal belongings. He looked under the bed. Nothing. When Abe walked into the bathroom, his pulse quickened. The window had been hastily repaired but still showed signs of damage around the frame where she must have pried it away.

So this is how you escaped, sweetheart. If only you had waited a few hours, I would have found you.

He sat on the edge of the bed, covering his eyes with a hand, overwhelmed by a feeling of emptiness, a heavy stone weighing on his heart.

We were so close.

After a few minutes, he put the pink dress back and left her toothbrush, soap, and comb—with a few of her black hairs still entangled in the bristles—where he had found them.

Abe made a list of everything in the room, then left. He knew the forensic team would be there soon to collect and analyze all the evidence. As soon as he stepped out, he heard shouting in the hall and the scream of a hysterical woman.

The fathers of the two Navajo girls hovered around the matron, demanding to know where their daughters were. Darcy's father held the woman's head back by her hair, and Charley had his skinning knife pointed at her throat. "Where are our daughters, you piece of white trash? My girl is sick. Tell me now, or I will remove your ugly hair quicker than I can skin a rabbit," Charley said.

Abe hurried toward the melee, reaching the woman seconds before the other posse members. "Put down the knife, Charley. This isn't going to help."

"She knows where they are. Lina could die. She needs her shots."

"We'll find them," Abe said. "We're getting close. Lina's counting on you to rescue her. She won't want you to go to jail. Give me the knife, man."

The other two Navajo men pulled Henry Benally away to a corner and spoke to him in Navajo. Benally held his head in his hands, looking at the floor. Stress had brought the Navajo fathers to the breaking point.

Abe held out his hand, and Charley Nez gave him the knife just before the sheriff and Will burst into the foyer.

"What the hell's going on out here?"

The woman, pale and shaken, opened her mouth to speak, but Abe gave her a menacing look and hissed, "Shut up." Charley Nez stared at the floorboards.

"Is anybody going to answer me?" The sheriff looked from one face to another, staring intently at the woman, whose own face had turned white as a sheet. No one uttered a word until Abe spoke up.

"It's nothing—a little argument. They worked it out."

"That woman knows more than she's telling," said Charley Nez.

"If she does, we'll get it out of her. Now get back to work." The sheriff narrowed his eyes and shook his head while he waited for an explanation from Abe.

"I found a dress and toothbrush in the room where we think they kept Emily," Abe said, changing the subject. "Marks along the edge of the window frame appear to have been made recently. Emily must have used the screwdriver Betty gave her to pry the window off."

Sheriff Turnbull nodded, inhaled deeply, and slowly blew air out of his mouth. "We're doin' the best we can to find your daughter, Mr. Nez." He scowled at the faces of his posse. "Did anyone else find anything useful?"

The men, silent and looking glum, shook their heads.

The sheriff rubbed the back of his neck, frustration showing in the drawn lines around his eyes and mouth. He sighed. "I hate to admit it, but this case is bigger than my department can handle. We've got possible rampant sex abuse, a kidnapping, fugitive flight, and who the hell knows what else. I'm calling for assistance from the state. The Navajo Tribal Police Department is sending as many extra men and equipment as they can spare as well. I don't like involving the Feds. Those assholes want to take charge, and they treat the locals like we're a bunch of country bumpkins who can't find our butts when they need wipin'. But now we have proof the perps took hostages across state lines, and that makes it a federal case. Also, we've got too much ground to cover and too little time. Finding those young girls and Officer Etcitty is our top priority."

The men perked up upon hearing the sheriff's words. This was what they wanted, to be actively searching for their loved ones. The tedious task of combing through buildings had led to growing tension, especially for Abe and the Navajo men.

"What do you want us to do now, Sheriff?" Abe said.

"Keep doing what you're doing until backup arrives. Tear this place apart, but follow procedure. Write it down, but don't disturb the evidence." He paused before adding, "Any hotheads who get out of line are going to be sent home for insubordination and not allowed in my county. Understood?" The sheriff turned his gaze on the Navajo men, who stared fixedly at the floor and nodded their agreement. "Freeman, I told Betty to wait in her room till we were ready to take her with us. She's a material witness. Make sure that no one bothers her and that she doesn't decide to leave. Lock the door."

24

Friday, April 13, 1990

Women's Compound

Harmony Home Ranch

While Abe and the rest of the posse continued scouring the women's room for evidence, five cars with the emblem of the Colorado State Patrol arrived on the scene. They were followed shortly afterward by four green-and-white Navajo Nation Police SUVs and a state forensic unit. A member of the K-9 Unit had accompanied the Colorado officers, bringing with him a large mixed-breed hound called Spike who answered to no one but his trainer. Abe recognized the trooper who had pulled him over and then led him to the courthouse, and he nodded in greeting. Sheriff Turnbull and Hosteen met with the new arrivals for a quick debriefing.

Afterward, the sheriff assembled all his posse members for an update. Evidence was turned over to the forensic unit or noted where it could be found, and the men were broken down into new teams. Some would remain at the compound to question cult members and complete the investigation. Another group consisting of Abe, Will, Hosteen, and the K-9 trainer with his dog made up part of the search party for Emily. The remaining Navajo men were staying at the compound with the sheriff and three state troopers to continue their quest. The fathers of the two girls felt convinced their daughters were hidden somewhere on the ranch, and they were more determined than ever not to leave until they found them.

Each member of the search party was issued a canteen of water, a flashlight, and a walkie-talkie. Spike sniffed Emily's dress until the trooper felt sure he had the scent and led the dog outside, under the window where Emily had made her initial jump. The dog immediately picked up the trail, and the men were ordered to fan out in the direction of his pursuit. When Abe spotted a single boot print in an apple orchard, and Spike barked verification, his adrenaline kicked in. He felt they were getting close, and the trail was easy to follow—until they reached Navajo Wash. Spike raced up and down the banks of the waterway, nose glued to the ground. After several minutes, the dog stopped and barked, looking at the other side.

"She crossed the wash," Abe said to Will. "She didn't want to walk on the road and be spotted, so she headed this way."

Will's slight nod showed his agreement. He gazed in all directions—at the mountains to the north, those in the west. Then he squatted down and picked up a handful of soil, rubbed it between his fingers, and smelled it. "This is the ancestral land of my people, the Diné," he said. "Emily would know; she'd recognize the sacred mountains and find her way home. She must have crossed there, where the dog lost the scent."

"Let's go," said Abe. He found a pile of rocks in the wash that acted as stepping-stones and waded through the swiftly moving current. Some parts had deep holes, but Abe reasoned last night's full moon had provided enough light for Emily to find the best crossing.

The other members of the group, including the dog, followed his lead. Once on the other side, Spike shook, and immediately put his nose to the ground again. The wash cut a twisting path through the bottom of a steep-sided ravine lined with slickrock and shale. Abe wondered how Emily could have managed the climb, even in the moonlight. And then he heard Spike barking.

The dog had picked up the scent and was climbing the side of the ravine, but he stopped midway and came back down. Spike sniffed excitedly at a rocky spot near the bottom of the ravine. Abe ran to where the dog stood and looked around. At first he saw nothing, but after a closer examination of the rocks and soil, he spotted the blood. His heart sank.

What happened? Did she fall? If she fell and hurt herself, where is she? Could a mountain lion or a bear take her? No.

He knew he couldn't think in those terms.

She scratched herself on some branches and bled before she moved on. She's okay, finding her way home, he silently told himself.

But he didn't feel reassured.

Abe saw the screwdriver under a salt cedar bush. "Will!" he yelled. "Over here. I found something. Emily must have dropped it."

Will stared at the screwdriver and the bloodstains. "Don't touch anything, Abe. They will need to dust it for prints—make sure Emily dropped it, and that this is her blood," he added in a quiet voice.

Although Will's expression remained neutral, Abe recognized the tightness in his voice, the tension in his body, as a sign of worry, the same concern he had.

What happened to Emily? And where is she now?

He left the screwdriver and summoned the state trooper.

To the search party's consternation, Spike lost the scent. He repeatedly ran to the midway point on the side of the ravine before returning to the bottom where the blood and screwdriver had been found. To make matters worse, a late-afternoon thunderstorm brewing in the west came crashing down with a driving force, obliterating any signs of the direction Emily might have gone beyond that point.

The men hunkered down under hats and raincoats to wait the storm out. Early April weather could be extremely fickle, ranging from warmth one day to an icy wind often bringing snow the next. There was a chill in this west wind, giving Abe goose bumps. Or was it the thought of Emily—out there, hurt and bleeding, cold and alone? He shook his head and told himself again she was all right, that they would find her. He could not sit still and wait. He noticed Will pacing along the edge of the wash, now transformed into a brown torrent strewn with branches and other debris. The water had begun to rise at a rapid rate. The other men scrambled to their feet.

Will and Abe might have been thinking the same thing. "Let's go," Abe said. "We can't stay here, waiting. Emily knows the danger of a flash flood in sudden rainstorms. She must have climbed back up the ravine."

A jagged bolt of lightning split the blackening sky, followed by a loud crash of thunder from the west. Torrential rains began to pelt the rocks and cliff sides, but Emily remained dry. She wondered why, then observed she had been lying under the overhanging lip of a shallow sandstone cave. The Ute woman reappeared and pulled the *travois* into the *wickiup*, which was at the back of the cave, completely hidden from view. The sudden movement sent spasms of pain through Emily's leg, and she clamped her jaws to keep from screaming. Beads of perspiration ran down her face and between her breasts. Once the woman settled Emily in the small space, she sat on a mat on the opposite side of the shelter. Emily pleaded with her once again to seek help when the storm ended.

"Listen to me. You can take me outside, away from your camp, and leave me. I won't tell anyone about you. Just let someone know where to find me. That's all I ask."

A stoic silence met her pleas.

"Who are you? I have to call you something," Emily said.

The woman looked as though she would not answer, then exhaled a weary sigh. "You can call me Chipeta, even though it is not my real name. It's the name of Chief Ouray's wife, so if you must call me something, Chipeta's good enough." She fetched an earthen pot from the fire and poured a fragrant liquid into a smaller container. After helping Emily to a sitting position, she handed her the small bowl. "Drink this. It will lessen your pain and help prevent infection."

Emily accepted the steaming cup. Though the aroma was familiar, she did not readily identify the herb. "What is it?" She felt light-headed and weak—as well as a bit suspicious—but it was a relief to be able to sit upright.

"Bear root. You know the bear is special to the Ute, and the root has potent healing properties."

Yes, of course, Emily thought, sipping the familiar bitter tea. *I should have known right away. Oshá, bear medicine, is often used by Grandfather. How could I have forgotten something so familiar?*

She drank her tea, wondering how she could convince the woman to send for help. The tea alleviated her parched mouth and throat, but not her full bladder. "I need to pee." She pushed the blanket off her legs but knew there was no way she would be able to stand on her splinted, broken leg.

Chipeta handed Emily a shallow crockery bowl. "You'll have to use this to take care of business until you can stand with crutches. I'll give you some privacy." She stood, covered her head with a shawl made of animal pelt, and walked out of the *wickiup* into the pounding rain.

Emily, grimacing with the effort, slid the dish under her body. She flinched when she bumped her broken leg but sighed with relief when her bladder emptied. After cautiously removing the crockery and setting it beside her *travois*, she fell back onto the rabbit-pelt pillow and closed her eyes, letting sleep overcome her once again.

In the dream, the bear crouched at the entrance to her grandfather's trailer. Emily wanted to go inside, but the bear blocked the door. Grandfather watched her from inside his old silver Airstream, waving his arms, cautioning her with gestures to be careful.

The huge, shaggy bear, saliva dripping from its mouth, roared. "You have greatly disappointed me, stupid woman." Emily shivered, cowering behind a juniper tree. "Haven't I taught you anything?"

"I tried!" Emily cried. "I tried my best to save the girls."

"You thought you could escape from me, but you have failed," the bear roared. "Failure, failure, failure. You know the price for failing." The huge bear stood on hind legs, saliva streaming from his open mouth, and lumbered toward her.

Emily tried to move, but in the dream she was still strapped in the *travois*, her broken leg, swollen to a grotesque size, oozing pus. "Please!" she cried. "Give me another chance. Tell me what I must do."

"No more chances," said the bear, moving closer and dropping back to all fours. "Now you pay."

The bear ran toward Emily, snarling, gnashing its teeth. As it neared, it transformed into Coyote, then into the form of a tall man in a dark suit with piercing black eyes. A steady tic caused him to blink his left eye. The man fixed his eyes on hers and laughed. Emily thrashed from side to side in a futile attempt to escape, screaming, "No, no, no!"

Chipeta rushed into the *wickiup*, a concerned look on her face. "What is it?"

Sweat dripped from Emily's forehead even though she could not stop her chattering teeth. "A dream."

It was a dream, but it felt terrifyingly real—more real than her life the last two days.

Has it only been two days?

Emily realized she did not know how long she had been in that strange place or how she had managed to get there. Her last memory was of waking up and staring into the almond eyes of the goat. She had been taken captive on Wednesday, and on Friday escaped from the cult house.

"What day is this? How long have I been here?" she asked the Ute woman.

"I don't keep track of the days of the week or time," said Chipeta, "but you've been here two days, counting today. You were out of your mind most of the time, jabbering and not making any sense. It was partly due to the medicine I gave you so I could straighten and splint your leg. Peyote and datura. Guess you saw and heard things that only existed in your head."

Emily looked at the rough buckskin dress covering her body. She saw her leg protruding from the dress, wrapped from her ankle to above her knee with a hard clay cast. "What happened to the clothes I was wearing?"

"They wouldn't do. They were sopping wet, caked with mud, and all torn up. I had to take them off so I could fix your leg. Broke your tibia *and* your fibula—snapped them right in two. Don't worry. I used to be a nurse's aide and have watched the doctors set plenty of bones. It's easy enough."

Emily became aware of the aroma of something cooking, and in spite of her discomfiture, her stomach rumbled with hunger. She leaned back and closed her eyes, too weak to continue the conversation. Her head throbbed and her brain felt scrambled. "I have to go home so the cops can find those girls," she said. "I'm begging you. Tell someone where I am."

"You aren't going anywhere, so just shut up and stop whining. I guess you're well enough to eat something. You haven't had nothing but broth and tea. I've got stew cooking in the pot."

Emily opened her mouth to say more, but the Ute woman was gone. "Damn," she muttered as another sharp jolt of pain shot through her leg.

Clouds clung to the night sky like a thick shroud, making visibility beyond the narrow beam of a flashlight impossible. The state trooper called off the search and told the men to head back to the compound. They would spend the night there and start fresh in the morning. The men were cold and had not eaten all day, except for water and granola bars the trooper had distributed. Discouragement showed in the faces and hunched shoulders of the men, none more so than Abe and Will. They had not been able to find a single clue as to where Emily had gone.

They trudged down the slippery ravine, barely speaking. Once the rains ended, the water in the channel subsided as quickly as it had risen, allowing them to cross in the same place as before. Small trees and shrubs, carried downstream by the force of the water, were jammed up against the rocks.

If Emily had been unconscious near the wash's bank, she would have been swept away just as quickly as those bushes, Abe thought, as a chill ran through his body.

"I've got to get hold of Mom somehow—let her know what's going on, tell her I'm staying here until we find Em," Will said.

The men walked single file, heads bent toward the ground as they turned back to the compound through the apple orchard.

Abe caught up with Will. "There's bound to be a phone somewhere you can use—one in the church office, for sure. I need to let Ellen know as well, but if she's at my place, she can't be reached by phone."

"Mom can drive over to your place. Probably be good for her to have someone to talk to."

They walked the rest of the way back to the ranch headquarters without further conversation, unable or unwilling to voice their worst fears.

Sheriff Turnbull stood in front of the temple, waiting for the men to return. After listening to their account of the day's events, he reported that he hadn't had any luck in finding the two Navajo girls either. "We'll bunk out in this here church for the night and continue searching for those young ladies. If they're around here, we'll find them."

He didn't say out loud what Abe was thinking and what the sheriff must have suspected: *Unless Langley took them with him on the plane.*

"I'll round up some blankets and pillows. There'll be more folks joining the search party tomorrow morning," the sheriff continued. After noticing their muddy, sodden clothes, he added, "And I'll have someone bring you all a fresh set of clothes—rain ponchos and socks, too. The women here, with some coaxing and a little down payment, of course, have reluctantly agreed to provide hot meals. I can't say they are the friendliest bunch." He looked at their drawn, dirty faces and said, "Go clean up before you eat. We're using the 'the Prophet's' bathroom—the son of a bitch. When you're fed and rested, I'll fill you in on what we did find."

Abe, Will, and Hosteen sat at one end of a long table in the women's compound. While they ate bowls of steaming beef stew and thick slices of homemade bread, Abe fired questions at Hosteen.

"What about those other two—Harris and Mackey? The ones who kidnapped the girls and Emily in the first place? Does anyone know their whereabouts?"

"We tracked down their wives and questioned each one," Hosteen said. "They had three each, and between them, nine kids. The women were noncommittal. I don't know if they were lying or didn't know anything. All they said was their husbands were traveling, and they didn't seem too sorry to see them gone. The sheriff is convinced they took off with Langley."

Will heaved a heavy sigh. "Did they track the plane? Anybody find out where it was headed?"

"No," said Hosteen. "The pilot didn't file a flight plan. They could have landed at any number of small, clandestine landing fields. The FBI's working on it. They're looking into another religious community to see if there's a connection."

Abe cradled a coffee mug with both hands and looked at Hosteen. "We can't let the bastards get away."

"They won't," Hosteen said with finality. "If that girl dies, I'll track them down and kill them."

That night, as he bedded down on the hard surface of one of the temple's pews, Abe stared at the ceiling. The clouds had cleared, and moonlight filtered through the tall stained-glass windows, casting eerie shadows on the prone bodies of the posse members. He kept going back over the events of the day and the sheriff's words. While they ate, Turnbull had explained that the FBI had taken the secretary and the matron, along with four of her women associates, into their local office for further questioning. They hadn't had any success in breaking their code of silence yet, as far as he knew. Betty Prescott was being held at the sheriff's office for her protection while they tried to locate her husband and son. Some of the other women at the compound admitted to having seen Emily and two younger Navajo girls, but they assumed the girls were runaways and had come voluntarily to serve their lord and master. They reported that one of the girls appeared sickly. None of them were allowed to speak to the girls or one another. Neither the Navajo men, the state troopers, nor the FBI had been able to find any trace of the missing girls, but they did find a vault with a cache of turquoise-and-silver jewelry and Native American ceremonial dress.

Will had called his mother from the secretary's office. She broke down when she learned Emily had escaped. Bertha agreed to drive to Abe's house and share the news with Ellen. Will told Abe his mother was already planning Emily's homecoming celebration, so sure was she that her daughter would be found. Abe knew his friend had presented an optimistic picture to his mother. Not wanting to worry Bertha, Will had not mentioned the blood.

Abe couldn't stop thinking about Emily. *Are you hurt? Where could you have gone? Why haven't you been able to contact anyone? Are you alive, Emily? Jesus Christ, if there is such a thing as God, if You exist at all, please help us find her.*

The alienation he felt from God and his Jewish heritage was accentuated even more in this so-called place of worship.

A holy shrine dedicated to the evil nature of humanity.

Abe had already witnessed the suffering and untimely death of his first love, Sharon, and could not bear the thought of losing Emily as well. A wave of melancholy enveloped him.

He looked at Will, in the pew across the aisle. His eyes were closed, but Abe knew his friend wasn't sleeping either. Maybe he was praying to *his* gods. Abe got up and carried his blanket and pillow outside. A few minutes later, Will, Hosteen, and the other Navajo men followed him. They spread their bedding on the grass under cover of a cloud-shadowed moon. Finally, one by one, the searchers dropped off to sleep.

25

Saturday, April 14, 1990

Chipeta Longtooth's Camp

Colorado Backcountry

Emily heard the familiar wop-wop-wop-wop of helicopter rotor blades and pulled herself into a sitting position. She surveyed her surroundings and saw that the sandstone cave was tucked behind a thick stand of Gambel oak and juniper. It would be impossible to spot from the air—but if she could make a fire, someone might see the smoke. The rain had ceased, and bright sunlight broke through the clouds.

Chipeta was nowhere in sight. Emily loosened the straps holding her leg steady and slid her body off the *travois*. Her broken leg, heavy with the weight of the mud cast, hit the sandstone floor with a thud, and Emily bit her lip to keep from crying out. After the first wave of pain had passed, she used her arms to drag herself to the rim of the fire pit, where a few remaining coals still smoldered.

She could no longer hear the helicopter, but thought maybe it would make another pass. She began looking for dry twigs or grass, anything that would burn. A basket sat near the edge of the pit, and Emily dumped the contents, tuberous roots of some kind, onto the rock floor. She put the basket on the coals and, lying down, blew lightly until the embers ignited the dry reeds. The grasses began to smoke, and a small flame appeared. Her eyes darted around the cave, looking for anything else to burn, when a large moccasined foot stomped on the basket.

"What the hell do you think you're doing?" said Chipeta as she retrieved her singed basket from the ashes. She carried two branches cut into crutches, but tossed them on the ground. "Do you have any idea how hard it is to make one of these?" She continued stomping until there was no longer any smoke.

Near tears, Emily lay on her back and closed her eyes. "They're looking for me. And all you care about is your stupid basket. I have to get out of here, Chipeta. Those girls . . ." She covered her eyes with a forearm so the Ute woman could not see her cry. "Why won't you help me so someone can get those children out of there?"

Chipeta sat on a mat, her legs folded under, and gave Emily a serious look. "The big ranch bordering the north side of the wash—is that the place you're running from?"

"Yes. A madman—calls himself 'The Prophet.' His followers believe he has a direct link to God, and if they obey him and practice his teachings, they'll be blessed with eternal glory or some other bullshit. They practice polygamy to increase the flock, and since there aren't enough women, they steal young girls as soon as they reach puberty."

"Well, how'd you end up there? I know you're way past puberty."

"I had been investigating an earlier kidnapping of a young Navajo girl while she was doing her final *Kinaaldá* run. You must have something similar in your tribe when a girl reaches puberty. When I learned another child was having a ceremony, I decided to dress in the traditional way and run with her, for protection. But . . . they took me, too."

"I rustled a calf or two from there, took some apples, but never knew what went on behind those walls. Shit, if I'd known, I would have stolen a lot more." Chipeta stood and put her hands on her hips, scowling at the dead fire.

"The women are used as slave labor. They turn all their money from government-assistance checks to the man who claims to be the Prophet, and they are forced to work all day. They have no voice, no choice, but they are so indoctrinated into the beliefs of this cult they don't resist."

Chipeta stopped pacing, sat down again, and exhaled a heavy sigh. "I will tell you a story because, before you can share it with anyone else, I will be gone." She settled herself into a comfortable position. "My grandmother raised me; I don't know who my parents were or what happened to them. Grandmother never talked about it. We lived much as I am living now. When I was a young girl, about thirteen, three men came to our camp claiming to be servants of the Lord. They stayed for a few days and tried to persuade my grandmother to let them take me away, to provide an education, a better life—'God's blessings,' the one in charge said. I didn't want to go, and Grandmother also had become suspicious. The men didn't act like men of the cloth. When she refused to give her permission, they stabbed her and tied me with rawhide straps. They stole whatever they could carry and took me away. When they stopped to set up camp, they raped me, took turns, then got drunk. One man, their guide, was a Ute. He did nothing to help me. At night, when they were passed out, I saw the knife the Ute carried and used it to free my hands. The Ute woke up, and I stabbed him and the one who called himself the 'head missionary.' I took the gun of the third man and prepared to shoot him, but he managed to get away in the darkness. I heard the thunder of his horse's feet and knew he would report what *I* had done, but not what happened to my grandmother and me. That same night, I took the other two horses and left the bodies to feed the buzzards. When I found my way home, grandmother was dying. She had a dream, she said, telling her I would come back. I stayed with her until the end, and then washed and wrapped her body—buried it in the mountains she loved and piled rocks on the grave so the animals couldn't find her. I burned her *wickiup* and stayed in this land, but never in one place for long."

As Emily listened to the Ute woman's tale, she felt the horror that young girl must have experienced, and a wave of compassion washed over her. "And you have been running all your life."

"Yes, running and hiding, always looking over my shoulder. When I was seventeen, I decided to leave the mountains, go to Denver, where no one knew me, and get a job. For a while, I worked as a nurse's aide at the county hospital. But one day a Ute patient, someone I went to the mission school with, was brought in. He recognized me, and I knew I had to leave. There is no place for me in towns or cities or on the reservation, so these mountains and canyons are my home. I know how to survive here. Running and hiding is the only life I know."

Emily waited silently for more, but there was nothing forthcoming. "I understand what you are saying, but if you turned yourself in and told your story, they might dismiss the charges."

"No. The cops would never believe me. Those men I killed were murderers. But now *I* am the hunted one, wanted by both the white man and the Utes. I no longer have a tribe."

"The place I ran from—it's also evil. They're raping young girls. I escaped so I could bring help for them."

Chipeta's face appeared calm, but she wrung her hands. "This man, you say he is called the Prophet, he is the devil's spawn. Someone should kill him."

"No one will know about him if you don't tell someone. Until then, he will keep doing the same thing," Emily said.

Chipeta stood. She looked down at the remains of the fire Emily had started, put a hand on her forehead, and shielded her eyes. She appeared to be in deep thought, perhaps considering Emily's words. But after a few moments she shook her head. "Impossible," she said and walked to the outer edge of the cave, gazing out at the thick undergrowth of oak and the two goats browsing on their leaves. When she turned to face

Emily again, all she said was, "I brought you some crutches. You need to get up and move around. I'm tired of cleaning up after you, and no more fires unless I make them."

It required an extreme effort to stand and use the crutches, but once she was on her feet, Emily felt less confined. She moved tentatively at first, then slowly hopped the length of the cave, testing her newfound freedom. She tired quickly and had to rest again. Emily used both arms to lift her leg so it stretched in front of her while she rested on a stump Chipeta used as a stool. She hadn't realized how weak her body had become in the short period of time since her fall, nor how burdensome the adobe-like cast around her leg was until she tried moving. Now her entire right side throbbed with pain. She had attempted to do too much. She closed her eyes and leaned back against the solid sandstone wall, thinking.

It was obvious to Emily that Chipeta had conflicting emotions concerning what to do. If she notified the authorities, it would result in her arrest for murder. But she surely realized there would be search parties, and they could stumble upon her camp at any time. Emily felt conflicting emotions as well. Chipeta had saved her life and nursed her back to health, but the Ute woman had never tried to tell her side of the story to anyone and remained wanted by the police.

Would I give her away or arrest her, given the circumstances?

She heard Chipeta's footsteps, sighed, and opened her eyes.

The Ute woman built a small fire in the pit, then skinned and skewered a rabbit she had trapped. Emily watched her as she pulled dandelion greens and tubers of Jerusalem artichokes out of her pouch. While the rabbit roasted over the coals, the greens and potato-like tubers simmered in a clay pot of water and herbs. Chipeta sat on a blanket and silently stared at the flames. Finally, she turned to face Emily and spoke.

"They're looking for you, and if they find you, they'll find me. I can't let that happen. I've seen the helicopters, and I know there's a search party. It's just a matter of time. I'm leaving in the morning. There will be enough food and water to last you a few days. Then you're on your own. You need to build up your strength, in case you have to walk out of here—though I wouldn't advise it. You'd have to climb down a cliff, and with a broken leg, you won't make it. Give me a day. When I am gone, make a big, smoky fire."

"I owe you my life," Emily said. "I would never have survived without your help."

"But you would arrest me if you could. It's what you do—you're a cop."

26

Sunday, April 15, 1990

Women's Compound

Harmony Home Ranch

Abe awoke as the sun peeked over Sleeping Ute Mountain, changing the sky from a rosy hue to dark lavender. He looked for Will or Hosteen. When he couldn't spot either man or the other posse members, he cursed himself for oversleeping and quickly got to his feet. A small crowd of men, women, and children stood a short distance away, staring at him. He rubbed his eyes and found the posse gathered inside the temple. Abe sat in a pew next to Will and said, "Why didn't you wake me? What did I miss?"

Will glanced at him, his scarred face looking as if he had not slept a wink all night. "Nothing yet. The sheriff is waiting for reinforcements to arrive before he fills us in."

As he spoke, a crowd began to gather—law-enforcement officers from both the Ute and Navajo nations, more state troopers in uniform, a SWAT team from Durango, an ambulance with medical personnel, and representatives from the sheriff's departments in neighboring counties. Phil Brewster and his wife, Tina, showed up, looking for the scoop on a breaking story. Civilians, and men and women from the Navajo and Ute Reservations, arrived as well, and among them stood Bertha Etcitty. She spotted Abe and Will and squeezed in between them.

"Hey, Mom. Why are you here?" Will said, a concerned look on his face. "There's nothing you can do."

"You don't expect me to stay at home, do you? How could I? If I can't go out on the search for my girl, I can make myself useful here—cook meals, clean, whatever. I want to be around when you find Emily."

Abe knew how stubborn Bertha could be when she had her mind set on something. He gave her a resigned smile and shook his head. "There's no talking you out of it, is there? But you're going to have to get clearance from Sheriff Turnbull. He's in charge."

Bertha crossed her arms. "I already did."

Once the newcomers had settled in pews and on benches along the wall, Turnbull cleared his throat to get their attention. "Thank you for making it out here so early in the morning. There'll be coffee and eggs in the dining hall after I finish my little speech. I'd like those of you who volunteered to go on the search party for Officer Emily Etcitty to sit on the left side, and the rest of you on the right. That way I've got some idea of what I'm working with."

Abe watched while people shuffled from one side of the nave to the other. As he expected, the Native American law-enforcement officers, including Joe Hosteen and most of the civilians, had joined in the search for Emily. Bertha appeared confused as to which side she should sit on but, in the end, remained where she was. They now had a team of about fifty people, with the trooper dog trainer and Hosteen in charge. Those individuals on the right consisted of lawmen better qualified to handle the forensics and logistics of an extensive search of the compound.

"I'm cordoning off the ranch," the sheriff said. "Buses are on the way to remove the women and children and take them to a community shelter until DNA testing can be completed. We have reason to believe underage girls were forced into what they call 'spiritual marriages' as soon as they reached puberty and were made pregnant." He paused, screwing his face into an expression of disgust before continuing. "The men will be taken into custody and questioned. If any is suspected of indulging in sex with a minor or committing bigamy, they will be charged and prosecuted to the full extent of the law. And to those good people who have come to lend their support by bringing food and supplies, I thank you. I appreciate y'all coming out here to help in any way you can. Now, the search team wants an early start, so you're dismissed to meet with your team leaders—Officer Joe Hosteen with the Navajo Police, and Colorado State Patrol Officer Mark Newman. Good luck, and God bless."

Bertha stood and addressed Turnbull. "I'm Emily Etcitty's mother. I talked to you on the phone, Sheriff. I'm willing to do whatever I can. Where would you like for me to start?"

"Mrs. Etcitty, first off, I want you to know our number one priority is finding your daughter and the two young girls. We'll be setting up a workstation in the women's compound. I'd like you to coordinate the volunteers' activities, if you don't mind. It entails communication, supplies, meals, running errands, and anything else that isn't police work. Think you can handle it?"

She regarded the other volunteers, a mixture of Native American women in long skirts and velvet blouses, Anglos in jeans and cowboy hats, and Mexican Americans from nearby communities. All nodded affirmatively. "Of course we can. If someone shows us the way, we'll get started."

The crew looking for Emily returned to the marked-off place where the dog had lost the scent and where they'd found the screwdriver and traces of blood. From there, they broke down into two groups to search a wider area. Both team leaders had walkie-talkies so they could communicate if anything turned up. Abe and Will joined Hosteen's group, along with a second Navajo officer. They were better prepared today with water bottles, sandwiches, and rain gear. Still, after six hours of climbing rough, rocky terrain, they had not found a single clue.

High winds blew out of the west, stirring up clouds of sand and threatening to bring a new storm. Hosteen stopped under a cluster of *piñon* trees and called to Will and Abe. "Let's take a break."

They sat on boulders, then pulled out their sandwiches and canteens. There didn't seem to be much to say, so they ate their meal in silence. A helicopter circled overhead.

Will stared at the rocky soil in front of him and squatted for a closer look. "Strange."

"What did you find?" Abe asked.

Will picked up a small pellet, rubbed it between his fingers, and smelled it. "Goat shit. What're goats doing out here? And look at this. The mesquite has been eaten down." He squatted down and studied the ground around the mesquite bush. "Goat tracks."

Hosteen looked skeptical. "Could be deer."

"Or mountain goat," Abe added.

Will straightened up, a glimmer of excitement shining in his eyes. "No. This print is a domesticated animal's—somebody's livestock. The only mountain goats in Colorado are further north, above the tree line. These hoof tracks are blockier than deer, and the front tips are rounded instead of pointed. Let's see if we can find more. If they're goats, someone is tending them, and maybe they know something about Emily."

"I'm all for tracking this person down, Will," Hosteen said. "But I've got to wonder. If someone did find her, why haven't they notified authorities?"

"We'll know the answer when we find Emily. Let's get moving on this," Abe said.

Hosteen pulled out his walkie-talkie and keyed in the number for Sergeant Newman. "Mark, Hosteen here. Do you read? . . . I'm up here about two miles northwest of Navajo Wash, near a stand of *piñon*. What's your 10-20? . . . Copy . . . Will Etcitty might have found something. It isn't much, but it's our first clue. Fan out and scour the ground for goat shit . . . Yes, you heard me right—goat shit. Let me know if you find anything. Freeman, Etcitty, and I will pursue this section . . . Roger."

Abe was surveying the area around the trees. "There's a lot of ground to cover. We need to break up."

Will squinted at the sun. It was beginning to drop in the west. "Each one of us can take a pie slice of this area, starting right here, and work our way northwest. Make a zigzag path so you don't miss anything."

"Good strategy, Etcitty," Hosteen said. "You should have been a cop."

"Goat dung, rabbit dung, sheep dung, deer dung—it all looks like the same shit to me," Abe said. Country life was still new to him. In spite of the time he spent managing the Churro sheep-breeding ranch, he knew he had a lot to learn. After all, he had been born and raised in Atlantic City, New Jersey, where he'd never had exposure to anything but bullshit.

"Maybe Newman should join us with his dog—track the scent of the goat?"

"Look for droppings that are not perfect spheres, a little elongated, and rounded at one end. It's easy to tell once you get familiar with it. Here, take some samples with you." He scooped up a few and handed them to Abe.

"Only for Emily would I do this," Abe said as he dropped the pellets in one of the small plastic bags he carried in his pocket.

"Don't take it all," Hosteen cut in. "Leave enough for the dog to get the scent. I'll radio Newman, see what he thinks." After a brief conversation, Hosteen told Abe and Will to go ahead and get started. He would wait for the state trooper and his dog.

"Sweep out wider as you go, Abe," Will said. "I'll flank your right side."

Abe surveyed the untamed expanse of land spread out in front of him. It would not be smooth walking. Hogbacks, gullies, and rocky cliffs lay ahead. "Okay," he said. He wished he had Patch with him. Even though his dog only had three legs, Abe thought he could track down a goat or even Emily better than any police-trained search-and-rescue dog.

Didn't Patch find me two years ago when I became trapped in a cave, and a crazed motorcycle gang leader tried to kill me? Patch, I need your help, boy.

Abe studied the ground, saw some pellets, pulled out his plastic bag, and decided they were too small and round. Probably rabbit. He climbed a rocky hillside and stood a moment to catch his breath. Even resting, he could not stop from scanning the ground's surface for any sign of Emily. If there had been prints, they had been erased by recent rains. The land lay barren and rocky, with only a few scatterings of pale grass and rabbitbrush.

When he reached the top of a knoll, he had a good view of the surrounding area. He looked to his right to check on Will's progress, then back to where he had left Hosteen before he started out again. Chamisa and mountain mahogany shrubs grew thicker there and made walking difficult. He bushwhacked his way through a patch of scrubby oak and spotted what appeared to be a deer trail a short distance ahead.

Any sensible goat would follow a trail, he told himself as he made his way to the path, expecting to see a lot of deer pellets. *And maybe some goat pellets?*

He walked a short distance farther and saw something unexpected—a line of large, dry, round dung. Not quite like a horse's, but maybe a mule or donkey. He didn't know if there were wild burros in this part of the state, but Will would know. His adrenaline kicked in, bringing with it a glimmer of hope. Maybe someone had found Emily and had taken her to a safe place. Abe put two fingers in his mouth and whistled—a loud, piercing call for help.

27

Sunday, April 15, 1990

Chipeta Longtooth's Camp

Colorado Backcountry

While Chipeta prepared for her departure, Emily continued to practice walking with her crutches, building her endurance. She hopped to the outer edge of the rock shelter to get a better look at her surroundings and discovered that Chipeta's camp perched on the brink of a high cliff. A narrow path cut through a dark crevice in the cliff's wall and led down to a thick patch of juniper and skunkbrush. The goats looked up at her and bleated before continuing to munch on shrubs. Emily knew it would be impossible for her to climb down the path on her own; she would have to use both hands to cling to the wall and hop on one foot. Her leg still throbbed painfully, and she had periods of dizziness. She scanned the horizon in all directions but saw no sign of Chipeta or her donkey. The Ute woman had gone out to gather food and supplies.

When Chipeta returned later in the afternoon, she carried a bundle of dry wood and green boughs of juniper. Emily had been resting on her pallet but lifted her head when she heard the woman's footsteps.

"For your fire," Chipeta said, as she dropped her load near the entrance of the cave. "You'll need this wood when I'm gone."

Emily stared at the small stack of brush and sticks, knowing it would not last long.

Then what? Please, don't leave me here alone.

"It's burro shit, all right," Will said. He kicked the rounded droppings. "See how dry it is? They're desert animals—know how to retain water. This scat is about two days old. It could be a wild one, but wild burros and horses aren't usually alone—like to herd for protection. Someone is herding a couple of goats and a burro."

"And that person could be taking care of Emily," Abe added hopefully.

"Maybe." Will turned at the sound of Hosteen and Mark Newman approaching. The dog was in the lead, pulling on his leash.

"Spike led us here after he picked up the goat's trail," Newman said. "Did you find anything else?"

"Donkey dung," Abe said. "How about on your side?"

"Nothing," Newman said. "It's like we had her trail, and she disappeared. Spike kept circling back to the blood spot. Strange." He kneeled on one knee and looked at the animal dung. "You say it's donkey?"

"Right," said Will. "Somebody's domesticated animal."

"Who would be living up here?" asked Hosteen.

"Could be people from the reservation out grazing their animals. Funny you would take a goat and a donkey this far from any Ute homes, though," Newman said. "There's better places than here."

Will crinkled his eyes as if in deep concentration. "I remember a story about a Ute woman hiding from the law out this way. She killed two men, stabbed them, but one escaped. Her grandmother was missing, maybe murdered as well and buried somewhere. They say the woman went crazy, though she was just a girl of about fourteen at the time. All this happened at least twenty years ago. You think it might be her?"

"Chipeta Longtooth is what she goes by," said the Colorado lawman. "She's legendary—elusive as all hell. I grew up on stories about her. No one's ever been able to track her down."

Abe saw the pained expression on his friend's face. "What makes you think she's still around here?" Abe said.

Newman scratched his head and scanned the horizon before answering. "Well, about twelve years ago, someone reported spotting Chipeta in a Denver hospital, but she disappeared again. The Utes believe she came back home and lives on her own in the wild. Although no one has ever seen her, they've stumbled onto remains of camps. It's all rumors and speculation, though."

"Have there been any more killings?" Abe asked.

Newman frowned as if he were pondering the question. "There've been killings, but none could be attributed to her. Hell, she's probably dead by now."

Hosteen studied the sky. "We don't have much daylight left. Newman, can your dog track donkeys?"

"Hell, yes," said the Colorado trooper. "There's nothing Spike can't follow." He radioed his team, asking if they had turned up anything, telling them his location and plan. After he had signed out, he turned to the other three. "Let's go."

The search dog pressed his nose to the donkey dung and ran ahead as he followed the scent, with the men trailing close behind. The path meandered in a roundabout fashion, sometimes doubling over ground they had already covered.

The sun dropped lower, casting dark shadows on the land. Abe's frustration grew as he realized they were traipsing over ground they had already covered. "What the hell? We're going in circles."

"The animals were grazing, wandering wherever they found food," Will said. "Look. More dung—maybe two or three goats."

The sun disappeared behind the western range, and dusk began to creep in. Abe pulled out his flashlight, looking for any sign of human footprints. He was still thinking about Chipeta Longtooth and her murderous rampage. How was it possible a child so young could kill three people? Spike tugged on his leash, but it soon became too dark to continue.

Neither Abe nor Will wanted to go back at that point. "We're onto something," Abe said. "If we quit now, we'll lose ground and have to spend half the day getting to this point tomorrow." He watched the rising moon disappear behind low clouds. "If it rains, the dog will lose the scent as well."

"I say we stay here, keep looking," Will added.

"Listen," said Newman, "I've got another crew back there I need to track down. I'll call in for horses tomorrow, and we can spread out more."

Abe shook his head. "I think we should sleep here tonight so we can get an early start in the morning."

Despite Newman's objections and the fact that they didn't have enough food or water, or even bedrolls, Will agreed with Abe. "We can manage. We'll ration our water and forage for food if needed."

Hosteen had remained quiet throughout the discussion, chewing his lower lip as if pondering what to do. "I'll stay with them, Trooper—make sure they don't get in trouble. Tomorrow morning, bring us some food and water with the horses. We'll mark the trail so you can find us. I agree we should keep looking for Officer Etcitty."

Trooper Newman shrugged. "Okay, Hosteen. I know she's your partner. It's your call; just be careful. You all are carrying, right?" He studied the darkening sky. "I'm heading back before it's too late. I'll find you tomorrow with a string of pack horses and supplies. Probably won't hurt to bring a first-aid kit as well."

"You know your way?" said Hosteen.

"I was born in this country, Joe, and I've got my radio and my dog. I'll be fine."

The three men watched Trooper Newman as he gradually grew smaller and finally disappeared in the dwindling dusk. They looked at one another—sweaty, dirty, and dog-tired. Abe blew out a whoosh of air. His bum knee hurt and he was thirsty, but he didn't pull out his canteen, thinking it best to conserve water.

"Well, we better continue searching while we have a little daylight," he said. Without the dog to lead them, they decided to stick together. No point in having someone lost or fall off a cliff.

They walked for another hour and stopped to make camp for the night at the base of a mesa. A blanket of clouds blocked any light from the moon and stars. Night, black as a tomb, engulfed them, and a cold wind blew from the west. Using a flashlight, Abe gathered deadwood for a fire while Will cut *piñon* boughs to form makeshift beds, and Hosteen radioed the control center to inform the sheriff and Bertha Etcitty they were spending the night. As they sat on the hard ground near the campfire with shared remnants of sandwiches and water, Abe stared gloomily at the flames.

"You told my mom we were staying here, looking for Emily?" Will said.

"Yeah," said Hosteen. "She's okay, glad she knows. She's sleeping at the ranch tonight. I asked her if they had found the girls."

"And?" Will said.

Hosteen took a bite of his bologna-and-cheese sandwich and chewed. "Not yet. The Feds are interviewing all the families. If they learned anything, they're not sharing. That's the way the FBI operates. But when we were interrogating Betty Prescott, she mentioned something interesting. Will and the sheriff had stepped out of the room because they heard the ruckus in the hall. I asked her if she had spent any time with Lina and Darcy."

Will leaned in toward Hosteen. "Oh, yeah? What did she say?"

"Said the one girl was sick, had been throwing up—told them she was diabetic and needed her shots. There's a woman there called Mary Jo who is also diabetic, so they called her in, and she shared some insulin with Lina. But when Mary Jo went back to check on her, the girl was gone."

"That's some comfort, at least," Abe said. "If Lina did get a couple shots, it gives her more time. I hope Langley didn't take the girls with him."

"Yeah." Hosteen knitted his brows. "The thing is, Emily and I questioned the mother of a girl who went missing several years ago—the daughter's name was Mary Jo. She was also celebrating her *Kinaaldá* when she disappeared, and *her* mother is diabetic. I'm betting this is the same girl."

Abe listened carefully to the conversation while he chewed bologna and bread. "Sounds like this has been going on for a long time. The bastard has to be found and stopped." Then his thoughts returned to Emily. "Hosteen? You think the Ute woman might have—"

Will cut him off before he could finish. "Shut up, Abe. Don't even talk like that."

Abe took a sip of water and wiped his mouth with his hand. It was the bleakness of the black sky, the skittering in the brush of night animals, the worry and uncertainty, that left him feeling helpless and unsure.

"You're right, Will. Just wish we had more than goat and donkey shit to go on."

Hosteen used his backpack for a pillow and settled onto his bed of boughs. "Get some sleep. We'll be up early tomorrow."

Abe pulled his jacket around him and lay on his back, his hands behind his head, his eyes staring into the dark. When he finally drifted off, he dreamed of Emily calling him. Her voice echoed off canyon walls and cliffs, seemingly coming from all directions. Abe rushed from one place to another in a frantic, futile attempt to find her. *I'm coming, I'm coming.*

He awoke in a cold sweat by a yell and a curse from Hosteen.

"Goddammit! Get off me, you sons of bitches!"

Abe sat up and, in the dim glow of the dying fire, saw Hosteen stomping his feet and brushing frantically at his arms and neck.

"What's wrong?" asked Abe, on his feet as well.

"Spiders, maybe scorpions. I don't know."

The noise woke Will. "What's going on?" He trained his flashlight on Hosteen. "Ants. You bedded down near an ant nest and got them riled up. You need to find a better place to sleep." He returned to the place where he had dug a groove in the sandy soil and lay back down.

"Shit," said Hosteen. "It could have been spiders or snakes. You don't know what's out here."

"I do know what's out here. You don't. You grew up in the city, spent all your life there except for the last two years, Hosteen. Now bed down closer to the fire, and let us sleep. Emily is what's out there, and we need to find her."

Will's right, Abe thought. *Hosteen and I are both out of our element— fish out of water—in the desert. All I know are the mean streets of Atlantic City, and Hosteen may be a cop, but he's not much different. The only one who knows what he's doing is Will.*

Abe shifted his body to the hard surface, trying, without luck, to find a more comfortable position. He thought he felt snowflakes brush against his face. He covered himself with the plastic poncho and hunkered down.

In the gray of early morning, Abe shivered and rubbed his eyes, groggy from his restless night. Will and Hosteen stood in ankle-deep snow studying the cliff wall and discussing whether they should scoot around or try to climb up the slopes. They both chewed on a granola bar and handed one to Abe. That and a sip or two of water to wash it down was breakfast.

"We'll be able to tell more about the lay of the land from a high vantage point," Will reasoned, looking up at the mesa top. "But we won't find any more goat or donkey shit until this melts off."

"Yeah, we'll see more if we manage to get up there without breaking our necks," said Hosteen. While they discussed options, sunshine broke through the clouds, providing hope for clear skies and good weather.

Abe emptied his bladder behind a nearby boulder, tried to ignore the pain in his knee, and said, "Let's walk around and see if there's an easier way to the top."

28

Emily shivered as a gust of cold wind whipped through the cave. She pulled the deer-hide blanket up to her chin and lay wide-awake in the pitch-black darkness. She could hear no other sound except the wind. She didn't know what time it was, or if Chipeta had left or not. The Ute woman had returned from her foraging in the afternoon with a bundle of roots and herbs. She divided out a portion for Emily and indicated a jug of water and a bag of elk jerky she planned to leave behind. A single clay pot and spoon sat on the stump by the dead fire pit. Her remaining possessions had been readied to pack onto the burro.

"When you wake up, I'll be gone," Chipeta had said. "Remember what I told you. Don't make a fire until daylight—no one will see it but me if you try." After a slight pause, she added, "I wish you well, Navajo cop, but I hope I never see you again."

What could Emily say? *Good luck, Ute woman? I hope I never have to arrest you?* She mumbled a "Thank you" when Chipeta handed her a steaming cup of herbal tea, and that was all.

Despite the tea, Emily had not been able to sleep. Along with the pain in her leg from the recent exercise, she could not stop thinking. *Is anyone going to see the smoke from my fire? Is Abe out there looking for me? And Will? If no one comes, will I be able to get down, or will I stay here and die alone?*

Once she thought she smelled smoke, but the fire in the pit had gone out hours before. She waited in the silence for what seemed like an eternity, and when she couldn't stand it any longer, she called out in a soft voice to the Ute woman.

"Chipeta?" Receiving no answer, she called once again, louder. Again, nothing. She had not heard any movement in the cave, but the woman moved as silently as a ghost. She must have slipped away during the night. Emily could do nothing in the complete darkness, so she burrowed under her blanket and tried to sleep. Eventually, she drifted off.

She opened her eyes to a gray morning light and brushed a layer of wind-driven white flakes from her bedding. A spring snowstorm had blown in with the west wind during the night. The wind had died down, leaving a blanket of fog hugging the cliff tops. From what she could see, the surrounding countryside remained sheathed in three inches of snow. Emily reached for her crutches and, bracing herself against the rock wall, staggered to her feet. Losing her balance, she fell to the hard floor of the cave and lay there for a moment, breathing deeply, catching her breath, and willing herself to stand again.

How can I survive here if I can't even stand on my own two feet? she asked herself.

She reached for the branches Chipeta had formed into crutches and pulled herself onto her good knee. Pushing with the one strong leg, she stood once again and gazed at a muted sunrise.

I'm alone, she thought. *Whatever I do, I do on my own. It's me out here; there's no one else.*

Fire. Emily shivered. *I have to build a fire.*

Chipeta had left a pile of branches, but they were dusted with snow. She shook the flakes off and looked around the enclosure. *Matches? Flint?* Of course, there were none. *Dry twigs?* They would have to be under the pile of branches. *When have I ever tried to start a fire by rubbing sticks? Never.*

She eased herself down on the stump near the fire pit and reached into the bundle of branches until she had a handful of dry twigs and needles. After placing them in a small pile inside the pit but within her reach, she searched for anything she might use to create enough friction to spark and make an ember. Beside the pit, she spotted a flat piece of wood with a V-shaped notch and a small depression. A smooth, rounded two-foot-long stick lay on top of the wood.

This must be what Chipeta used to start fires, Emily thought, and silently thanked her for leaving it behind.

She put the notched piece of wood near her nest of tinder and inserted the spindle stick in the groove. Putting as much pressure on the wood as possible, Emily swiftly rolled the rod back and forth with her hands. After several minutes, no spark had been produced, and her arms ached from the effort. She rested, catching her breath, but tried again after a few moments.

Don't give up. This fire is your only hope.

Emily continued rolling until blisters formed on her palms. Finally, after a long, agonizing time, she saw the glow of a small ember in the nest of dry straw and twigs—only to see it die out before it caught. The blisters on her hands broke open and began to bleed, but Emily knew she couldn't quit. After several more agonizing minutes, another spark glowed, followed by another. A curl of smoke arose, and she fanned it lightly with her hand until the twigs ignited. She settled back with a sigh of relief, almost smiling when small flames appeared. The fire was a major accomplishment, but there wasn't time to waste basking in her success. Tending the fire and making sure it did not go out was an immediate concern. As the tinder burned, she gradually added larger sticks and branches until she could smell and feel the welcome warmth of a *piñon* fire.

Chipeta had left her water in an earthen pot. Emily heated it on the coals and soon was warmed inside by a steaming cup of Navajo tea and deer jerky. Feeling stronger and more hopeful, she gathered up her makeshift crutches and hopped to the outer edge of the cave. The fog had burned off, for the most part, leaving patches of blue sky and bright sun. Still, she knew she couldn't walk down the steep, slippery slope of the canyon wall.

Fearful she might run out of firewood before anyone spotted her smoke, Emily looked around for more branches and dead limbs—anything that could burn—but the sandstone base was nearly devoid of vegetation. She would have to watch her wood carefully. She returned to the fire pit and put a green branch of juniper on the flames, letting it smolder, watching the thick, gray smoke rise. While the wood slowly burned, Emily practiced walking with her crutches, resting when she became too tired or the pain was too unbearable. Emily knew that once she ran out of wood and had not been spotted by searchers, starvation or frostbite would be her fate.

I need to build up my strength, she thought, grimacing and pulling herself to her feet once again. *Whether I walk or have to drag my body, I'll have to find a way to get down this mountain.*

Will laid out an arrow of branches and stones indicating to Mark Newman they were following along the canyon wall from the left side. They clambered over clusters of large boulders that had broken and fallen from the sides of the wall as they made a gradual ascent to the base. The vertical wall appeared inaccessible from their position, as it shot straight up a few hundred feet. Abe took a pair of binoculars out of his pack and studied the top of the mesa. He focused on something—clinging fog, clouds, or smoke?

"Will!" Abe said, grabbing his friend's shoulder, "look up there. What do you make of it?"

Squinting his eyes in the bright sunlight, Will took the proffered binoculars and looked in the direction Abe pointed.

"It's smoke from a campfire," Will said, excitement in his voice. "Hosteen, I think we've found something."

Abe licked his dry lips, his heart pounding. He wanted to yell Emily's name at the top of his lungs but thought of the other woman who might still be with her.

As the three men studied the canyon crest, the smoke thickened, rising high in the now-pristine sky. "It has to be Emily, or the Ute woman—or both," Hosteen said. "We've got to figure out how to get up there without being seen."

"We'll find a way," Will said. "If someone else could get up there and make a fire, there has to be a trail. Come on. Keep looking."

They picked up the pace, not knowing what lay ahead, but feeling they had found their best indication as to Emily's whereabouts.

The fog burned away, allowing an unobstructed view of the surrounding cliffs. The top of the mountain appeared to be a broad flat stretch of land—a mesa with sandstone and shale outcroppings. As the three men approached the back side of the tabletop mountain, the slope became more gradual and the undergrowth denser. Shrubby rabbitbrush and mountain mahogany pricked at their skin—daggerlike yucca leaves jabbed their shins.

"How could Emily, or anyone, have made it to the top of this mesa with all this brush?" Abe asked as he bushwhacked through the dense growth. "There's no sign of a trail, and before we reach the top, it'll turn into a straight-sided cliff again." He had his eyes trained on the crown, searching for the gray stream of smoke he had seen before, but a single cloud of fog hugged the mesa top, obscuring his view.

Will stopped to sweep his gaze out over the land. As the snow melted, steam rose from the warmed earth and rocks. The men's pants and shoes were soaked through and caked with claylike mud. "See that patch of scrub oak?" Will pointed. "I think there's a definite break in the brush. Might be a deer trail or something."

Lifting his arms shoulder high to keep from being stabbed by the yucca spines, Will led them to the spot he had seen. It was indeed a trail that gradually made its way to the top. By the time they finished the climb, the position of the sun indicated it was between noon and two o'clock. Abe took off his ball cap and wiped sweat from his forehead. The plume of smoke was clearly in view, but not its source. It appeared to come from a lower point on the far opposite side. "There's a campfire on the back side. I'm headed that way," he said. Will took off right behind him. Abe glanced back to see Hosteen try his radio, then shake his head. They were out of range. Hosteen hurried to catch up with the other two.

Feeling exhausted and defeated, Emily slumped on the stool and held her head in both hands. There were only a few remaining branches, and the errant fog had obliterated most of her smoke. Worry had caused her to pace the length of the cave until she was on the verge of collapse. If smoke failed to draw the attention of searchers, she knew she could die. But, before that happened, she would attempt to climb down herself—at whatever cost. She placed her only remaining branch on the flame and prayed to all her grandmother's gods that someone would come for her. Once the last limb was smoldering and emitting a stream of smoke, she laid down on her makeshift bed on the *travois* and closed her eyes.

I may never see my family or Abe again. I'm going to die on this mesa top, alone.

Her eyes filled with tears as she recalled a Navajo prayer taught to her by her grandmother, and silently mouthed the words:

> Grieve for me, for I would grieve for you.
> Then brush away the sorrow and the tears.
> Life is not over but begins anew.
> With courage, you must greet the coming years.

Her energy spent, she intended to rest awhile before looking for more limbs, but when her eyes closed, she fell asleep.

When the three men were approximately a hundred yards from the source of the faint wisps of smoke, Hosteen raised his hand for Abe and Will to stop, cautioning them not to make any noise. They hunkered down behind a large boulder while he gave them instructions. "Get your guns out, and be ready," he whispered. "We need to take a look at what's down there without drawing attention. There must be an access trail to the campsite. We'll split up. Abe, you take the left, Will, the middle. I'll be on the right. Reconnoiter the area, but don't go after anyone on your own. We'll meet back here in about an hour."

"What if I see Emily and she's alone?" Abe asked in a tight voice.

"Don't do anything. You won't know if Emily's alone or who made that fire. If the Ute woman is there, Emily could be in danger. Got it, Freeman?"

Abe nodded, tense and steely-eyed. He took the short-barreled shotgun from the shoulder case looped over his shoulder and inserted two shells into the loading flap, one into the chamber. He clicked off the safety and hoped like hell he wouldn't have to use it.

Will loaded ammo into his grandfather's pistol. His eyes gleamed with excited anticipation and hope, erasing the worry lines on his burn-scarred face.

He thinks we've found her, Abe thought. *God, I hope he's right.*

Abe felt it, too, and although he was no lover of guns and had no training in their use, he was ready to use one. He licked his dry lips, crouching low, and held the shotgun in front of him as he ran a zigzag pattern to the next large boulder. Movies were all he had to go on, and instinct, plus the desire to reach Emily.

Freeman, he told himself, *fuck it. If you have to shoot a crazy killer to get Emily back, do it.*

29

Monday, April 16, 1990

Chipeta Longtooth's Camp

Colorado Backcountry

Abe dropped to his stomach in a washed-out gully at the edge of the mesa top. He listened carefully for sounds coming from the area where the diminishing streams of smoke were visible, but all he could hear was the cackling of crows and the thunderous beating of his heart. He looked to the right to check the location of Will and Hosteen, then belly-crawled to the rim. Cautiously peering over the edge, Abe noticed that the vertical cliff flattened after about fifty feet onto a rock shelf. He caught a whiff of smoke. He knew no one could scale a solid wall without rock-climbing gear. There had to be a trail.

He crept along the rim of the mesa, looking for an opening, trying not to make a sound. Something ahead caught his attention. Mesquite and snake brush clustered around what appeared to be a fissure on the solid surface. The break was nearly three feet wide and led down the cliff with a series of natural rock steps. Abe signaled to Will to follow him and moved forward. He could not see Hosteen.

"Should we call Hosteen?" Will asked.

"The hell with Hosteen." He was nowhere in sight, and Abe didn't want to waste time looking for the lawman. Will agreed, and using hand signals to communicate, the two men crept down the mountainside. The path was well used and smooth for the most part, with occasional scratches on the sandstone surface. Goat and donkey scat dotted the trail. It appeared to Abe that someone had recently dragged a heavy object along the surface.

Will put a finger to his lips and pushed back with his palm, urging Abe to go slow and remain quiet.

They inched down the path until reaching a flat outcropping of smooth sandstone that ended in the broad overhang of a natural cave. Abe felt his body tighten and his pulse quicken as he pushed his back flat against the wall of rock. Both men remained as still as death, barely breathing while they listened for any sign of movement inside the cave. Will held his pistol in the ready position and nodded for Abe to do the same. The smell of burned wood hung in the air, and a soft moan came from the dark entrance—accompanied by the sound of something thumping on the rocky surface.

Will raised three fingers. On the count of three, the two men burst into the entrance of the cave with their guns cocked and ready to fire.

"Put your hands behind your head and step forward!" Abe shouted.

Then he heard a shriek and looked on, stunned, as Emily let go of her crutches and fell to the floor.

"Emily?" Will said, dropping to his knees. "`Adeezhi, my little sis-ter, I was afraid we would never find you."

Abe ran toward her, calling her name. "Emily, Em! My God, it's really you." He looked at her leg encased in the makeshift cast, dropped to his knees, and brushed the hair from her tearstained face. "You're hurt, baby. What happened?"

Emily sobbed and clutched at both Abe and Will.

"Sister," Will whispered, "who brought you here? The Ute woman, Chipeta Longtooth?"

Emily nodded.

"Where is she now?" asked Abe, looking around the cave, noticing the barely smoldering wood in the fire pit, the pot of water, and the crutches.

"I don't know," Emily said. "She left sometime during the night. Abe, I fell and broke my leg. She found me, took care of me, put this cast on my leg, gave me food and tea and firewood. I had almost given up. How did you find me? Did you see the smoke?"

Abe looked at her braided hair, tanned buckskin dress, and soot-smudged face, and shook his head in wonder. "We saw the smoke, Em, but it wasn't easy to find the trail. It's unbelievable she managed to bring you here. Let me help you up. There's so much I want to know, but first we have to get you out of here and to a hospital."

"What about the girls?"

"They're still searching, sweetheart," Abe said. "The FBI, state police, and local agencies are tearing the ranch apart and questioning all the cult members. They'll find the girls, but the so-called Prophet skipped out—took off in a private aircraft." No one wanted to cause Emily any more pain by mentioning Lina's diabetes.

Emily's mouth turned down. "I wish I could go after him myself. If I hadn't run away, maybe he wouldn't have fled. Someone might have found the girls. He was probably afraid I'd make it back and lead the authorities to him—and I would have if I hadn't broken my damn leg."

"Don't blame yourself. You were trying to save them," Abe said. He picked her up and carried her to the stool, knelt, and held her in his arms.

Will had turned toward the eastern sky and was chanting a prayer, his voice breaking at times. He clutched the medicine bag, the *jish* he always carried across his shoulder, and extracted a small handful of white corn pollen. After scattering it to the east, he concluded his prayer and turned back to gaze at Emily and Abe.

"They say the Ute woman killed two men," Will said.

"She had her reasons for killing those men," Emily said in Chipeta's defense. "She's gone now, vanished in the night."

"Joe Hosteen is with us," Abe said. "We have to let him know we found you so he can radio for a rescue chopper. A Colorado state trooper on horseback is tracking us. He should be here soon with more help."

"I want to stay here with my sister, Abe. Find Hosteen."

Abe hated leaving Emily, but seeing Will's face, he reluctantly agreed. "I'll be back soon," he said, softly brushing at a smudge on her cheekbone. He kissed her forehead and hurried toward the path.

When he emerged at the crest, Abe saw no reason to remain silent, so he whistled several times, hoping to get Hosteen's attention. "Joe Hosteen, we found Emily!" he shouted. After getting no response, he headed in the direction where he had last spotted the Navajo cop. "Hosteen! Where the hell are you?"

The sound of a groan led him to a narrow opening between a split in an immense boulder. Six feet inside, he nearly stumbled over Hosteen's protruding legs. The cop sat on the ground holding a hand to the back of his head. Blood oozed between his fingers.

Abe knelt beside Hosteen. "Jesus. What happened to you?"

"It had to be Chipeta Longtooth. I saw some moccasin prints in the snow and followed them. She hit me from behind with something heavy; the murdering bitch knocked me out. Oh, man."

"We found Emily. She said the Ute woman left sometime during the night. Emily has a broken leg. Can you stand, Joe?"

"Yeah, give me a hand. Where is she? Thank God the Ute woman didn't kill her."

"I'll take you there," Abe said, helping Hosteen to his feet. "Are you sure you can walk?"

"Yeah, yeah. Let's go." Hosteen staggered, leaning against Abe to steady himself.

"When we get out in the open, try your radio, Joe. We need a helicopter to get Emily out of here and to a hospital. Someone should look at the cut on your head, too."

By the time Abe and Hosteen reached the level plateau on the mountain, Mark Newman and three more men on horseback were cresting the ridge. "Over here!" Abe shouted, waving his arms. Newman turned his sorrel packhorse at the sound of Abe's voice, and the four riders, led by the search dog, rode to meet him.

"We found her," Abe said. "We've got Emily."

"Is she okay?" Newman asked.

Abe nodded in affirmation, panting to catch his breath. "She has a broken leg, but otherwise seems okay. Can you call in a chopper?"

"No service," Newman said. "I've been trying to make contact with you all morning." His eyes lingered on Hosteen's bloodied head. "What happened, Officer?"

"She found me," said Hosteen. "And I don't mean Emily. I didn't get a look at her. I heard a noise like a donkey braying and followed it. She hit me from behind. Must have been Chipeta Longtooth. Guess I got too close. I'll be all right—lucky she didn't kill me. Abe and Will found Emily," he said with a droll expression. "I'm some cop. You ready to take us to her, Abe?"

Relieved that help had arrived, Abe could hardly wait to get back to Emily. "Behind those bushes," he said, pointing in the direction of a clump of scrubby, wind-twisted trees. "A hidden path leads down to a cave. Emily's there with Will. Follow me."

"Hold on just a second." Mark Newman pulled out his handheld and tried to reach the compound headquarters. After receiving nothing but static, he handed it to one of the men on horseback. "Take my radio and ride back until you can get reception. Call control center and give them our 10-20. Let them know we found Emily Etcitty and need a medic and chopper up here on the mesa top ASAP. And you might mention Officer Hosteen had a recent encounter with Chipeta Longtooth."

Emily, still marveling at her sudden rescue, let the stream of tears run down her cheeks while she stared intently into her brother's eyes. Will squatted beside her, his back to the opening of the cave. He wanted to know everything—how she broke her leg—whether she had any other wounds—if she'd been treated well—and how Chipeta Longtooth managed to bring her to such a remote place.

Emily smiled at her brother and held tightly to his hand. "I'll tell you all about it later. Is Mom okay?"

While she listened to his reassurances, Emily thought she saw a slight movement behind Will. She caught a fleeting glimpse of Chipeta's face peering in at the edge of the cave. It disappeared again, as swift as the glance of a falling star. It could have been a hallucination, but her reaction did not escape Will's keen eyes.

"She saved your life," he said with a knowing look.

30

Monday, April 16, 1990

Chipeta Longtooth's Camp

Colorado Back Country

Medics placed Emily on a stretcher and whisked her to a waiting medevac chopper ready to transport Hosteen and her to University Hospital in Albuquerque. She held tight to her makeshift crutches, insisting on taking them along. Hosteen would have stayed on the mesa if his captain, who arrived with a contingent of Navajo police officers, had not ordered him to get medical clearance from the hospital before reporting back to duty. Will and Abe climbed aboard a second helicopter and headed back to the compound. Though hungry and exhausted, they were so excited about sharing the news of Emily's rescue with Bertha that they'd forgotten the sandwiches and thermos of coffee Mark Newman carried in his saddlebags. Newman remained on the mesa top with his dog, Spike, and two other Colorado state troopers until dusk, futilely searching for any clues leading to the location of Chipeta Longtooth. But the elusive woman had disappeared like a shadow on a cloudy day, and they were forced to give up the search.

Bertha Etcitty fussed over Will and Abe like a mother hen with two precious chicks. She burst into tears of happiness after listening to Will's account of Emily's rescue, and his reassurance she was going to be all right. It seemed she couldn't stop talking.

"Here, eat another bowl of stew. Do you want some more coffee? I brought you clean clothes. After you take a hot shower, we gotta go to Albuquerque. I'll drive. I know how tired you must be." Bertha beamed at Will and Abe. "I am so proud of you boys."

Abe said, "No need, Bertha. I'll take my truck and clean up at home before I go to the hospital. I need to check on my place and see if Ellen and Danny can hang around a little longer. If you get to the hospital before me, tell Emily I'm on my way. Will can ride with you."

"Okay, Abe." Tears threatened to spill once again from Bertha's eyes. She blinked them away and smiled. "I know I have a reputation for being a tough old Navajo woman, but I'm just so relieved and happy right now—knowing my baby is alive. Emily can come home." She no longer tried to restrain the tears flowing down her cheeks in rivulets and running past her beaming smile.

Before he left, Abe caught up with the sheriff and updated him on Emily's condition and rescue.

Sheriff Turnbull's eyebrows rose a half inch when Abe mentioned that Chipeta Longtooth had found Emily and set her broken leg. "How'd she manage to do that, and where do you suppose she went?"

"I don't know. Emily said she took off during the night. Newman and a couple of other state troopers are looking for her."

"Huh. Don't that beat all? Well, great work finding Officer Etcitty. I'll release you from posse duty now if you like. We've got enough men here to cover our bases, but you're free to stay—earn a little more money for your hard work."

Abe extended his hand. "Appreciate it, Sheriff, but I'd like to head on out to Albuquerque to see Emily. How's the investigation going here? Did you turn up any clues as to the whereabouts of the girls?"

Newman scratched his head before answering. "We know they were here, and now they're not. The woman who calls herself 'matron' broke down and admitted as much. We found the white van used in the kidnapping of Emily Etcitty and Lina Nez, but those two dirtbags who pulled it off are missing. The white utility van was decked out with folding cots secured to the sides, constraint straps, automatic locks on the doors, and shaded windows. The FBI is giving it a thorough going-over for prints and DNA, or anything else they can use. Since the head scumbag took off to parts unknown in a private plane, those other two might have gone with him. We'll find out, and I'll keep Hosteen posted. Heard he got whacked on the head and is down in Albuquerque, too."

"They'll probably keep him overnight for observation, Sheriff. Make sure there's no concussion. Tomorrow he'll be chomping at the bit to get back on the case."

The sheriff grinned. "Yeah, he's a go-getter, all right." After a pause, he added, "You know, son, on my first impression, you didn't strike me as the lawman type. You've got a studious, intellectual air about you. And I don't believe you've had much experience with guns. But, by God, you proved yourself out there. Found your girlfriend. Listen, you take care of her and yourself from now on."

Abe bid the sheriff good-bye and drove away from the compound. When he reached the highway, he sped up, as he was anxious to get home, take a hot bath, and put on a change of clean clothes before making the three-hour drive to Albuquerque. Knowing Emily was safe had lifted a heavy burden from his mind. But he worried about the girls and whether they had been forced to go with the leader of the cult.

There might be other young women in the compound who had been kidnapped at some point, too. The thought was chilling.

He mulled over other aspects of the conversation with the sheriff. One of the women in the compound appeared to be Navajo. She had been given to a cult member as his third wife several years ago and had borne four children. So far, the woman hadn't revealed how she came to be at the ranch, but Abe suspected she had been so indoctrinated by the Prophet's propaganda that she no longer knew what was real. He recalled a term—Stockholm syndrome—when a victim becomes emotionally attached to his or her captors.

There had also been references made to a so-called hideout, the whereabouts of which no one knew—or wouldn't tell. There was a hell of a lot of unraveling to do, but Abe was ready to let the experts handle it. He was relieved but tired, and all he wanted was to see Emily and go home to his dog and bed.

As the sun disappeared behind the western mountains, and a waning moon rose in the east, Abe pulled into the driveway of the sheep-breeding ranch he managed. Before the truck came to a stop in front of his quarters, he was greeted by yips of joy. As soon as he opened the door to his truck, Patch jumped onto his lap and, squirming with joy, planted kisses all over his face. Abe sat there awhile, talking to and petting his dog, enjoying the moment. He looked up and smiled when Ellen and Danny appeared at the door of his house.

"Hi, Abe," said Danny. "I took good care of your sheep and Patch."

"Great, Danny. I knew you would, and I've got your pay right here."

Danny beamed with a broad grin.

"Glad you're back," Ellen said. "Any news?"

Abe limped from the truck, bone weary and bleary-eyed, but still smiling.

"We found Emily. She's safe now, at the University Hospital in Albuquerque."

"What fantastic news. I'm so relieved you found her. What happened?"

"Yay!" Danny interrupted. "Abe's a hero. He found Emily."

"No, not a hero. She fell and broke her leg while escaping from the ranch compound. There were lots of people looking for her and the two girls. Will, Hosteen, and I got lucky. But no one has found a trace of the girls yet."

"Oh, dear. Those poor babies," Ellen said.

"I have one more favor, Ellen—if it's not too much of an imposition. After I clean up, I want to drive to Albuquerque tonight, to be with Emily. Could you manage to stay around for a couple more days? I can pay you and Danny now for your time and help, and give you the rest when I get back."

"Don't even think about it, Abe. You can settle up with Danny later, and of course we would be glad to stay on."

Danny erupted with another loud "Yay!" and clapped his hands.

Ellen said, "But don't you think you should sleep at home tonight and get a good rest? By the looks of your face, you sure could use it. By the time you drive to Albuquerque, you can bet your boots the doctor will have sedated Emily and she'll be sound asleep. If you leave at six in the morning, you'll be there before ten."

Abe thought about it. What Ellen said made sense. What good could he do by arriving in the middle of the night? He could use a soak in the hot tub, a cold beer, and a good night's sleep. He nodded his head and grinned.

"You've got a point, Ellen. Think I'll follow your advice. Thanks."

"Well, we'll be heading home. I left some fried chicken and potato salad in the refrigerator. Danny will be here by seven in the morning if I can drag him away tonight. He loves it here with the animals so much, he never wants to leave."

After Ellen and Danny had left, Abe decided to call the hospital to check on Emily and leave word that he would be there in the morning.

226

When he got to the phone, he noticed the message light blinking and pushed the play button.

Mattie Simmons's strident voice drawled across the lines: "Mr. Freeman, I'm calling to inform you I will be arriving at the ranch in two weeks to check on my breeding stock and buy a new shipment of rugs. I plan on spending a week visiting the weavers and evaluating their work, and I am counting on you to be my driver. I am assuming my ranch is in top-notch condition, and you will oblige my request. Those Indians aren't real friendly to me and seem to expect more money than I am willing to pay. Very well, I will see you in one week."

"Shit," Abe muttered.

I don't need Simmons around, especially now, he thought. *Of course the Navajo people don't like her. She's ripping them off by not paying a fair price for those high-quality rugs. But, damn it, she's my boss. What would she do if she came back and found me missing and Danny Jorgenson taking care of the sheep? She'd fire me.* He let out a long sigh. *Nothing I can do to prevent her coming out here. She pays the bills.*

Abe called the hospital and left a message for Emily about his arrival time. The ward nurse reassured him Emily was comfortable and sleeping peacefully. He locked the door to the main house and walked to the barn to make sure everything was all right before heading for his quarters. Patch, still excited, followed closely on his heels.

It felt good to be home, especially knowing Emily was receiving proper care, and he felt even better when he opened the refrigerator expecting to find his last beer and saw a full six-pack of his favorite brand. Abe gave Ellen a silent thank-you, thinking how much he owed her, and filled a plate with chicken, potato salad, and sliced tomatoes even though he had eaten earlier. Settling back in his most comfortable chair, plate on his lap, he glanced appreciatively around the room. His place was far tidier than before—in fact, it was immaculate. Following a long, hot soak in the bathtub, he crawled between clean sheets and fell asleep minutes after his head hit the pillow. Patch curled up beside him and snored in unison with his master.

A persistent knock on the door brought them both to their feet—Patch barking and Abe grumbling. "Who in the hell could that be?" The alarm clock on the bedside table said eleven thirty-five. "I'm coming. I'm coming." He opened the door and squinted through half-closed eyes at the figure of Joe Hosteen.

"I spoke to Bertha Etcitty before she and Will left for Albuquerque. She said I'd find you here," Hosteen said.

"What are you doing in Bloomfield?" asked Abe. "I thought they were keeping you for observation?"

"I talked them into discharging me and caught a ride back with my mother. She's spending a couple days in Farmington, visiting her sister."

Abe stepped aside and held the door open. "Come on in. What's up?"

Hosteen sat on the couch and looked at Abe as he sat in the rocker. "Want to ride with me to Albuquerque tomorrow morning? I was ordered to take some time off. We can stop by and see Emily. I got a possible lead on the two men involved in the kidnapping. There's an apartment complex in Albuquerque I want to check out. Just thought since we're going in the same direction . . ."

"What's so special about this place?" Abe asked.

"I didn't give it any significance at the time and had forgotten about it until now. When Will and the sheriff were out in the hall, Betty told me her son had been sent to a place in Albuquerque as punishment for listening to rock music. She said one of the Prophet's bodyguards accompanied him, and he had to stay there for a week. Her boy said it was awful, and he was scared to death. The Crosstown Apartments, I'm pretty sure is what she called it. Maybe someone we're looking for is using it as a safe place to hide out for a while."

Abe considered the offer. "You want me to be your backup?"

"Not officially, but yeah. Hell, why not? As long as it doesn't get back to my boss. Do you want to nail these bastards or not? And I figure

228

you've got a personal interest in finding these assholes—not to mention a history of assisting a rogue cop."

Abe figured Emily must have told Hosteen about his involvement in tracking down the killer of Easy Jackson two years ago. He shrugged. "I don't know. I'm not good at this, and I don't like using a gun. As long as I don't have to shoot anyone, I'll consider it. But what am I supposed to be doing?"

Hosteen stretched his long legs, stood, and walked to the door. "Well, I'd want you to pack something, just for your protection, but I don't expect you to have to use it. Just be there as a lookout."

After another lengthy pause, Abe said, "Isn't there another cop who can help you?"

"I'm on leave, and no one but me knows the location of the apartment."

"Why don't you tell the authorities in Albuquerque, or the FBI?"

"Because they have a way of screwing things up. There'll be delays—paperwork, a warrant, wasted time, and the perps could get away before they did anything. Besides, this is my case."

"It wouldn't be because you want to make sergeant and are trying to look good?"

"That has nothing to do with it. Emily is my partner—those two girls are my people. It's personal. Are you coming or not?"

Abe gave Hosteen a long, hard look. He began to wonder if Hosteen's interest in Emily was more than professional. "Okay, I'll go with you."

"I'll be by at six," Hosteen said as he went out the door.

As soon as Hosteen left, Abe began to question his decision.

What the hell am I getting myself into now? I got involved in this amateur police work once before and nearly ended up dead. I swore I'd never do it again. Freeman, you're a damned idiot.

He returned to bed with troubling thoughts and misgivings, but fatigue got the best of him, and he fell into a deep sleep.

31

Tuesday, April 17, 1990

University Hospital

Albuquerque, New Mexico

As Hosteen's Chevy Silverado pickup sped southeast along Highway 44 toward Albuquerque, Abe stared out the window at another beautiful sunrise. Brilliant hues of orange and pink crowned the mesa tops as the sun spread its light across the eastern sky. Traveling along this highway evoked memories of when he had first arrived in New Mexico and was taken into custody by Emily as a suspect in a murder case.

Flashbacks of the FBI interrogation and the overnight lockup with drunks and petty criminals hounded him as they passed the Huerfano Substation. Bright sunlight glittered on the top of the sacred mountain called *Dzith-Na-O-Dith-Hle*, where, according to Navajo legend, Changing Woman gave birth to First Man and First Woman. As they cruised past the Nageezi Trading Post, he recalled the night he and Will had turned off there two years ago when they followed the road to

Chaco Canyon, before heading on to Bisbee, Arizona, in search of the Mexican Mafia gang leader Rico Corazón.

"Ever been to Albuquerque?" Hosteen asked, breaking the silence.

Abe continued gazing out the window, mesmerized by the surreal landscape of the Northwest Plateau. Grotesque mushroom-shaped rocks, or *hoodoos*, ranging in color from deep gray to shades of purple erupted through the khaki-colored desert floor. Spring had brought patches of green to the usually parched earth, and wildflowers lined the gullies and *arroyos* where recent rains had filled their banks.

"Not really. Only drove through there on the interstate once. What's it like?"

"Modern urban sprawl and old-time territorial New Mexico all jumbled together. There are some great places—interesting mix of cultures, good food, beautiful architecture. And there are some dangerous neighborhoods as well. We'll go to the University of New Mexico to see Emily, which is nice, but sections of nearby Central Avenue are the worst—prostitutes, pimps, drug dealers, runaways, you name it."

"What kind of neighborhood is this apartment in?"

"I looked up the address of the Crosstown, and I've gotta say, not one of the better ones."

As soon as they left Highway 44 and merged onto I-25 near Bernalillo, traffic became bumper-to-bumper and continued past the "Big-I" intersection and the low-profile city center. Abe couldn't help observing that many New Mexican drivers didn't bother to use turn signals or come to full stops at intersections. Nor did they follow the speed limit. They reached the grounds of the University of New Mexico Hospital in a little less than three hours.

When they entered Emily's room, it was nine thirty, and she was sitting up sipping a glass of water, her leg swathed in a brand-new cast, a drip attached to her wrist, rehydrating her body.

Henry Forbes, an FBI agent out of Albuquerque, sat in a straight-backed chair beside her bed. When Abe and Hosteen entered, he gave them a curt nod, closed his notebook, and stood. "Thanks for your time, Officer Etcitty. If you think of anything else, give our office a call. Hosteen, how's it hanging?" he said on the way out.

Hosteen ignored him and stood behind Abe, his arms crossed, his head tilted at an angle.

Emily had recently showered, and her gleaming black hair fanned out on the white pillowcase. A broad smile spread across her face when she saw Abe and Hosteen.

Abe matched her grin with one of his own and strode across the room. "Hi, sweetheart," he said, and kissed her on the lips. "You look like an angel. I should have brought flowers, but we were in a hurry to get here." He glanced at Hosteen, who still stood near the door shifting his weight from one foot to the other, looking somewhat uncomfortable.

Emily smiled at her partner. "Joe. Did you two come together, or is it just a coincidence you both showed up at the same time?"

"Abe came with me. After checking my head, the hospital decided I hadn't lost all my marbles yet and released me. My mother gave me a ride back to Farmington. I wrote my report, and the boss told me to take a couple of days off. I wanted to come back to see how you're doing, so I figured, 'Why don't Freeman and I ride together?' So how're you?"

"Pretty good. The tibia and fibula were broken, but X-rays showed the bones had been aligned correctly before someone applied the temporary cast, and they didn't have to reset it. I don't know how she, um, how—"

"Someone being Chipeta Longtooth?" said Hosteen.

Emily smiled and quickly changed the subject. "Sit down, both of you, and catch me up on the case. I'm sorry I ran from the cult when I did and caused so much trouble, but you found the girls, right?" She grasped Abe's hand and looked expectantly at his face.

Abe pulled up a chair alongside the bed, his grin fading. Before he could answer, she saw the answer in his cobalt-blue eyes and asked again, "Have the girls been found, Abe? Joe?"

"They're not at the ranch, Emily," said Hosteen. "They were nowhere on the premises, and neither was the son of a bitch who calls himself the Prophet. The Feds, state police, and all local law enforcement they can spare are looking for them."

Emily slumped back against the pillow, the smile gone.

"They'll find them, Em. There's no way Langley's going to get away," Abe said.

"And in the meantime, what's happening to Lina and Darcy? I should have done a better job protecting those girls. I have to get out of here." Emily pulled herself upright and reached for the nurse call button.

Abe held her arm. "Stop it, Em. Don't be crazy. What could you do now besides cause more harm to your leg? Think about it. There is an army of lawmen looking for those girls."

"Listen to the man, Emily," Hosteen said. "He's right. You need to sit this one out, partner. I'll keep you up to date, but a one-legged cop can't be much help."

Emily closed her eyes, defeat showing on her face. "Shit."

The door opened, and Will and Bertha entered the room. Bertha hurried to the other side of the bed.

"*Shich'é'é.* My daughter," Bertha said, patting Emily's cheek. "Just look at you, my beautiful girl." She turned and acknowledged Abe and Hosteen with a nod. "I heard what you were discussing. I'll tell all of you this: when Emily leaves this hospital, she will go home with her mother. And there will be no argument," she added, looking sternly at Emily. "We need to have a long family talk."

Abe took the hint. "I think I'll find the cafeteria and get some coffee," he said. "I'll be back later, sweetheart." He squeezed Will's shoulder on his way to the door.

"I'll join you," Hosteen said. "These folks need some time alone. Let your leg heal, Emily, so you can stop loafing and get back to work. Will, Mrs. Etcitty, take care of our girl."

Jealousy rose like green bile in Abe's throat. Once they were in the hallway, he gave Hosteen a scornful look. "What's this 'our girl' shit? Maybe your interest in Emily isn't purely professional. Are you trying to make a move on my girlfriend?"

"Cool it, Freeman. It's a figure of speech. You don't have anything to worry about—except for the fact you're not Navajo."

His words stopped Abe in his tracks. He grabbed Hosteen by the shoulder and swung him around. The two men stood glowering at each other. "When we're done, you and I need to get something settled."

Hosteen was a good three inches taller than Abe and outweighed him by thirty pounds.

"Right . . . ," he said, pushing Abe away. "Fuck that for now. I've got work to do. You can stay here and figure out a way home, or come along. What's it going to be, Freeman?"

"I'd do anything to help Emily. Let's go."

"Coffee and breakfast first. If anyone is at this hideout, they'll stay put a little longer."

Abe swallowed his anger, for the time being at least, and grabbed a burrito to go with a Styrofoam cup of black hospital coffee. "Ready?"

When Abe and Hosteen left the cafeteria and turned the corner toward the elevator, Will caught up with them. "You two have something up your sleeve. I want in on it."

"What about Emily?" Abe said.

"Mom's staying with her. The doc told me she can be dismissed tomorrow if her vitals are good. It was a clean break, so there should be no complications. Keeping her from being too active will be the hard part. Knowing my sis, she'll want to jump right back into work. So what's up? Why'd you two leave in such a hurry?"

"I got a tip about a place here in Albuquerque where the two fugitives might be hiding. I'm supposed to be off duty, but I want to follow up on it."

"And Abe?" Will said.

"I'm coming along for backup, in case Hosteen needs help," Abe said.

"I'm going with you," Will said. "I'll tell Mom I'm riding back with you two after we take care of some business."

Will returned a couple of minutes later. He grinned. "Mom and Emily gave me 'the look' but didn't ask questions. So, where is this hideout?"

Hosteen walked toward the hospital exit, Will and Abe following closely on his heels. "On a side street between Wyoming and Eubank. A tough neighborhood with a lot of gang activity, slumlords, boarded-up businesses. I can't figure out why Langley would want a place in such a rough neighborhood."

"Maybe he wanted to impress on the kid how terrible the rest of the world was. If he didn't straighten up, that's where he'd end up. The kid probably didn't know any other life than that compound," Abe said. He opted for the small backseat of Hosteen's Silverado, granting Will the extra legroom in front. Hosteen took a handgun out of his glove compartment and handed it to Abe. Then he retrieved a shoulder holster containing his Glock from under the seat and put it on.

"You'll have to be unarmed, Will—unless Abe wants to give you his weapon."

Although he disliked the gun, Abe would rather carry it than give it up and look like a wuss. He checked out the Beretta 92G, found the safety, opened the chamber, and saw that, except for the firing chamber, it was loaded. He made sure the safety was on and stared straight ahead, adrenaline pumping through his veins like an oil gusher.

Albuquerque was a big city with a small-town attitude. Adobe structures contrasted with modern shopping malls. The old blended with the new, the run-down with the upscale. Abe was no stranger to big cities and traffic, having come out West from Atlantic City, but this place had a different feel. The quaint "Duke City" boiled with vitality and unbridled testosterone.

They turned onto Central Avenue, where groups of young men wearing hairnets or do-rags eyed them with menacing looks. They didn't have far to go before they found the single-story apartment complex with scantily clad girls and homeless men standing out front. The name on the billboard, with two letters missing, read THE CRO ST WN. A quicky-loan building bordered one side of the cheap pink building, and there was a pawnshop on the other. Panhandlers squatted in front of a fast-food joint across the street.

"You sure this is the place?" said Abe. "It's a skid-row dump."

"But it's cheap and off anyone's radar," said Hosteen. "Who'd ever think of looking for fugitive religious cult members here?"

"You got an apartment number?" said Will.

"Not yet, but I've got mug shots of those two dickheads. I'll find the manager and see if he recognizes them."

A sign in a window near the front read REASONABLE RATES: MONTHLY, WEEKLY, DAILY, OR HOURLY.

"Wait for me here, and keep an eye out for anyone coming or going," Hosteen said as he lumbered toward the office.

32

Tuesday, April 17

Crosstown Apartments

Albuquerque, New Mexico

The manager, unshaven and exposing a slice of bare belly where the bottom of his dirty T-shirt fell shy of the top of his pants, stood in the office door pointing toward a unit near the back.

"Number eleven," Hosteen said when he returned to the truck. "It's a studio apartment with a kitchenette and front and back exit. The guy wasn't going to tell me anything, so I flashed my badge and threatened to call the vice squad and have him arrested for pimping a whorehouse. When I showed him the mug shots of the suspects, he verified it's Harris and Mackey, though they used false names and driver's licenses. The manager said they checked in last Saturday. They must have made a run for it when they found out Emily escaped."

Will stared at the apartment, his eyes as hard and cold as ball bearings. "Are they in there now?"

"Came in late last night with two women, and the manager hasn't seen anyone leave."

Abe felt his adrenaline kick in, his heart pounding in his chest. "What are we waiting for? The girls could be in there with those men."

"There's no hurry now," said Hosteen. "Here's what I want. Abe, go around to the back. Keep the door covered, in case they make a run for it. If they do, have your weapon ready, but don't shoot unless you're threatened. I don't know if they're armed, but my guess is probably. Will, come with me to the front, but stay off to the side until we know what we're dealing with. Abe, I'll give you time to get around there before I rush the front."

The two men nodded. Abe pulled the Beretta out of his pocket and scooted to the back of the building. Once there, he found himself in an alley full of dumpsters, weeds, and garbage. Five separate doors faced the alley.

Shit, which one is number eleven? he wondered before recalling it sat dead center in the back line of apartments.

He crept up to the middle door and pressed his back against it, took a deep breath, and waited for the ruckus.

A few minutes later, a loud banging came from the other side of the room, and Hosteen's muted shout, "Open up. Police."

He heard the sound of scrambling bodies, the crashing of furniture, a woman's scream, and the slam of the front door as it was forced open and banged against the wall. A gunshot rang out, more shouts, a scuffle. Abe thought, *The hell with this gun!*

He jammed the Beretta in his pants at the small of his back. He had taken up boxing as a teenager to defend himself against bullies in his neighborhood and had won a couple of lightweight Golden Gloves titles. What mattered was speed, catching your opponent off guard, and the element of surprise. Abe waited for the door to open, not sure who would be behind it. He placed himself against the side of the wall so he would be hidden when it opened.

The moonfaced, balding Midwesterner stuck his head out and scanned the alley. He looked slack-jawed and hungover. A revolver dangled from his right hand. As soon as he stepped out, Abe shoved on the door, slamming it into the left side of Mackey's head. An upper-cut caught the stunned fugitive squarely under the chin, and a quick one-two punch to the solar plexus finished him off. Mackey, soft as a marshmallow, dropped his weapon and collapsed in a heap. Abe picked up the abandoned gun and pointed it at him.

"Get to your feet, asshole, and put both hands behind your head."

"I'm hurt," Mackey whined, holding his chin. "You broke my jaw."

"Shut up," said Abe. "Hosteen? Will?" he shouted. "What's happening? Are the girls in there?"

"It's under control," Will answered. "No sign of the girls here. There were a couple of prostitutes in the room, though. You okay?"

"Yeah, I'm bringing Mackey in. Where's Hosteen?"

"Right here beside me. Harris threw a lamp at him when Joe busted through the door, and his gun went off. The women grabbed their clothes and ran outside half-naked. I'm sitting on this skinny little shit until Hosteen's ready to cuff him."

"Get in there," Abe said to Mackey, prodding him with the gun this time. "Hey, Joe. I've got another present for you." Mackey, his hands behind his head, stumbled into the room.

Hosteen had a sheepish grin on his face. He dabbed a handkerchief at a small stream of blood trickling from a goose egg–size bump on his forehead. "Second time in two days I've had my head in the wrong place. Must be losing my touch."

Satisfied there wasn't much blood, he pulled a pair of PlastiCuffs from a pocket and fastened them to each of the perps' wrists.

Mackey let out a yelp. "He tried to kill me. Watch it."

"You're not even bleeding, you pussy," said Hosteen.

"Can you make an arrest here in Albuquerque, Joe? Aren't you out of your jurisdiction? Maybe we need to call the locals."

"That's right," said Harris. "You got no right to do this. You broke into our place."

Hosteen smirked. "There's a couple of exceptions to the rule of territorial jurisdiction. One is when in 'fresh pursuit' of a suspect who committed a crime within their territory, and the other is a 'citizen's arrest.' Since one of you assholes assaulted an officer, and the other pulled a gun on a citizen, an arrest is warranted. I could add that a felony was committed in my jurisdiction, and I am pursuing your sorry asses. I'll make a phone call to my boss just to be sure this arrest sticks—after I read you your rights."

When Hosteen finished reading the fugitives the Miranda Warning, Will jerked Harris to his feet and shook him like a dirty rag. "I know this cop said you have the right to remain silent, but just between you and me, I want to know what happened to those two young Navajo girls you kidnapped."

"I don't know anything about no Navajo girls," Harris stammered.

Mackey kept his head down, sniveling between whimpers and rotating his jaw back and forth.

"Where are we dumping these two sacks of shit, Joe?" said Will.

"We're tossing them in the back of my camper and taking them all the way to Crownpoint—giving them to the Navajo Nation. I'm not dealing with the locals or the FBI. I'll bet they'll start talking once they're locked up with a few Diné."

"I'll ride in the back with them." Will pulled a sharp skinning knife from a sheath attached to his belt. "Did you ever see a Navajo dress a sheep out?" he asked, smiling at Harris and Mackey. "A skilled herder can take the entire hide off a sheep in less than five minutes. Did I mention *I* raise sheep?" Will tested the blade's sharpness on the tip of his thumb and chuckled.

The accused kidnappers paled.

"Hey, no. You can't do this. We've got rights," Harris said.

Abe stifled a grin. He knew Will was bluffing, but those two didn't. "Sounds like a decent plan. Let's load them up."

Hosteen shoved the two men into the camper. "Stay with them, Will. Make sure they don't make too much noise. Abe and I are going to search the room, and I need to check out the manager's records. Try not to rough them up too much. Well, not so it's noticeable. I don't want blood inside my truck."

Still brandishing his knife, Will smiled and crawled into the camper.

Abe and Hosteen reentered the room and rummaged through the drawers and wastebaskets. It appeared the two men had left in a hurry and not brought much with them. Hosteen confiscated two wallets with fake drivers' licenses and credit cards, plus a set of car keys. Abe combed through a trash container overflowing with the detritus of derelicts—crumpled fast-food wrappers, beer cans, cigarette butts, used condoms. Not the sort of things you would expect from religious fanatics. But there were no receipts or other incriminating papers. He pulled gray sheets off the sagging beds and lifted the mattresses, wrinkling his nose at the acrid smell. "Doesn't anyone ever clean these dumps?" he said. Soiled clothing and towels lay in a heap on the floor. Abe kicked the pile until it scattered. "Guess that whining piece of shit will have to keep wearing his wet pants," he said. "Nothing decent here."

Hosteen finished checking the bathroom. "Let's have a talk with the manager. See how the rent gets paid."

Back in the office, Hosteen tapped on a bell until the manager waddled back in. "Whadda ya want now?"

"I want to know who pays the rent for apartment eleven," said Hosteen.

"I don't know. Bill's paid in advance. Some guy sends a check to cover the year. Different people show up with the key. Whadda I care, long as I get my money?" He scowled at Hosteen. "You didn't shoot the room up, did you?"

"Nah," said Abe. "It's in as good a shape as it was when we got here."

Hosteen got in the manager's face. "Go through your files. Find a name, a canceled check, or some proof of payment."

"I don't have time for this shit," the manager grumbled. "I got work to do."

"You'll have nothing *but* time, in a jail cell, if you don't cooperate with us," said Hosteen.

The man huffed and walked to a metal filing cabinet. He pulled open a drawer and began rummaging through a stack of files. After several minutes, he retrieved a manila folder and opened it. "Here it is. Some guy calls himself Rupert Langley."

"I need to borrow this file," said Hosteen, taking it from the man's hands.

"Hey!" the manager yelled. "Whadda ya think you're doing? Them's my business records."

"This is evidence in a criminal investigation. Thanks for your help," said Hosteen. "I'll let you know when you can have them back."

"Fucking cops," said the man as Abe and Hosteen turned to leave.

Will waited outside the open door of Hosteen's camper. "Good, you're back. I didn't want to spend any more time than necessary with those stinking assholes. Anyway, I got what I wanted, and they don't have a mark on them. Still crying for their mamas, though."

Abe perked up. "What do you mean, Will? You got some information about the girls?"

Hosteen joined the two. "What's up?"

"I think I know where Langley might be hiding out. He has another ranch. Same kind of cult thing going on there, too. Only he goes by a different name."

Hosteen, his eyebrows lifted, put his hands on his hips. "Tell me about it, Will."

"Ever been to South Dakota? I understand they've got a lot of Native Americans up there, Ojibwe and Sioux. And a pervert who likes little girls—this time calls himself Jason Blakely, but to his followers, he's known as 'the Prophet.'"

Hosteen let his mouth hang open while he digested this information. He shook his head in disbelief. "I don't even want to know how you persuaded them to fess up, but we're going to check it out. I need to make a couple of calls before we take these dirtbags back to the reservation and book them on kidnapping charges." He smiled broadly, a rarity for Hosteen. It showed his brilliant-white teeth. "Did you happen to catch the name of that ranch?"

"Get this, and try not to puke—'Heaven's Gate: A Rest Stop for Disadvantaged Girls.' It took all my willpower to keep from pigsticking those two slimeballs. They've been helping Langley-Blakely commandeer young girls for a long time. I think they're hired guns without a lick of religious leanings."

"Shit." Abe shook his head. "Where in South Dakota are you talking about?"

"My sources tell me it's about forty miles north of a nowhere place called Faith."

"The irony never stops, does it?" Abe said. "Faith—hard to believe. What's the next move, Joe?"

Hosteen scribbled the information in his notebook. "We only have one move left, partner, and you can't take part in this one. I'm going to contact Sheriff Turnbull in Montezuma County. He's in charge of the investigation, and he's earned the right to be in on the takedown. The Feds will have to be involved—they'll most likely secure an arrest warrant for Langley and raid the ranch. They could use Emily up there to make a positive ID of the perp. After they're done, Turnbull can have them extradited to Colorado. With the captain's permission, I'll book a flight to South Dakota and bring those little girls home. Will, you sure as hell came through. Even if I can't report it the way it happened, I have to give you and Abe a hell of a lot of credit for your help. Damn, I need to find a telephone ASAP."

Will chuckled. "Can't divulge how I got them to talk. Shaman's secret."

While Hosteen returned to the Crosstown office to make his calls, Will and Abe checked on the two prisoners under the camper shell. When Abe lifted the door, he saw both men cowering in the far corners. Will had found a coil of rope and tied their hands to D rings on the inside of the camper so they couldn't move around.

"Don't let that Indian near me. He's crazy!" Harris shrieked.

Mackey began to whimper once again. "Stay away from me. I already told you what I know."

"See what cowardly bastards they are when they're not dealing with helpless, drugged little girls?" Will said, slamming the door of the camper shell shut. "These white scum disgust me."

Abe leaned against the back of the truck, thumbs in his pockets. "You sure as hell put the fear of a crazy redskin in them, Will."

Will grinned. "I always thought you were kind of soft, but you didn't even use a gun to stop Mackey. Nice going."

"Huh." Even though he had nothing but contempt for Mackey and Harris, inflicting pain on another living being still left Abe feeling uneasy. He ran a hand through his hair before speaking. "You know what I think, Will?"

Will cocked an eyebrow and looked at Abe. "What's up, buddy?"

"If those two girls are in South Dakota, you and Emily should go up there with Hosteen and bring them home. Joe's right, the Feds need her on that trip to make a positive identification once they find Langley. Emily said the hospital would discharge her tomorrow, and she can use a wheelchair or crutches, as long as she isn't on her feet too long."

"Hmm," Will said, slowly nodding. "I know they'd feel a lot more comfortable if a woman they knew was with them, but why me?"

"Because those young girls are going to be traumatized and in need of a lot of support, and you are a spiritual leader, someone they look up to and feel safe with." He glanced up to see Hosteen emerging from the manager's office. "Let's get Hosteen to make a quick stop at the hospital so we can give Emily the news."

33

Thursday, April 19, 1990

En route to Faith, South Dakota

The plane touched down at the Pierre, South Dakota, airport and rolled to a stop. From there it would be a two-hour drive to the small rural town of Faith, where Rupert Langley allegedly maintained a private ranch. Emily felt tired but emotionally pumped. This time Langley would not get away, and she would be there to help nail his ass. She sighed and closed her eyes, calming herself, silently mouthing the words of the Beauty Way Prayer:

> Today I will walk out, today everything evil will
>   leave me,
> I will be as I was before, I will have a cool breeze
>   over my body.
> I will have a light body, I will be happy forever,
>   nothing will hinder me.
> I walk with beauty before me. I walk with beauty
>   behind me.

I walk with beauty below me. I walk with beauty
    above me.
I walk with beauty around me. My words will be
    beautiful.

The biggest thing in the flat prairie town of Faith was a life-size metal sculpture of Sue, the most complete *Tyrannosaurus rex* skeleton ever found, which was discovered only fifteen miles outside of town. Emily stretched her injured leg on the backseat of the rented jeep while Hosteen cruised the main street. Will swiveled his head to get a better look at Sue as they drove past. He had said little on the long trip from Albuquerque.

"What are you thinking about, Will?" Emily asked.

"That's one hell of a big lizard. I'd like to see the site where they found her—take a look at the rock type and depositional environment," he said, the trained geologist in him coming out. "Someday, when all this is over."

When a convenience store/gas station appeared on the right, Hosteen pulled in. They needed directions to the fishing camp on Durkee Lake where they would meet with Sheriff Turnbull and the FBI agent assigned to the Colorado crime scene. The two men had arrived in Faith the day before to set up plans for the raid on Langley's "Heaven's Gate."

Hosteen returned with directions to Durkee Lake and a temporary South Dakota fishing license. "I didn't want to arouse suspicions," he said. They had been forewarned not to be seen in uniform until the actual raid so that no one in town could alert Langley. A mile out of town, they checked into a motel, The Broken Arrow, a single strand of eight rooms plunked down in the prairie. After unloading their bags and freshening up, they continued on to the fish camp. The short trip took them down a dirt road and through a wooded area that ended at a lake bordered by a small cluster of buildings.

"Here we are," Hosteen said as he stopped the jeep near the front of a bait-and-tackle shop. Four unmarked, midnight-blue Chevrolet Suburbans were parked near a campground close to the lake's shore. Hosteen stepped out of the jeep and stretched while Will unloaded the rented wheelchair.

"I don't need a wheelchair," Emily said. "I'll use the crutches."

Will flashed her a big-brother look. "Don't argue with me, sis. Yes, you do. I promised Mom I wouldn't let you overdo it. Now sit in this chair and be quiet."

Hosteen went inside the bait shop and returned a few minutes later with a plastic container of red wrigglers.

"What are you going to do with those?" Emily said.

"Set them free. I told you I want to appear authentic, so I asked a few questions about the best spot to catch the big ones, and so on. You know, just shooting the bull."

Emily and Will chuckled.

"Let's meet the team," Hosteen said. "They're expecting us for the briefing."

Six men and two women sat at two picnic tables pulled together. All heads turned at the sound of Will wheeling Emily down the gravel path. At the far end of the table, Sheriff Turnbull stood and welcomed them.

"Glad to see you made it," said Turnbull. Addressing the group, he added, "This is the rest of our team: Navajo Police officers Joe Hosteen and Emily Etcitty. Emily, as I told you earlier, was kidnapped and held hostage along with the girls. She broke her leg when she escaped from the cult compound in Colorado. Her brother, Will, is a Navajo shaman. He's here to accompany Emily and to provide spiritual guidance and comfort to the girls after we rescue them. He's a good man—not law enforcement, but he was part of my posse, and he, along with another feller, found Emily. He can be trusted. Feel free to discuss anything in front of him."

The FBI agents, dressed in cargo pants and long-sleeve black T-shirts, mumbled greetings.

Emily rolled the wheelchair up to the table and studied their faces. "Henry," she said, nodding her head in recognition of New Mexico agent Henry Forbes. The lead Colorado agent sat at the far end, near a cluster of Styrofoam cups, soda cans, and used paper plates. The smell of burned coffee rose from an old-fashioned percolator sitting on the grill.

Hosteen slid into a folding lounge chair beside Emily. Will remained standing and leaned against a tree, his arms folded across his chest. He gazed impassively at the group of lawmen.

"How is this going down?" asked Emily.

"We've got a federal arrest warrant for Rupert Langley, alias Jason Blakely," said Agent Forbes. "Based on the information gained by Officer Hosteen and investigations by South Dakota State Police into the affairs at the cult ranch, we believe we have probable cause. Also, we have the warrant to search the premises for the missing Navajo girls and any evidence indicating illegal activities at the ranch—including the financial records and personal property of all cult members. We'll conduct a full-scale raid at five a.m. tomorrow, to catch Langley when he's least expecting it."

Emily smiled. "Sweet. What about backup?"

Sheriff Turnbull turned his attention to Emily. "Faith can spare a couple of men, and local law enforcement from neighboring towns will provide some help. Pierre is sending in a helicopter and SWAT team. Langley won't get away this time, guaranteed."

"Do you have any reason to expect armed resistance?" Emily asked.

"You never know," said Turnbull. "I understand one of the kidnappers was carrying a weapon when Hosteen arrested him in Albuquerque. It's best to be prepared."

Hosteen flashed a quick look at Will, whose face remained unreadable. "Right, Sheriff. I believe he would have used it if I hadn't caught him off guard."

The South Dakota lead FBI agent, Bill McCallister, cleared his throat. "I guess I don't need to familiarize the new arrivals with the nuts and bolts of this case, and I assume the rest of you have read the summaries handed out. Our local FBI will bring their evidence team, so the primary role of the sheriff and other law-enforcement officers will be to conduct a search for Langley and the Navajo girls—which will involve more than thirty officers. Based on the information supplied by Sheriff Turnbull, all women and children will be bused to a community shelter for age determination and DNA testing. We'll hold the men at another facility until we complete the investigation, and they can be tested to determine paternity. I don't want word of this to get around town, so be discreet. Again, we strike in the morning, at five a.m., and speed is of the essence. Any questions?"

"Sir?" Emily said. "How far away is this ranch, and what information do you have concerning the number of residents?"

"Our sources tell us there are approximately one hundred men, women, and children. An accurate number is hard to ascertain because the group is extremely reclusive. The location is near the Cheyenne River Reservation, ten miles out on Highway 73, and about five miles from the discovery site of Sue. Paleontologists found the *T. rex* on Indian land, so there's still some hard feelings about Faith's claim to being the home of her discovery and the tribe being robbed. They aren't too friendly with anyone trespassing on their land." He stood, looking at the assembled group. "Unless you have questions or plan on fishing, get out of here, get some rest, and meet back here at four thirty tomorrow morning. There are two motels in town, and campsites here on the lake—take your pick."

Back in the jeep, Will spoke up. "I want to take a ride out of town before we check in to the motel. Maybe we can scope out the ranch—this so-called Heaven's Gate."

"All right," said Hosteen. "As long as we don't look conspicuous. Emily, you up for this?"

"You bet, but I could use a bite to eat and some good coffee first. We can get directions to the site afterward." It had been a long time since the bean burrito she'd grabbed before boarding the plane in Albuquerque.

When they were on the outskirts of Faith, Will pointed to a fast-food place called Lulu's Drive-In.

Hosteen pulled into a slot in the half-full parking lot and went inside to find a menu.

"They've got burgers, fries, corn dogs, chicken dinner, cheese balls. What the hell are cheese balls?" he asked when he returned to the jeep.

"Don't know," said Emily. "But I'll pass. I could handle some chicken."

Will nodded in agreement.

"Chicken dinners all around," said Hosteen. "Sit tight. I'll order."

"I'll help you," said Will as he followed Hosteen into the café.

Emily rolled down the window and gazed across the prairie at the Black Hills lining the western horizon. Faith sat in the middle of nowhere, but she felt at home in the vast remoteness of the landscape. It reminded her of Navajo country.

A battered Ford truck with three occupants—two women and a man—pulled to a stop beside the jeep. Country music blasted from the pickup's speakers. The man, barrel-chested, brown-skinned, with high cheekbones and straight black hair tied in a ponytail, went inside the café while the women waited in the truck.

Lakota, Emily thought. She decided to strike up a conversation to see if she could learn anything useful.

"Hi," she said through the open window. "I wonder if you could help me. I think we're lost."

The two women twisted their heads around to peer at Emily.

"Where're you from?" a round-faced woman said. "You're sure not from around here."

"Nope," said Emily. "Navajo, from New Mexico."

251

The Lakota women chuckled and turned down the volume on the radio. "You're a long ways from home—no wonder you're lost," the younger of the two said.

"I'm here with my brother and a friend. We're just traveling through, doing a little sightseeing, and heard about the *T. rex* skeleton discovered somewhere around here. Sue, they call it. You know where the site is?"

"Humph," said the older woman, her mouth turning down. "Private land. Big 'No Trespassing' sign. Besides, they took it all away; nothing left. They shouldn't have dug up those bones. Messed with the spirits."

"Yeah," Emily said. "My brother, Will, is a geologist and wanted to analyze the soil. What's your tribe?"

"Cheyenne River Lakota," the younger woman said. "We live on the rez. The exact spot where they found the bones is on the reservation, too, but a private rancher owns it. The Lakota got ripped off."

Not the first time, Emily thought.

"Damn, that's not right. But isn't that the way it works in the white man's world? Hey, I heard a white man bought a big chunk of land near here, and he's set up some kind of weird religious community."

The younger woman sneered. "You must be talking about the crazy ranch out on Dunston Road near the rez. They built a big wooden fence all the way around so no one can see inside, but they make plenty of noise."

"Trucks going in there day and night," said the other woman. "One time I saw some of the people in town—the women dressed in funny clothes, long dresses, real old-fashioned. But most of the time they stay behind the tall fence. What do you want to know about them for?"

Emily thought about telling them she was a Navajo Police officer and was here to investigate the cult, but remembered the need for discretion. Will and Hosteen came out of the restaurant carrying three Styrofoam boxes and a paper sack. She smiled at the two Lakota women. "Thanks for your help. We better get going. Have a great day."

"Yeah. You, too. Try not to get lost, Navajo," said the one Emily figured must be the mother. The woman laughed as if she had just told a joke.

Will tipped his scruffy hat to the ladies, and Hosteen nodded. When the Lakota man returned with his order, the women rolled their windows up.

"What was that about?" said Will, handing one of the Styrofoam boxes to Emily.

"I found out where the ranch is," Emily said. She opened the lid of her box and peeked at a plate piled with fried chicken, mashed potatoes with gravy, and a biscuit. "Keep the lids on the coffee. Sue's site is on private land, but Langley's ranch is not far. Let's find Dunston Road and have a little picnic out there."

A short cruise down Highway 73 West brought them to the sign drilled with bullet holes that once read "Dunston." They traveled five more miles past scattered clapboard farmhouses that had seen better days before the pavement turned to gravel. Fenced fields of hay and prairie grass with grazing beef cattle became more dominant as the houses thinned out. When the jeep reached the top of a bluff, Hosteen swerved to the shoulder and turned off the ignition. An eight-foot plank fence broken only by a tall steel gate announced their proximity to "Heaven's Gate."

The Black Hills, outlined in silver by the setting sun, went unappreciated as Emily stared at the compound gate. She grasped the Styrofoam coffee cup with trembling hands and took a small sip before the bile rose in her throat. Her appetite was gone, replaced by a flashback of the leering face of the Prophet as he examined the young girls in the compound.

34

Thursday, April 19

Mattie Simmons's Sheep Ranch

Bloomfield, New Mexico

Sitting on the front stoop with Patch curled at his side, Abe sipped his coffee and contemplated the recent developments in the kidnapping case. Emily was in South Dakota with Will and Hosteen, intent on arresting Rupert Langley and bringing the girls home. Abe worried about the girls, especially Lina, but also about Emily. He hoped everything would proceed quickly and safely. Emily had assured him she would stay in the background. Just the same, she planned to wear her uniform and carry her Glock when they conducted the raid on the compound.

The kidnappers, Harris and Mackey, were incarcerated at the Navajo Nation Corrections Department, and with Emily as the star witness, Mackey and Harris wouldn't have a chance.

And he had worked things out with Hosteen. After the lawman had delivered his prisoners to police headquarters, Abe and Hosteen had that talk. Abe felt like a fool for his ridiculous outburst of jealousy. He was satisfied the Navajo officer did not have any romantic interest in Emily. Hosteen told him about his fiancée, who was finishing her master's degree in education at Kansas State, and how they planned to marry when she returned.

Abe shook his head with disgust and thought, *I know I'm a moody son of a bitch sometimes, prone to jumping to conclusions. I wonder why Emily puts up with me.*

Shaking off his self-deprecating thoughts, Abe picked up the newspaper from the coffee table and reread the ad. The latest edition of the *Farmington Daily Times* lay open to the help-wanted page, a single item circled in pen: "San Juan College seeking instructor in piano and voice." It had him thinking. He knew three things for sure. He was in love with Emily, he missed playing the piano, and he wasn't cut out to be a sheep rancher. Abe had decided to set up an appointment with the head of the music department.

He emptied his cup and went out to the barn to begin his chores, then shook his head in amazement at what he saw. Danny Ferguson had done a kick-ass job of taking care of the sheep in Abe's absence—better than he would have done. The barn and stalls were cleaned, and fresh hay was scattered in the pens. The animals appeared calm and well maintained under Danny's supervision. The kid had even assisted in the delivery of two new lambs and repaired some sagging fence.

"Shoot, Danny would have done this for nothing. Working with animals has been good for him. It's the happiest he's been since the accident," Ellen had said.

Later that evening, Abe thought about the upcoming meeting with the owner of the ranch. Mattie Simmons would arrive in about ten days, and the small kernel of an idea began to form in his mind. He would need some help from Emily, and a little time. She had promised to call at eight, and it was seven thirty now. He hurried over to the main house so he wouldn't miss her.

He was playing the piano when the telephone rang. Abe grabbed it and smiled when he heard her voice.

"Hey, sweetheart. How was your trip?"

"Long, Abe. I didn't think we'd ever get here. Faith is tiny—smaller than Bloomfield. All the law-enforcement officers are hanging out at different places outside of town so no one from the ranch gets wind of what we're up to. We raid the place in the morning, at five."

Abe picked up on the tension in her voice. "What is it, Em? What are you worried about?"

"We found out where the compound was and drove out there this afternoon. When I saw the fence and gate, I got chills and the shakes. It brought me back to that place they kept me, and I thought about the girls and all of their suffering."

He wondered if Emily had been told about Lina's diabetes. "You shouldn't have had to put yourself through this again. In a couple of days, this will all be over, and you can put it behind you—we can get on with our lives." He hoped this was true. "Are you feeling better now?"

"Yeah. I recovered, but it'll be different for those kids. After we find them, they'll need counseling for a long time. How about you, Abe? How's Patch and the sheep?"

"It's all good here. Patch and the animals are doing fine, but I miss you. Be careful, and call me as soon as you can."

"I will, Abe. Love you."

"I love you, too. Where are you staying, Em? In case I need to get in touch?"

"Broken Arrow Motel, room number seven."

After she hung up the phone, Emily checked the time. A little past nine in Faith, South Dakota, an hour ahead of Abe. She desperately needed sleep, but edginess about tomorrow's raid kept her wide-eyed. The faint sound of television came from the adjoining room, shared by Will and Hosteen. Emily couldn't concentrate on TV. She put on a jacket, picked up her crutches, and stepped outside into the chilly night air. A cold wind blew down from the north. Emily shivered and pulled her jacket tighter.

How am I going to react if I come face-to-face with the bastard? She shuddered. *I'd like to shoot him. But if we don't find him—if the girls aren't there—what will we do?*

Emily knew she shouldn't think about that. She had to put her mind on something else. All the thinking wasn't helping her sleep. She sighed and went back inside to get ready for bed. The four thirty meeting would mean getting up at three.

35

Friday, April 20, 1990

Heaven's Gate Ranch

Faith, South Dakota

The blaring of the radio alarm interrupted a dream Emily didn't want to end. Abe had been slowly undressing her, kissing his way down her body. She fumbled with the radio, willing it to stop, trying to find the off button. Then she sat up and turned on the bedside lamp. Three o'clock—only two in New Mexico where Abe, no doubt, slumbered peacefully. Having finally located the switch, Emily shook off the remnants of her dream and pulled herself out of bed. She had been waiting for this day—the chance to find the two Navajo girls and arrest the pedophile who called himself a prophet. She took an awkward shower, cursing while balancing herself on one leg and trying not to get her cast wet. Her mother had opened the seam in the right leg of her uniform pants so she could pull them over her cast, but dressing still took extra effort. Emily combed and fastened her hair into a tight bun, squared her campaign hat, and frowned at her reflection in the mirror.

She made her way to the motel office, where Will and Hosteen sipped Styrofoam cups of burned-smelling coffee. Will offered to get her some, but after one whiff, she declined.

Outside, the Milky Way split a trail through the black sky. It might as well have been midnight, as dark as it was. Hosteen drove to the fishing camp. Other officers had arrived before them. He parked beside a cruiser marked with the emblem of the Meade County Sheriff's Department.

Emily rubbed her arms and shivered. Winter had not released its grip on South Dakota. She zipped her coat up to her neck but refused the wheelchair and grabbed the crutches. Men and women dressed in a variety of uniforms and leather jackets sat at the long table, on benches or folding chairs. Boxes of store-bought doughnuts and take-out coffee were scattered on the table. Some, who couldn't find a seat, leaned against trees or squatted on the ground. All wore somber faces. A deputy sheriff offered Emily his seat; Will and Hosteen opted for a log.

Bill McCallister, the lead South Dakota FBI agent, stood and began to address the assemblage.

"You all know why you're here. There's an evil son of a bitch out there who glorifies himself by seducing and having sex with young girls. And there are two young Navajo girls, recently kidnapped from a traditional ceremony marking the beginning of their womanhood." McCallister paused here, looking uncomfortable, and took a breath. "A pair of dirtbags, under the orders of a pedophile who calls himself 'the Prophet,' took these girls—and who knows how many others—to serve as his wives and bear his children. I don't want to leave here until we get the son of a bitch. Your job is to help me find those young ladies and anyone else who is a victim of this sick bastard so we can return them to their respective homes. The FBI has been aware of Heaven's Gate Ranch for some time, but we've had no substantial reason to conduct a raid until now. Thanks to the testimony of Navajo Nation Police officer Emily Etcitty and information garnered by Navajo officer Joe

Hosteen, we now have substantial evidence the aforementioned is hiding out here—plenty of information to justify a raid on the compound. You know the procedure when serving a warrant. Report any interesting find to the FBI evidence team; don't try to collect it yourself. Agent Carillo is the man in charge of forensics. Remember, as soon as you locate the girls, radio the medics immediately so we can get Lina Nez to a hospital."

The agent called Carillo, swarthy with a narrow face, raised his hand and gave a partial salute to the group.

"The SWAT team will lead the way, followed by federal agents and me. Once inside, I'll issue further instructions on how to proceed. All right, if there're no questions, let's roll."

Emily gave Will a questioning look. "What was that about Lina?"

"She's a diabetic, Em."

Emily took a sharp intake of breath.

"Oh, shit, Will. Why didn't anyone tell me?"

Once the Feds presented their ID to the gate guard, they entered the ranch without resistance, and left a man at the guardhouse to prevent anyone from leaving. The buildings on the compound were similar to those in Colorado, but fewer in number and smaller in scale. Outdoor lights illuminated frame houses clustered around a center temple. Various buildings bore signs such as COMMUNITY MEETING HALL, FOOD STORAGE AND EXCHANGE, MAINTENANCE. A school with an assortment of playground equipment sat adjacent to the temple.

Agent McCallister dispatched three men to a hangarlike building. Emily looked for a structure similar to the woman's compound at Harmony Home Ranch, but could see none. Though dawn had not broken through the dark sky, lights burned in kitchen windows of houses where women, dressed in the familiar long dresses, prepared breakfast. The first look of the compound gave the impression of a peaceful community waking up to a new day.

Emily and Will leaned against the jeep as lawmen went from house to house, rousting people out of bed, separating the men from the women and children. The officers rounded up the men and herded them toward the temple. Women and children, looking frightened and confused, were taken to buses for transportation to a community center where they would be held until DNA tests could be performed. Local police officers agreed to feed livestock in their absence. The raid took everyone by surprise but was able to be conducted in a professional and systematic manner.

"See any familiar faces?" Will asked as the men paraded in front of her to mount the steps of the temple.

Emily shook her head. *Was our information correct, or had the kidnappers lied and intentionally led us astray?*

"Langley's going to be inside the temple if he's anywhere. He'll have living quarters there. I want to go in."

"How're you going to get up those stairs?" Will said, appraising the twelve steps leading up to the temple door.

"You're going to carry me, big brother."

"Hold on," Will said as he lifted her in his arms and climbed steps of the temple.

Emily grasped the crutches with one hand and clung to Will with the other. "You made that seem easy," she said as he gently lowered her to the floor in the vestibule. She used the crutches to hop to an out-of-the-way spot near the front of the congregational seating area where she could easily study the faces of each man. This temple did not compare in size or opulence to the one at Harmony Home Ranch, and as the men shuffled in, glancing around with bewildered or angry faces, the pews quickly filled. More were brought in, a few protesting, and demanding to know what was going on, but most were fuming quietly, waiting for answers.

The men, having been rousted from bed at an earlier-than-usual hour, had dressed quickly, most in work clothes—overalls or dungarees and muslin shirts. A few had donned khakis and shirts with button-down collars, but none wore the shiny black suit of the Prophet. None appeared to have his slicked-back, gray-streaked hair or those piercing dark eyes that had seemed to look into her soul.

Where the hell is Langley? Emily thought, her eyes searching the features of each new arrival, her nerves on edge.

The last man seated wore blue jeans and a plaid shirt, his short-sheared hair a dull brown, his body stooped, possibly from hard labor or age. He sat at the end of a pew, near one of the many side doors. A pair of glasses covered milky, blue eyes. Emily turned away, distracted by Sheriff Turnbull as he prepared to address the group, and then looked back. The old man's mouth began to twitch—the left side. He glanced her way, and their eyes locked. Emily caught her breath as recognition set in. "That's him!" she shouted. "The one at the end, wearing glasses."

Will turned to where Emily pointed, but before he could respond, the old man stood up straight and slipped through a side door nobody had noticed. Emily's cry had also caught Hosteen's attention. Both men rushed to the door and tried to push it open, but it appeared to be locked and reinforced with steel and didn't budge. Emily joined her brother and Hosteen and began beating on the door with one of her crutches.

The sheriff stopped speaking when he heard the ruckus. "What's going on back there?"

"I saw him!" Emily said. "Rupert Langley. He's in disguise, but I know it's him. He recognized me and disappeared through this door."

The men in the pews began to stir, but not one said a word. Several officers rushed to Emily's side in the effort to break down the door.

"Hold it. Listen to me, all of you," the sheriff said, addressing the cult members. "Someone tell me how to open this door and what's behind it. D'ya understand?" When no one responded, Turnbull shouted at the lawmen, "Get a crowbar and a battering ram in here. We'll get the damn door open if we have to blow it up with dynamite."

36

Friday, April 20, 1990

Heaven's Gate Ranch

Faith, South Dakota

It took five minutes after an agent keyed his handheld for a unit to come into the temple with a battering ram. During that time, Emily felt her heart pounding in her ears like a herd of wild horses, and beads of perspiration appeared on her forehead. Feeling like she couldn't get enough oxygen, she sucked in air through her mouth in short gasps as she paced back and forth, ranting to anyone within hearing.

"Hurry up. It was him. We had him in our hands, and he slipped away, damn it."

Will tried to calm his sister. "Listen, there's no place for him to go. They have men posted outside, at the gate, and in front of the hangar. He won't escape this time."

After another ten minutes, they broke the lock, and the door swung open, revealing a long passageway lit by overhead, recessed lighting.

Agent McCallister ordered three of his men to guard the cult members inside the church and make sure no one entered or left. He pulled a 9mm Luger from the holster at the small of his back and cautiously made his way into the passageway. Sheriff Turnbull and Officer Hosteen followed with their weapons drawn.

"I'm going in there, Emily. You stay here. I mean it," Will said to his sister.

"I'm not staying here, Will. I'll keep out of the way, but I want to be there when they find him."

"Look, you can't keep up, can't draw your weapon fast enough, and even if you could, you wouldn't be able to aim—not with those crutches and a broken leg. Now stay put."

Emily fumed, shaking her head at her brother. As soon as Will disappeared down the hallway, she followed the men. The lights cast eerie shadows along a cinder block–lined wall. She could hear the echoes of their feet ahead of her as they pounded the cement floor, and the thumping noise her crutches made. Fifty feet in, a set of steps leading down into a tunnel halted her progress. Inhaling slowly, she threw her crutches to the bottom, and by balancing her weight on the cast, slowly descended the six steps. At the bottom, a searing bolt of pain shot through her leg, and she leaned against the wall of the tunnel to rest and catch her breath. The men's footsteps sounded far away now, and she could no longer hear their voices. Evidently, they had not encountered Langley.

Soon, she thought. *We'll have him, and he'll have to tell us where the girls are. But what if there is more than one exit? No one knows where this tunnel ends.*

She placed her hand on the side of the passageway to brace herself as she bent down to pick up the crutches. As soon as she put pressure on the wall, she felt movement and jerked her hand back in surprise. A portion of the wall had slid open, revealing a hidden entrance to another tunnel. Emily stood stock-still, listening. Blood rushed to her organs, leaving her prickling with a cold sweat. She could no longer hear the footsteps of Will and the other men, only the pounding of her heart.

Emily took her gun from its holster and carefully picked up one crutch to balance herself. Common sense told her to turn back and notify the other officers, but as she turned and took a step, careful not to make a sound, she heard whimpering, a groan, a girl's voice. The girl said something in Navajo and began sobbing. Or, was it two girls?

It's Lina and Darcy!

She knew she had to go to them.

She passed through the opening and entered the dark, narrow hallway. Her belt held a penlight, but Emily could not hold both it and the Glock with one hand while she had the crutch in the other. Besides, it would give her position away if Langley was near. There was nothing to do but inch her way along the wall in the direction of the voices as quietly as possible. Any slip or false move could alert Langley.

The texture of the wall changed, and she realized she had reached another door. But the girls were not in there—their voices, though louder, were still distant. Thinking Langley might be inside as well made Emily pause.

What if he is in the same room with the girls? I'll find them, and I'll wait and listen until I'm sure he's not there. If he is with them, I'll wait until he comes out. There are so many "what ifs." Will, Joe, and the FBI could come back down the hallway anytime, and they will notice the opening. I can't think about any of this. I need to reach those girls.

As the voices became more distinct, Emily knew she was getting close. Inching her way along the wall, she felt the smooth surface of another door. The gun felt loose in her sweaty palms, so she tightened her grip. Emily wanted to tell them she was there and she would get them out, but it was too soon. She had to remain cautious, so she pressed her ear against the door and listened while her heart raced like a stampede of wild horses.

She could hear them talking, half in Navajo and half in English. Darcy's voice came in a forceful whisper while Lina's reply sounded weak, like a frightened child.

"Lina, you can't show him fear. It's what he wants—to break us down so we will see him as a god. We can't let him do that to us."

"I'm not as brave as you. *To-bah-ha-zsid*, Darcy. I am afraid. If I have to stay here, I'm going to die. I want my mom and dad. I want to go home."

Emily thought her heart would break while she listened to the girls—both so young—one putting on a brave face while trying to comfort the other, a terrified child in need of medical attention, unable to hide her fear. Still, listening to them gave her hope. It seemed unlikely they would talk so freely if Langley were in the room, and Lina was at least conscious. She waited a few minutes longer, her mouth like a dry *arroyo* bed, and her stomach clenched into a tight fist.

Emily tapped on the door with her Glock and heard the girls gasp.

"Darcy, Lina. It's Emily Etcitty. I've come to help you. Is there anyone else in the room with you?" she asked in a hushed voice.

She waited in the ensuing silence.

"How do we know you are who you say?" Darcy whispered.

They don't trust anyone, Emily thought.

She answered them in Navajo: "My mother is Bertha Etcitty, the teacher; from the Turning Mountain People Clan. My brother, Will Etcitty, was the *hataalii* at Lina's *Kinaaldá*. You know you can trust me. I'm a police officer. I've come here to bring you home."

"Emily?" came the tentative cry.

"Yes. We have to be careful. Now, keep your voices low. Is there anyone else in the room?"

"Just me and Lina," Darcy said between sniffles. "I'm okay, but I'm scared for Lina. She's been throwing up, and she is so weak."

Emily bit her lip, shifted her weapon to the hand holding the crutch, and patted the door with the other. There was no indication of a doorknob or latch. "Is the door locked from the inside?"

A different voice responded. "Are my mom and dad here?"

"They will be at the airport when we fly back home, Lina. They can't wait to see you. Now, we have to be quiet and work quickly. The man who brought you here—how did he open this door?"

"I don't know. He had something in his hand. When he shut it and left us here, we tried to open it again, but it wouldn't move."

Emily remembered she had found this passageway by accidentally pressing a spot on the wall. She used her free hand to pat all the surfaces around the door, wondering where Will and Hosteen were, knowing speed was essential if she was going to get the girls out.

"Perhaps I can be of some assistance," said a chilling voice behind her.

The blood drained from Emily's face, and the hairs on her neck prickled like a frightened animal whose hackles were up.

"But first, you will have to put your little weapon down."

She slowly turned around, her Glock grasped clumsily in the hand with her crutch, and faced Langley—and the barrel of a pistol pointed squarely at her heart.

"Drop the gun, now," Langley repeated.

Emily let her Glock clatter to the floor. "You can't get away. Cops and federal agents have the place surrounded. Your best bet is to give yourself up and let these girls go. Lina needs immediate medical attention."

Langley sniggered, a sound like rusty gears. "You have been trouble since the first minute they brought you to my ranch, but you underestimate me. I have prepared for the possibility of someone's meddlesome heathen intervention."

I have to stall him, keep him here until Will and Hosteen and the others come back, keep him talking, Emily thought. *Where are you, big brother? I need you now.*

"If you or anyone else hasn't harmed the girls, the law may go easier on you. Don't make matters worse."

"Be quiet." Langley pressed a series of numbers on a remote, and the door slid into the wall. "Well, there're my little red-skinned beauties. Now, no more talking. Let's go on in and join these young ladies."

A single overhead light cast ghostly shadows on the cinder-block walls. The two girls huddled on a cot in the corner, crying, arms around each other, still clothed in the now-soiled long white dresses and high-top boots, their eyes wide with terror. Lina appeared wan, barely able to lift her head. Another cot lined the opposite wall, and a curtain partitioned a small area near the back. Emily assumed it was a place the girls could relieve themselves using nothing more than a chamber pot. The room had a small vent in the door for air circulation or for looking inside, but a damp, foul odor permeated the clammy space.

"Hurry up," said Langley, poking Emily's back with the barrel of the gun, causing her to drop her crutch. His voice turned cold and menacing. "Everything would have been fine if you hadn't meddled in my affairs. A spiritual marriage with these young squaws would have pleased my Lord and master and increased the Almighty's flock for his everlasting glory. And they would have been happy, joyous. But you had to ruin it. Now we have to leave again."

This monster is insane, Emily thought.

She hopped to where the girls sat and turned around to face Langley. "I don't know what your plans are, but take me and leave the girls. Don't let murder be added to your crimes." Lina and Darcy clung to her like ivy on a rock wall. "If you have any compassion at all, think of how these girls' parents must feel. Please, let them go."

"Now, now." The Prophet took a remote from his pocket and aimed it in the direction of the back wall. Another opening appeared, dark and smelling of damp earth. "After you, ladies."

Both girls sobbed as they cowered behind Emily.

Emily said in a measured voice, "I can't walk without my crutch."

"Well, we don't want you slowing us down, do we girls?" Langley picked up the crutch and handed it to her.

37

Friday, April 20, 1990

Heaven's Gate Ranch

Faith, South Dakota

E mily felt the change. Calmness and clarity of mind settled over her like a warm embrace on a winter night. Her nerves steady now, she knew it was time to make a move, but there was no room for error. She had to be quick and decisive. When Langley handed her the crutch, she grasped it firmly with both hands and, rousing all the strength she could muster, let out a fierce yell before shoving the crutch into the pit of his stomach. Langley gasped, his hands going to his abdomen, and folded like a crumpled napkin. Acting before he could recover, Emily pulled the crutch back and brought it down on his head—not once, but twice. Langley writhed on the floor, moaning in pain. Darcy saw him lose his grip on the gun and reacted quickly, picking it up and rushing to the other side of the room. Lina made her way beside her.

"Darcy, can you keep the gun pointed at him?" Emily said.

The young girl nodded while Emily spoke to the other girl. "We need to get out of here as fast as we can, Lina. There are rescuers outside. Can you walk?"

Lina looked terrified, but she grasped Darcy's arm and whispered, "Yes."

The only problem was that the door to the main hallway had closed, and Emily couldn't open it. They were trapped in the room with Langley. She lowered herself to the floor and dug through his pockets until she found the remote, but it had a keypad, and she didn't have the combination.

"Help me look for a switch or lever that might open the door," she said to the two girls. "There has to be one somewhere. Did you ever watch him when he opened it?"

Both girls shook their heads. "He always used the remote," Darcy said. But she put the gun down and began pounding the wall around the entrance.

Langley stirred and moaned. "Stupid woman." His breath came in labored gasps. "All three of you are doomed to rot in hell. God will see you whipped with a thousand lashes and buried under a volley of stones—your heathen heads crushed."

"Yeah, well, if I shoot you, it'll be worth it," Emily said. She picked up the pistol and aimed it at Langley. "Tell me the combination to the door, or I'll blow your damn fake face off."

Langley sneered at her and laughed.

"I'll count to three."

The voice of a possessed demon came from Langley's mouth. He laughed again, a guttural rasp. "You won't do it."

"One."

"You'll never get out of here alive, stupid bitch."

"We will, but you won't. I have the remote. Do you want it in the head or the gut, or would you rather I left you here to die slowly?"

"You wouldn't."

"Two. I like the idea of a head shot so no one ever has to look at your evil face again. I'll aim at that twitching eye." Emily pointed the pistol squarely at Langley. "Three."

The blood drained from Langley's face, his twitch palpitated the corner of his mouth, and rivulets of sweat dripped from his forehead. His voice came out in a high-pitched whine. "Wait. I'll tell you the code. Don't shoot."

Emily kept the weapon trained on the man. "Keep talking."

"Seven—four—six—nine—zero—five."

With her eyes pinned on Langley, Emily handed the remote to Darcy. "Point this at the door and press these numbers." She slowly repeated the code. "If it doesn't work, Langley, you're a dead man."

They heard a click, and the door leading to the passageway slid open. The movement made the girls gasp in joy, and Darcy led Lina to the entrance.

Langley scooted to a corner, looked toward his imagined heaven, and beseeched God's intervention. "My Lord," he pleaded in a plaintive voice, "do not abandon me now in my time of need. Haven't I been your faithful servant? Everything I have done is for your exaltation."

Emily narrowed her eyes and spit at him. "You miserable, slimy bastard. I have no sympathy for you—wish you would have given me the excuse to shoot. Get to your feet."

"I can't. My leg . . ."

"There's nothing wrong with your leg, asshole." Emily hobbled closer to Langley and jabbed him with her crutch. "Stand up and put your hands behind your head." She heard the girls calling from the corridor and diverted her eyes for only a second.

Langley had been watching, waiting for his moment. He made a guttural sound and sprang into action as quickly as a crouching mountain lion. He threw himself at Emily, knocking her to the floor. He wrestled the gun from her grip. "I knew the righteous and mighty Jehovah would not abandon his faithful servant. Retribution is mine, whore. An eye for an eye." Langley stood over Emily, laughing like a madman, and slammed the crutch down on her wounded leg time after time.

Emily screamed and grasped her leg. She thrashed on the floor, trying to escape the blows as explosions of white-hot pain shot through her body. Her cast offered little protection, and as the strikes moved from her leg to her arms and head, she struggled to remain conscious. Despite her agony, she heard the girls crying and calling her name.

Lina. Darcy. I can't let him take them again.

"Wicked harlot, abomination to all that is sacred. I would shoot you now, but it might bring unwanted attention." Langley delivered a final blow and tossed the crutch to a far corner of the room. "I don't think you will be following me now," he hissed.

"No!" Emily yelled as she watched Langley grab Darcy by the arm and run out the door.

She rolled to the wall, trying to use it as support, gritting her teeth as she tried to pull herself to a standing position. Emily swallowed the sour taste of bile as a wave of nausea swept through her body. Grimacing with pain, she dragged her body to the door just in time to see Lina on her knees holding Emily's police-issued Glock with two shaking hands. "Lina, don't shoot."

Lina's voice sounded high and hysterical. "He's got Darcy!" A shot rang out, echoing through the chambers of the long tunnel, and Emily saw Langley look back in disbelief before he stumbled to the floor in a pool of blood. Darcy was running back toward her, and Lina, still on her knees, held tightly to the weapon.

Emily inched her way to the trembling girl. "Give me the gun, Lina." She put her arms around her and held her tightly. "Don't say anything when the police come. Let me do the talking." She wiped the girl's prints off the gun and glanced at Darcy. "Are you all right?" The girl gave her a barely perceptible nod and, weeping as well, hurried to Lina's side. They sat on the floor, clutching each other. "It's going to be okay. Don't look at the man. Just turn your heads away."

You monster. What new hell have you wreaked on these children?

She pulled herself to a standing position, and despite the throbbing pain in her leg, hopped to where Langley had fallen and felt for a pulse. He was alive. The bullet had passed through the left side of his chest but appeared to have missed vital organs. The sound of the shot must have alerted the search party, because Emily heard thundering footsteps running down the corridor in her direction.

Will was the first to reach her, followed by Hosteen.

"Is he dead?" asked Will as he knelt beside Emily. He checked Langley's wrist and showed relief after finding a pulse.

The Navajo have strong aversions to touching the dead, believing the evil in a person stays with the physical body. It is deemed bad luck—even worse if the dead man is a *bilagáana*.

"No, it's a clean wound, no organs—losing lots of blood. There're blankets and a towel in the room where the girls were kept," Emily said.

"What happened, Emily?"

"Later, Will. Joe, call it in. It's the perp. He needs an ambulance."

Hosteen already had his handheld out and had keyed in the code. "I have a 10-53, man down. It's a 10-72. Victim is Rupert Langley. Send in the medics for Lina Nez." He gave his location, checked Langley's wound, and tried to curtail the bleeding by applying pressure.

Will entered the small enclosure where the girls had been and came out with a towel and two wool blankets. He handed the towel to Hosteen, who placed it over the wound, then covered Langley with one blanket and put the other under his head.

"She tried to kill me," Langley hissed through clenched teeth. He began to shake convulsively, and his breathing came rapid and shallow.

"Don't talk," said Hosteen. He shot Emily a questioning look, but her face revealed nothing. His eyes traveled to the two Navajo girls, who crouched in the shadows against the wall, their hands hiding their eyes. "How'd it happen, Emily?"

Lina had fired at Langley's back while he tried to flee, dragging Darcy with him. He had fallen facedown, never knowing who pulled the trigger. The fact Hosteen thought it was Emily who fired was the way she wanted it. "It'll be in my report, Joe. I want to get these girls out of here."

"What shape is Lina in?" Hosteen said.

Emily frowned. "Lina is holding on, but she's frail and in a dazed condition. I don't think she would have lasted much longer. We need to get her to a hospital right away." Will knelt beside Lina and Darcy, speaking to them in soft, reassuring tones. "Will, would you get my crutches? One is in the room, and the other is around here somewhere."

After Will helped her to her feet and handed her the crutches, Emily made her way to the girls. "Let's go. There's nothing to be afraid of now."

Will picked up Lina and carried her to the approaching medical-team stretcher.

38

Friday, April 20, 1990

Mattie Simmons's Sheep Ranch

Bloomfield, New Mexico

Abe awoke to sunshine streaming through the bedroom window and realized he had overslept. He had lain awake the night before, working out a strategy for dealing with Mattie Simmons. His suspicion the ranch owner was cheating Navajo rug makers out of their fair share of the selling price had been fomenting for some time, but he had no proof—just rumors and grumblings from Churro sheep raisers and weavers. But if Emily could somehow gain access to Simmons's sales records and bank accounts, they'd have substantial evidence, and he could move ahead with the second part of his plan.

He stretched, feeling rested, secure in the knowledge that Emily would be back soon. It had been his first decent night's sleep in a week. Abe pulled on his jeans, put the coffee on, let Patch out, and saw the open barn door. He could have sworn he had closed it after he checked the livestock the evening before.

"Damn," he muttered. "What's this about?" After putting on his shoes, Abe walked toward the barn—and met Danny Ferguson as he herded the sheep out to pasture.

"Danny, what're you doing here? You didn't have to come to work today."

"I wanted to, Abe. I like taking care of them. You don't have to pay me anything. Can I stay? Please."

Abe scratched his head. "Sure, you can stay. I'll help you, though, as soon as I grab some coffee."

The smile spreading across Danny Ferguson's face gave no doubt the young man with the intellect of a boy loved the sheep. And the animals responded to his quiet voice and manner of dealing with them. "Thanks, Abe. You can drink your coffee and eat breakfast, too."

"Does your mom know you're here, Danny?"

"Yep. She said, 'If you're going to go to Abe's, just be quiet so you don't wake him up.'" A worried look crossed his features. "Did I wake you up?"

"No. Don't worry about it. The sunshine told me it was time to get up. I didn't mean to sleep so late. Have you had breakfast?"

"Yes, sir. Oatmeal with applesauce, and toast and jelly." He patted his belly.

Abe helped Danny herd the sheep and llamas in their separate pastures, thinking the entire time about a plan to expose Mattie Simmons. As soon as he completed some chores, he would make a list of all the Navajo weavers who had sold rugs to Mattie Simmons and pay them a visit.

The work didn't amount to much. Danny had already done most of what needed doing. And it looked like Ellen had paid him another housecleaning visit during his absence. Abe took a bath, put on clean clothes, and grabbed the notebook he used for listing the buyers of Navajo sheep.

Not all had commissioned Mattie Simmons to be their dealer. But after studying the list, he had several sellers he wanted to follow up on: George Tsosie, Marvin Joe, Malcolm Henry, Ben McDonald, Arlen Martinez, Charley Nez, and Herman Tallbrother. Herman had been the last person to receive a check and two yearlings. The Navajo families scattered themselves throughout the reservation. It was going to take time to visit them all. He decided to begin today with the most recent buyer, Herman Tallbrother, at Teec Nos Pos. He had noticed the beautiful rug Herman's wife was working on, and wondered how much Mattie Simmons would offer for it.

He wanted to start right away, but first he decided to make a call to the head of the music department at San Juan College and then pay a visit to Ellen Ferguson.

Later that morning Abe looked for Danny and found the young man sitting under a cottonwood tree, watching the sheep graze. "Let's call it a day. I can finish up later and bring those sheep in tonight."

At first Danny's face fell, but then Abe added, "I want to take you and your mom to lunch. And we're going for a drive afterward. How does that sound?"

"Good, Abe," Danny said, securing the gate between the two pastures. "Where're we going? I like hamburgers and french fries."

"Come on—I'll give you a ride home, and we'll talk about it. Is your mom there?"

"Okay. Yeah. Mom is always home. She makes things to sell so we can have a little more money. Sometimes we don't have enough, and the gas company turns off the heat. It gets cold, Abe, so Mom wants to be sure we stay warm next winter."

Abe pondered Danny's circumstances. He hadn't thought much about how difficult life must have been for Ellen and her son since her husband died. "Climb in the truck, and tell me where's your favorite place to eat."

Danny sat on the passenger side, with Patch hopping in beside him. *It might get a little crowded in here,* Abe thought. *But we'll manage.*

The short trip to Ellen Jorgenson's house took them down a rough side road. A small blue bungalow sat at the end of a dirt driveway between two willow trees.

Ellen stood out front, a shovel in her hand, and waved when they drove up. The house looked tidy but run-down. Missing shingles dotted the rooftop, and plastic had been nailed over the windows to help keep the cold out.

"I'm getting some flowerbeds ready, mixing in some sheep manure—gonna try to pretty this place up a little. I'm about done and was going to pick up Danny for lunch. Come on in and have a cup of coffee and lunch with us. It'll only take a minute to put something together."

"Why don't you let me take you out to eat? If you don't mind going for a drive afterward, I'd like to introduce you to some friends," Abe said.

"Now, Abe. You don't have to buy us lunch. You just paid us a bunch of money for watching your place."

Although preoccupied with thoughts of Emily and what might be happening in South Dakota, staying home and doing nothing while waiting for her call racked his nerves. "I insist. Come on. Hop in."

Danny looked at his mother with pleading eyes. "Come on, Mom. Hamburgers and french fries!"

"Well, just give me a minute to wash up a little. Who're we meeting?"

"Some Navajo families out on the reservation. They buy breeding stock from Mattie Simmons's place so they can build their Churro sheep herds. They're herders and weavers. Honest, hardworking people."

When Ellen returned, she carried a cardboard box that she placed in the bed of the truck.

Abe called Patch around to the back and lifted him into the bed. "You're going to have to ride back here, buddy. Make room for the humans." Glancing at the box, he added, "Whatcha got in there, Ellen?"

"Just a little something I like to give to new people I meet—some of my homemade pickles from last summer."

Abe had never heard of giving pickles to new acquaintances. He couldn't suppress his smile. "Okay. Where're we going, Danny?"

"Junior's Super Burgers. And can I have a big root beer float, Abe?"

After lunch, Abe navigated the truck past Teec Nos Pos and onto the dirt road that would take them to Herman Tallbrother's sheep camp. Danny gazed out the window, mesmerized by the sight of Indian ponies—pintos, chestnuts, and roans grazing languidly on new spring growth or gathered at watering holes—and frolicking colts trying out their legs. Scattered hogans squatted far from the road, isolated markers of human habitation in the sweeping landscape. Red sandstone mesas and steep canyons punctuated the rolling plains. As they began to ascend the mountain leading to the Tallbrothers' camp, bright patches of wildflowers cropped up, adorning green slopes where multicolored sheep grazed. The animals lifted their heads and stared with curious faces as the truck passed.

He found the Navajo herder and his son filling jugs of water from a tank in front of their temporary shelter. Two women worked near the side of a lean-to, one carding and cleaning wool, the other adding plant material to a large kettle of boiling water.

"*Yá'át'ééh*, Herman Tallbrother," Abe said from the open truck window.

Herman returned the greeting. A question such as "What brings you here?" might have been on his mind, but the Navajo was too polite to ask. "Welcome, Abe Freeman. Come in, rest a spell," he added, acknowledging Ellen and Danny.

The women looked their way, smiling shyly at the strangers, and beckoned Ellen to come over. Before Ellen joined them, she retrieved two quart-size jars of dill pickles from her box. In a matter of minutes, they were talking and laughing like old friends. Abe had left Patch in the back of his truck because of the protective nature of the Tallbrothers' sheepdogs—he didn't want trouble. Danny immediately headed toward the dogs, walking unabashedly into the herd of sheep, speaking in a soft voice to the animals. The dogs wagged their tails as he approached.

"That boy," Herman Tallbrother said, pointing with his lips at Danny. "He knows how to work with the sheep—talks to them, and the animals listen to his words."

"Danny is an exceptional young man." Abe explained how Danny had been in an accident and lost his father, and how his mind would never see the world as an adult.

Tallbrother solemnly nodded. "His spirit is blessed. The animals know. See how the sheep and dogs respond to him."

Abe knew not to rush the Navajo man. While the women drank coffee and chatted, Abe cautiously inched toward his reason for being there.

They talked about the case of the missing girls, but the Navajo grapevine had filled Tallbrother in on most of the available details. He planned on bringing his family to join the other Navajos at the Albuquerque airport for the girls' homecoming. The small talk continued with a discussion of weather, sheep, wool, and finally, weaving.

"I know this is none of my business," Abe said, "but, I am curious to know how much you were paid for the last rug you sold to Mattie Simmons."

After he had garnered the information, Abe jotted it in his notebook by the herder's name. They shook hands, and he said good-bye to the Tallbrother family. He began driving toward the next name on his list.

"Those ladies have so much skill," Ellen said as they bounced along another dirt road. "Did you see the rug they were weaving? I've never seen such exquisite work, and they color their yarn with beautiful shades of homemade dyes. Just amazes me how they do it."

They visited four more sheep camps before Abe decided it was time to go home. He had documented the information he needed and introduced Ellen and Danny to the Diné herders and weavers. Ellen continued to give out her pickles, winning the women's approval, and Danny impressed the men with his natural ability to work with animals.

It looked to be a good match for his plan. After putting more than a hundred miles on the truck, and a few hours talking sheep, he was more than ready to head back. Primarily, he was anxious for Emily's call. Abe dropped Ellen and Danny off and hurried to Mattie Simmons's house to check the messages on the answering machine. Nothing. He tried to call the Broken Arrow Motel where Emily was staying, but no one answered. He left a message on the answering machine—a sense of foreboding settling over him like an ominous cloud.

39

Friday Evening, April 20, 1990

Mattie Simmons's Sheep Ranch

Bloomfield, New Mexico

Abe waited an hour before calling Emily's room again. After receiving no answer, he tried contacting her mother. Bertha picked up the phone on the first ring.

"Emily, is that you?"

"No, Bertha. It's me, Abe. I wanted to know if you had heard anything from Emily or Will. I haven't been able to reach either of them."

Bertha's voice sounded tight with restrained emotion. "Me neither, Abe. Do you think anything is wrong?"

Wanting to reassure himself as well as Bertha, Abe tried to put a positive tone in his voice. "No, I'm sure everything is fine. They're probably busy and can't get to a phone is all. Are you doing all right?"

"I never should have agreed to let her go. Her body hasn't had time to heal, and she is still exhausted."

"They needed her, Bertha. No one has a picture of Langley, and she's the only one who could identify him. Will and Joe Hosteen are with her. Don't worry, she's okay." He wanted to believe his words, but he couldn't shake the fear gnawing at the pit of his stomach. "Let me know if you hear anything, and I'll do the same."

"I will."

"Is anyone staying with you?"

"Yes, I am thankful that Grandfather Etcitty is here, and he is going to perform a Protection Way prayer for Emily. It is a special ceremony that will empower her to be clear-minded and to make positive and life-affirming choices. He's helping me keep my spirits up. I will be all right now. And you, Abe?"

Abe Freeman wished he had Bertha's indomitable faith in prayers, but he had lost his belief in God after watching his first love, Sharon, suffer and die. He tried again to sound upbeat. "It's all going to work out fine, Bertha. I'm glad Grandfather Etcitty is there with you."

When he hung up, Abe remained sitting by the phone, holding his head in his hands, willing it to ring, wishing he could pray. After a while, he went to the piano, his only solace, and began to play Mozart's *Concerto No. 23*. He played it again and again, wanting to lose himself in the music, striving for perfection.

Abe grabbed the phone as soon as he heard the first ring. The pendulum clock in the foyer chimed nine times. He had not wanted to miss the call, so he had been playing the piano for the last four hours, only taking a brief time-out to feed Patch. His dog sat at his feet as if waiting for news from Emily as well.

"Hello?" he said.

"Abe, it's finally over. We found the girls and got Langley. Lina is in the hospital, and her parents are being flown out here. She's going to be okay."

Abe exhaled a huge sigh when he heard her words and felt an immediate release of tension. "Thank God, Em. I've been worried sick. Are you all right?"

"Yes, a little sore, but I'm okay." Emily hesitated, and her voice broke. "Langley's in the hospital, too—Abe, I shot him, but he's going to live."

Abe waited for more. When nothing came, he said, "You did what you had to. How are you handling it, sweetheart?"

He heard her sigh. "I'm all right. Darcy is staying in the room with me tonight. It's been a long, tough day; a lot has happened. I can't tell you the whole story now, but we'll be home Sunday. We should arrive around two thirty on the Delta flight from Minneapolis. Lina will have to stay in the hospital a little longer, and I won't leave until her parents are here with her. They should arrive tomorrow."

"How did Lina manage to beat the odds and stay alive without her medication?"

"Another woman who is also diabetic brought her insulin while she was at the Harmony Home compound. After Langley took her away, she basically started starving herself. Darcy said all she would take was water. It would have just been a matter of hours before ketoacidosis set in and she died."

"What an amazing child." Abe felt his heart swell for the sweet girl who had struggled so cheerfully and determinedly through his piano lessons. She hadn't given up, then or now. "Em, I'll be at the Delta gate waiting for you—the guy right up front. I think the whole tribe is going to be there as well."

"I can't wait to see you. I have to go now. I need to call my mom so she can let everyone know the girls are safe. I just wanted to tell you . . ."

"What, Emily?"

"I love you, Abe Freeman."

After he had placed the phone receiver back in the cradle, he picked up his dog. "Patch, did you hear the news, old boy? Emily's on her way home, and she said she loves me. She's never said that before." A smile spread across his face, and he laughed out loud. Abe returned to the piano and began playing with abandon. His selected piece, Beethoven's *Ode to Joy*, rang out in clear, bright tones.

40

Sunday, April 22, 1990

Albuquerque International Airport

Albuquerque, New Mexico

When Emily, Will, Hosteen, and Darcy Benally emerged from the passenger boarding bridge and into the Albuquerque Airport waiting room, a cheer erupted from the crowd. Darcy spotted her parents and rushed to their waiting arms. It appeared as if half the Diné had shown up for the homecoming. Tears of joy flowed from the emotional crowd of greeters; drums and chants drew the attention of other travelers as they stared with curiosity at the gathering.

Emily had gone shopping for Lina and Darcy the evening before they left Pierre, even though Lina remained in the hospital. She had purchased jeans, T-shirts, underwear, socks, tennis shoes, pajamas, and jackets for them using her credit card. She didn't care about the money. They also needed basic toiletries and hairbrushes. After showering and donning new clothes, Darcy looked like a typical teenager instead of the traumatized victim of a madman. She had held up well during questioning from the FBI and the ordeal of a doctor's examination in South Dakota and, finally, was released into Emily's care. Lina had been spared the interrogation. Thankfully, the girls had not been sexually molested, but there would be scars only time, love, and counseling would heal.

The FBI had questioned Emily as well. "Yes," she said. "I shot Langley when he attempted to escape. He was armed and had threatened the two girls and me. He pushed me down and tried to run away, taking Darcy as a hostage. I believed he had access to another secret room and a way out. I couldn't let him get away." She signed a statement of her account of the incident, fully aware there would be an internal investigation and that she would be put on administrative leave as per procedure with a police shooting. She could handle it—as long as the girls were spared.

Emily scanned the crowd and saw Abe standing by her mother and Grandfather Etcitty. Their eyes locked, and for the first time since all the trouble began, Emily felt at peace. Will had spotted his mother, too, and started pushing the airport wheelchair toward them as they came rushing forward. Emily could not reach them fast enough, and when she did, her relief and joy were so great she didn't know whether to laugh or cry.

Emily had been home for three days before Abe was able to pry her away from her mother's protective care. He brought her to the guesthouse on Simmons's sheep ranch and fixed her a steak dinner. After the meal, they sat together on the couch, their feet propped on the coffee table, their bodies close, and sipped brandy from round-bowled snifters. Newspapers cluttered the table. The *Albuquerque Journal*, the *Farmington Daily Times*, and the *Santa Fe New Mexican* had all run front-page stories covering the abduction and rescue of the Navajo girls.

But the *Cortez Journal* was the only paper that featured a full front-page story complete with pictures of Emily and the rescued girls.

Abe asked her about the incident leading up to the shooting and capture of Rupert Langley. She hated to lie but did not divulge, even to him, that it had been Lina Nez who shot Langley.

She told him both Sheriff Turnbull and the Navajo Nation had filed papers to extradite Langley, and how the *Cortez Journal*'s managing editor, Phil Brewster, and his wife, Tina, had flown out to South Dakota to get the scoop on the story. Their headline came out first, followed a day later by an in-depth report on the activities at the Harmony Home Ranch.

"How many underage girls were in the women's compound at the time you were there, Em?"

"I'd estimate thirty. I haven't heard the official count. The investigators are trying to determine exactly how many of them Langley had sex with. Right now, they've learned enough to charge him with statutory rape as well as kidnapping. They were also able to identify two other young Navajo women besides Mary Jo, and are working on reuniting them with their families. It's going to be a long process of reintegration, Abe. They've been so brainwashed—some don't want to come back."

Abe nodded. "Like Patty Hearst and the SLA," he said. "The mind can be easily manipulated. What about the other men who lived on the ranch?"

"They'll all be tested, as well as the children, to determine who fathered them. If the mother was underage at the time she became pregnant, the father will be charged as well. Then there's the question of polygamy. It's officially illegal for Mormons, but everyone knows it goes on anyway. That's probably part of the reason Langley decided to split off. We'll have to see how a judge handles it."

Emily held out her empty glass, and Abe poured her a second drink. She stared at the contents, a faraway look in her eyes. "Do you know if anyone found Chipeta Longtooth?"

"No one has seen hide nor hair of her. Last I heard, she had vanished like a wisp of smoke. You don't have any idea where she might have gone, do you?"

"No, not a clue," Emily said, and she meant it.

"Something strange happened out at the Harmony Home Ranch, though."

"What?"

"The place was deserted—the families are still being held in Cortez for DNA testing and questioning, I guess. An unexplained fire burned the temple to the ground, but all the other buildings remained undamaged. I hear some of the cult members want to go back there, rebuild the church, and wait for their leader to return."

"Weird. I wonder how the fire started." Emily had a hunch but kept it to herself. "Now tell me what else is on your mind." She swirled the amber liquid in her glass before taking a sip.

"I think Mattie Simmons is screwing the Navajo people," Abe said. "I don't believe she's giving them a fair share of the sale of their rugs and blankets."

"Well, you're not the only one who feels that way. The Navajo have been grumbling about her for a long time."

"Emily, can you get access to her financial records? Find out who she is selling to, and for how much? Take a look at her business transactions, bank deposits, and such?"

"Hmm, she's based in Dallas, right?"

"Yeah. Em, listen. I want to put some pressure on Simmons—make her pay the Navajo families their fair share."

"I'm listening."

"There's something else. I have an interview for a job at the college. If it comes through, I'll leave this ranch, but I'd like to see someone I trust taking my position."

"Ellen and Danny?"

"They'd be perfect. Ellen lost her home after the accident. Hospital bills were too much, and she couldn't keep up her mortgage payments. Now they can barely make ends meet living in their little rental. And she can't hold a full-time job because of Danny, so she does housecleaning on the side and sells produce. Danny is a natural with the sheep, and with Ellen's supervision, he can do just about anything."

"You don't like raising sheep, Abe?"

"Sweetheart, I don't have anything against the sheep or herding. I love animals; I love the outdoors. But I want to play more music than I can squeeze in on a borrowed piano. It's not enough to have a spare moment to get in some practice at Mattie Simmons's place. I want to teach—I want to play for an audience once in a while. I like making people happy with my music. Do you understand?"

Emily nodded, and her lips curved into a slow smile. "I think I know someone in Dallas who can help us. I'll make a few calls, see what we come up with, and let you know."

Abe tilted Emily's face up and kissed her long and hard. "I knew you could, Super Woman."

He let his hand slip down to the buttons on her shirt and began undoing them while continuing to plant kisses on her lips and neck.

Emily let out a low groan.

"Do you want me to stop?" asked Abe as his mouth caressed the tops of her breasts.

"No. Don't you dare." As Abe ran his tongue around the areola of her breast, her nipples hardened like small precious stones. "God, I've missed you. I just don't know how much I can do with this damn cast."

"You don't have to do anything. I'll do all the work." Abe stood, picked her up, and gently laid her on his bed, his erection fighting against the confines of his jeans.

"Help me out of these clothes, Abe. I need you so badly."

"Oh, baby, it will be my pleasure."

The following morning, Abe and Emily awoke early and took their coffee to the back patio. The rising sun glinted off the pale grass, transforming the morning dew into iridescent pearls. Abe had promised to bring Emily home early, and he had chores in the barn, so they didn't have much time. In the afternoon he wanted to practice a complicated piece of music he planned to play for his audition at the college. But, for now, he was content to sit there with Emily and marvel at her beauty.

Emily and Abe didn't talk much that morning; they didn't need to. Whenever their eyes met, each would shyly smile as if they shared a secret. For Abe, the previous night's lovemaking had been different somehow—more intimate, bringing them closer together. He felt sure that Emily shared this newly found intimacy as well. Even Patch seemed to sense their mood and sat watching them, his tail wagging—some would even say his thin black lips curved into a knowing grin.

The following day, Emily called Abe. He grabbed a pen and piece of notebook paper.

"Hi, sweetheart. What's happening?" He waited, listening to the sound of shuffling papers before she responded.

"I've got something that may interest you. Simmons's cheating is even worse than anyone imagined, Abe. Listen to this. A Two Gray Hills rug sold six months ago to a collector in Germany for thirty-five thousand dollars. Your boss's check to the Navajo weaver—two thousand. A large Teec Nos Pos rug went to another collector in The Netherlands. Her selling price—twenty thousand. Nina Benally's share was one thousand. And there's plenty more. Do you know what kind of contract she has with the weavers?"

"The people I talked to said it's supposed to be a forty-sixty deal, with sixty percent going to the Navajo rug makers. The greedy bitch has been scamming them big-time. Were you able to get copies of the business transactions?"

"Yes. I spent a day at my desk. Told my boss I needed to catch up on some paperwork. My source faxed me copies of all her deals and bank statements."

"They can get those without a warrant?"

"Yep. All they need is a mere subpoena—not even a judge's signature. It's amazing what those government agents can get their hands on."

"We just might have Mattie Simmons between a rock and a hard place. Thanks for coming through, babe. I talked to a couple of herders who knew they had been underpaid but couldn't do anything about it. If they were desperate enough for gas or food money, an authentic Navajo rug might go for as little as two hundred fifty dollars."

"Simmons turns around and sells it for a five hundred percent markup. It's bad enough there are all those cheap knockoffs of Navajo patterns reproduced abroad. They undercut the Diné weavers by selling their merchandise at a lower price." Emily's voice took on an angry tone. "I never imagined the extent of her greed. We should have investigated this woman a long time ago. Any design woven by a Navajo weaver within the six sacred mountains is sanctified. The plants, animals, rocks, mountains, as well as the sheep, wool, dye plants, and *piñon* pine used to build the weaving loom were given to the Diné by their Holy People. I'm pissed at this woman, Abe."

"Will you be my backup when I confront her with this information?"

"You bet. I wouldn't miss it for the world. I'm still officially on administrative leave, but give me a date. We'll put together a case Mattie Simmons won't be able to buy her way out of—no matter how much money she has."

"I only want her prosecuted if she doesn't agree to some terms I've worked out," Abe said.

"What do you mean? What terms?"

"She pays back all the money she ripped off from the weavers in the past and agrees to uphold the sixty-forty agreement. I want it down in writing."

"Hmm. Might be sweeter than jail time. Anything else?"

"She offers my job to Ellen and Danny Jorgenson and raises the wages."

"Whoa. You drive a hard bargain. And if she doesn't abide by these terms, we'll throw the book at her? I like it that we have tangible evidence."

"She'll be here in a little less than two weeks."

"Good. That will give me time to put a strong case together. I have a bit more digging to do."

"Em, on a different subject—when is the sergeant's exam coming up?"

"In about two weeks. I'm going to have to pass on this one, Abe. Joe Hosteen has earned it. He told me he was going to ask for a transfer to the Tohajiilee Indian Reservation near Albuquerque so he can be closer to his mother and fiancée. She applied for a teaching job there, and they're planning a wedding."

Abe reflected on his petty jealousy of Hosteen. He hadn't known anything about the man at the time and had jumped to some stupid conclusions. Hosteen had gained his respect. "Are you disappointed—to miss the chance for a promotion?"

"Nah. I'll have other opportunities. Next time, I won't break a leg."

"Emily, I love you."

"Thanks for loving me, Abe Freeman. I know I can be difficult at times."

"A wild woman—especially in bed."

"Does that mean I'm bad?" she asked in a teasing voice.

"Oh, no. It means the opposite. You are amazing, both in bed and out. I wouldn't want you any other way, sweetheart."

41

Monday, April 23, 1990

Ellen Jorgenson's Home

Bloomfield, NM

After Abe had outlined his proposal, Ellen stared at him, her mouth open, the coffee cup suspended in midair. "Why would you give up your job for Danny and me?"

"I'm applying for a position in the music department at the college, Ellen. It's the sort of work I love, and I've had some positive feedback from my interview with the department head. Besides, Danny is better at sheep raising than I'll ever be."

"That's why you took Danny and me with you the other day, out to meet those herders and their families, isn't it?" Ellen said with a knowing grin. "You were already setting things up."

"All right, I confess. Yes, I was. Look, I know the guesthouse has only one bedroom, but there's a good-size storage room you can convert, and the place is comfortable. Plenty of space for two."

"I know. I loved working there while you were gone."

"Well, what do you say? I won't be moving for at least a month, so you could give your landlord notice and have plenty of time to get ready. You and Danny can ride with me when I deliver new lambs to the buyers so you'll become more familiar with the operation. The pay is twelve hundred a month, with free rent and paid utilities."

"I'd be crazy to turn it down. Danny will be out-of-this-world happy," said Ellen. "He's gonna miss you and Patch—and I have to say, especially Patch. He's become very attached to that dog." Ellen brushed a wayward strand of hair out of her eyes. "How do you know she'll hire us?"

"She will. Trust me."

42

Monday, April 30, 1990

Mattie Simmons's Sheep Ranch

Bloomfield, New Mexico

The color drained from Mattie Simmons's face as she read the copies of her business transactions with the Navajo. She sat in a nearby chair and grasped the papers in one hand, shaking them at Abe as if to scold him. "How . . . how dare you snoop into my personal affairs? You won't get away with this. My lawyers will see to it."

The words that spewed from her mouth were cold and venomous, but her eyes lacked conviction.

Emily stood beside Abe, her arms crossed over the shirt of her Navajo Nation Police uniform. "Do you deny you sold Navajo rugs at an inflated price to European collectors and lied to the Diné about the selling price, thereby cheating them out of thousands of dollars?"

Simmons stared at her with narrowed lids, her steel-gray eyes hard as ball bearings.

"Do you want to call a lawyer?" Emily said. "There's going to be quite a scandal when we arrest you and this story hits the newspapers."

Biting her lower lip, Simmons turned and riveted her eyes on Abe, her mouth a tight, thin line. She glowered, breathing heavily, before turning away.

Emily and Abe waited in the tense silence while Mattie Simmons fumed. When she answered, Abe read the defeat in her voice.

"No. A scandal will ruin my business, and I have an extensive list of very prestigious clients waiting for an authentic Navajo rug. You are blackmailing me, you bastard." Mattie Simmons inhaled deeply. "What do you want?"

Abe handed her another paper. "I've made a list of the people you owe money to and how much. Contact your bank and start writing checks. I will be your driver and witness when you deliver the checks to the families. I'm also giving you notice—I will no longer be your employee after this month. I have someone I want you to hire in my place, however. I'm sure you will be pleased with their work, as they've already shown themselves to be more than capable of handling this job."

"What? You think you can dictate to me who to hire? Go to hell. You're fired, and I want you out of here."

"Well, here's the deal, Mattie. It's all or nothing. If you don't hire Ellen Jorgenson and her son, Danny, and if you don't repay the weavers, copies of these business transactions go to the FBI, the United States Fish and Wildlife Service, the Navajo Nation, and the *Farmington Daily Times*."

"Get out of my sight," the woman hissed.

"Yes, ma'am," Abe said with a small grin. "Tomorrow morning we need to deliver two yearlings to Sammy Begay, so you can put his check first on your list. I believe his mother, Sylvia, made the beautiful Yeibichai rug you sold for eighteen thousand."

Mattie Simmons's cheeks flared bright red.

Abe thought it was time to back off. "We'll leave at nine, and you'll have a chance to meet Ellen and Danny."

He heard the door slam behind him as soon as he and Emily stepped outside.

Emily shook her head and gave Abe a wide-eyed look. "You amazed me in there—you were tough as old boots with that broad."

"Guess I'm growing a thicker hide—and I had you as my backup, sweetie pie."

"Well, I'll tell you what, white man. You can be my backup anytime."

Abe kissed her on the forehead. "I need to get in the barn. Three ewes are about ready to give birth. You know, a pregnant ewe was having a hard time the other day. She had twins, and one was breech. She couldn't deliver until Danny turned it and pulled the lamb out. He reached in and brought the head forward—saved both lambs. I'm not so good at delivering babies, but it didn't even faze Danny. He's in the barn waiting for me now."

The following morning, Abe and Ellen rode in the front seat of Abe's truck as they made their way to Luckachukai, the home of Sylvia Begay, master weaver of Yeibichai Navajo rugs. Danny and Patch opted to ride in the back with the two yearlings. Mattie Simmons, not wanting to spend any more time with Abe than necessary, followed in her rental car. Abe wished he'd had a camera to catch the expression on Sammy Begay's face when Simmons handed him a check for $10,000, the amount due on the selling price of the last rug. After the shock had worn off, the new sheep had been integrated into Begay's flock, and the coffee had been drunk, Abe looked around for Danny. He spotted him sitting on the ground under a lean-to shed, surrounded by six wriggling puppies. He knew the mother must have weaned them because they had a food dish, and the Blue Heeler mix didn't appear concerned about visitors.

"How much would you take for one of those pups, Sammy?" Abe said. "I think I know someone who would give a young sheepdog a real good home."

EPILOGUE

On a hot and dusty Sunday afternoon in August, four months after Emily Etcitty and the two kidnapped Navajo girls were returned to their homes, Abe Freeman smiled down from the stage as the audience rose to their feet in a standing ovation. Abe had been working as a piano teacher at San Juan College for the past three months, but this was his first concert—a program he called "Five Not-So-Easy Pieces," which he had memorized. He had played compositions by Chopin, Bach, Beethoven, Satie, and Bartók to the appreciative crowd. As he gazed out at the audience, his eyes searched for one familiar face—Emily's. Unable to spot her, and uncomfortable with the cheers of acclaim from the audience, Abe wanted to get off the stage as quickly as possible. After an awkward bow, he headed for the sidelines, where he found Emily waiting with open arms. A flush of warmth spread through his body as he gave her an ear-to-ear grin.

"You were magnificent," said Emily.

"Sweetheart, I was scared shitless. Let's sneak out of here so I don't have to do the meet and greet."

"You're skipping out on the reception?"

"I'll make an excuse."

As he spoke, a tall blond woman wearing a little black dress and bright-red lipstick approached. Abe had also dressed in black slacks and shirt, as required.

"Marvelous," she said, stretching her lips into a broad smile. "The audience loved you. See you in McKinley Hall? That's where the reception is being held."

"Thanks, Margo, but something important has come up. I'll have to bow out. Please give my regrets."

Her mouth turned into a pretty pout. "Oh, Abe, I know you are merely shy." Her eyes flickered over Emily, who was wearing blue jeans, tennis shoes, and a T-shirt. "And this is . . . ?"

"My girlfriend, Emily Etcitty. Emily, the chairwoman of the music department, Margo DeVries."

They shook hands, mumbling niceties and appraising each other with their eyes before Emily spoke up. "Abe, we better get going. Very nice meeting you, Miss DeVries."

Once they slipped out the back door, Emily poked him in the ribs. "I think she's got the hots for you."

"No way. She has a husband and is at least ten years older than me."

"Doesn't mean a thing to these 'artist' types. Anyway, I've got my Bronco on a side street. Let's go to your place so you can change into something more practical, like jeans and hiking boots. I'm taking you someplace special."

"Great. Where's that?"

"You'll see."

Abe's rented bungalow sat on a bluff within walking distance of the college, but he took advantage of Emily's offer of a ride, and they got there in five minutes.

"I'll wait out here for you. Bring Patch."

A half hour later, they left Farmington behind and headed toward Shiprock, then split off to Indian Service Route 13. Abe never tired of the scenery on the Navajo Nation, a mystical land blessed with red rock mesas, natural sandstone arches, and incredible eroded rock formations in every color and form imaginable. They crossed into Arizona near Red Valley, with Emily still secretive about their destination.

"You are very mysterious today, sweetheart. What's up?"

Her eyes sparkled with mischief. "It's a surprise. Be patient, though I've noticed that isn't always your strong suit."

Abe knew that occasionally he was hotheaded and impulsive. "I hope my finer qualities outshine my faults." Grinning, he glanced at Patch, perched beside a covered basket on the backseat.

"Lucky for you, they do." Emily guided the Bronco along a twisting mountain road and over a high pass. "We're almost there."

"It's beautiful country. Wherever we're headed, I'm happy to be going there with you. By the way, I haven't seen Will in a while."

"He's accompanying Grandfather on his quest to the six sacred mountains. Will is still an apprentice *hataalii*, and Grandfather is showing him where to find items he needs to replenish his *jish*."

"*Jish?*"

"Bundles of sacred soil, herbs, and various other things for his medicine bag. Only the *hataalii* knows the contents of the *jish*, and each item must be renewed every year. Grandfather is blessed with many years of experience as a *hataalii*, but he is feeling those years. This may be his last trip to our sacred mountains, and he wants to pass on all his knowledge and prayer songs to Will."

Abe didn't understand the magic of Navajo healing ceremonies, but he had witnessed the transformation in Will after the sweat-lodge cleansing ceremony performed by his grandfather. Will no longer felt the need for alcohol to achieve what the Navajo called *hózhǫ*—a state of harmony, peace, and balance.

Emily grinned. "And I have more news. There will be another *Kinaaldá* for Darcy and Lina. This time, they will celebrate and run the races together. We're invited, of course."

"That's great. I'm glad they're doing it together." He smiled back at her. The girls had won their race against time. Now, they would go full circle. "I can't wait to see them, but you are going to sit this one out, Em."

They drove on, through the village of Luckachukai, then veered onto Indian Route 64 toward Chinle, on the rim of a long three-armed canyon with spectacular vertical walls.

"Wow. What is this beautiful place?"

"Canyon de Chelly—the only national park on Navajo land. It's administered jointly by the Diné and National Park Services and has been an ancestral home for the Anasazi, the Pueblo Tribes, and the Navajo. There are still about forty Navajo families living and working here for the park services. We can walk along the rim and hike down into the canyon. This is also the place where Kit Carson trapped the Diné, leading to their surrender and the devastation of the long walk."

"It's amazing and haunting at the same time. Ghosts of the past."

"Yes. Best not to disturb them. See that tall pinnacle? That's Spider Rock, home of Spider Grandmother, *Na'ashjéii Asdzáá*, creator of the world. Our legends say she was responsible for the stars; she took the web she had spun, laced it with dew, threw it into the sky, and the dew became stars."

"Very romantic."

"I love our legends. I never tire of these stories."

"I love it when you tell them."

"Get that thing out of the backseat, and let's walk along the edge here."

"I hope there's something good to eat in there. I'm starving."

Emily laughed, a sound like tinkling bells. "We can eat in Chinle. I wanted to bring you to this place for another reason."

Puzzled, Abe fetched the bulky item from the Bronco and returned to where Emily waited.

"We can sit on this boulder overlooking the canyon. Put that down between us." As Abe watched, Emily took the blanket from around the object.

He stared, his mouth hanging open, at the ponderosa-pine frame looped with buckskin laces. "Emily, is that what I think it is? Are you . . . ?"

"It's a cradleboard, passed down through generations in my family. And, yes, I am. You're going to be a father, Abe Freeman."

ACKNOWLEDGMENTS

I would like to recognize some of the wonderful people who have helped make this novel a reality. To the loyal gang of fellow writers in my critique group who have spent countless hours poring over my manuscript and providing feedback—Pat Walsh, Steve Anderson, John Johnson—a sincere thank-you. I am indebted to an amazing Navajo *hataalii* and healer, Rita Gilmore, who has so generously shared her wisdom and knowledge. Her stories have given me a greater understanding of Navajo spirituality.

Eternal thanks also to acquisitions editors Jacquelyn BenZekry and Jessica Tribble for believing in me, and to developmental editor Charlotte Herscher for her sound advice and patience in helping me polish this piece of work. I am exceedingly grateful to the entire team at Thomas & Mercer for all their input. And, as always, I want to give gratitude to my family for their continued support. I am truly blessed to have these people in my life.

ABOUT THE AUTHOR

Sandra Bolton's novels are based on her real-life experiences with diverse settings and cultures, as well as a desire to right racial inequality. Her first novel, *A Cipher in the Sand*, was inspired by her work in the Peace Corps in Honduras; while *Key Witness* and her follow-up novel, *Abducted Innocence*, were inspired by her years spent teaching Navajo children.

With twenty-five years of teaching experience and a master's degree in guidance counseling, Sandra is no stranger to compelling stories, but her love of writing truly began with a passion for reading. Then, her skills were honed under the tutelage of southwestern mystery writer Steven F. Havill.

Originally from California, Sandra has traveled the globe with her military husband and three kids. She now resides in Raton, New Mexico, where she divides her time between writing, hiking, photography, and gourmet cooking. Sandra is currently at work on a third novel in the Emily Etcitty Mysteries with the help of her coauthors—her cat, Fidel, and her dog, Sam.

For more on the author and her work, visit her website, www.sandrabolton.com, or find her on Facebook at www.facebook.com/sandraboltonauthor.